Dedicated to the memory of Eric John Haydock.
Bass player and one of the founder members of The Hollies.
1945–2019. Rock on, dear Eric, along with the rest of the
fantastic band that now resides in Rock'n'Roll heaven. Xxx

THE
NURSES
of LARK LANE

PAM HOWES

bookouture

Published by Bookouture in 2019

An imprint of StoryFire Ltd.

Carmelite House
50 Victoria Embankment
London EC4Y 0DZ

www.bookouture.com

ISBN: 978-1-78681-473-9
eBook ISBN: 978-1-78681-472-2

Chapter One

Aigburth, June 1955

Alice Dawson put down her knitting needles, stretched her arms above her head and yawned. She dropped the navy blue cardigan she was making into a tapestry knitting bag on the floor beside her armchair, got to her feet and switched off the television set. She'd picked up a bargain pack of wool down at Paddy's Market last week and was trying to get ahead with school uniforms in readiness for September's new term. Poor kids, she thought, they hadn't even had their summer holiday break yet and she was ready for packing them off back to school. But at least it would save her some money later in the year. There was enough wool to make two new cardies each for her daughters, Sandra and Rosie.

Alice tapped on the front sitting room door and popped her head round. The cosy room now did duty as her eldest daughter's bedroom. Cathy was curled up on the single bed under the window, reading a battered copy of *Anne of Green Gables*. 'I'm making a bit of supper, Cathy. Do you want anything?'

Cathy smiled and sat upright. 'Toast, please, Mam, and a cuppa. I'll come through to the back room while we have it.'

In the small kitchen Alice put the kettle on the gas stove and leaned against the sink, feeling drained. Her thoughts wandered back over the last few years, which had been nothing short of disastrous, both financially and emotionally. She and her second husband Jack had been in charge of the Aigburth British Legion until February this year, when due to him abusing his steward's position, drinking away all the profits and then fiddling the books to try to cover his tracks, he'd lost them every penny they'd ever had. They'd been evicted by the brewery from the flat they'd lived in above the club. Jack was currently residing in a convalescent home, recovering from an operation to amputate his right foot. It had been damaged during a wartime shooting accident and infection had developed in the bone above his ankle; he'd have been at risk of septicaemia if the operation wasn't carried out. Alice and her eldest daughter Cathy, from her first marriage, and Sandra and Rosie, the two younger daughters Alice had had with Jack, had managed to find a new home in a small terraced house on Lucerne Street, next door to Millie, Alice's best friend. Millie and her husband Jimmy had bought Alice's old family home a good few years ago and Alice now loved being almost back where she felt she belonged. And to make things complete, her and Millie's close friend Sadie now lived opposite them with her teenage son Gianni. Alice felt that, although tiring, life couldn't be better at the moment after the very unsettling time when she thought she'd be homeless.

She enjoyed the peaceful times she and Cathy spent after the evening chores were done and the little ones were asleep. She loved their new home, and the younger kids were so much happier now that Jack was out of the way, hopefully for quite a long time. He'd never wanted children, had very little patience and shouted at them far more than was necessary. She'd tried hard to make the marriage work but he'd cheated on her with Sheila, an ex-barmaid, and she'd found it hard to forgive him. Now she was enjoying being almost single, for the time being anyway. They'd all settled really quickly into the cosy little house and it was easy to run and look after. Working all day as supervisor over the cosmetics department in

Lewis's store didn't leave her much time for doing anything else, so it was perhaps as well it was easy to cope with.

Every other weekend Jimmy's brother Johnny had taken to coming over from Blackpool, where he lived, and staying next door, and on those nights Millie always invited Sadie and Alice over for a bit of supper and a drink. It was a nice social break in an otherwise busy life and Alice looked forward to having that one night out of the house with her friends.

'Can I have jam on my toast, please, Mam?' Cathy called from the back sitting room, breaking Alice's reverie.

'Yes, love.' Alice buttered two slices of toast, poured mugs of tea and put the lot, along with a small pot of strawberry jam, onto a tray.

'Soon be the long school holidays and then we won't need to get up so early,' Cathy said, scraping jam onto her toast. 'Just one more year and then I can leave and hopefully I'll have enough good O level grades to start my nurse training.'

Alice smiled and looked at her daughter. She was so like her late father, Terry, who had survived the war, only to be killed in an accident on his motorbike the following year. She had his thick dark hair and big blue eyes, and the determined set of her mouth was Terry's. Alice hoped her daughter would get the chance to achieve her dreams one day. Nursing had always been her own dream, but the war and the need to help support her widowed mother and young brother Brian had put paid to any plans she'd had.

*

Jack Dawson frowned as the doctor at the convalescent home spoke to him. 'What, you mean I've got to go home? And how am I supposed to manage with the stairs? No matter how much I try here with the physiotherapist I can't balance right to get up them.'

The doctor shuffled the papers on his knee and looked at Jack over his glasses. 'We will make sure you have all the help you need. A home visit from district nurses a couple of times a week will be arranged. They will help you with taking baths and if you can't manage the stairs, maybe a room can be equipped for you downstairs.'

'But the bathroom is upstairs, so that's no good.' Jack shook his head.

'We'll contact the housing authorities to see if suitable accommodation can be arranged for you and your family, Mr Dawson. Maybe a flat all on one level or a bungalow can be allocated. Anyway, I'm about to call your wife and tell her that you can be taken home tomorrow. It will give her a day to get prepared. I'll see you later with your discharge letter that can be handed to your own doctor.'

Jack stared after the doctor as he left the room. He let his head fall back against the chair and let out a long breath. He really didn't want to go home to Alice and the houseful of brats, but what choice did he have? He could just imagine Alice's response to any suggestions that she may need to move out of her new home, so he could be all on one level. That would go down like a lead balloon. She'd told him in a letter that the front room was now a downstairs bedroom for Cathy. Well she'd have to bugger off out of it, because it would be ideal for him. And she'd said there was still a working outdoor carsey with the property that she was using as storage space. He'd have to make do with that. He'd manage to wash himself at the kitchen sink and maybe they could get a tin bath that could be filled when he needed it. It would be better than nothing. If only he had the money to get a decent place all on one level that was big enough for him and his bit on the side, Sheila, it would be ideal. Sheila's bedsit was two floors up in an old house with a steep staircase, so would be totally unsuitable for his needs. Hopefully, in the not-too-distant future, there might be a chance they could be together. Living with Alice again was not going to be easy – she'd made sure he knew how much she hated him for losing all their money – but he had no choice at the moment. He was her husband, and while they were still married he had rights and Alice had better remember that. He hoped Sheila would come over to see him this afternoon and bring him some more fags. With it being Sunday he knew Alice wouldn't come, as she'd made it clear that she was too busy with the kids and housework to visit him on her only day off, which suited him fine, and he was looking forward to seeing Sheila again anyway. She was the only good thing in his life at the moment. Though how the hell he'd get to see her once he was at home, he had no idea, but they'd work something out to suit, he was sure.

*

Cathy pulled back her bedroom curtains and slid open the sash window. The day felt warm already, but a light breeze fluttered the sparkling white net curtain that gave her a bit of privacy from passers-by. She could hear her mam talking quietly to her half-sisters in the back sitting room. The faint aroma of freshly made toast coming through the gap at the bottom of the door made her mouth water. She hurried to make her bed, but then the sound of a motorbike being revved up outside caught her attention. She peered through the nets and then ducked back behind the curtain as Gianni Romano raised his hand to his mother from the pillion seat and he and his friend set off down the road. Cathy saw her mam's friend Sadie place her hands on her hips, slowly shaking her head from side to side, watching as the boys rode out of sight. Her shoulders seemed to slump and then she walked across the street and knocked on their front door. Cathy rushed into the hall to answer it and let Sadie in. 'Mam's in the sitting room with the little ones,' she told her, noting the worried expression on Sadie's face. 'Go on through.'

'Thanks, love,' Sadie said and tapped on the door leading to the back room. 'Only me,' she called out.

'Ah, Sadie.' Alice looked up from her mug of tea and smiled. 'Come on in and park yourself. I'll make a fresh pot in a minute. Cathy love,' she called out, 'go and knock on for Millie please.' As she spoke a knock and another 'It's only me' sounded and Millie let herself in at the front door. Cathy pointed to the back sitting room and then went back into her bedroom and closed the door. She knew Sadie didn't like Gianni riding pillion on his friend's bike and was terrified they'd have an accident. But she also knew bike-riding was in Gianni's half-Italian blood and Cathy was certain that as soon as he was old enough he'd be saving up to buy his own motorbike.

She finished her bed-making, hung up some clothes that were lying on a chair and went into the back room for breakfast and a listen-in to what her mam and her friends were talking about. 'I'll make a fresh pot,' she said and picked up the empty tea pot from the table.

Her little sisters were outside playing with a skipping rope and not squabbling for a change. Cathy cut two slices of bread and popped them under the grill. She brewed the tea and, when it was ready, buttered her toast. Reaching for three clean mugs from the cupboard, Cathy filled a tray and carried it through. She caught the tail end of what her mam was saying to Millie.

'Tomorrow? They want me to go and pick him up tomorrow? But I can't get there. It's Monday. I'll be working all day.'

'What's up, Mam?' Cathy frowned.

'The convalescent home has rung Millie with a message. They want to discharge Jack tomorrow.'

Cathy felt her jaw drop. 'Does that mean he'll have to come and live here with us?'

Alice nodded. 'Unfortunately, yes. He has nowhere else to go and I *am* still married to him. I've got to ring back and make the arrangements with them.'

Millie patted Alice's hand and gave her the front door key. 'Go and phone them now and then we can decide what to do. Jimmy said he will give you a lift up there and then bring Jack home.'

Alice sighed. 'I'm so sorry, Millie. That means Jimmy will have to take a bit of time off work as well.'

'It can't be helped,' Millie said. 'It'll only be an hour or so. Go and get the call over and done with and come back and we'll have this brew and talk some more.'

Cathy stared after her mam as she hurried away. Her toast lay uneaten on her plate, her appetite gone in an instant. She really didn't want her stepfather home. She hated him and his bullying ways. They'd been so happy and contented here for the last few months. She was aware of Millie saying something to Sadie and tuned an ear in to their conversation.

'They're too steep. He'll never manage them,' Millie said. 'He was struggling last time Jimmy and I went over to visit him. He needs to be all on one level.'

Sadie looked at Cathy and shook her head. 'Fortunately the outside toilet is still in working order and he'll just have to make do with strip washes in the kitchen.'

Cathy's eyes widened as it dawned on her what they were implying. Jack would need her bedroom. He couldn't manage the stairs. She'd either have to share with her sisters or move into the tiny room that was kept for Uncle Brian when he came home from university. Her eyes filled at the thought of giving up her lovely bedroom. She and her best friend Debbie had spent happy hours in there chatting and listening to records. They wouldn't be able to do that any more; any noise upstairs would disturb her sisters. At that moment, she didn't think she could hate Jack any more than she already did. And if anyone thought she was being selfish for that, then tough. Jack had wrecked their lives, taken all her mam's money and fathered two kids he simply wasn't interested in. And now he was coming home to wreak more havoc and no doubt would expect to be waited on hand and foot, well one foot, at least.

Alice came back after a few minutes, her eyes red-rimmed and her shoulders sagging, like she was carrying the weight of the world on them. She looked at Cathy, who chewed her lip and tried not to cry.

'I'm sorry, Cathy love. I have to go and collect him at three thirty tomorrow. I told them it couldn't be any earlier as I'm working and will need to arrange to take an hour or two off, as will Jimmy. This afternoon we'll need to spend time rearranging the house to fit him in. I'm afraid you'll have to give up your room, love.'

Cathy's eyes filled. 'I know. Maybe I should just go and stay at Granny Lomax's then.' She choked on a sob and ran from the room, slamming her bedroom door shut, calling out, 'I hate that man. I don't want him to live here with us.'

*

Alice shook her head after Cathy's departing back and sat down at the table. She picked up the mug Millie pushed towards her and took a sip, feeling close to tears. The few months of feeling happy and in control of her life, and the money side of things, were almost over. Jack would be tetchy and horrible to live with if he didn't get alcohol and cigarettes and her already tight budget wouldn't stretch that far. All she could do, against her better judgement, was bring him home and take a day at a time. His disabled soldier's pension wasn't much, but better than nothing. If he could master the crutches and maybe even manage to get around on just one he might be able to find a job doing the work he was used to; helping out in a pub or club. Then at least he'd be out of the house at night. Poor Cathy. Alice didn't blame her for wanting to go to her Granny Lomax's. Terry's mother would always give her granddaughter a roof over her head. Alice would go herself if only she could. But

Cathy's place was here with the family and only if things became unbearable would she allow her daughter to leave home.

'I've got some boxes from my move in the shed,' Sadie said. 'I'll go and get a couple for Cathy to pack her books and things in and we can take them upstairs.'

Alice sighed. 'There's no room to swing a cat up there. I don't know where we can put her desk or anything. I think they'll have to stay in the front room for now. But then Cathy won't want to do her homework in there if he's in. Bloody Jack. I could swing for him.'

Millie patted her arm. 'He might have changed, you know. Losing his foot and learning to walk again might have mellowed him a bit.'

Alice snorted. 'Well, there's been no evidence of it so far. It'd be a miracle, and I can't see it somehow.'

'Benefit of the doubt,' Millie said. 'Everyone deserves a second chance.'

'Millie, this will be more than a second chance for him. After everything he's done to me and mine, he doesn't really deserve another chance. But I'm his wife and I don't have a choice. One step out of place though and that's it. He can get out and I'll divorce him somehow or other. I'll find the money from somewhere.'

'I've just had a thought,' Sadie said. 'Why don't we bring your double bed downstairs and take Cathy's single up to your room with her desk and bookcase. Then you and Jack can have the front room and she can have privacy upstairs for her friends to visit and do her schoolwork in peace.'

'That's a good idea,' Millie agreed.

Alice felt her face draining. 'Oh, I, er, I wasn't planning on sharing a bed with him,' she stuttered.

Millie raised an eyebrow. 'He's your husband. I thought… well, after you had Rosie that things were okay on that front, until he went into hospital.'

Alice chewed her lip. 'They were, until I found out he was still seeing Sheila.'

Millie pursed her lips. 'Well, he won't be doing that again, will he? You saw that one off good and proper and if he's living here and can't get round to going out and seeing her, he's hardly likely to start the affair up again. And besides, you need to make sure he doesn't. Start as you mean to go on. Let him know you are watching his every move, and you can see how it goes.'

Alice got to her feet and cleared the mugs away into the kitchen, her thoughts racing. Could she forgive Jack? Start again, only this time take more control of things. And make sure he knew he was on a final warning at making their marriage work. She supposed there wasn't an awful lot of choice. She called Cathy into the room and explained what they'd just discussed. Cathy shrugged at the suggestion but went across the road with Sadie to help carry the boxes over. Millie went next door to fetch Jimmy, who had been out fishing for the day with their young son Paul, and by teatime the rooms were swapped around. Cathy had her little sanctuary upstairs, and Alice had a room she was going to reluctantly share with Jack.

Chapter Two

August 1955

Jack flung down the *Echo* and got gingerly to his feet, wincing as the wooden one rubbed against the scarred tissue at the bottom of his leg. He limped across the room and lifted the net curtain, peering out at the gloomy day, and sighed. Beginning of bloody August and it was peeing down. Unusual weather for the time of year. Still, it kept the nosy neighbours indoors, which meant they wouldn't see Sheila arriving shortly. Having her visiting him was like planning a military operation, but Alice was at work and the kids all at school so he had the house to himself for at least another four hours. Plenty of free time for Sheila to come and cheer him up.

There was no one in at Millie's next door either, and Sadie across the street and her lad were also out for the day. It was all working out rather well, Jack thought. In the few weeks since he'd been back living with Alice, Sheila had managed to come round a couple of times a week and he looked forward to seeing her. She was the one light in his otherwise boring existence. On the days in between he had sessions with the nurses who were trying to help him cope with the stairs, but he was quite happy just staying in his room, reading, listening to the wireless and dozing when he could. He took a daily stroll on his crutches up the street, going a bit further each day. When he felt confident enough he'd go and show his face at the Legion. See how the new steward was doing. He'd missed the Legion more than he'd missed Alice and his kids. It was the only place he'd ever really felt he belonged in and now it was all gone. He was still in a lot of pain and needing strong pain relief that seemed to knock him for six at times, which was why he dozed a lot, but he hadn't taken any today yet. He didn't want to fall asleep while Sheila was here. She'd be expecting him to be on top form, demanding his body like she always did, and he would do his best not to disappoint her and waste her visit. At least she was loving towards him, not like Alice, who looked on his advances as though she was being punished for wrong doings and made it clear she was glad when he'd finished. If he was honest, he'd been surprised to find himself sharing a bed with her when he arrived at the house. But in a place this small he guessed there wasn't much choice. Not that it bothered him, because his thoughts were always elsewhere anyway when he made love to Alice. He lit a cigarette and limped into the kitchen to brew a pot of tea while he waited for Sheila to arrive.

*

'You okay, Alice?' Millie's voice echoed through her thoughts and Alice turned and smiled. She put down her clipboard and pen and rubbed the back of her aching neck.

'Just a bit tired. Be glad to get home tonight.' She stifled a yawn. 'I could do with a few days' holiday somewhere nice, but I think it would be too much of a struggle with Jack and his crutches and the kids playing up. Hardly worth the bother. But even a day away on my own would do.'

'Why don't you come to Blackpool next Sunday but one with me, Jimmy and Paul? We're going to see Jimmy's mam and dad. Johnny will be there and you can bring Cathy too if you like. Ask Marlene if she'll have the kids.'

Alice's face lit up. 'I might just do that. I'll see what Marlene says. I should be able to leave them with Jack, but they'd hate that and so would he. Not sure that Cathy would come though. Since Jack moved in, Sunday is her day for going over to see Granny Lomax and then her and Debs usually go hanging around the café on Seffy Park, lad-spotting. Well Gianni-spotting in Cathy's case.'

'Aw, they'd make a lovely couple, if both ever overcome their shyness and pretence that they don't fancy one another.'

Alice laughed. 'Well, you remember what it was like to be a teenager, all that angst and fluttering eyelashes, and butterflies in the tummy, and then when lads dared to look at us, we'd look the other way.'

Millie smiled. 'We did indeed. But it didn't take you and Terry long to get it together.'

Alice sighed. 'I suppose not.' She chewed her lip as Millie rubbed her arm. 'I do miss him. It feels like such a long time ago since he died. Another lifetime even.'

Millie nodded. 'It does,' she said quietly. 'We miss him too.'

By the middle of August, after plenty of practising, a determined Jack had managed to walk up to Aigburth Road. He was met there by Sheila, who accompanied him to the Legion. He felt exhausted by the time they got there and Sheila helped him to a seat at a nearby table and went to get them a drink from the bar. Jack watched as she talked for a while to the barman and threw her head back, laughing at something he was saying. Jack felt a twinge of jealousy twist in his stomach as he watched the man making eyes at her. She turned and pointed at Jack and the man nodded and lifted his hand in a wave. Jack raised his hand back as Sheila waltzed across with the drinks and placed a pint of mild on the table in front of him. She sat down and took her cardigan off and had a sip of her gin and tonic.

it's a yes from both of us and then we can get back to mine for a couple of hours before they all come home.'

Alice and her neighbours set off for Blackpool at nine thirty after first dropping Sandra and Rosie round at Marlene's. She'd left Cathy doing her homework before going to her granny's. Jack had managed to get a few hours' paid weekend work at the Legion, which had surprised Alice, but he'd been quite animated as he'd told her he was to be in charge of entertainments on Saturday and Sunday nights. That meant peaceful weekends for her – well, until he came home stinking of booze in a taxi paid for by the steward, anyway. He was always on the defensive and aggressive side when he'd been drinking and she knew that being on his feet for any length of time caused him pain, for which he still took more than his prescribed dose of painkillers. Trying to keep him sweet so that he didn't cause any rows that would disturb the sleeping kids upstairs, Alice reluctantly gave in to his demands. If she didn't then she was sure he'd force himself on her like he'd done when she got pregnant with Sandra a few years ago. This way she was at least prepared with her diaphragm in place, as Jack wouldn't even think twice about contraception as long as he got his way. As far as she was concerned, it was a case of shut up and put up for now. But one day in the future, she dreamed of being free of him. She allowed her thoughts to turn to Jimmy's brother Johnny and how much she was looking forward to seeing him again.

*

Sadie hurriedly pushed the letter back into its envelope and put it away in a drawer as she heard footsteps on the stairs. Gianni was back early from his Sunday-morning ride on his pal's bike. She didn't want him to see the latest letter from his father Luca. All Luca's letters were hidden away in a shoebox in her wardrobe, along with birthday cards that he'd sent regularly for his son. One day, probably when she popped her clogs, she knew he would find them, but that would be years off yet so for now, out of sight, out of mind to be on the safe side.

She fixed a bright smile on her face and looked up as he dashed into her bedroom.

'What time are we having our dinner?' he asked, cheeks flushed from the ride and his usually neat quiff looking windswept.

'In about half an hour.'

He nodded, glancing out of the bedroom window.

'Just gonna walk to the corner with Cathy then,' he said and shot off down the stairs.

Sadie peeped out of the window and saw Cathy locking the front door as Gianni approached her. Cathy smiled and her face lit up as he spoke to her. He fell into step with her and they strolled along Lucerne Street. Sadie nodded her head with satisfaction. At least the pair were speaking a bit more to each other these days, more than they'd done throughout their primary school years when Gianni preferred to play with his friends rather than girls. Fingers crossed. They were only young, but her son could do worse than Cathy.

*

Cathy said goodbye to Gianni as they reached her granny's white-painted bungalow on Linnet Lane. She waved as he walked back the way they'd come after arranging to meet up later near the Palm House on Sefton Park. Debbie was calling for her after dinner – the pair had taken to going to the park on a Sunday. Cathy couldn't stand being in the house alone with Jack Dawson and today her mam had gone out with Millie, and the kids were at childminder Marlene's. Cathy had tried to keep out of his way while she'd done her homework and tidied up the kitchen. He still couldn't get up the stairs in any hurry but he'd deliberately pushed up against her in the kitchen and put his hand on her bottom, with the excuse he was steadying himself while he opened the back door. She didn't believe him for one minute and she wouldn't trust him as far as she could throw him. He was a dirty old letch and she'd heard some of the filthy things that he shouted at her mam when they were in bed and thought Cathy was asleep. He repulsed her and she didn't know how her mam could stand him near her. It wasn't something she had the confidence to speak to anyone about either, but maybe one day she would, and meanwhile she'd do her best to keep out of his way. At least he'd be at the Legion doing his new job tonight. She hoped he'd be gone before she went home to wait for Marlene to bring her sisters back.

'Only me, Granny,' she called as she let herself in at the front door. The lovely aroma of roast lamb and apple pie wafted down the hall and her stomach rumbled in anticipation.

Granny Lomax held her arms out and Cathy melted into them.

'Lovely to see you, sweetheart,' Granny said. 'Sit down and I'll make you a cup of coffee. Did you get your homework finished? It's important you keep on top of it now you're getting close to your final year. You need the best results to go nursing.'

'I know, and yes, it's all done. Mam's gone to Blackpool with Millie for the day and Marlene's got the kids. Jack's going to work at the Legion later.'

'Yes, I heard word in the post office that he'd been offered a few hours' work there. At least it gets him out from under Alice's feet, although let's hope he doesn't drink this new steward dry. I overheard someone saying that Sheila is working there again as well. I bet he hasn't told Alice that.'

'Is she?' Cathy groaned. 'Oh Gran, for God's sake don't tell Mam. Otherwise she'll tell him he has to give the job up and then we'll have him under our feet all weekend. It's so nice when he's not there. We can watch the telly in peace. He moans if we watch *Sunday Night at the London Palladium*, because he knows me and Mam enjoy it.'

'Does he indeed?' Granny raised her eyebrows. 'He's a miserable devil. My lips are sealed. What Alice does is nothing to do with me these days. But at least you're armed with the knowledge should you ever need it.'

*

Alice strolled along the prom with Johnny by her side and Millie and Jimmy just in front. Paul had been taken out on a fishing boat by his granddad. The sun was warm and it was good to feel the heat on her bare arms and legs. Might get a bit of colour to them today. Millie had painted Alice's toenails a pretty pink last night and Alice thought they looked lovely against the white of her leather sandals. She'd put on a pink and white striped sundress and felt like she was on holiday, even if it was to be short-lived. The prom was crowded with families making their way onto the piers and beach.

'Shall we have a drink on the pier and then go on the Pleasure Beach?' Jimmy called over his shoulder, but his words were drowned out by the tooting of a tram. He repeated himself, laughing, as another tram passed, going in the opposite direction and tooting just as loudly; but Johnny caught his words and nodded. He looked at Alice and held his arm out for her to link it. She hesitated momentarily, but then shyly slipped her arm through his and strolled along beside him, feeling her heart skip a beat in a way it hadn't done since Terry had been alive. She took a deep breath and said a silent prayer for a future in which they would all be happy once more.

Chapter Three

December 1955

Cathy pulled the pillow around her head, trying to drown out the sound of her mam and Jack arguing. It was the same every night, ever since he'd started working at the Legion and drinking heavily again, and it was getting worse. His aggression was out of control. He'd ruined their Christmas by drinking all day and falling into the Christmas tree this afternoon, knocking it flying. He'd smacked Rosie hard on her legs because she'd left her new roller skates where he didn't spot them. And when Sandra had given him a kick on the shin for hurting her little sister, who was crying heartbrokenly, he'd ordered them both to bed without any of the nice tea her mam had prepared. If he hated them all so much, why didn't he just leave and go and live on his own somewhere? Probably because he had no money and it was down to her poor hard-working mam to keep him. He spent his entire disabled pension and the wages he got on drink and fags; he certainly didn't give any of it to her mam to help out. They were worse off than they'd ever been right now.

'I don't care what she wants; she can forget the O levels. She'll have to leave school and get a job,' Jack yelled as Cathy lay there listening. 'You were working at fifteen and so was I. We need a wage coming in from her and the sooner the better. Now get out of my way, you useless bitch.'

Cathy sat up as she heard his bedroom door slamming shut and her mam running up the stairs and going into the bathroom. She could hear her crying and then Sandra calling out 'Mammy!' She slid out of bed and crept across the landing into her sisters' room, putting her finger to her lips to shush Sandra from waking Rosie, who had sobbed herself to sleep. Jack still couldn't get up the stairs properly in a sober state, never mind drunk, but he had a habit of shouting and swearing and throwing things and if Millie and Jimmy heard him they'd come knocking and Jack would get even angrier and take it out on her mam. She gave Sandra a hug and told her to go to sleep. 'Everything will be fine in the morning,' she promised the worried little girl. 'We'll have a nice day because Jack will be going to the Legion.' Cathy didn't actually have a clue if he was working or not tomorrow, but if it helped her sister to sleep peacefully, it was a good white lie.

She closed the bedroom door and knocked on the bathroom door. Her mam opened it and gave her a watery smile. 'Sleep on Brian's little spare bed tonight, Mam,' she suggested. 'Leave *him* to wallow in his drunken pit. You can't go back down there. He's still awake; I can hear him banging about. Sandra's settled back down and Rosie's still asleep.'

Alice gave her a hug. 'You're a good girl, Cathy. I don't know what I'd do without you. I can never forgive myself for getting us into this mess.'

'Mam, it's not your fault. It's his. He's evil. Why can't you just chuck him out?'

Alice shrugged, tears running down her cheeks. 'And how would that look to the authorities, chucking a disabled man out with nowhere to go? If only he didn't drink so much, it would help. He's throwing good money away that I need for food and rent. I just don't know what to do, I honestly don't. And it *is* my fault. I married the swine. If only I'd listened to people who tried to warn me, like your granny. It's too late now, I'm stuck with him.'

Cathy sat down on the side of the bath. 'I heard what he said, about me getting a job. Does that mean there's no point in me doing my O levels? Will I have to leave now I'm fifteen?'

Alice sighed. 'I hope you *can* stay on. But let's see what happens over the next few months, shall we? I'll go and put some sheets on Brian's bed and we might as well as try and sleep on it tonight and hope he forgets what he was ranting about by tomorrow.'

Cathy nodded. 'Okay. Goodnight, Mam.' That was the trouble with Jack. He could never remember any of the hurtful things he'd said, and often woke up in a reasonable mood as though nothing had happened.

Back in her own room, Cathy listened as the house fell silent, but she couldn't sleep. She was thirsty and needed a glass of water. She went back out onto the landing. Hardly daring to breathe, she crept downstairs, flinching as the door to the back room made its usual slight squeak. In the kitchen she filled a glass and stood facing the sink, sipping water until she'd had enough. She tipped the rest away and went back into the sitting room. She jumped with shock as Jack appeared in the doorway.

'What are you doing up?' he demanded, moving towards her.

Cathy was conscious of the fact she was only wearing a short frilly nighty that her granny had given her for Christmas and folded her arms around herself. 'I was getting a drink of water.' She fixed him with a mutinous stare and shivered as his eyes moved over her body and a smirk spread across his face. She felt nervous, but he was blocking her way out of the room and she didn't want to squeeze past him in case he touched her. But he just stood there looking her up and down with an unfathomable look in his eyes. Then he stood to one side and said, 'Get up the stairs out of my sight, now.'

Cathy shot out of the room and flew upstairs, her heart thudding in her chest. She wedged a chair beneath the door handle and climbed back into bed. She tossed and turned and hoped she'd eventually fall asleep.

*

Jack lurched back into his room, a glass of whisky in his hand. He sat down on the bed and swigged it down in one. He was so pissed off. Being stuck in the house all bloody day with Alice and the brats had been a nightmare. No work to relieve the monotony; the Legion was closed for two days over the holiday period. Daft idea really; he'd always opened Christmas Day and Boxing Day, as had Arnold and Winnie before him. There was money to be made by serving dinners and buffets. But Martin had told him his wife insisted they close and go to visit family in North Wales. There was no Sheila to comfort him, and that hurt because he knew she'd be all on her own while he was stuck here. She'd given him earache about it, saying he should be able to get at least an hour to himself. But the opportunity didn't arise for an escape and he'd got so drunk he'd destroyed the Christmas tree by slipping on Rosie's skates and falling on it. He knew that Alice wouldn't come down again now. She'd keep her distance. If he could only get up the stairs he'd drag her down to his bed. She had no right to be turning her back on him when he needed some comfort. And that little bitch Cathy, standing there looking all innocent while showing him all she'd got in that fancy nightdress. She'd get her comeuppance one of these days. He'd make sure of it. He blamed her for Alice not paying him attention for most of their marriage. But he'd get his own back, he was determined.

By the time the new term started, Cathy had resigned herself to the fact that she would have to leave school in the summer and give up any idea of a nursing career. Her mam had told her that she might be able to do her O levels at night school sometime in

'Bottoms up, gel.' He downed his whisky in one. While she sipped her sherry he took his wallet from the pocket of his jacket over the chair and pulled out two one-pound notes. He put them on the table. 'I've had a bit of a rise,' he said. 'Put that in your purse, get that drink down you and then you can come to bed with me and show me how grateful you are for a bit of extra money.'

Alice felt sick inside but did as she was told and finished her drink. He pulled her to her feet and propelled her into the bedroom, giving her no time to protest. It was only as she was falling asleep later that she remembered with horror that she hadn't been prepared with her diaphragm tonight.

*

Jack slid out of bed and went into the sitting room to light a cigarette, his mind in a whirl. He poured himself another whisky and sat on the sofa. That bloody Sheila. Fancy the dozy cow dropping her earring like that. Alice seemed to have bought his act of dumb innocence though. He always warned Sheila to make sure she'd left nothing lying around and not to wear any strong perfume. Alice would be sure to smell it on the sheets and know it wasn't hers. Wait until he saw her tomorrow. He'd give her what for, almost landing him in Shit Street. Alice would chuck him out if she found out he'd had her in their bed. And although living here sometimes drove him mad, during the day, when he was alone, it was an okay place to be. Always clean and tidy and he was well fed considering Alice was always saying she had hardly any money for food. He doubted he'd get that with Sheila. She got on his nerves at times with her neediness. To keep her sweet, he'd let her think he wanted to live with her, for now anyway. Otherwise she might stop him having his way at work when they got the chance, as well as here. He'd love to ask Millie next door to sing at the club again, like she used to do on a Saturday night, but if he did that, Alice and Sadie and their friends would come in and that would be it. All the people

Alice had worked with went to another club now, so he didn't cross paths any more with any of her old pals, who would be sure to tell tales. If he could just manage to keep the balance right, things were bearable. The little kids were growing up and were a bit more manageable. Alice had a good job, and later this year Cathy would be bringing money in. Life wasn't all that bad, even if Alice *did* occasionally look at him as though she'd like to kill him.

Chapter Four

July 1956

After dropping her youngest pair off at school, Alice and Cathy hurried up Aigburth Road to the bus stop where Debbie was waiting for them. Instead of going to school today, the teenagers were off to the city for a job interview at Lewis's department store. Alice had put in a good word with the store manager for the pair, who were leaving school next week. She hoped they'd both be taken on; it would soften the blow for Cathy if Debbie was working alongside her.

'Morning, Debs,' Cathy greeted Debbie and gave her a hug. 'You ready for this?'

'As I'll ever be,' Debbie replied, her long auburn hair, held in place with a black velvet band, gleaming in the bright sunlight. 'Do I look smart enough for an interview?' She looked down at her black and white checked pencil skirt topped with a black fitted jacket. Cathy was wearing a similar outfit and they both wore black low-heeled court shoes. Cathy's dark brown hair sat neatly on her shoulders with the ends flicked into soft curls.

'Yes, you both look very smart,' Alice said, nodding her approval. 'Quite grown up with your nice hairstyles. Now remember what I told you, the bosses like good manners and a neat and tidy appearance. I think we can safely say you'll pass muster on both those counts, so fingers crossed. Right, here's the bus. At least it's on time today. We don't want to be late before you've even started the job.'

*

Cathy stared out of the bus window, her mind on anything but the job interview. She was still disappointed that she couldn't stay on at school, but she wouldn't let her mam know. She'd only blame herself again. As far back as she could remember, Mam had encouraged her to think about a nursing career, something she'd been unable to do herself because of the war and needing to help support her family. But now Cathy's dreams had been taken away too. Without five good grades in her O levels it would never be possible. Her clever Uncle Brian, who'd just finished at Oxford University, had always instilled in her the need to work hard at school and she'd done just that with his encouragement and extra tutoring. She'd passed her eleven-plus and gone to grammar school, where most pupils stayed on to do O levels.

'You okay, Cathy?' Debbie asked, breaking into her thoughts as the conductor called out Ranelagh Street. 'I know this isn't what you really wanted to do, but at least it helps your family out for now, and you never know what the future will bring.'

Cathy nodded. 'We'll have to see.' She looked up as her mam got to her feet and ordered them to keep up with her as they dodged the crowds on the busy street.

Lewis's store, finally stripped of the scaffolding that had been in place for years, stood proudly on the corners of Ranelagh and Renshaw Streets, and Alice took them to the room where the interviews were being held. A group of boys and girls, all school leavers by the looks of it, were waiting to speak to a woman who was taking details at a desk in the corner. Extra staff were needed now the store had undergone the redevelopment. Standing at a huge nine floors, including the basement, it was finally nearing completion.

'Good luck, girls,' Alice said as she left them. 'When you've finished, come and find me in cosmetics and let me know how you've got on.'

After Cathy and Debbie had given their details to the woman at the desk they were told to take seats and their names would be called in due course. Cathy looked around and spotted empty seats under the window, next to two smartly suited lads who looked about the same age as her and Debbie.

'May we?' Cathy indicated the space and the boys nodded and shuffled up slightly. 'Thanks,' she said as the boy next to her flushed and muttered 'S'kay.'

Debbie smiled at him and he smiled back. 'Good morning. I'm Debs and she's Cathy. Are you two ready for leaving school too?'

He nodded. 'I'm Davy and he's Mike. We're hoping to be offered jobs in the television and electrical department.'

'We'd like cosmetics, but anything will do to get us in really, eh, Cath?'

'I suppose so.' Cathy sighed loudly.

'You don't sound very sure about that,' Mike said.

'She wants to be a nurse.' Debbie spoke for her. 'But her mam needs her to work and she'd have had to stay on at school for O levels.'

'Hard luck,' Mike sympathised, and then looked up as his name was called by a tall man with a clipboard. Davy's name was also called and he turned to Debbie and said, 'Good luck then. Meet us back out here after. Maybe we can go and have a coffee.'

Debbie stared after them, a big smile lighting up her face. 'I'm going to marry him,' she said, almost to herself. 'That Davy one, I mean.'

In spite of her nerves, Cathy burst out laughing. 'What? Don't be so daft, Debs. You don't even know him and you've only spoken half a dozen words to him.'

'I am. I tell you.' Debbie stopped as a woman with a clipboard peered over the top of her glasses and called their names. A badge fastened to her smart navy blue jacket declared that she was Miss Dolores Redfern.

'Follow me,' Miss Redfern instructed and led the way through one of several doors that led off the waiting room. 'Please take a seat.' She pointed to two chairs positioned on one side of a desk and sat down on the opposite side, facing them. She handed them a sheet of paper and a pen each, gave them instructions about details they needed to list and sat back in her chair while they completed the forms. When they'd finished she read through the lists and nodded as though satisfied by what she saw. 'First jobs then?' she muttered as she read. 'Ah, school leavers and both fifteen next month; jolly good. Now, as you can see from all the work going on within the store, we are expanding and require extra staff to take up positions as and when the new departments are ready to open.

'I'm particularly looking for young ladies to work on cosmetics, where Miss Lomax's mother is supervisor over the whole floor, and I have,' she consulted her list, 'vacancies for two junior sales staff on the Max Factor counter. The hours will be nine until six with two fifteen-minute breaks and an hour for lunch. The wages are two pounds two and six a week to begin and after six months' satisfactory service that will increase to two pounds and five shillings with annual increments to follow. There's two weeks' paid holiday along with bank holidays and a uniform will be provided. This will consist of a smart skirt and jacket in navy blue with two white blouses. We expect you to keep the uniform clean and well pressed and to wear our cosmetics. There's no need to plaster them on, but shoppers like to see our products used by staff and what they look like if worn correctly. You will be expected to demonstrate, so training will be given on the job. Now, Miss Lomax and Miss Jones, any questions?'

Cathy and Debbie stared open-mouthed at her and shook their heads. 'Er, does that mean we've got the jobs?' Debbie asked as Cathy stared in shock at the woman.

'It does indeed.' Miss Redfern got to her feet. 'Your mother spoke very favourably for the pair of you, Miss Lomax, as did the school references we asked for before inviting you for interview. They inform me that you are both bright pupils. I'll show you where to go to order your uniforms, and we will see you on the first Monday in August. Report to reception as you arrive and someone will bring you to the correct department.'

Davy and Mike were waiting for the girls as they emerged from the room. The wide smiles on each boy's face made Cathy smile also. 'You got taken on then?'

'We did,' Mike replied. 'White goods and tellies. Just what we wanted. What about you two?'

Cathy nodded. 'Max Factor cosmetics.'

'Smashing. Coffee then?'

'Just got to pop down to the cosmetic department and tell my mam,' Cathy said. 'She's supervisor down there. We'll only be a few minutes. We'll meet you by the entrance doors.'

'See you shortly then.' Mike and Davy left, and Cathy and Debbie made their way down the stairs to see Alice.

'Well done, girls,' Alice said when they told her their good news. 'What are you doing for the rest of the day?'

'Having coffee with two lads we just met upstairs and then a bit of a wander round town,' Debbie said.

Alice nodded and chewed her lip. 'Okay. Well, I might be a bit late today, so will you pick the kids up from Marlene's for me?' she asked Cathy. 'I've got to go somewhere before I get home. I'll definitely be back in time for tea.'

'Of course I will, Mam.' Cathy frowned. 'Where are you going?' Her mam never went anywhere without telling her. She wasn't meeting her eye and looked a bit shifty.

'Nowhere important.' Alice dismissed Cathy's query with a wave of her hand. 'There's just something I need to do, and I also want to call in and speak to Sadie at the library, so doing all that will take me over my usual time. Right, I'd best get on; enjoy your coffee with your new friends. See you later.'

Cathy linked arms with Debbie as they made their way outside the store. It was still early, so plenty of time to have a stroll around the city as well as coffee. Idle Jack could have got the girls from Marlene's for Mam. Not that he'd ever think to offer, and he had still been in bed when they'd left the house earlier. He hardly did anything to help with the kids, lazy bugger.

Mike and Davy were waiting for them and led the way to the Kardomah coffee shop, where Mike ordered frothy coffees all round and a plate of toasted teacakes. He refused Cathy's offer of paying their share. They chatted about their new jobs; they were all due to start work on the same day in August.

'Where do you two live?' Mike asked. 'Never seen you in town on a Saturday night.'

Cathy shrugged. 'Near Lark Lane in Aigburth. We sometimes go to the pictures, the Mayfair near us, or for a walk in Seffy Park. We don't really come into the city though.'

'Perhaps you could join us this weekend,' Davy suggested. 'Saturday nights we meet up in the Rumblin' Tum coffee bar on Hardman Street. Nice crowd and they have a great jukebox. Mike and I love all the new music that's starting to come through from America.'

Debbie dug Cathy in the ribs before she had a chance to refuse. 'We'd love that, wouldn't we, Cathy? I don't know where the Rumblin' Tum is though. So where shall we meet you?'

'I'm not sure that I'll be able to,' Cathy muttered, knowing full well that if she asked to go out Jack would throw a hairy fit about her wasting money on gallivanting. She might ask her granny if she could sub her. 'Have to see how the land lies at home first.'

'Okay, well, if you *can* come along, Davy's folks have got a telephone.' Mike wrote down Davy's number and passed it to Debbie. 'Give him a call on Saturday morning about dinnertime and tell us where to meet you.'

Davy winked at Debbie, who smiled and slipped the paper into her handbag. 'I will do.'

Chapter Five

Alice stared in horror at the doctor. He had just told her that the result of her recent pregnancy test was positive. She'd known deep down it would be, but even so, she'd been praying for it to be negative. Jack would go absolutely mental. Drunken rages and forcing himself on her had resulted in the conception of Sandra. Rosie had been unplanned and this one was from the earring saga night, as she'd come to think of it. The one night she'd been unprepared and given in to his demands so that arguing with him didn't waken Cathy and the little ones and frighten them.

She worried about Cathy and the way Jack leered at her now she was growing up. She'd stick a knife in his ribs if he so much as laid a finger on her girl. She wished she had the energy and courage to throw him out once and for all and cope alone. After all, it was pretty much what she'd been doing for years. And then he wouldn't be able to demand money for booze when she needed it to feed their children. Cathy working would help a bit, but it wasn't the answer. She was aware of the doctor speaking to her and blinked. How long had she been sat there in silence with her jumbled thoughts?

'Mrs Dawson, I gather from your shocked reaction that this isn't good news for you?'

Alice covered her face with her hands. 'It's a disaster,' she wailed. 'I simply can't have another baby. I won't be able to cope. My husband, he's er, he's unable to work due to him missing a foot, and he will go mad when I tell him. I don't want it, I really don't.'

The doctor was new to the practice and Alice hadn't seen him before, so he would have no idea of her past life and how this, her fourth child, like her last two, was so unplanned and unwanted. He shook his head and shuffled through her notes, nodding slowly, while she composed herself.

'I think you need to go home and talk to your husband. Once he's over the initial shock, I'm sure you'll both come round to welcoming this baby into your lives. You're still a young woman at thirty-five. Book an appointment to see me in two weeks' time and we'll assign you a midwife with whom you can talk over any worries or problems you may have.'

Feeling dismissed, Alice dragged herself out of the surgery and along Aigburth Road towards Sefton Park library, where she was meeting Sadie for coffee and a sandwich. Sadie had recently been promoted to her dream job of chief librarian. She'd worked alongside Millie and Alice in Lewis's, but had always wanted to work in a library. How Alice wished she'd taken a leaf from Sadie's book and stayed single, with just Cathy to worry about. Marrying Jack had put paid to her daughter's dreams of training to be a nurse, just like the war had put paid to Alice's own dreams of nursing. She hoped there would come a time when Cathy would realise *her* dreams and that there would be a future where they would be rid of Jack Dawson for good.

Sadie was waiting anxiously in the foyer of the beautiful black and white timber-framed library for her and greeted her with a hug. Alice felt her eyes filling again. Apart from Millie, Sadie was the only other person privy to her secret worry; there was no need for words.

'Oh, Alice, no!' Sadie cried. 'Not again. How the hell are you going to cope? Come on, let's go through to the staffroom rather than out. I'll send one of the girls to get us a sandwich and we can make coffee back there.' Sadie led the way, calling out to Linda at the desk to follow her. 'Get us two cheese salad rolls and a couple of vanilla slices from down the road, Linda, please.' She handed the girl a ten-shilling note and gestured for Alice to sit down while she put the kettle on and busied herself making two mugs of coffee. 'Right, get that down you,' Sadie ordered, handing Alice a steaming mug. 'I've put an extra spoonful of sugar in it.'

'Thanks.' Alice looked around the pleasant little room. It was painted primrose yellow with a green carpet and matching curtains that fluttered in the slight breeze from the open window, which overlooked the park. The heady scent of rose bushes drifted in and birds twittered in the trees. It felt peaceful and restful. She took a sip of coffee. There was a tap on the door and Linda came in carrying two white paper bags.

'I timed it right,' she said, putting the bags onto the coffee table and handing Sadie her change. 'They'd just finished the dinnertime rush. Rolls are in the bigger bag.'

She left the room as Sadie took two small china plates from a wall cupboard over the sink for their sandwiches. 'Here you go. Get this down you. You need to keep your strength up and I know you don't eat as much as you should in favour of feeding the kids.'

'Thank you,' Alice said, taking the plate. 'I am a bit peckish, I must admit. I've only had time for a slice of toast all day.'

'Well, it's not enough,' Sadie said, 'especially now, feeding two. You'll be fainting all over the show.'

Alice sighed. She never really felt too nauseous and faint while pregnant, which was just as well when she was trying to hide it from Jack and Cathy. She hated him almost as much as he proclaimed he hated his family when he was drunk. On days when he was sober his moods lightened and he could still be charming, but those days were getting rarer as time went on.

'So when will you tell him?' Sadie asked gently.

Alice shrugged. 'I don't know. I'll think about it tonight. I'm just about four months – it was the last week of March – so I've got a bit of time before I start to show properly. It'll be due about

Christmas or just after. I'm so annoyed with myself. I love being at work, as you know. Now I'm going to have to take time off again, without pay, and there's no way I can afford to put a baby in the nursery now Marlene's stopped full-time childminding. Jack should be the one doing the minding to save us some money, but I can't trust him. One drink and he'd forget he's got kids.'

Sadie shook her head. 'It's easy to say with hindsight, but I do wish you hadn't married him, Alice.'

'That makes two of us.'

Alice finished her coffee and Sadie put the vanilla slices on the plates. 'I'll make us another brew,' she announced. 'You were doing fine on your own and before you sold your mam's house to Millie. You'd have managed somehow.'

Alice shook her head. 'I couldn't afford to put my brother through college and university without the money from the house sale. Brian worked so hard, he deserved every penny of his share. Putting my half up as a bond for the Legion was the big mistake. Jack wasn't fit to be running his own club. When I think back now, and if only I'd stayed single, Cathy and I could have lived at Terry's mother's while I got on my feet. Brian could still have done exactly what he has done and I might even have been able to buy another little house, like you did, in time. I had enough for a deposit and I had a full-time job, so I could have paid a small mortgage. Cathy could have stayed on at school. I feel dreadful that my stupid choices and decisions have ruined her future.'

Sadie patted her arm. 'Don't blame yourself. Cathy will be fine. She might need to wait a while to do what she wants to do, but she'll get there one day. She's a determined girl, like my Gianni's determined to do what he wants to do. Oh, and that reminds me. We're going away during August bank holiday. Romano's Fair is coming to Sefton Park for a week so I've booked the time off work. Gianni's on holiday anyway so we're having a week at Butlin's in Pwllheli.'

Alice looked up. 'Does he know his father is coming to town?'

Sadie shrugged. 'Not as far as I know. I saw posters being pasted up, so when it was dark I tore them down. They're in the bin outside. There may be others around the city, but there's nothing around here where he's likely to see them. The fair hasn't been to Liverpool since the end of the forties, so I've been lucky really. I don't want them to meet up. Gianni is of an age where he's easily influenced and he's driving me mad now he's got that bloody motorbike. Not much I can do about it – he saved up the deposit from doing odd jobs for people, and I'm helping him to pay the rest on hire purchase instead of him having any birthday or Christmas presents for a couple of years. He knows it worries me to death when he's out on it, but he's growing up. I've got to learn to let go a bit, and he'd find the money from somewhere else if I didn't help. If he knew Luca was involved in a wall of death ride I'd never hear the end of it. After what happened to your Terry, I couldn't bear it.'

'I don't blame you,' Alice said, getting to her feet. 'I suppose I'd better let you get back to work. Cathy and Debbie got the jobs, by the way. Max Factor counter. They seemed really pleased with that.'

'Oh that's good. They'll enjoy it, I'm sure. Is Dolores still doing the interviews?'

Alice smiled. 'She is. She doesn't change, still as efficient as ever. Tickles me how we all knew her as Dolly at school but she insists on Dolores now. She looks all intelligent with her new posh frame glasses.'

Sadie laughed. 'Ah well, good for her. Will you tell Cathy about the baby before you tell Jack?'

'I think so. She can be there to support me when I tell him. He'll keep his fists under control if Cathy's around. She stands no messing from him.'

'You should chuck him out, Alice.'

Alice stared at the ceiling. 'I know. But he's disabled. Where would he go?'

'That's not your problem.'

Alice said goodbye to Sadie and set off to walk to Lucerne Street. It was a lovely warm day and she removed her jacket, enjoying the feel of the sun on her arms. Outside the Lark Lane post office she bumped into Granny Lomax. Her stomach plummeted, but she fixed a bright smile on her face as her ex-mother-in-law raised a hand in greeting.

'Alice, my dear. How are you? How did Cathy get on today?'

'I'm fine, thank you,' Alice replied. 'Cathy got the job. No doubt she'll be over to tell you later.'

Granny Lomax nodded. 'Well, it could be worse. You've done okay there and Lewis's is a nice enough store to work in, although I'm not sure what the owners were thinking when they allowed that naked statue to grace the front of the building.'

Alice half-smiled at the reference to Nobby Lewis. The nickname had been given to the Liverpool Resurgent statue by many young people in the area. 'That statue is meant to celebrate the resurgence of the store and the city after the Blitz. We're all quite proud of it, actually.'

'Hmm, well that's as may be, but the sculptor should have put some clothes on it. It's quite indecent. Anyway, it's such a shame Cathy can't achieve her nursing goals. She's a bright girl, she's worked hard and she really does deserve better.'

'I agree with you, she does. But at the moment it's not possible. I hope you're keeping well. I'd better go. I've a lot to do and I need to get home to the children. Goodbye.' She dashed away before Mrs Lomax could say any more on the subject.

Alice hurried into her house to hear raised voices coming from the back sitting room. She sighed, hung her jacket on the coat stand and took a deep breath. Fixing on a smile, she opened the sitting room door. Jack was in his usual chair by the fireplace, clutching a mug. His unshaven chin and untidy appearance meant he'd not left the house all day. If he'd been out to the Legion he would at least have made an effort to smarten himself up. Cathy was standing by the table clutching her handbag to her chest, a mutinous expression on her face.

'What's going on here?' Alice demanded.

'He's sulking because I won't lend him five bob.'

Alice shook her head. 'Cathy doesn't have five bob to her name, Jack. And if she did, she wouldn't lend it to you to go out and waste on beer. If you want money, then get a few more hours' work at the Legion. We need every penny I've got coming in to pay bills and keep the roof over our heads. I can't do it on fresh air.' Alice stopped as he glared at her. She wouldn't have dared to speak to him like that if they'd been alone and he knew it. But her daughter's presence always made her feel a bit stronger.

He got to his feet and slammed the mug down on the table. 'I'll have a wash and shave and then I'm going down the club. A bit of glass-clearing and they might sub me a pint.' He limped off and shut himself in the kitchen.

Alice turned to Cathy. She had a face like thunder. 'What?'

'Him. He could have got off his backside and picked the girls up. Me and Debs would have liked a bit longer in town. We're back in school tomorrow.'

'I know, love, and I'm sorry. But I can't trust him to do a simple job, you know that. Where are the girls, by the way?'

'Playing hopscotch round the back. He's a waste of space, Mam. I don't know why you don't get a divorce. He's horrible to you, me and the kids. He started shouting as soon as we walked through the door. He scared Rosie half to death and then smacked her legs for crying. He was always nasty to me when I was little and I hate him for what he's done to us all.' Cathy's lips trembled and Alice gave her a hug.

'One day it'll all be over. I promise you.' But when would it? Alice thought. With a new baby on the way things were about to change yet again, God help them all.

Cathy shrugged. 'Huh. You reckon. And pigs might fly.' She changed the subject. 'Er, Mam, is it okay if I go out with Debs into the city on Saturday night for a couple of hours? Those lads we had a coffee with asked us to meet them to go to a place that has a jukebox. It's called the Rumblin' Tum coffee bar.'

'I suppose so,' Alice said. 'But don't mention anything to Jack. He'll be at work anyway, so there's no need for him to know. Saves causing another row over money. Not that he gives you any to spend anyway, but it keeps the peace. I'll have to get used to you going out, maybe doing a bit of courting now and again. Does Gianni go in there? I'm sure I've heard Sadie mention the name.'

Cathy shrugged. 'No idea. Be nice to see him if he does though.'

Mike and Davy met Cathy and Debbie off the bus and they made their way to the Rumblin' Tum on Hardman Street.

Cathy gazed around as they entered the shop with its unusual decor of newspaper pages plastered all over the walls like wallpaper, and coated with shiny varnish to protect it. Everything, including the Formica-topped tables and chairs and tiled floor, was black and white. A few leather-jacketed lads with immaculately quiffed hair, and wearing tight denim jeans, clustered around the silent jukebox, smoking and discussing what record to choose next. It was very different to anywhere she'd ever been before and there was an exciting atmosphere in the air. She shivered with anticipation.

'Frothy coffees or Coca-Cola?' Mike asked as Davy led the girls to a table.

'Coffee for me, please,' Cathy replied and Debbie said she'd have one as well. They sat down and Davy went to help Mike carry the drinks across.

'We can try a Coca-Cola later,' Debbie said with a grin. 'Looks great, doesn't it?' she said, pointing at the walls. 'Although I couldn't see my mam agreeing to have copies of the *Echo* papered onto our sitting room walls.'

The jukebox burst into life and Bill Haley and the Comets belted out 'Rock Around the Clock.' Several couples got up to dance in the small area of floor clear of tables. Cathy watched them cavorting around. It all looked very energetic and she wondered if she'd ever be able to dance like that. She'd heard it was called jiving and the Americans had invented it. Although the other week, when some dancers were on the telly, Jack had pointed his cigarette at the screen and said that was nothing compared to the jitterbugging they'd all done during the war. The thought of her crabby stepfather with only one full foot moving about like that took a definite stretch of the imagination.

'Do you want to dance?' Mike asked.

Cathy shook her head and took a sip of coffee. 'I don't know how to do it.'

'I do. Come on, you.' Debbie grabbed Davy by the hand and pulled him onto the floor.

Cathy and Mike watched their friends giggling, twirling around and ducking under one another's arms, Davy almost tripping Debbie up at one point. The song ended and then Elvis Presley's 'Blue Suede Shoes' came on and Cathy smiled. 'I love Elvis,' she said dreamily.

'Well come on then, let's give it a go.' Mike held out his hand. She shyly took it and he led her to the small dance area.

Cathy was so busy trying to concentrate on her moves and get her feet right that she didn't see Gianni and a small girl with long blonde hair strolling in, holding hands.

The next song on the jukebox was the Dream Weavers' 'It's Almost Tomorrow' and was declared too slow to dance to by a breathless Debbie. Davy went to the counter for more drinks as the others sat down.

Cathy gazed around and caught Gianni's eye. He smiled and raised his hand in greeting. The girl he was with turned round and frowned at Cathy, who smiled and waved back anyway.

'Who's she frowning at?' Debbie muttered as Davy came back to the table with a tray of bottles of Coca-Cola with straws.

'Me, I think,' Cathy replied. 'Because I waved at Gianni.'

'Well, he's your friend. Why shouldn't you?'

'Know him, do you?' Mike said, handing Davy a cigarette and his lighter.

Cathy nodded. 'He's my neighbour's son and my friend from since I was a little girl.'

'Right flirt, by all accounts. Thinks he's God's gift.' Mike curled his lip in disgust. 'Good job you're not his type or he'd hurt your feelings.'

Debbie frowned, took a sip of her drink and coughed as the bubbles hit the back of her throat. Davy patted her on the back and she caught her breath. 'What makes you think Cathy isn't Gianni's type, Mike?'

Cathy stared at Mike as his jaw tightened. He shrugged. 'Well, it's obvious. She'd have said he was her ex, not her neighbour. He'd have asked her out by now if he fancied her. Who wouldn't?' he finished, smiling at Cathy, who chewed her lip, feeling embarrassed.

'We're just good friends,' she mumbled and concentrated on her drink. Mike's observations had hurt a bit. Maybe Gianni didn't fancy her and that's why he'd never asked her out, held her hand or kissed her on the odd occasion they'd been alone. Time to put him to the back of her mind and get to know Mike a bit better, although if she was honest, he was a nice enough lad, but not really her type. She couldn't even begin to imagine what her type was, though, except… She looked across at Gianni again and saw him running his hands through the blonde girl's hair. She sighed inwardly. Well, that was something she'd never be in a month of Sundays, a blonde.

Chapter Six

August 1956

By mid-August Alice was struggling to conceal her pregnancy, no matter how tight a girdle she squeezed herself into. It was such a relief on Sundays when she didn't have to get ready to go to work. She'd taken to wearing a loose floral cotton overall to do her housework in and it covered her secret as best it could, but Cathy had made a comment yesterday about her putting weight on, and she knew she'd have to come clean sooner rather than later. Her baby was due the last week in December, according to the midwives, which sounded about right when she worked it out for herself. Strange that Jack hadn't noticed her gaining weight – or if he had, he didn't mention it.

In the kitchen she attached the hose to the tap, filled the washer with water and switched it on to heat up while she sorted out the washing into piles of darks and lights. The little ones were down the street at their school friend Betty's house and Cathy was getting ready to go to her granny's as usual. Jack had left early for the Legion as there was a bowling match on this morning, so he'd be out for a good few hours.

She sprinkled in the Omo powder and dropped the first wash pile into the machine, closing the lid while it agitated the load. She caught her breath momentarily and put her hand on her stomach. Butterflies, the stirrings of movement. She thought she'd felt it last night in the bath, but then the feeling went away so she'd put it down to a touch of wind. She looked up as the door from the sitting room opened and Cathy came in.

'Hi, Mam. Shall I make us a quick brew before I go to Granny's?'

'I'll make it.' Alice popped her head round the kitchen door. 'You look very nice. Is that the dress you got from Paddy's Market last week?'

Cathy looked down at her black and white spotted dress with the full skirt. 'It is. I mended that split in the seam and took the hem up a bit and bought this black waspie belt from work. Sets it off nicely and it all goes with my black jacket. Deb's said she can't believe how lucky I was to pick this up for next to nothing – it's the latest style coming in from America. It's what everyone's wearing to do that new jiving dance now. When we went to the Rumblin' Tum with the lads from work all the girls were wearing something similar.'

'Some people have more money than sense. Whoever gave it to the fella on the market obviously couldn't be bothered to mend it,' Alice said. 'Your gain, their loss.'

Cathy sat at the table and her mam brought in two mugs of tea and sat down opposite. 'Before you go out there's something I need to talk to you about. But I don't want it going any further than here, for now. No telling your granny,' Alice warned.

Cathy raised an eyebrow. She sipped her tea, looking over the top of her mug.

Alice took a deep breath and began. 'You've noticed I'm putting on weight, because you mentioned it yesterday. Well the reason for that is – I'm expecting a baby—' She stopped and burst into tears.

Cathy gasped and put down her mug. 'Oh, Mam. I can see you're not very happy about it. Does Jack know?'

Alice shook her head. 'Not yet. And if I'm honest, I'm dreading telling him. He'll go absolutely mad.'

'Well, it's half his fault; and you can't keep it to yourself. When is it due?'

'December,' Alice replied. 'And it means I'm going to be off work with no pay for a few weeks before and afterwards. I really have no idea how we're going to manage.'

Cathy chewed her lip. 'Granny might help us.'

'Cathy, no, we can't ask her and I don't want her to know yet. I've already told you that.'

'Does Uncle Brian know?'

'Not yet. I'm going to write to him this week. There's only Sadie and Millie knows. I need to tell Jack before anyone else finds out. You get off to your gran's now. But will you make sure you're home when Jack finishes work? He'll be finishing earlier tonight as he went in early for the bowling match. Come back for nine at the latest and you can sit upstairs. I'll call out for you if I need any backup.'

Cathy got to her feet. 'Try not to worry, Mam. Jack might be okay.'

'Hmm, and pigs might fly. Off you go, enjoy your roast dinner and your stroll around Seffy Park later.'

*

Cathy walked up Lark Lane, her head in a whirl. She was oblivious to his whistling to catch her attention until Gianni stepped into place beside her.

'You were off a bit sharpish today,' he said, catching his breath. 'Thought I'd missed you, until Mam said she'd seen you leaving while I was out the back.'

'Oh sorry, Gianni. I got delayed.' He'd taken to walking most Sundays with her to Linnet Lane and back. It was the only time they got to catch up with each other's news.

'The usual way, Jack, the usual way.' She sat back and waited for the outburst that was sure to come. But he just continued to stare at her, looking like the stuffing had been knocked out of him. When she'd told him she was expecting Sandra he'd told her to get rid of the baby at first, until he'd calmed down, but when she'd told him that Rosie was on the way, he'd just nodded and accepted it. Not happily, as time went on, but he'd been calmer. This time it seemed he was speechless.

'How do you feel about it?' she dared to ask.

He shrugged. 'I'm shocked,' he admitted. 'When's it due?'

'December. Jack, you do realise I'll have to give up work, don't you? For a few months, anyway.'

He nodded slowly. 'I daresay I can get more hours at the Legion. We'll be busy over Christmas so that won't be a problem. I can offer to take over on Christmas Day and Boxing Day. Martin will want to close again, no doubt, but I can run the place for him with the help of the staff. They just need supervising, that's all.' He was quiet for a while as though thinking things over. 'It'll probably be best if I stay there while Martin's away and then I'm on site for any problems. You and Cathy can manage here with the kids and I'll be out of your hair. It's a while off, I know, but plans need to be put in place for Christmas dinners and what have you. That should earn me a nice bit of extra that we can save towards the rent for the few weeks you're laid up.' He finished his drink and gave Alice a hug. 'Don't you worry, gel, we'll manage somehow or other. Get yourself off to sleep now while I nip up the garden for a pee. I'll have a quick wash in the kitchen before I come to bed.'

Alice nodded and hurried upstairs to the bathroom, but first popped her head round Cathy's door. Her daughter was sitting on the bed, her face etched with worry.

'Everything okay, Mam?'

Alice nodded. 'Oddly enough; yes, unless it's the calm before the storm. But he doesn't seem all that bothered. I'll tell you tomorrow when we're on the way to work.'

*

As he washed the scent of Sheila from his body, Jack felt numb from the shock of Alice's news. Another bloody mouth to feed. He really didn't need it. But they'd manage somehow or other. Sheila wasn't going to be very happy when she found out that Alice was up the duff again. He'd told her that due to lack of rooms they shared a bed, but there was no hanky-panky between them. It kept Sheila happy, but this news would go down like a lead balloon. He'd try to keep it to himself for as long as he could and just make sure her and Alice's paths didn't cross. Looking after the Legion over Christmas had been mentioned earlier by Martin, and Jack had already agreed to do it. He'd been wondering how to tell Alice he'd be missing for a couple of days without arousing suspicion. So that was one problem solved, at least.

Sheila was going to stay with him and that would stop her complaining again about spending Christmas on her own. Plus he wouldn't have to go through that awful frustrating time of being cooped up with Alice and the brats. If the new one had arrived by then it would no doubt whinge all the time, like babies do. He knew that Alice and Cathy would probably be happier if they didn't have to share the day with him. Cathy could look after her mother for a change. She was always moaning on about wanting to be a bloody nurse – well, she could get a bit of practice in at home. All being well, the arrangement should keep everyone happy and the bonus was that he'd be able to cough up a bit more money to help with the bills.

*

By the time December rolled round, Cathy had been forced into the role of main breadwinner, with Jack begrudgingly tipping up some of his disabled soldier's pension and the odd few shillings from his wages when the mood suited him. Alice was resting for most of the day with her feet up as they, along with her ankles, were slightly swollen. Her blood pressure was higher than her midwife would have liked as well. With the baby due in the last week of the month she was taking no chances. Her other three had all arrived early, so with every day that passed she expected to go into labour. Apparently the baby was a big one and had been lying in the correct position with its head engaged at her antenatal appointment yesterday. It had stopped kicking and wriggling a bit now it had swapped position and Alice felt a bit more comfortable. She was never off the lavvy though, as it insisted on playing football with her bladder, and she was so grateful for the one outside, as trawling up the steep stairs to the bathroom was a job and a half.

Marlene was picking the girls up today and taking them to her house for tea. Her old friend was so good and even though Alice had told her she didn't need to help with them any more now she'd finished work and she had no money to pay her, Marlene insisted she still wanted to do her bit. Alice struggled to her feet from the armchair and put her hands on her aching back. Sadie was finishing work earlier today and had told her she'd pop in with a couple of cakes on the way home.

Time to put the kettle on and then she could have the tea brewed ready. She put the little white matinee jacket she was making back into her mam's old tapestry knitting bag that she'd never had the heart to throw away. She'd do a bit more tonight when the kids were in bed and Cathy was round at Debbie's. Jack would have his tea with Martin and his wife, he'd told her, so there was only Cathy and herself to feed and she'd made a pan of scouse earlier. What was left would do for tomorrow's tea. She filled the kettle and leaned against the sink, waiting for it to boil.

'Come in,' she called to a knock on the door.

Sadie let herself in and came through to the sitting room. She put down a white paper bag and went into the kitchen to help carry the tea pot and mugs to the table. Alice brought the milk jug and sugar bowl through and gingerly lowered herself onto a dining chair.

'Oh, I've forgotten the little plates, Sadie. They're on the side.'

Sadie brought the plates through and opened the paper bag. Alice's eyes lit up as she saw her favourite vanilla slices in there.

'Oh yum. Just what I need to cheer me up.'

'Not long now, Alice,' Sadie said, pouring tea into the mugs and handing a vanilla slice to her. 'How are you feeling today?'

'Like I'm ready to pop,' Alice said. She took a bite and then licked the sticky icing from her fingers. 'I'll be so glad when it's over. It feels much bigger than any of the girls did. Makes me wonder if it's not a boy this time.'

'Gianni was only tiny, just over five pounds, so it doesn't always follow that big babies are boys.'

'The movements feel different though. More forceful and heavy.'

'Well, if it is a boy, Jack might be thrilled. It would even things up a bit.'

Alice rolled her eyes and sighed. 'I think thrilled is pushing it a bit, no matter what it is. All he's interested in is the fact the family allowance goes up by another ten bob a week once it's here! Give him his due, he's keeping out of the way and not arguing as much. I don't know what I'd do without Cathy to help me. She's been so good seeing to the kids and getting them off to bed once Marlene brings them home. She's bought all the Christmas stuff, wrapped everything and put the tree up. All I've had to do is write the cards. What are you and Gianni doing for Christmas?'

'Oh, he'll be out with his mates on Christmas Eve, and we're at my mam's on the day. Millie's going to Blackpool this year to Jimmy's mam's.'

'I know.' Alice nodded. 'Jack's in charge at the Legion all over Christmas so it's just me, Cathy and the girls. I'm hoping for a better time for them this year.'

They sat in companionable silence, finishing their tea and cake, and then Sadie got to her feet and washed the plates and mugs.

'I'd better be making tracks and get something on the go for his lordship's tea. I'll see you in the next day or two, Alice. If you need anything, send one of the kids over.'

The shrieks of excitement as her sisters unwrapped the few things she'd managed to buy for them, and that Father Christmas had delivered in the early hours, brought tears to Cathy's eyes. She had a distant memory of early childhood when her dad had been alive and Uncle Brian lived with them. Just one Christmas they'd shared as a family after the war and before her dad had died. At least she *had* that memory; all Sandra and Rosie had experienced so far was a grumpy dad who'd managed to spoil their last Christmas and had never been much fun on the previous ones either.

Jack had seemed almost delighted last night as he'd left the house with a small suitcase in readiness to spend the next couple of days managing the Legion. Not sorry at all that he'd miss spending it with his family. He kept going on about how much more money he'd be earning doing this extra work. And of course he'd be spending the extra time in Sheila's company. He had no idea that Cathy knew about that, and she hadn't said a thing to her mam either as there was no point in upsetting an already rocky applecart.

She looked up as her mam shuffled into the sitting room, clutching her stomach, a pained expression on her face. 'You okay, Mam?'

'I will be as soon as I've been out the back to the lav. Oh, God almighty, the little bugger is playing football with my bladder something shocking. Won't be a minute.' She lumbered away, groaning.

'Right, girls,' Cathy addressed her sisters, who were looking at the chocolate bars in a selection box. 'Screw the torn wrapping paper up and I'll put it on the fire. Let's have our breakfast and then I can get on with making Christmas dinner. You can show Mammy your nice presents. Do you like your dollies?' Cathy had managed to get two almost identical baby dolls and had shown them to Granny Lomax, who kindly knitted them an outfit each. Sandra's dolly was dressed in pink and Rosie's in pale lemon. They nodded enthusiastically. They'd also got a storybook each, boxes of crayons and colouring books, tops and whips, a large jigsaw puzzle between them and the selection boxes. Cathy smiled; they seemed happy enough with their little haul and it would keep them quiet for most of the day.

Alice dried the dishes that Cathy had washed and put the last plate in the cupboard. 'Thanks, Cathy, that was a lovely meal. I really enjoyed it. It was so nice to have it cooked for me for a change.'

'I couldn't have done it if you hadn't been here shouting your instructions, Mam.' Cathy laughed. 'God knows what sort of burnt offerings you'd have been served up. I feel quite pleased that I managed to do it and it didn't spoil.'

'Well, there's plenty of chicken left for sandwiches later and there's a tin of pears and Carnation milk in the cupboard for afters, so we should go to bed with full tummies tonight for a change,' Alice said. 'Paying into the butcher's Christmas club was a good idea of yours. We couldn't have afforded that chicken or the bacon and eggs we had for breakfast otherwise…' Alice stopped as someone knocked on the door. 'Now who the heck can this be?'

Cathy hid a smile. She'd been keeping a little surprise for her mam, not to mention an extra dinner stored secretly in the oven between two plates. She got a set of cutlery from the drawer and went to lay a place at the table as her mam waddled down the hall

and flung open the door. Her surprised yell made Cathy laugh out loud and Sandra and Rosie looked at one another as a deep voice shouted out, 'Merry Christmas, ho, ho, ho!'

'Uncle Brian!' the little ones squealed, and flung themselves at his legs as he tried to get into the sitting room.

'Girlies,' he said, bending to take them both into a hug. 'My, how you two are growing. Cathy.' He stood up and held his arms out. She melted into them and was squeezed so hard she squealed. 'Sorry,' he said, releasing her, 'don't know my own strength.' He laughed and put his arms round his sister. 'And how's my lovely Alice?'

'Fat,' she said, tears of joy running down her face. 'I can't believe this, I really can't. What a wonderful surprise. I thought you were going away for Christmas? You said you were in the letter you put in your card.'

'This is away for me, coming home. But Cathy and I wanted to surprise you. She said if you knew I was coming you would be dashing around like a mad thing and you are in no fit state to do that. So when you wrote back and invited me I had to tell a little white lie because Cathy and I had been plotting.'

'But your bed needs making and, oh God, we've no dinner for you.'

'His bed's been ready for days, Mam, and,' Cathy waltzed into the kitchen and came back with a plate full of Christmas dinner, 'I'd hidden his dinner in the oven out of your sight. Sit down, Brian, and I'll get you a drink. We can take your case upstairs later.'

'I'll eat first and then I'll unload the car,' Brian said, his face beaming with happiness. He looked around. 'Er, where's Jack?'

'Believe it or not, he's working at the Legion all over Christmas,' Alice said as she joined her brother at the table, still unable to believe her eyes. 'You'll have to pop in and see him tomorrow afternoon. But right now we're not letting you out of our sight.'

Chapter Seven

Alice breathed a sigh of relief as, after a long game of snakes and ladders and two stories, Sandra and Rosie were taken up to bed. Cathy settled them down and came back to join her mam and Brian round the fire. The sitting room positively brimmed with happiness; so very different to last Christmas Day, Alice thought. Brian had produced a large bag of gaily wrapped parcels that he told the little ones Father Christmas had left under his tree by mistake, which was why he'd had to drive all this way to deliver them by car rather than sledge. The girls had excitedly unwrapped a compendium of games and a large box each that contained dollies' prams. Sandra and Rosie's excitement reached a peak of almost hysteria as they put their dollies in the prams and strolled proudly up and down the length of the narrow hall as it was too dark to play outside. Brian promised to take them and the prams to the park in the morning if they were good girls and went to bed nicely.

Brian had also brought a beautiful iced Christmas cake in a fancy tin and Cathy made three mugs of tea and sliced pieces of the cake to have with them.

'What a treat. We haven't had a Christmas cake for a few years now,' Alice said. 'Well, not since we moved into here.'

'You're going to be awfully cramped here when the baby arrives,' Brian said. 'Where will you put it?'

'It'll have to go in your little room when it's old enough and sleeping through,' Alice said. 'Then we'll squeeze it in with Cathy when you come to stay over.'

Brian nodded and took a sip of tea, looking thoughtful. 'That might not be for quite some time,' he said. 'I've er, I've been offered a teaching position at an American university, to begin in March. It's an initial two-year period and then we'll see. It's such a wonderful opportunity and I can't afford to turn it down.'

Alice nodded. She'd be sorry to see him go away, but had been expecting him to up sticks and leave England at some point in the not-too-distant future. She looked at Cathy, whose lips were trembling at Brian's news. She felt so bad for her daughter. Her girl's ambitions were on hold all because Alice had married the wrong man. If only she could turn back the clock and Cathy could be freed from her present life and begin her nurse training. Damn bloody Jack Dawson and his thoughtless ways. She finished her tea and cake and got to her feet. 'I'll nip out the back and then I'm off to bed. I'll leave you two to catch up properly. Thank you both for making today so very special. I won't forget it in a hurry.' Alice's eyes filled as she made her way to the outside lavvy.'

*

Cathy woke from deep slumbers to hear her mam calling her name. There were no fingers of light peeping through the curtains yet, so it must still be the middle of the night. She squinted at her bedside clock. Just after five am. She slid out of bed, put her slippers on and grabbed her dressing gown, which was draped over the bed for extra warmth. She clicked the landing light on and saw her mam sitting on the stairs a quarter of the way up. She hurried down, squeezed past and knelt in front of her. 'Is it the baby? Is it coming?'

'I think so, but let's go into my room so we don't wake Brian and the kids up.'

Alice heaved herself to her feet and Cathy slid her arm round her waist and led her into the bedroom. She helped her onto the bed and stood back feeling anxious as her mam let out a low, deep groan.

Alice looked up. 'Don't look so worried, chuck. It's just a small contraction. It's passed now. I've a while to go yet, but we need to get things ready.'

'Shall I go to the phone box and call the midwife?' Cathy asked; her eyes wide with fear. Her mam had decided to have this baby at home rather than the hospital, because she knew Cathy would end up doing everything if she was away for any length of time. And she had her job to go to.

'Not yet,' Alice said. 'We'll wait until the pains are closer together. Let's just get everything ready,' she repeated. 'Put some more coal on the fire, love, and some twists of paper. There's a few glowing embers in the grate. It should soon get going again. The new white bowl and bucket are under the kitchen sink. They'll need those. The birthing pack the midwife brought round last week is on top of the chest of drawers and in the bottom drawer is a new baby towel and blankets and some baby clothes—' Alice stopped and took a deep breath. She grimaced as another pain took her breath away.

Cathy hurried into the kitchen and put the kettle on. She'd read somewhere that midwives need plenty of boiling water, but she'd make her mam a cuppa first. She grabbed an old copy of the *Echo* and the coal scuttle and dashed back into the front room to bank up the fire, which was soon roaring up the chimney. She got to her feet, drew back the curtains and saw ice on the windowpanes. At least with a good fire going it would be a nice warm room for the new baby to arrive into. She wondered if she should suggest ringing Jack at the Legion, but decided against it as he'd be annoyed at being woken at this time and he wouldn't be much help here either.

Her mam hadn't mentioned getting him to come home yet. No doubt she would later. After making sure she was okay and resting on the bed, Cathy hurried back into the kitchen and brewed a pot of tea and then refilled the kettle in readiness. She cocked an ear at the bottom of the stairs. Silence. That was good. The longer they all slept in the better. Thank God Brian was here; he could see to the little ones while she helped with her mam. In spite of her mixed feelings of apprehension and nerves, she also felt excitement at the prospect of being on hand when her new sibling came into the world.

'Would you like a slice of toast, Mam?' Cathy asked as she took her a mug of tea through.

'No thanks, love. You get something though. It could be a long morning. Hopefully Brian will take the kids out later, like he promised to. Check in your purse and mine that we've got some change for the phone box. I would have to start now when Millie's still away and we can't use her phone.'

By mid-morning the midwife on duty, accompanied by a student nurse, were ensconced in the front room with her mam. Brian and the little ones were on their way to Sefton Park with the new dollies and prams.

Cathy anxiously hovered between the hall and the kitchen listening to her mam calling out for and cursing Jack in equal measures. She wished Millie and Sadie were home, but her mam had told her that Sadie would be back sometime this afternoon. No one had called Jack yet, although Brian had offered to pop into the Legion later and let him know. A gentle knock sounded at the front door and Cathy ran to answer. Sadie hurried in.

'I saw the midwives' bikes at the gate,' she said. 'Is everything okay? Is the doctor here? There's a posh car outside.'

Cathy beckoned for Sadie to follow her into the back room. 'It's Uncle Brian's car,' she said. 'He arrived on Christmas Day. Mam didn't know he was coming – we surprised her. She was thrilled to bits. He's taken the kids to the park out of the way.'

'Oh, how lovely!' Sadie exclaimed. 'But I bet the shock of seeing him has sent Alice into labour.' She looked up as the young student nurse popped her head round the door.

'May I use the toilet?' she asked, smiling.

'Of course,' Cathy said. 'There's one upstairs in the bathroom and another down the garden. Take your pick. But be careful out there, the path's a bit icy. I haven't had time to sprinkle hot ashes on it yet.'

'I'll nip down the garden, thank you. Your mother was asking for you, Cathy. Do you want to pop your head in?'

Cathy took a deep breath and looked at Sadie.

'Go on, I'll stop here,' Sadie said. 'Go and see what she wants.'

Cathy slipped into the front room and Alice held out her hand.

'Sit with me,' she whispered. Cathy sat down on the side of the bed and took her hand. 'Is there anything I can get for you, Mam?'

The midwife smiled at Cathy. 'Your mother is doing really well, shouldn't be too much longer now.'

Alice blew out her cheeks and was about to speak when Sadie hammered on the closed door and dashed inside. 'Your young nurse has slipped outside,' she began, looking at the midwife. 'Her leg's bent under her at a funny angle. Looks like a nasty break to me.'

'Oh Lord!' The midwife jumped up. 'Stay with your mother, dear,' she instructed Cathy. 'I'll just be two ticks.' She followed Sadie out to the back garden.

As the midwife left the room, Mam let out a long low moan. 'Oh God, I need to push,' she groaned.

'What do I do, Mam, tell me what to do,' Cathy said as her mam's chin sank into her chest and she went red in the face.

'It's coming out,' Alice cried. 'Cathy, the head's coming out. Get ready to catch it any minute, I can feel another pain coming. Grab that towel next to you.'

Cathy took one look at the small head with dark hair that was protruding from her mam's nether regions and took up position at the bottom of the bed. She yelled for help but was drowned out by her mam's loud cry as she pushed as hard as she could. Within seconds Cathy was holding a wet and slippery baby boy. She wrapped him in the towel and laid him between her mam's legs as he let out a yell.

'Oh, Mam, it's a little boy,' she gasped, feeling totally overwhelmed as the door flew open and the midwife and Sadie practically fell into the room.

'Oh, my goodness,' the midwife said as Cathy burst into tears and pointed at the newly delivered baby. 'Well done, Cathy. And you too, Alice. I'll finish off here and Sadie will go and ring for an ambulance. I'm afraid my young nurse appears to have broken her lower right leg. We've managed to get her onto your sofa in the back room. She's in a lot of pain and I'll need to make sure she gets to hospital as soon as I can. Cathy will you go and sit with her, love, while I finish off here. Don't let her fall asleep; keep her conscious by talking to her. Maybe you could make us all some tea with plenty of sugar. We're all in shock, except for this young man here.'

*

In between deep breaths, the young nurse told Cathy her name was Jean and that she was a second-year student nurse and wanted to train as a midwife eventually. This was her first week helping on the ward. Her face was white with shock and she was shivering, and Cathy could see she was in a lot of pain. She popped the knitted throw from the back of the sofa over her and kept her talking.

'All my life I've wanted to be a nurse,' Cathy told her and went on to explain why it was no longer a possibility.

'It's a shame, Cathy. You really kept your cool today. And now you've even delivered a baby. That's amazing at your age. The Royal operates a scheme where you can get taken on as a cadet nurse from sixteen and do a preliminary nurse training course without needing to do O levels. It's advertised in the local paper twice a year. Keep an eye open and apply that way. You'll need to take an entrance exam and pass an interview, but I'm sure you'd walk that no problem. You also get paid while training. That's how I started.' Jean took a deep breath and grimaced as the door opened and two middle-aged ambulance attendants came in with a stretcher. 'Ah, thank goodness it's you two.' She smiled weakly as they greeted her and wrapped her in a blanket. One of the attendants put a mask attached to a cylinder over Jean's face and instructed her to take deep breaths.

He turned to Cathy as Jean closed her eyes. 'Gas and air,' he explained. 'It'll help make her comfortable while we get her to the infirmary. Thank you for looking after her. One of the best nurses we've got at the Royal, is our Jean.' When Jean had closed her eyes the mask was removed and the pair gently lifted her onto the stretcher and carried her out to the waiting ambulance. One of them nipped back inside for the gas and air cylinder and then away they went with the bells clanging.

Cathy closed the front door and went back into the front room, where her mam, Sadie and the midwife were admiring her new little brother.

'Just over eight pounds, Cathy,' her mam said. 'Bigger than all you girls. I had a feeling it was a boy; an Everton player in the making. Thank you, love, for being there for me, and for him. It was a very brave thing you did and I hope it hasn't scared you to death. Would you like to choose his name? I think it's only right that you should after all that.'

Cathy picked the little bundle up from the bed. He was clean and dressed now and smelled of baby powder and soap. His thick dark hair was freshly washed and stood up on top in a miniature quiff. His chubby cheeks were framed both sides by his clenched fists and he had a little dimple in his chin. His blue eyes stared at her and she could see he had a look of her mam and Brian; he was nothing like Jack at all. That was good. She smiled. What a day. And Brian still hadn't come home with the girls. It was late afternoon now and was bitterly cold outside. 'What about Rodney, Mam? After the brother you lost in the war. We could call him Roddy or Rod when he's older.'

Her mam's eyes filled with tears. 'That's a lovely and thoughtful idea, Cathy.'

'Roddy it is then,' Sadie said as the front door flew open and the thundering of little feet sounded in the hall.

Brian popped his head round the door. 'Any luck?' he asked as Sandra and Rosie poked their heads through his legs.

'Come and join the party,' the midwife said. 'I'm going to get off now, Mrs Dawson,' she announced. 'I'll leave you with your family and see you in the morning. Congratulations again and well done once more to Cathy. You'd make a grand nurse, lass. Maybe it's something you might think about in time.'

Cathy handed her brother to Sadie.

'Thank you for looking after Jean,' the midwife went on. 'Would you ask your uncle to put her bike in your back garden and I'll get it picked up tomorrow at some point.'

'I will do,' Cathy replied. 'Will you be able to find out how Jean is and let us know tomorrow?'

'Of course I will. I'm going to ride to Casualty now and make some enquiries. It's been quite a day all round. Good luck tonight. I'll not worry too much about your mam now I know what a very capable daughter she's got looking after her.'

Cathy waved goodbye, feeling filled with pride, and went back into the chaos that was her mam's bedroom.

*

Brian rang the bell connected to the Legion's private quarters. It was still fairly early in the morning, but he had a long drive back to Oxford tomorrow and today he wanted to spend a bit of time looking up old school friends as well as taking Cathy shopping for some bits and bobs that Alice said she needed. He'd left Cathy getting ready and Sadie had taken the little ones over to hers for the morning. Sadie had called Millie at her in-laws' last night with the baby news and she and Jimmy were driving home today, so he knew that between them all, Alice and baby Roddy would be well cared for. And after work today, Jack would be making his way home. Sadie had tried to call the Legion last night after hours to let Jack know he had a son, but she said she'd got the engaged signal every time she dialled. Maybe the phone was faulty or it had been accidentally knocked off the hook. Whatever, Jack was in for a nice surprise when Brian gave him the news.

After a few more rings on the bell a man's voice yelled, 'All right, all right, hold yer bleeding horses!' Then a bleary-eyed Jack answered the door. He frowned at Brian. 'What the hell do you think you're—' he stopped and stared and then his mouth fell open. 'Bloody hell, Brian. I didn't recognise you, mate.'

'Morning, Jack. Aren't you going to ask me in?' Brian asked, stamping his cold feet.

'Yeah, yeah, come into the kitchen,' Jack said, shooting a furtive glance over his shoulder. He practically pushed Brian into the kitchen and closed the door. 'Coffee?' He picked up a kettle and waved it in Brian's direction.

'Please,' Brian said, wondering why Jack wasn't questioning him immediately as to why he was here. He knew the baby was due any day.

Jack made two mugs of coffee and pushed one across the worktop to Brian. 'Didn't know you were coming home,' he said, and offered him a cigarette and a light.

'Cathy and I planned it between us as a surprise for Alice,' he said. 'But I'm the one who got the surprise.' Brian took a deep drag on his ciggie in readiness for his big announcement. Neither he nor Jack was aware of the door opening quietly as he spoke. 'And boy have I got a lovely surprise for you, Jack. Congratulations. You have a new baby son, Rodney, born yesterday. But we couldn't get hold of you after he arrived. Think something's wrong with the phones in this place—' He stopped abruptly and turned his head as a strangled shriek came from the doorway. A scantily clad woman with untidy red hair stood with her hands clasped to her mouth, her face drained of all colour and her eyes almost popping out of her head.

'Jack!' she screamed and launched herself at him, raining blows to his face and body and knocking him to the floor.

Brian grabbed hold of her and pinned her arms to her sides as she kicked out at his shins. Fortunately she had nothing on her feet. Brian held her tight as she collapsed sobbing into his arms. He sat her on a kitchen chair and went to help Jack up off the floor. His lip was bleeding and his face bore deep scratches to each cheek from her long sharp nails. The double look of shock on his face would have been comical if the situation weren't quite such a mess. Brian recognised the woman now as Sheila, Jack's ex-mistress, who he'd fired years ago; or not so ex, it would now seem.

Tears were streaming down Sheila's face and she fired hysterical questions at both Brian and Jack. 'Did you just tell him he's got a new son?' she screeched.

Brian nodded. 'Yes, he was born yesterday.'

'How, Jack, how? You told me you didn't sleep with Alice and that you were leaving her to be with me. You lying, cheating bastard. How could you do this? After we've had such a lovely Christmas here as well. You've been lying to me all this time, using me, and all the while you knew Alice was expecting again and you never said a word. Well, that's it. We're over. God, I hate you. I hope Alice chucks you out when she knows how you've lied to her too. But a baby! And you don't even like the two kids you've got.' Sheila got to her feet and ran out of the room. Brian heard her talking on the phone to a taxi company. He guessed that the pair had left the phone off the hook all last night so as not to be disturbed. She thundered upstairs and was gone a few minutes before coming back down, dressed and holding a small suitcase. 'Don't you ever come near me again. I don't want anything more to do with you.' She went into the concert room and waited for her taxi.

Jack sat in silence with his head in his hands as Brian stared at him, wondering what the hell he should do or say. He got to his feet, poured two small whiskies from a half bottle on the worktop, tapped Jack on the shoulder and silently handed a glass to him. Brian knocked his back in one go.

Jack drank his whisky and then looked sheepishly at Brian. 'Is Alice okay, and the baby?' he asked quietly.

Brian nodded. 'They're both doing fine. It was a bit of a chaotic time back at your home yesterday.' He told Jack what had happened and how Cathy had helped to deliver his son.

Jack let out a deep breath and looked at the ceiling. 'So, are you gonna tell Alice about Sheila?'

Brian chewed his lip. His sister's marriage to Jack had never really been a happy one, but for some reason she'd been adamant that she couldn't walk away from it. But this was something else. 'How long have you been seeing Sheila again? I know you were keeping her for a long time, but I presumed when you came home to Alice it was to make a new start. I'm guessing Sheila never left the picture. And no, I'm not going to tell her, Jack. *You* will do that. I want you out of my sister's life before March, when I travel to America to work. You make up an excuse, any excuse, as to why you have to leave her, but leave her you will. She doesn't need you. All you've ever done is drag her down and waste her money. You've also ruined Cathy's future. Well, that's it. No more. I'm not going to break my sister's heart when she's just given birth and neither are you. But over the next couple of weeks I want you to get a plan into place and just get lost. I'll help Alice to get on her feet again, but I'm sending nothing until you're gone.'

Brian stood up, feeling more angry than he'd ever felt in his life. He could punch the living daylights out of the pathetic excuse of a man sitting in front of him; but Jack already had to go home and give Alice a good reason as to why he looked a mess, without Brian adding to it. 'Now go and get yourself cleaned up before you come home to see the baby and Alice. I'm going back to Oxford tomorrow, but I'll be watching your every move until I do.'

Brian drove back to Lucerne Street and, leaving Alice with the midwife, who was doing her mid-morning call, picked up Cathy for the shopping trip. He told her what had happened at the Legion when she asked him what time Jack was expected home.

'I knew Sheila was back working at the Legion,' Cathy said, 'Granny Lomax told me ages ago, But I thought it best not to say anything, especially when Mam told me she was expecting. I didn't know she and Jack were still having an affair, although it doesn't really surprise me.'

Brian also told Cathy of his threat to Jack and not to be surprised when he announced he was leaving them all, but to be as supportive as she could to her mam when it happened and not to worry about money, as he would be sending some home each month to help out as soon as he was sure that Jack had gone. 'Alice has always refused my help before and I reckon that's because she knew Jack would get his hands on any money I sent and waste it.'

Cathy nodded. 'No doubt. Can we just pop into Granny's?' she said as they pulled onto Linnet Lane. 'I'll tell her about the baby and there's something else I want to tell her as well. And she'll be so thrilled to see you. We don't need to dash back while Mam's got the midwife there. Don't say anything about Jack and Mam though. Or she might interfere and that would only cause more problems, because Jack hates her.'

Granny Lomax greeted them both with hugs and kisses and, as Cathy had predicted, she was so happy to see Brian again and thrilled that he had a new job in America lined up.

'We've got more news for you, Granny,' Cathy said, a big smile lighting up her face. She told how she'd helped to deliver baby Rodney yesterday after Nurse Jean's accident had thrown everything into disarray. And she also told her about the possibility of doing cadet nurse training without needing O levels and how the information would be in the *Echo*.

'That would be marvellous, Cathy. I have the *Echo* delivered daily; I'll scour it page by page. They usually have an intake for training in September. I bet we can get you signed up for that one and you'll be sixteen by then. You could do both the nurse training and then midwifery, seeing as you've got a bit of experience under your belt now. Weren't you terrified?'

Cathy laughed and shook her head. 'To be honest, Gran, it had happened before I could even think about it. Roddy took us all by surprise. He's lovely. I'll bring him round to see you when he's allowed out in the pram. It'll have to be a bit warmer than it is now though.'

'Of course.' Granny Lomax got to her feet and opened the sideboard cupboard. She pulled out a gaily wrapped parcel and gave it to Cathy. 'Some clothes I've been busy making for the new arrival. Nothing blue, because we didn't know what he would be, but nice pastel shades. I'll get some blue wool when I next go into the city.'

*

Jack let himself in at the front door. Brian's car wasn't outside so he felt a bit of hope that the lad had kept his word and not blabbed to Alice. The house was quiet as the grave. Nobody in the back room or kitchen either. The door to the front room he shared with Alice was closed. He tapped gently and walked in. Alice was lying on her side with her back to the door. His new son was by the side of the bed in a little white wooden cradle that Millie had lent them. He was awake, but lying quietly sucking his fingers. As Jack peered into the cot two bright blue eyes peered back at him. Jack smiled and nodded at the baby.

He felt a swell of pride as he gazed at his son. He'd not felt like that with either of his daughters – well not as strongly as the 'something' that was gripping his heart right now. 'Well, you're a grand little fella, aren't you?'

Alice stirred at the sound of his voice, then turned and half-smiled at him. He marvelled that she looked a lot less rough than Sheila did after a night on the tiles, and Alice had just given birth! He felt a rush of shame and guilt that he'd not been around yesterday and last night when they'd needed him. That was bloody Sheila's fault, insisting they take the phone off the hook so no one would disturb their night of passion. But, he reasoned, they seemed to have managed well enough here without him. He'd have only got underfoot.

'Jack, you're home,' Alice mumbled as she tried to sit up. 'What's happened to your face?'

'Had to separate a couple of women fighting over a fella last night,' he lied. 'Anyway, never mind that, well done, queen. He's a lovely little fella.' He bent to peck her on the cheek.

'Glad you approve. At least you'll have someone to side with you now when all we females are ganging up.'

'I will, gel, I will.' And no matter what your bloody brother says, I'm going nowhere, Jack thought. This is my house, my wife and my lad, and no one tells *me* what to do in my own home. He'd keep his nose clean, keep away from Sheila and reclaim what was his by rights. It was nearly New Year's Eve, so time to get his act together and try to make a fresh start.

Chapter Eight

June 1957

Cathy closed the till and forced a bright smile. The sour-faced woman gave a curt nod, snatched up the paper bag containing her purchase and dropped it into her shopping bag.

'Goodbye,' Cathy called, watching her squeeze her bulky hips past the Friday-morning shoppers. 'Miserable devil,' she muttered. 'No matter how much you try and help, some people are never satisfied.'

'Satisfied?' Debbie raised an eyebrow. 'She wouldn't know the meaning of the word. Anyway, Pan Stik's a waste of time for *those* wrinkles.'

Cathy laughed and took advantage of the lull in customers to turn her attention elsewhere. She began arranging Max Factor Crème Puffs and lipsticks on a stand covered with black velvet and became so absorbed in her work she was unaware that Debbie was speaking again.

'Well – are we?' Debbie wiggled her hips. When she got no answer she waved a hand in front of Cathy's face.

'What?' Cathy said, startled. 'You scared the life out of me.'

'Sorry. You were miles away. I said, are we dancing tonight?' She wiggled her hips again and spun round on her kitten heels.

'Oh, Debs, I'd love to, but I'm not sure if I can. I'll have to see how the land lies. Mam might need help with the little ones. She's really tired cos Roddy's cutting teeth and keeps waking up in the night.'

Debbie frowned. 'It's Friday. Can't Jack help? It's not your fault they've got kids coming out their ears.' She smirked. 'Surprised he can still manage it, the way he complains.'

Cathy felt her cheeks heating and twiddled a gold-coloured lipstick tube between her fingers. *She* was surprised Jack could still manage it too, considering he never stopped moaning about his foot and his leg and how he could hardly move some days. He shifted himself fast enough when the Legion opened, though.

'Well, he *should* be past it at his age,' Debbie said and pulled a face. 'Ooh, thinking about it's enough to make you cringe. I know you do a lot at home to help, Cathy, but they shouldn't stop you having a life.' She paused and looked at her watch. 'Have you finished mucking about with those lippies? It's almost one. I'm starving. I fancy beans on toast.'

'Again?' Cathy placed the final lipstick on the stand. 'No wonder you're a redhead.' She glanced up, looking over Debbie's shoulder. 'Look busy, here comes Dolly.'

Dolores Redfern, the staff recruitment lady who had interviewed them, bore down on them, long thin nose in the air. Her dark hair was scraped into a severe topknot, and her black tailored suit made Cathy think of funerals.

'Miss Lomax, Miss Jones.' Dolores consulted a clipboard and pushed her glasses up her nose. 'I'd like you to tidy up the Max Factor shelves in the stockroom after lunch. How you girls can find anything in there is beyond me. I'll put Miss Clark and Miss Taylor on your counter from two until four. That's plenty of time to do what's necessary.'

'Yes, Miss Redfern. Thank you, Miss Redfern,' Cathy muttered as Dolores swanned away.

'Gets us off the counter for a bit,' Debbie said. 'We can do our nails. I've got a nice bright red in my handbag that'll go lovely with your dark colouring. Make you look dead posh.'

Cathy sighed. 'Now why would I want to look dead posh? I'm not going anywhere.'

'Yes, you are. One way or another you're coming to the Rumblin' Tum with me tonight and you're going to enjoy yourself even if it kills me first.' She shot Cathy a sideways glance. 'Gianni's going tonight too. You know he fancies you, Cath.'

Cathy felt her cheeks heating again.

'See, you're blushing. You fancy him like mad.'

'No, I don't. We're good friends, that's all.'

'You could do worse than Gianni. He's nice-looking and he's fun. Anyway.' She changed the subject. 'It's one o'clock. Are we ready?'

'We are,' Cathy said. 'Grab your bag. Let's go.'

As she and Debbie hurried arm-in-arm down Ranelagh Street, Cathy's thoughts wandered. She wished she were still a much-cherished only child with her mum and dad around, like her friend.

Every night lately she went home to utter chaos. After being on her feet all day, the last thing she felt like was tackling the mountain of dirty dishes cluttering up the kitchen. It was usually left to her to cook the tea and sort out the washing, too. By the time she'd got the kids fed and ready for bed, and the twin-tub on, she felt fit for nothing, while Idle Jack, who recovered at times to suit, sat with his wooden foot propped up on a footstool reading the *Echo* until the Legion opened. In spite of Brian telling Jack he had to go, he'd made no attempt to leave, and with Brian in America now there was no sign that he would any time soon either. Cathy had recently written to Brian and told him Jack was still there at the house. She was waiting for a reply, but didn't hold out much hope that he could do anything from so far away. It really was up to her mam to tell the lazy bugger to get lost once and for all, and she couldn't see that happening in a month of Sundays at the moment. Since Jack wasn't seeing Sheila any more, as far as she knew, Cathy didn't know how to persuade her mam to get rid of him.

Cathy hardly kept a penny of her wages, Jack saw to that. He always had money in his own pocket for a bet and a pint, though – mostly her money. If it hadn't been for Granny Lomax, who slipped her a pound spends each week, she'd have nothing to her name. She lay in bed at night consumed with resentment, and then guilt for feeling that way. She could never invite friends home any more, not even Debbie. She'd be too embarrassed. The only thing that kept her going was looking forward to the secret future she'd got planned, and she said a silent prayer every night to help it all come true.

In the Kardomah Café Cathy and Debbie found a table by the window and sat down. Debbie fidgeted uncomfortably.

'What's wrong?' Cathy frowned.

'It's these new seats. They're sticking to my thighs.'

The brown plastic seats and matching melamine tables had been part of a recent refurbishment and the seats weren't the most comfortable to sit on.

Cathy picked up a menu. 'Pull your skirt down a bit then.'

'I can't.' Debbie tugged at the skirt of her suit, Lewis's staff uniform, except the skirt was supposed to be knee length, but Debbie's was shorter. 'I turned the hem up a bit last night.'

'Debs! Well, what more can you expect?' Cathy shook her head. 'Stop moaning. Let's order or it'll be time to go back.'

'What are you having?' Debbie ran her finger down the menu and selected, by way of a change, beans on toast.

Cathy hoped she had enough money in her purse to eat. She was down to her last few shillings until they got their pay packets. 'Cheese on toast, I think.'

While Cathy placed their orders the café began to fill with regulars. By the time she returned to the table, Debbie had been joined by Mike and Davy. Mike winked at Cathy as she slid into her seat.

'How are you, Cath?' Before she had a chance to answer he continued, 'Debs tells us you're going to the Rumblin' Tum tonight with her. I'm going too, with Davy, so we'll see you there.'

'I think I am,' Cathy said. 'Just hope I can get out.'

'You're going, and that's all there is to it,' Debbie said. 'She's going!' she directed to Mike as the waitress brought their food to the table.

'Consider yourself told.' Mike grinned at Cathy.

'Why don't you both meet us near Lime Street Station at seven thirty?' Davy suggested. '

'Fine by me,' Debbie said. 'That all right with you, Cath?'

Cathy nodded and tucked in to her cheese on toast. 'Damn it, I forgot to order our drinks.' She hadn't, but the contents of her purse had only stretched to the food. She and Debbie took it in turns to pay for lunch and she was too embarrassed to tell her friend that she was skint.

'Would you like a frothy coffee?' Mike stood up.

'Please.' They nodded in unison and Cathy breathed a sigh of relief.

'How about doughnuts for afters?'

'No thanks, Mike,' Debbie said. 'I have to watch my waistline.'

'I'll watch it for you.' Davy laughed, adding, 'It's a nice waistline, and just right for a squeeze.'

'Cheeky.' Debbie smacked his hand.

Cathy smiled. Debbie and Davy were made for each other. They had been casually dating for a few months now and were always flirting. After Debbie's flippant remark on their interview day that she was going to marry him, Cathy had no doubts that she would one day.

Mike came back to the table with coffee and doughnuts. 'Here you are, girls, enjoy.'

'Thanks, Mike,' Cathy said. 'We can split Debbie's doughnut between us.'

Cathy jumped off the bus on Aigburth Road and hurried towards home. If Jack started moaning about her going out she was ready to walk away and stay at Granny Lomax's. He'd go mad that she'd already taken five shillings out of her wage packet and given it to Debbie to look after for tonight, just in case he left her with none. Well, he could just get lost. It was her money. She needed her bus fare and enough for a couple of drinks too. The café sold soft drinks, but they still needed paying for and she liked to buy a round at least. She wasn't the sort of girl who'd let a lad do all the buying. They'd expect something in return and there was no way she was doing that.

She intended to make something of her life, go places and see the world. Not end up like half the girls from school, married too young, babies on the way, accepting their lot. That wasn't the life for her. Anyway, she hadn't met anyone she wanted to get to know better yet, except maybe Gianni. They'd always been really friendly as young children and still were, but in spite of what Debbie said, she was certain he couldn't be interested in her romantically at all. He'd never shown that he was, apart from the time outside her gran's ages ago when he'd said he was glad Jim wasn't her boyfriend; that had been it.

Her footsteps slowed as she approached her home, if you could call it that. Slave camp more like. The tiny front garden had recently become a dumping ground for the scrap metal Jack had acquired. She wished he'd hurry up and sell it on. The rusting pieces were dangerous to leave lying around where her little sisters played. The flower bed had vanished from neglect and the privet hedge was overgrown. The black front door was shabby and chipped, and to a passer-by the whole place probably looked like the scruffy hovel it now was. She hated it and heavens knew what Millie must think now, when her own home next door looked like a palace by comparison.

In the narrow hallway the sound of raised voices met her, accompanied by the stench of a dirty nappy. She gritted her teeth to stop herself gagging. It was always the same lately. How wonderful it must be to come home to a house where your mam had the tea ready and welcomed you with a hug and, 'Have you had a nice day at work, chuck?' That's what it was like at Debbie's home. She'd had tea there a few times recently and Debbie's mam always had the welcome mat out, and the aroma of home-cooked food wafted up your nose as you walked in at the front door. There was always a cuppa waiting in the pot and flowers on the table. Granny Lomax's place was the same and smelled of freshly baked cakes and lavender furniture polish. How she'd love to live with her. Granny had suggested a few times that she move in, and she was tempted, but always worried about how her mam would cope without her.

Before she met up with Debbie at the bus stop tonight Cathy planned to pop in to her granny's to see if the long-awaited letter had arrived. It was due any day now. Her stomach did a little flip and her heart raced at the thought. That letter could either dash all her hopes or be her passport to freedom, and then her mam would just have to learn to cope the best she could. She took a deep breath and went into the back sitting room.

''Bout bloody time too. Where the hell have you been?' Jack shouted from the confines of the fireside chair, where he seemed to have taken root; dirty plates, cups and newspapers surrounded his feet. Baby Roddy lay on the rug in front of him, stinking and crying. Her mam was sitting at the dining table looking weary as usual and Cathy's heart went out to her, but not for long. Frustration took over. Why couldn't she see the state of the place and pull herself together? Make Jack do something instead of waiting on him hand and foot. The lazy sod.

'Sorry!' Cathy turned and glared. 'Were you talking to me?' She wouldn't allow him to intimidate her like he did her mam. He didn't scare her with his aggressive manner. After all, she had the upper hand tonight. She knew he was waiting for her wages so he could clear off out. 'I've actually been to work, Jack. You know; that place I go to each day to earn money to keep your kids fed and watered. You should try doing a bit more yourself some time.'

'Cheeky mare. I paid the rent this week, and I kept *you* for years.' He got unsteadily to his feet and lunged towards her, but Cathy sidestepped and he fell forward, banging his ribcage against the spindly back of a kitchen chair. He howled with rage and Cathy fought hard to suppress a giggle. He was horrible. She hated him for what he'd done; dragging her mam into the gutter after she'd tried so hard to do the best for them all. Cathy took off her jacket; put it on the table with her handbag. Ignoring Jack, she picked up Roddy and carried him upstairs to the bathroom, changed his nappy, wiped his sticky face and tickled him under the chin. He gave her a half-smile.

Poor little mite, he didn't smile much; maybe because he was left to cry for most of the day. This couldn't go on. She tucked him under her arm and marched back down to the sitting room. She fastened him into his high chair and placed a cushion behind to stop him slipping.

Jack had emptied the contents of her handbag onto the table and was rummaging feverishly through old bus tickets, a lipstick, a comb, a packet of chewing gum and her diary. He was looking for her wage packet, but Cathy wasn't that daft. It was tucked safely into the waistband of her suspender belt. 'Looking for something, Jack?'

'Where is it?' he shouted, face close enough to knock her out with his stale breath. 'Hand it over, you little cow!'

'Jack, stop, please,' her mam said, voice little more than a whisper.

Cathy stood behind her mam's chair and put her hands on her shoulders as Jack scowled at the pair. 'He's not getting it this week, Mam. Not a penny. I'll pop to the chippy for something for the kids' tea. Have we got any bread?'

Mam nodded and got to her feet, seeming glad that Cathy was once again taking charge. 'I'll butter some and wash the plates.'

Jack grabbed Cathy by the upper arm and dug his fingers into her flesh. 'Money, now! I need a pint.'

The stench of his sweaty body overwhelmed her. 'Then get yourself a proper bloody job,' she yelled. 'And take your filthy hands off me.' She saw a sly smile cross his face and he changed tack and pulled her closer.

'Come on, Cathy, gel. You don't begrudge your old dad a drink with his mates, now do you?' Her mam's back was turned and Cathy shuddered as he looked down the front of her blouse and leered. He put an arm round her shoulders, slid it down and squeezed her backside.

'You're not my dad.' She brought her knee up sharply and slammed him in the groin. His face contorted but he didn't cry out. He grabbed a chair-back to stop himself stumbling. Cathy knew he wouldn't dare yell. It wasn't the first time since Rodney was born that he'd groped her and it wasn't the first time she'd jarred him with her knee. He'd be out on his ear the next time he tried that one. She'd just about had enough. If she didn't sort this mess out soon there'd be no chance of her moving on. She hoped that when Brian wrote back he'd advise her what to do. But her mam needed to take charge and tell him to get out of their lives once and for all. 'Just get lost,' she snapped. 'Ask your so-called mates to buy you a drink and I'll feed your kids.' She grabbed her jacket and ran out of the house as Jack lunged for her again.

Chapter Nine

Gianni proudly rode his Triumph Bonneville up Lucerne Street and parked outside the terraced house he shared with his mam. He let himself in to the sound of clattering pots and the wireless playing in the background, his mam singing along to Doris Day's latest hit. He sniffed the air. Nice smell. 'I'm home!' He popped his head round the kitchen door.

She turned, a smile lighting up her face. She was a good-looking woman for forty, her hair neatly fastened back with a big fancy slide, but her blue eyes had dark circles beneath them, in spite of her makeup. 'You okay, Mam?' He frowned and gave her a hug. Looked like she was in for one of her bad heads again. She'd been complaining of headaches a lot lately.

'Hello, love. Yes, I'm fine thanks. I had to stay behind for a meeting, but tea won't be long. I've put it in the oven to heat up. Good job I made a shepherd's pie last night.'

'Ah, wondered why you still had your suit on.' His mam always looked smart for work but usually changed into something casual as soon as she arrived home. 'Have I got time for a wash and change before we eat? Need to be out early tonight.'

'Go ahead. It'll be a while yet.' She smiled up at him, tiny at five foot four to his nearly six-foot frame.

He hugged her again, kissed her cheek and ran up the narrow flight of stairs that separated the front room from the kitchen. In his bedroom he rooted in the wardrobe, found clean jeans and a black silk shirt and laid them on the bed. He rubbed his chin. Bristly, could do with a shave. In the windowless bathroom, built into the bulkhead between the two bedrooms, he washed and then squinted in the mirror while he ran the razor over his olive skin. The room was airless and lit by a single bulb that cast a gloomy light. He hated this tiny house and wished he could take his mam to live somewhere really nice. She often said she fancied a bungalow by the sea, with big rooms and a big garden, but this was all she could afford after years of living at his gran's when she left his dad. One day he would buy her that bungalow, when he was qualified and designing aircraft that would fly people all over the world, but for now, this place would have to do.

Gianni hadn't seen his dad since he was a little boy but often thought about him. There had been letters and the occasional birthday card sent to his gran's address. Romano's Fair still travelled the country – he'd seen the posters, but he'd never told his mam. She still wouldn't allow contact and had usually taken him on holiday when she knew the fair's Whit Week visits to the area were imminent. Gianni was aware that his dad had no idea where he was living now and there'd been no desire to look for him when he was younger. But since starting work at the aircraft factory he'd become bored and restless and fancied a change, wondering what life with the fair would be like now he was grown up.

He couldn't tell his mam though. She'd go crazy. She'd worked hard to make sure he'd had a decent education, passed his O levels, secured an apprenticeship and had prospects for a good future. She was always saying she was glad she'd got him away from what she considered to be a dangerous way of life. Her greatest wish, and she never missed an opportunity to drop a hint, was that he'd find the right girl one day, settle down and start a family. 'You'll be lucky,' he muttered as he splashed on Old Spice aftershave. He was doing no settling down any time soon. The only girl he cared about was Cathy Lomax. He wished that she'd look at him in any way other than just as a friend, but she never did. He'd love to ask her out, but lived in dread of her turning him down, because then that would put paid to his dreams of her one day being his girl.

He pulled on his clothes, pushed his feet into Cuban-heeled boots and dragged a comb through his thick dark hair. He was looking forward to tonight. A few pints with his mates and then a dance at the Rumblin' Tum. Cathy would be there, he hoped. He'd bumped into her mate Debs last week and she said they were dancing tonight. Hopefully Cathy would dance with *him*. He was desperate to get closer to her now that she'd grown up into such a beautiful girl. They'd been really good pals as kiddies but then grown apart when they changed schools. He'd tried everything he could think of to encourage her to talk to him more. Debs had told him she was convinced that Cathy fancied him, but she gave no indication to him that she did, wouldn't even meet his eye most times when he walked round to her gran's with her on a Sunday.

Ah well, he'd give her another crack of the whip tonight and if she didn't bite then he'd have to try elsewhere. Plenty more fish in the sea, as his mates were always saying.

*

Jack staggered down the street towards the Legion, leaning heavily on his walking stick. He was limping badly tonight after that little cow had kneed him between the legs. He'd always hated her, and blamed her for his marriage to Alice not working out. They'd have been fine if she hadn't had the brat to look after and had paid him a bit more attention. He'd always got on well with young Brian, but Cathy had been needy and clingy and had driven him mad. What with her and that bloody mother of Terry's telling tales and watching his every move, the pair had ruined everything. Ma Lomax and her accusations over Terry's death had made him drink more than he should, and the constant pain from his injury needed to be drowned out as well. No wonder he'd become an alcoholic. The only one who'd stuck by him was Sheila, and now that was all over because Alice had had Rodney. Sheila wouldn't even answer her door to him when he'd tried to apologise. He was stuck with Alice and the brats for now. But that was his choice as he had nowhere else to go and he knew Alice would never chuck him out. As soon as he could find another woman who could give him a roof over his head, though, he would be off. Nobody wanted him there. Cathy treated him like shit on her shoe. One day that girl would get what was coming to her, her *and* that bloody grandmother of hers. It was only a matter of time before he got his own back, and time on his hands was something Jack had plenty of lately.

*

Millie looked out of the window and spotted Jack shuffling off up the street. Good. She'd pop in on Alice and see how she was doing. Since Roddy arrived her friend seemed to have gone downhill. *Bit of baby blues,* she thought. Millie had read about that in *Woman's Weekly* and it seemed to fit Alice's recent moods. Having Jack there was not helping either. And poor Cathy was the only one bringing in money at the moment, apart from Jack's pension and the few bob from the Legion that he drank most of. But Millie had a bit of news tonight that might just cheer Alice up.

She hurried up the short path, shaking her head at Jack's untidy scrap metal junk piled on the front garden, knocked and walked straight in. They had worked so hard to get the little house immaculate when Alice moved in. Now it was a tip and Jack's presence was in every flipping corner. No wonder her friend was depressed. 'It's me, Alice,' she called out.

'In the kitchen,' Alice called back. 'Come through, I'll put the kettle on.'

Millie sat at the table and smiled at Roddy, who was strapped in his pram. Judging by the noise coming from upstairs, the younger girls were in bed, but fighting.

Alice appeared with two steaming mugs of tea and sat down opposite Millie.

'Have you decided what you're doing about coming back to work yet?' Millie asked. 'You need to hurry up or they'll give your job to someone else.'

Alice shook her head. 'I need to find someone to look after Roddy.'

Millie nodded. 'Right, well that's one reason why I'm here, that and the fact I've just seen his lordship going out. There's a woman on Bickerton Street opposite my mam who's started to look after kids. She's still got a place free for one more, so why don't you call in tomorrow and grab it while you can.'

Alice's face lit up. 'Really? Oh that would be great. I need to get out to work before I go mad. And we need the money so badly. I can't rely on Cathy for much longer. It's not fair to keep taking all her wages and I know she's getting really fed up with the situation.'

Millie smiled. 'It would do you good to spend time away from Jack as well. He might buck his ideas up and do a bit more around the house if he's left to his own devices. Can't believe how downhill he's gone since Roddy's birth and he's dragging you with him, Alice.'

Alice sighed. 'I know he is. I need to claw my way back. Cathy needs her own life as well. She's too young to be stuck here with all this drudgery.'

'Where is she?' Millie looked around.

'Gone out to meet Debs and some pals from work. But she was calling at Granny Lomax's first. I can't wait to tell her that I might be going back to work soon. Fingers crossed the woman will take Roddy.'

'I'm sure she will.' Millie clinked her mug against Alice's. 'Here's to a brighter future all round.'

'I'll second that,' Alice said. 'And here's to the back of Jack in time as well.'

'I'll third that,' Millie said with a grin. 'As soon as you are on your feet, you'll have to pluck up the courage and tell him to go. The time has come.'

*

Cathy let herself into the little white bungalow and smiled. The place was spotless and smelled of lavender polish, fruit and fresh baking. Granny was asleep, glasses slipping down her nose, slumped in an armchair in front of the TV. A cold cup of tea with a skim on top was sitting on the coffee table. 'Gran.' Cathy shook her gently by the shoulder. Granny opened her eyes and pulled herself upright.

'Hello, love. I must have dozed off,' she muttered. 'It's been a busy day, what with making cakes for the church hall bring-and-buy, and shopping in the city.' She pushed her glasses up her nose. 'There's a bag on the table for you. Just a bit of something I thought you might like.'

Cathy picked up the carrier bag with 'Blacklers' emblazoned across the front. Inside were a black and white tweed pencil skirt and a red cotton top with a sweetheart neckline. Tears pricked her eyes at the kind gesture. 'They're lovely. Thank you so much. You always know exactly what I like. I'll get changed into them now. Much nicer than this old black dress I'm wearing. And look.' She held out a hand and laughed. 'The red top matches my nails.' She'd given in to Debbie's earlier insistence that she have her nails painted and quite liked the bright colour.

Granny Lomax smiled and her eyes twinkled. 'You'll look lovely. I might be an old woman these days, but if I was young again like you I'd wear something fashionable like that and show off my nice legs. And see,' she pointed to the mantelpiece. 'Up there, behind the clock.'

Cathy clapped a hand to her mouth and took a deep breath. 'Is that it?'

'I reckon so. It's addressed to you, anyway.'

Cathy took the white envelope down. 'Liverpool Royal Hospital' was stamped across the top. She tore at the flap, hands shaking, and pulled out a single white sheet of paper. She scanned the page, then punched the air and jumped up and down. 'Yes! Oh yes! I'm in. I start in September.'

'Oh well done, love.' Granny got to her feet and wrapped Cathy in a bear hug. They danced a little jig around the living room. 'I'm so proud of you. I knew you could do it, mind. You're a bright girl. You take after your dad and your Uncle Brian for your brains. You'll make a smashing nurse.' She gave her another hug. 'Good job you spoke to that nurse Jean and she told you about this way in to do your training.'

'I'll feel a bit bad about leaving Mam alone to cope,' Cathy said, chewing her lip.

Granny Lomax pursed her lips. 'If you go, it might spur your mam on to go back to work. She needs to get a divorce and stand on her own two feet. She's leaning on you too much. She's pulled herself up before and she can do it again. She should put Roddy in a nursery and go back to work. You, my love, have a fresh new future to look forward to and neither your mam nor Jack Dawson are going to stop you doing this, or they'll have me to answer to. It's what your dad would have wanted for you too. And Brian will be so thrilled for you. Go out there and grab it with both hands. Don't let anything or anyone stand in your way. You will make us all so proud.' She raised her teacup. 'Here's to you and your new adventures, Nurse Cathy Lomax.'

Chapter Ten

Cathy touched up her lipstick in front of the mirror in the ladies' in the Rumblin' Tum. She teased her hair higher on top, and when she dropped the tail-comb back into her handbag her heart did a little skip at the sight of the letter nestled in there. Her dream was now within her grasp. In just a few weeks' time she'd be a nurse in training.

She was bursting to tell someone; dying to, in fact. Maybe she'd tell Debbie on the way home and swear her to secrecy, make her promise not to say anything at work until she was ready to hand in her notice. The course starting date was a few weeks off and she didn't want Lewis's getting wind of it or they might ask her to leave straight away so they could train someone else, and she needed her wages for the foreseeable future. She smiled as she thought about how Jack would react when he knew he'd no choice but to get a proper job once she'd left home for good.

She made her way back into the café and heard Debbie calling her name. She, Mike and Davy were seated down the bottom end of the room. She skirted around jiving couples until she reached her friends. Out of the corner of her eye she saw Gianni and a couple of lads come in and sit down near the jukebox. He hadn't seen her. Another couple of lads walked in with guitars and announced they were going to play a bit of skiffle music. Another lad joined them with a washboard and thimbles on his fingers. Halfway through 'Rock Island Line' Davy and Debbie got up to dance and Mike announced he was nipping round the corner to the Philharmonic pub to get some cigarettes. He asked Cathy if she wanted to walk round with him but she shook her head. She was enjoying watching the boys play and didn't want to miss anything. As the boys began to sing another Lonnie Donegan song, 'Putting on the Style', Cathy turned at a tap on her shoulder. Gianni, looking nervous, Cathy thought, reached for her hand and asked her to dance. She got to her feet and let him lead her onto the little dance floor, butterflies cartwheeling in her tummy at the touch of his hand on hers. She caught Debbie's smile and raised thumb and did her best to keep up with Gianni's quick steps. She almost fell backwards at one point when he whizzed her under his arm and back again, but he caught her and pulled her close. The tempo of the next song, 'Love is Strange', was slower, and she relaxed with her head against his chest. Cathy didn't see Mike coming back in and glaring at them before going to sit down at their table. Davy and Debbie rejoined him. Gianni escorted Cathy back to sit with her friends and thanked her for the dance. 'Maybe another dance later before we go home?' he asked, raising an eyebrow.

She nodded. 'I'd love to.'

'Coca-Cola?' Davy asked, getting to his feet. Cathy and Debbie nodded.

Scowling, Mike stood up and put on his jacket. 'Not for me. I'm going back round to the pub,' he announced and walked away without a backward glance.

Davy frowned after him. 'What's up with him?'

Cathy shrugged. 'Gianni asked me to dance when Mike had gone out to get ciggies. He's obviously annoyed with me.'

Debbie shook her head. 'Well, you're not going out with Mike or anything. He's just a mate, so why shouldn't you dance with Gianni? Not like you've led Mike on, is it?'

Cathy shook her head. 'I would never lead any lad on. Not knowingly anyway. It was nice dancing with Gianni.'

'Good. Well, let's hope he asks you again then,' Debbie said.

Davy came back with the Cokes and Gianni asked if he could join them. Cathy nodded and he sat down next to her. 'Did me asking you to dance put the cat amongst the pigeons?' he said. He offered cigarettes around, but only Davy took one. 'With the other fella, I mean?'

Cathy shook her head. 'We work in the same place, I already told you that. But Mike's not my boyfriend.'

'Good.' He squeezed her hand and she smiled. There was no sign of the little blonde girl tonight and that pleased her.

After a short break the boys with the guitars performed another couple of songs and again the friends got up to dance.

'Can I take you home, Cathy?' Gianni whispered later as they swayed together to the last song on the jukebox before closing time. 'Young Love' by Tab Hunter was one of her favourites and right now the words and the way Gianni was holding her made her head spin.

She smiled. 'Well, seeing as we live right opposite each other, I don't see why not.' She felt her stomach churn as she looked into his eyes. The way he held her gaze made her feel a bit strange inside. Did he fancy her or what? Was he just teasing her? How would she know? She'd never had a boyfriend. She looked away in case she made a fool of herself. Her heart was beating so loud she was certain he'd hear it. She had jelly legs and a looping stomach and had never felt so close to anyone as she did at that moment. He smelled so nice, and as the song ended and he bent and kissed her lightly on the lips and whispered 'Thank you', she felt she might burst. She tried to relax in his arms, her head resting on his silk-covered chest as he hugged her to him again. Debbie and Davy appeared beside them and Cathy pulled away from Gianni's embrace. Debbie had a dreamy expression in her eyes.

'We're getting off now, Cathy,' Debbie said. 'Are you ready to go? We can get the bus together and then Davy will walk me home.'

'I'll take Cathy home,' Gianni said, pulling her back into his arms. 'We'll get the later bus.'

'See you at work tomorrow then,' Debbie called as she and Davy strolled away.

Left alone, Cathy and Gianni finished their drinks. She put on her jacket and popped into the ladies', feeling suddenly nervous. She stared at her pink cheeks in the mirror. Her eyes looked over-bright. What if Gianni tried it on down a dark alley and wouldn't take no for an answer? She wouldn't know what to do. She wondered where the mates he'd come in with earlier had got to. Could she sneak out of the café without him noticing? Go and find Davy and Debs? She slipped out of the cloakroom, praying he wouldn't see her, but he was facing in her direction and, although he was talking to a few people, he spotted her and waved her over.

*

'I'm walking Cathy home,' Gianni told Nigel. He'd hardly seen his mates all night as he'd been determined to get to know Cathy better. 'You go on without me and I'll see you tomorrow.' He stopped as someone tapped him on the shoulder. He spun round. Brenda stood right behind him, her blonde hair hanging to her shoulders, eyes twinkling as she slipped an arm round his waist. She must have sneaked in as his back was turned and, judging from her glazed expression, had spent the night drinking in the Phil. 'You walking me home, Gianni?' she asked, chomping on a mouthful of gum. She licked her glossy lips suggestively and blew a bubble that popped before it had even begun.

'Er, not tonight, Bren. Nige will walk you home. Won't you, Nige,' he said pointedly.

'Will I?' Nigel spluttered as Gianni dug him in the ribs and whispered, 'You will.' 'Oh all right then. Come on, Bren, let's get going.'

Gianni breathed a sigh of relief. Tempting though Brenda was, he had another nut to crack, one he'd waited for ever for, and he wasn't going to screw up this chance to be with Cathy. He spotted her making her way towards them. 'Go on,' he urged Nigel. 'Enjoy yourself. I'll catch up with you tomorrow.'

He turned and caught Cathy's hand as she reached his side. 'Just saying goodnight to my mates,' he said. 'You ready to go?'

On the way to the bus stop they passed a shop doorway and Gianni pulled her inside. Cathy looked up as he gazed into her eyes. She felt a little thrill run through her and her stomach flip-flopped around. He was so handsome he could have any girl he chose. So what the heck did he want with her? She was useless at kissing, didn't have a clue what to do with a boy really, but his face was close and his lips on hers before she even had time to take a breath and the kissing just came naturally. He forced her lips apart with his tongue and explored her mouth and she found herself responding in the same way. It was easy really, not such a mystery after all. As they drew apart, Gianni smiled and ran his hands down her back, squeezed her bottom gently and pulled her closer. He pressed her up against the shop door and kissed her again. Her first instinct was to push him away as he caressed her breasts through the soft fabric of her top, but she was enjoying the overwhelming feelings he was giving her as he kissed her again, and she didn't want him to stop.

'We'd better go,' he whispered into her hair. 'Or we'll miss the last bus.'

Cathy nodded and straightened her top. She felt certain her cheeks were almost the same shade of red. Would he think her cheap for allowing him to touch her breasts? She hadn't meant to let that happen. She wasn't that sort of girl.

'Can I take you out tomorrow night?' he asked as they stood in the bus queue. 'We could go to the pictures if you fancy it. *Love Me Tender* with Elvis Presley is on at the Mayfair.'

'Yes, please, I'd like that,' Cathy said. He wanted to see her again. And Elvis as well. Oh God. Wait until she told Debbie at work tomorrow. She felt alive inside tonight, nervous – but happy at the same time. He did fancy her after all. But what if she couldn't get out tomorrow night? A feeling of panic washed over her at the thought of not being able to meet him. Sod it; she'd make sure she did by not going home after work. While Gianni held her in his arms her mind worked overtime. She'd take fresh clothes to work with her, get washed and changed at her granny's and stay the night at her bungalow. The bus pulled up and her stomach looped all over the place again as Gianni helped her onto the platform. He found them a seat and held her hand tightly all the way home.

Chapter Eleven

Saturday dragged on for ever. The store was busy, as always, but that didn't stop Cathy clock-watching and by five thirty she was desperate to escape. She hoped that Jack wasn't hanging around outside waiting for her. He'd done it before when he wanted money. She'd told her mam that she was going out and then staying over at Granny Lomax's tonight. She'd asked her not to tell Jack, but he had a way of wheedling things out of her mam and Cathy knew she was too weak to stand her ground and say nothing. She sighed, wishing he'd walk under a bus, and then felt bad, because at the end of the day he was the little ones' father. She'd asked Gianni as they'd said goodnight to pick her up from her granny's later.

'Still looking forward to your date tonight?' Debbie interrupted her thoughts.

'Yeah.' Cathy smiled and twiddled her hair around a finger. 'Not to mention Elvis Presley. I can't wait.'

'You won't have eyes for Elvis when you're sitting next to Gianni Romano.'

'Debs!'

'What? Bet he'll kiss the face off you.'

Cathy turned away as the heat rushed to her cheeks and she thought back to last night in the shop doorway, when Gianni kissed her passionately, and her not wanting him to stop. She moved to one side to let Dolores into the small space behind the counter. The supervisor opened the till, took the day's takings out and pushed them into a cloth bag, dropped the bag into a small tin box, locked it and tucked it under her arm. 'Looks like you've had a good day, girls. Well done. Off you go and enjoy your weekend.'

'Weekend?' Debbie scoffed as they made their way to the staffroom to collect their belongings. 'There's only tonight and Sunday left. Anyone would think she's giving us a holiday or something.'

Cathy grinned. 'I think she means well.'

'Huh, you reckon.' Debbie waved at Davy, who was hanging around waiting for her.

Cathy felt pleased to see he was alone. Mike must have left already. Then the door swung open and he appeared; a smile lit up his face as he spotted her.

'Hi, Cathy,' he said as Davy pulled Debbie into his arms and dropped a kiss on her lips.

'Hi.' Cathy fiddled with the strap of her shoulder bag, avoiding his gaze.

'Doing anything tonight?' He leaned against the doorframe, jingling loose change in his trouser pocket.

She nodded, sensing he was nervous and hoping he wouldn't ask her out. She didn't want to offend him. 'Excuse me please; I need to get my things from my locker.'

'Of course.' Mike took a step away from the door and caught hold of her arm. 'Just wondered if you erm, fancied going into town.'

'Another time, maybe.' Cathy shrugged his arm away. She hurried into the staffroom, hoping he'd be gone by the time she left. She thought again about Gianni. The memory of being in his arms and kissing him sent a thrill right through her. She shivered and grinned to herself. It had felt so right. She wondered if he felt the same. It was good to be going out, rather than her usual Saturday night stuck in at home.

Mike was still hanging around outside the staffroom door. 'You said another time. So what about tomorrow night instead?'

'Oh, I, er, don't think I can,' Cathy stuttered. 'I was out last night and my parents won't like it if I'm out tomorrow night as well. Sorry, Mike.'

'You're going out with him, aren't you?' he said, taking her by surprise. 'That Gianni guy. Why didn't you tell him you were with me when he asked you to dance the other night?'

'But I wasn't – with you – I mean. We weren't on a date or anything.'

'I met you off the bus, walked you to the Rumblin' Tum.'

'What?' She glared at him. 'I was with Debs and Davy as well. Why are you being like this?'

Mike shrugged. 'Thought we might have something going for us.'

'Well, *I* certainly didn't give you that idea.'

'Is it him you're seeing tonight then?'

'Gianni? Yes, it is.'

'Why would you wanna go out with a fella who's always with other girls?' he sneered.

Cathy shrugged. 'He isn't. And I like him.' She tried to push past him, but Mike wouldn't budge. 'Will you move out of the way, please? I'm in a hurry.'

He moved to let her pass. 'He's not right for you, that's all I'm saying.'

'It's nothing to do with you who I go out with,' she called over her shoulder and ran to catch up with Debbie and Davy as the bus pulled up. She sank onto a seat at the back, feeling annoyed. What gave Mike the right to dictate to her like that? They'd never fallen out before, so why start now? Then it dawned. Perhaps he was jealous. He was a nice enough lad, but she didn't fancy him. In the time she'd known Mike, being near him had never brought her out in a sweat like Gianni did.

*

Cathy let herself into her granny's bungalow and sniffed the air. Something smelled good. Her stomach rumbled at the prospect of a decent meal. She popped her head round the kitchen door. The yellow Formica-topped kitchen table was set for two. A crusty loaf stood in the centre on the breadboard, just waiting to be sliced into doorstops. She'd pushed a note through the letterbox on her way to catch the bus this morning, rather than disturb her gran at such an early hour.

'Come on in, love. I got your note. It's a good excuse to feed you up a bit.' Granny wiped her hands down the front of her flowery apron. 'Home-made chicken soup,' she said. 'And I made us that nice loaf to have with it.' She bent to pull something out of the oven. 'Apple pie for afters.'

'Oh, that looks lovely and the soup smells delicious. I'm starving.'

'Take your jacket off and sit down. Won't be a minute. Pour us both a cuppa while you wait.'

Cathy did as she was told and sat back in a chair at the table, sighing blissfully. If only she could do this every night. She thought fleetingly of her mam, struggling to organise tea for the kids, but banished the thought before guilt took over. They weren't her problem tonight. She had to stop this worrying about them all. Soon she wouldn't be there to sort them out, because her nurse training required that she live on site in the nurses' home at the hospital. Then they'd *have* to cope.

'Here you are, my love.' Granny put a laden bowl in front of her. 'Get stuck in.' She cut a hunk of bread and handed it to Cathy. 'Slather it with butter.' She pushed the dish across the table. 'I wish you'd move in with me, Cath. Just to give yourself a break before you start your training.'

Cathy sighed. 'You know I'd love to, but Mam really struggles with the little ones. I'll hang on a bit longer and see what happens when I give them my news.'

Granny Lomax pursed her lips. 'I've said it before, but Alice was a fool to marry Jack. Betty Moss at number thirty said she saw him coming out of the Legion with a bottle-blonde floozy on his arm the other night. Betty said she looked a sight. Hair like a haystack and heels so high she could hardly stand up.'

'Really?' Cathy raised an eyebrow. The thought of him going home with the woman and then getting into bed with her mam afterwards made her cringe. 'I wish he *would* go off with someone else. Leave poor Mam in peace. Trouble is, she's so low at the moment that she thinks she can't cope without him. Now she's found a minder for Roddy she's going back to work soon and then hopefully her confidence will come back and she'll chuck him out. Otherwise I'd have no chance of taking up my place on the course.'

'Nothing's going to stop you starting that course, Cathy. I'll make sure of that. Now get your soup down you, and then you can have a nice bath in peace. The immersion's been on all afternoon so there's plenty of hot water.'

'You've no idea how good that sounds,' Cathy said. 'I've had to share my baths with Roddy a few times lately.' There was also the time Jack walked in on the premise of getting the baby out of the bath to dry him. He'd never before offered to help with the kids and she knew he'd only done that so he could stare at her. She'd covered what she could of herself with her hands and the flannel and yelled at him to get out. Her mam had been at Millie's next door for a while that night. The thought of Jack's eyes on her body made her stomach turn. She pushed it away and tucked into her soup.

Granny watched her for a while before speaking. 'So – this lad you're off out with tonight, nice, is he?'

'Yes.' Cathy felt her cheeks warming at her granny's inquisitive tone. 'He's *very* nice. It's Gianni.'

'Oh, Sadie's boy. Oh well, he's a lovely young man. And he's very handsome too.'

Cathy smiled and cut a bit more off the loaf to wipe up the last dregs of soup.

'But you can never be too careful,' Granny Lomax went on. 'Just make sure he looks after you. You've a good future ahead and you don't want any lad spoiling things.'

Cathy grinned. 'I'll be fine. I can look after myself,' she said as Granny put a dish of apple pie in front of her and lifted a jug of custard from the oven.

'Help yourself, but use that cloth cos the handle's hot.'

'Thank you.' She could get used to this. She hoped her skirt would fasten after all this food.

Cathy was surprised when Gianni pulled up outside the bungalow on his motorbike. She'd been expecting him to be on foot. She walked down the garden path to meet him. He climbed off, gave her a hug and kissed her long and hard, making her heart race and her legs turn to jelly.

He held her close and whispered into her hair, 'I've waited all day for that and boy was it worth it.'

'Was it?' She smiled up at him. He was tall, just over six foot, and she was five foot five, so he was just right for her. She loved the way he looked tonight, tight jeans, a black polo-neck sweater, topped with a black leather biking jacket.

'Oh, it was.' His brown eyes twinkled. 'Right, well I had to pop over to my mate's before coming to you, so I'm on the bike as you can see. So we can go to one of the cinemas further afield or leave it here and walk to the Mayfair.'

Cathy chewed her lip. 'Can we walk to the Mayfair please? I'm a bit scared of getting on your bike after what happened to my dad. And Granny's at the window watching us. She'd have a fit if I got on it in front of her. Maybe another time?'

'Of course.' He held her hand as they walked the short distance to the Mayfair picture house. 'Are you looking forward to seeing Elvis Presley?'

'I am. Very much.'

'All you girls seem to have a crush on him.'

'You do have a look of him, you know.' Cathy glanced sideways at Gianni, whose dark quiff was styled exactly like Elvis's. He had the same deep-set hooded eyes, too, but Elvis's were blue and Gianni's as dark as plain chocolate.

He laughed, but looked pleased at her comments. 'Debra Paget plays Elvis's wife in the film,' he said. 'She's a looker.'

'She's very pretty,' Cathy agreed, thinking, if he fancied redheads, why didn't he ask Debs out instead of her? She felt a bit jealous, but for no good reason.

'So are you,' he said softly and stroked her cheek with a finger. 'Pretty, that is.'

Cathy's legs felt like they were about to give way. She couldn't believe how he could stir up such strong feelings in her and she felt a bit panicky inside, like she was about to lose all her common sense in one go.

They arrived at the Mayfair and he threw his arm round her and led her inside.

Cathy sighed and snuggled closer to Gianni. They were seated on the back row of the circle, his arm round her shoulders. The place was crowded; Elvis a popular choice. Gianni tilted her chin with his finger and kissed her. They'd hardly come up for air through the newsreel and the short support film, apart from allowing people to get to their seats further along the row, but now the main feature was about to start.

They watched the opening scenes, but then he kissed her again and slid his hand under her top. She gasped and looked into his eyes. Debs had been right. From the look he was giving her, she doubted they'd see much of Elvis tonight.

'Someone might see us,' she whispered.

'They're too busy watching the film,' he whispered back.

She lost herself to his kisses and caresses. The feelings made her tummy tingle and between her thighs feel warm, like nothing she'd experienced before.

'Like it?' he murmured, stroking her thighs.

'Yes. But I still think someone might see us.'

'It's dark, stop worrying,' he assured her.

*

When they left the Mayfair, arms round one another, they strolled towards a small coffee bar down the road that was still open. 'Would you like a coffee?' Gianni nodded towards the steamed-up windows. 'Bit too early to call it a night, and if you don't have a curfew… at least there's no irate dad waiting up to give me the third degree.'

'No but there's Granny,' Cathy said with a laugh. 'I'd love a coffee though, thank you.'

He took her hand and they found a table by the window. Gianni ordered frothy coffees at the counter and brought them over. Cathy had cleared a circle in the steam and was staring out of the window.

He watched her spoon sugar into her cup and stir it as though her mind was elsewhere. 'What is it? Did I say something to upset you?' They'd been getting along just fine and he'd felt really close to her as he'd held her. A feeling like he'd never experienced before with a girl. She was perfect. Pretty and slim, but curvy in all the right places. Her bright blue eyes had little flecks of light green in them and an air of amusement, as though she might burst out laughing at any minute. Now they were downcast and she looked a bit sad. He wondered if he'd gone too far with his groping, but she'd seemed to like it and had responded with soft sighs and moans that he'd found a real turn-on.

'It's not you,' she said, breaking his thoughts. 'It was when you said about my dad. I often wonder what life would be like for me and Mam if he was still alive. I only knew him for a very short time. You know I don't get on with my stepdad Jack.'

'I know.' He reached for her hand across the table. 'I haven't seen my dad since I was little.'

'Does it bother you?'

He never spoke of his father to anyone. Most of his mates thought his mum was divorced, if they thought anything at all, and he'd never told them that his parents were still married. 'Occasionally it does,' he said. 'I'd love to see him again, catch up with his life and have him catch up with mine.'

'Do you know where he lives?' Cathy took a sip of coffee.

The froth stuck to her top lip. It made her look vulnerable, like a child, and he wiped it gently away with his fingertips. 'He belongs to a family of fairground owners and he travels all over the country. I daresay I could find him if I tried.'

'And will you? Try and find him one day?'

He shrugged. 'Not sure. I don't want to upset my mam. She's made a lot of sacrifices to bring me up on her own. The fair pitches up on Sefton Park occasionally, but I've never been able to see it as my mam has always taken me away on holiday at the same time. But I'm a bit big for a bucket and spade holiday now!'

'Oh, fancy that!' Cathy exclaimed. 'I've seen Romano's Fair on Seffy Park but I never associated them with you, in spite of the name. I went for a wander around it with Debs last year and we watched the wall of death ride. I remember thinking how dangerous it looked. It made my stomach turn.'

'One of those riders must have been my dad. It's what he does. That's why Mam hates me riding the bike. She thinks I'll turn out like him.'

'So, if he's around each year, how come you've not seen him for ages?'

He sighed. 'Like I say, Mam wouldn't allow it. I don't want to upset her by going behind her back. One day, maybe, when the time's right, but not just yet.'

They finished their coffees and Gianni looked at his watch. 'I'd better get you home or your gran will be on the warpath.'

He held her hand as they walked to the white bungalow. 'Can I see you tomorrow afternoon? We can go for a little ride on the bike. I'm sure you'd enjoy it and I'll go slowly and look after you. We can park up and have a walk.'

Cathy chewed her lip. 'Okay then. I'd like that. But meet me on the corner of Lark Lane, Seffy Park end. I'll be home from Gran's by then but I don't want Mam and Jack to know where I'm going.'

She smiled up at him and he caught his breath. No girl had ever made his heart beat so fast.

Chapter Twelve

July 1957

Following a peaceful Sunday morning breakfast with Granny Lomax, Cathy got a shock when she arrived home. Her mam was standing in the kitchen peeling potatoes, but instead of her usual stained old clothes she was wearing clean beige slacks and a green and white striped blouse. Her light brown hair was fastened back in a neat French pleat and she'd even powdered her face and put a bit of lipstick on. The little ones were playing with a ball in the back garden, on a bit of lawn that was free from Jack's clutter. Baby Roddy, in his pram, was giggling at the line of washing blowing in the slight breeze. Of Jack, thankfully, there was no sign.

'Blimey, Mam, you're up and organised early. Are you trying to get into a routine for going back to work?' Cathy put her bag down on the table and pecked her mam on the cheek. 'Shall I make us a quick coffee before his lordship gets up?' She filled the kettle and popped it on the stove. 'You okay, Mam?' she asked when there was nothing forthcoming.

'I'm fine, chuck.' Alice looped a strand of escaping hair behind her ear. 'He's not here – his lordship, that is. He didn't come home last night. I slept like a log so I didn't know until this morning.

That's why we're all up and ready. I only had the kids to see to. And yes, I'm trying to get psyched up for going back to work.'

Cathy nodded. 'Aren't you bothered that Jack stayed out?' He'd no doubt spent the night with his floozy, but it wasn't her place to say anything.

'Not at all. It gave me a bit of peace. He'll have gone to one of his mates, or stayed at the Legion with Martin and his wife and fallen asleep. At least he didn't disturb us banging around. He'll be back when he's good and ready.'

Yeah, Cathy thought, when his floozy chucks him out. He'll be back, stinking of her and his usual sweat and stale breath. How any woman, least of all her mam, could get into bed with him and do anything intimate, she didn't know. The thought was enough to make her gag. The kettle boiled. She made two cups of coffee and sat down at the table.

'And is that why you've got yourself dressed up a bit?' she probed. 'For him, when he comes back?' She knew she'd hit the nail on the head when her mam blushed and the colour added a bloom to her cheeks, giving a glimpse of the pretty woman she once was.

'I've done it for me, but I'm sure he must get fed up of seeing me looking a mess with baby sick on my clothes and no time to do my hair nice or anything…' She trailed off as Cathy stared at her, and then muttered, 'I can't manage without him.'

'But you can, Mam. You've done all right this morning. You looked almost happy when I walked in. Jack does nothing to help you. Without him around you'd have a lot less to do. You're always fetching and carrying for him. You won't be able to do everything when you're working.' She finished her coffee, picked up both empty cups and rinsed them. 'Anyway,' she turned to face her mam and leaned against the worktop, 'what did he say when he found out I wasn't coming home last night?'

'He didn't seem bothered. I thought he'd go mad, but he'd had a win on the horses and had money in his pocket. I told him you were staying at Mrs Lomax's and he didn't even ask why.'

It amused Cathy that her mam now called her ex-mother-in-law, Mrs Lomax, instead of Mam as she'd done prior to marrying Jack.

'How did your date with Gianni go, love?' Mam changed the subject. 'Where did he take you?'

'It was lovely. We saw Elvis at the Mayfair, and then went for a coffee.' Cathy smiled, savouring the memory of her first date. 'Mam, do you miss my dad?'

Alice blinked and nodded. 'I do. Terry and me were teenage sweethearts. Although I get so little time to think about him now,' she said wistfully. 'Are you seeing Gianni again? Sadie will be thrilled to bits. We've been hoping for this for a long time. You two getting together and settling down.'

'Mam, we've had one date.' Cathy smiled. 'And we're far too young for settling down. We both want to do things with our lives first. Yes, I'm seeing him later.'

'That's nice. Are you having some dinner with us first? I can make the sausages spin out a bit.'

Cathy shook her head. 'No thanks, Mam, give them to the kids. I had a big cooked breakfast. I'll get something to eat while we're out this afternoon. There's bound to be a tea-shop open somewhere.'

'Will you make some gravy before you go out, love? Mine's always lumpy and you know how the kids like yours best. I've made a big Yorkshire pudding so they can have some with their sausage and mash and the rest with a bit of sugar sprinkled on for afters.'

'That'll fill them up,' Cathy said, reaching for a saucepan and the bottle of gravy browning. 'Have you got something in for their tea? I bet Jack never thought to share his winnings for food.'

'I've got some potted beef and bread,' her mam said quietly.

'He didn't, did he?' Cathy shook her head. 'I'll try and get them some cake while I'm out. *He* should be keeping you and the kids, it's not *my* job. I bet you didn't even ask him for any money.'

'He was in a good mood. I didn't want to risk a row when you weren't here to stand beside me.'

Cathy rolled her eyes and wondered how the hell she could even consider leaving home when her mam would clearly struggle to cope. But she'd have to manage come September. She looked up as the kitchen door flew open and Jack, big smile on his unshaven face, strolled in looking as though he hadn't a care in the world. Anger flared inside her. The arrogant sod.

'Alice, my love. What's for dinner?' Jack slapped her on the backside and she blushed and giggled like a silly girl. He deliberately ignored Cathy, who watched her mam fawning around him, feeling the disgust welling up inside.

Cathy banged the pan onto the stove, wishing Jack's head were underneath it, and proceeded to make the gravy. She could sense Jack's eyes on her back, watching her every move. He was willing her to turn round, she could feel it.

Then a scream of 'MAMMAAAAY!' from the garden had her mam running for the door. Cathy followed. Her sisters had ganged up on Teddy, a little boy from down the street, and tied him to the washing-line post with a skipping rope. He was sobbing and they were whooping around him, doing a war dance.

'Shoo, go on, you naughty girls,' Cathy shouted, untying Teddy and giving him a hug. 'Go inside and ask Daddy to play.'

Cathy took Teddy home and dashed back to see Jack looking aghast as the girls jumped on his knee. Sandra told him, 'Caffy said you have to play wiv us.' Rosie nodded and wiped her snotty nose on the front of his shirt.

'You dirty little beggar,' he growled, tipping them onto the rug and lurching to his feet. 'Watch my suit. You'll get it filthy.'

Cathy raised an eyebrow and looked him up and down. The suit had seen better days; beer stains and fag burns decorated the jacket.

'Why are you looking down your nose at *me*, Miss Hoity-Toity!' he shouted. 'And where the bloody hell was *you* last night. Out 'til all hours. And who with? That bloody half-breed from across the way, that's who! I saw you; bet you didn't see me though, eh? Eh? He was all over you outside Ma Lomax's. You think you're a cut above everybody else, you do. You're nowt but a little tart, that's what you are. And you needn't think you can come crying to me and your mam when he knocks you up!'

Cathy took a step towards Jack, who backed up against the wall. 'How dare you call me a tart and Gianni a half-breed,' she yelled in his face. 'You ignorant pig. And what were you doing near my gran's? None of your friends live up there. It's too posh for the likes of you and them. Were you spying on me, Jack?' She stopped, aware of her mam trying to herd the little ones out of the room. 'You come waltzing back in here and ruin everything Mam's done today. All the things you take for granted.' She took a deep breath, anger coming from within. She wanted to scratch his eyes out and run her nails down his stubbly face. She lowered her voice, hoping she sounded menacing. 'I know where you went after you saw me, and where you spent the night. Shall I tell Mam about your bottle-blonde, or will you? And also I know that you were working with Sheila for months behind Mam's back, so you just watch your step or you'll be out of this house, and I mean that. I also know that Brian told you to get out. I'd think about doing that if I was you.' She stepped back with satisfaction as his face paled and she saw his Adam's apple bob nervously up and down. She hoped her mam hadn't heard what she'd just said. The door was closed and the kids were making a noise, so it was unlikely.

'I don't know what you mean,' he spluttered, his eyes shifting from side to side. 'Don't you dare stir up trouble for me or you'll be sorry.'

'And don't you dare threaten me. Now, go and look after your kids while Mam finishes making the dinner, or I *will* say something.' She pushed past him and ran upstairs to her bedroom. She flopped down on the bed, heart thudding and hands shaking. She'd got the better of him again, but she didn't like the look in his eyes as she'd shoved him out of the way. She hoped he wouldn't take it out on her mam while she was out with Gianni.

Chapter Thirteen

The heavens opened and heavy spots of rain falling on his face made Gianni gasp. He jumped up and pulled Cathy to her feet. The big black cloud overhead had come from nowhere. They huddled together under a tree, his leather jacket over their heads, while he silently cursed the sudden downpour that had put an end to their romantic afternoon.

'Let's make a run for the bike,' he suggested. 'We're not far from home. And in this rain your mam won't be staring out the window so she won't see you on the bike. We can get dried off at mine.'

'Will your mam mind?' Cathy shook the raindrops from her hair.

He shrugged and looked at his watch. 'She'll still be out. Goes to my gran's on a Sunday afternoon.' Grabbing her hand, he pulled her along the path to the car park. He dried the saddle with a hanky before helping her on.

By the time they got to Lucerne Street they were wet through. He hurried her inside and switched on the sitting-room electric fire. Cathy shivered and took off her sodden jacket. Her white T-shirt stuck to her body and Gianni caught his breath. In spite of her bedraggled appearance she looked as sexy as hell. He pulled her into his arms and kissed her. 'Take off your T-shirt and I'll hang it over the fireguard in the kitchen to dry. The fire's lit in there.'

Her eyes opened wide. 'I can't do that.'

'I'll get you one of mine to slip on. Do you want a towel for your hair?'

'Please.'

He led her up the narrow staircase and into his bedroom. He got two towels from the bathroom and handed her one, watching as she rubbed her hair and self-consciously took off her T-shirt, holding the towel in front of her.

He pulled her to him and kissed her again, running his hands down her back. 'Your jeans are soaked,' he whispered, tugging at the towel in between them and letting it drop to the floor. She immediately covered her breasts with her hands and he pulled those away too. 'Don't hide yourself. You're beautiful.'

She looked at the floor and mumbled, 'I'm not taking my jeans off.'

'You're gonna get a chill if you leave them on.' He got a T-shirt from the chest of drawers and gave it to her. 'Here, it's long enough to cover your backside if that makes you feel better.'

'What if your mam comes back and finds us half-dressed.' Her teeth were chattering now and she shivered.

'I'll tell her we got wet in the rain and I'm drying your clothes. If they're on the fireguard steaming she'll see it's the truth.'

'Okay, if you're sure.' Cathy kicked off her shoes and peeled off her wet jeans. She slipped Gianni's T-shirt over her head and sat down on the narrow bed, pulling the hem down over her knees while he went to hang up her clothes.

*

Left alone, Cathy gazed around the simply furnished bedroom. She hoped Sadie wouldn't come home before she'd got all her clothes on again as she might say something to her mam and she'd go mad, thinking they'd been up to something. The white-painted walls were covered with motorbike pictures, some cut from magazines and forming a montage and others hand-drawn and coloured with poster paints. There were books on the bedside cabinet about bikes and models on a shelf.

A record player stood in the corner on a small table alongside a pile of singles. She got to her feet, wondering what sort of music he liked besides Elvis Presley. A quick look told her that he was a fan of Lonnie Donegan, Chuck Berry and Buddy Holly. He definitely liked his rock'n'roll music. On top of the record player lay a sketch pad and pencil. She peeped inside. He was good. Drawings of animals, houses and bikes filled the first few pages. Pen-and-ink likenesses of Elvis and Buddy Holly were as good as photographs. She stared at the next page and felt her cheeks heating as he came back into the room, carrying two steaming mugs. He stopped by the door, staring at her. 'When did you do this?' she asked, feeling wobbly inside.

'This morning,' he replied. 'Do you like it?'

'Like it?' she said softly. 'It's lovely. You've – you've – made me look really beautiful.'

'Well, you are.'

'Not like this.' The head-and-shoulders sketch had full lips, wide dewy eyes and long, windswept, face-framing hair. He'd even got the light sprinkle of freckles on the bridge of her nose just right.

'Yes, you are,' he said. 'That's exactly how I saw you last night after the breeze had whipped your hair around your face. You could be a model.' He put the mugs down on the bedside cabinet, took her in his arms and kissed her.

Cathy felt flattered and overwhelmed. She could be a model? No one had ever said anything as nice to her. She put her arms up round his neck and the T-shirt rode up her thighs as she kissed him back. Gianni clutched her buttocks and pulled her closer. She could feel his wet jeans dripping on her bare feet, and that wasn't all she could feel. 'You're very wet yourself,' she said, pulling back a little, worried, because she wasn't sure what to do. 'You'd better get changed or you'll get a cold.'

He groaned and let her go. She sat down on the bed again and he handed her a mug of coffee.

'Two sugars, like you had last night. Drop of whisky in it too to warm you up.'

'Thank you.' Fancy him remembering how many sugars she'd spooned into last night's coffee. And she'd never had alcohol before. She watched him take clean jeans off a hanger and a T-shirt out of the drawer.

'I'll, er, change in the bathroom,' he said and dashed away.

She sipped her coffee, feeling nervous now, sitting there half-naked. He might want her to go further than the kissing and cuddling they'd done earlier and she didn't know what to do. She just couldn't go any further than petting, even though her body told her it wanted to. The way he made her feel, it would be so easy to get carried away, like she couldn't give a damn about her principles when she was in his arms. She'd made a vow to herself ages ago that she'd get married before she went all the way. But that was then, before Gianni. She'd also promised herself a future that didn't involve getting too close to a boy. Otherwise, her wonderful new life would be over before it began. She looked up as the door opened and he came back in wearing faded jeans and a black T-shirt, his hair glistening and brushed back. Her heart leapt and her stomach churned as he looked at her with a twinkle in his dark eyes.

*

Gianni picked up the second mug and sat down beside Cathy. She looked a bit warmer now and her cheeks had a glow, thanks to the whisky. He could sense her nervousness and he smiled as she pulled the T-shirt down as far as it would go. He finished his drink, took her empty mug and put them both on the bedside cabinet. He pulled her close, smoothing her damp hair from her face. Then she was in his arms and kissing him and he pushed her back onto the pillows and lay down beside her. His mam would be home any minute now. Dare he take a chance? He looked into

Cathy's eyes and saw panic there. He sat up and swung his legs off the bed. It was too soon and, desperate though he was, there was no way he was risking losing her by rushing things.

'I'm sorry, Cathy.' He pulled her T-shirt back down.

'It's okay.' She stroked his arm.

'I really like you; you know that, don't you?'

She nodded.

'I know we're only young, but I think we might have something special happening between us.' He stopped and swallowed hard. Bloody hell, he'd never said anything so mushy to a girl before. He wanted to tell her how he felt and that he was willing to wait until she was old enough and ready. But how could he say it so that she wouldn't think that all he was waiting for was to get his leg over? 'What I'm trying to say is… will you go out with me? You know – like – be my girl?'

She smiled and knelt beside him. 'Yes. I'd like that.'

He put his arms round her and kissed her. 'Sit up the top of the bed then. I can't keep my hands off you and I know you're not ready for anything too heavy yet.'

'Okay.' She shuffled up and sat with her back against the headboard. 'Shall we just talk then?'

'If you like.' Anything to take his mind off what he really wanted to do.

'Where did you learn to draw so well?'

'School.' His eyes lit up. 'I've always enjoyed drawing. I'd have loved to go to art college but Mam insisted I have a trade after school. So when I got offered the draughtsman's apprenticeship it was too good to turn down. I draw plans for parts of planes. Not quite what I had in mind, but once I'm qualified I'll earn good money.'

'Do you enjoy it?'

He shrugged. 'Yeah, to a point. I feel a bit restless at times. As though there's more to life, I mean. It'll be a nine-to-five job and I'll have to wear a suit for the rest of my working days.'

'Still, it means you'll never have to struggle,' she said. 'You'll always have a decent wage coming in.'

'True.' He shrugged again, dismissively. 'What about you? Do you plan on climbing the sales ladder any further at Lewis's?' He frowned as she looked away for a moment, then he saw excitement in her eyes and she smiled at him.

'Can you keep a big secret?' she said. 'I mean, you can't even say anything to your mam or Debs, not just yet anyway.'

'Cross my heart and hope to die,' he said with a grin.

He listened as Cathy outlined her plans for the future.

'Will you have to go away for training?' He hoped she wouldn't. Not when he was just getting to know her, and he already knew he was halfway to falling for her in a big way. The thought that he might not be able to see her for weeks on end made him feel a bit sad.

'No, I'm training at Royal Liverpool. They have their own school of nursing.'

He breathed a sigh of relief. 'Oh good, so we can still go out together.'

'Course we can. I'll have to study and won't be able to go out too many nights a week, but I'm sure we'll manage. I don't start until September, so we've got a few weeks to get to know one another better.'

He reached for her and held her. They had all the time they needed. And once she was trained, and *he'd* got to grips with his nine-to-five routine, the world would be theirs.

*

Cathy peered across at her home to make sure the front room curtains were closed before she dashed up the street out on to Lark Lane and then hurried back again to make it seem as though she was on her way back from Granny Lomax's, should anyone be looking out for her. She was a lot later than she'd planned to be because Sadie had arrived back and insisted she have something to eat while her clothes finished drying.

She was out of breath and had a stitch in her side by the time she let herself in at the front door. She could hear the low murmur of adult voices coming from the back room, but no kids. They must be in bed. Then she remembered she'd promised to bring them cake. She felt a bit guilty for forgetting. Never mind. She'd bring some home after work tomorrow.

Her mam was sitting at the table, eyes red-rimmed, hands wrapped round a mug. Her earlier look of being in control had disappeared. Jack, glass in hand, slouched in his usual chair by the fire, which had been lit to finish drying the washing hanging above on a clothes rack. He puffed clouds of smoke in the air in an agitated way and it mingled with the steam from drying nappies. Cathy didn't like the look on his face. He'd obviously been having a go at her mam over something. He slurped the last of his beer and banged the glass down on the tiled hearth, where it shattered. Mam flinched and let out a little whimper.

He pulled himself to his feet and lurched towards Cathy, who took a step back towards the door.

'Here she is,' he began. 'Lady bloody Muck!'

Cathy frowned. 'I beg your pardon?'

'Oh you do, do you?' He jabbed her with his finger. 'Where've you been until now? Out with that biker lad again?'

'It's got nothing to do with you where I've been.' Cathy tried to get past him but he grabbed her arm and she stumbled back against the door. His face was close enough for her to count the blackheads on his blotchy nose and smell his foul breath. She gagged as he pushed his body against her and, using both hands, she shoved him as hard as she could. He wobbled but didn't lose his footing, which gave her seconds to dodge past him and stand behind her mam. 'You keep away from me, you filthy pervert.

Mam, he just pressed himself up against me. He's disgusting, and it's not the first time he's done it.'

'You're a lying little slut,' Jack yelled. 'She's making it up, Alice. You know I wouldn't do that.'

'He would, Mam.' Cathy burst into tears, feeling more angry than she'd ever felt. 'He even comes into the bathroom when I'm naked.'

'He wouldn't do that, Cathy,' her mam said, sounding a bit unsure. 'Why are you saying these things?'

'Yes, he would,' Cathy cried. 'Why do you believe him and not me?'

'She's lying, Alice. She always gives me the come-on when you're not in.' Jack fixed Cathy with a sly look, rooted in his pocket and threw something down on the table. 'And we know something else about her, don't we?'

Cathy's hand flew to her mouth. She'd left her handbag at home, hidden under her bed, so she wouldn't have to carry it on the bike while she was out. For all his struggling to get upstairs, Jack had found it. And that was the letter from the Royal Liverpool Hospital School of Nursing he'd thrown on the table.

'So, when were you going to tell us?' he spat.

She took a deep breath and said, 'When I was ready. But you've saved me the bother. How dare you go through my things? You've no right.'

'I've *every* right. This is *my* house and you do as you're told while you're under this roof.' Jack's face was mottled purple now and Cathy hoped he'd burst a blood vessel and drop dead.

'Well, if it's *your* house why don't *you* pay the rent and feed your kids!' she screamed.

'I'm sorry, but you can't take the place on the course, Cathy,' her mam said quietly. 'It means you living out and we'll need you here to help us when I go back to work.'

Cathy stared at her mam, her mouth open. She couldn't believe she'd take Jack's side. She knew she was scared of him, but even so. Somehow she replied with as much determination as she could muster: 'I've already accepted the place. I'm starting in September. I'll be leaving home and I won't be coming back. I'm sorry, Mam, but I can't cope with living here any more.'

'And you think your mother *can*?' Jack snarled. 'You're a selfish little cow. No thought for anybody but yourself.'

'How can you say that when you take nearly every penny I earn?' Cathy launched herself at Jack, kicking and yelling and pulling his hair. He fought her off and slapped her hard round the mouth. She screamed and so did her mam, who picked up her mug of hot tea and threw it over him, shocking him into stepping backwards.

'That's it,' Cathy cried, hands over her swollen lips, blood seeping through her fingers. 'I'm out of here now. I'm going to my granny's and I'm not coming back until he goes.' She ran out of the room and up to her bedroom to grab some clothes and her work uniform. She pushed everything into a small suitcase and picked up her handbag. Luckily she'd hidden the remainder of her wages in her uniform pockets and it was still there. Her heart sank as she heard the thud, thud of Jack's wooden foot on the stairs. The door opened and he came in, glaring at her.

'You're going nowhere,' he said in a menacing tone. 'Put that case down.'

Cathy stood her ground and held on tight to the case handle. 'Move, let me out.'

'Cathy, come on,' he said, his tone more wheedling now. 'Don't be like this. You know I love you like you're one of me own. You need to stay with your family. You're too young to be thinking of leaving home.'

'Let me out,' Cathy said again, through gritted teeth.

'I'm sorry I hit you. But you hit me first.'

'You're an adult. I'm only fifteen,' she said, a sob in her voice. She wished Gianni was here. He'd soon sort Jack out. She felt like crying again but knew he would see it as a weakness. 'I could report you to the police for attacking me.' Her lips were stinging like crazy now, blood drying on them. They needed bathing with warm water and the sooner she got to her granny's the better. She hoped he hadn't loosened any of her teeth. She ran her tongue round inside her mouth to check and all the time Jack was staring at her, leering almost.

He stepped forward and put out a hand.

'Don't you dare touch me!' she yelled, waking her little sisters in the next room, who started crying. 'Let me out.'

'See, you've woken the kids now,' he said, grabbing the hand that was holding onto the case. He twisted her wrist and she gasped and let go of the handle. He pulled her close and breathed beery fumes in her face, his hand fondling her backside.

Her stomach turned and she brought her knee up sharply and jarred him in the groin. It worked, as always. He let her go and bent double, clutching himself between the legs.

'You vicious little mare,' he growled, dropping to his knees.

Cathy grabbed her case and handbag, gave him another quick boot between the legs for good measure and hurried as fast as she could down the stairs, suitcase bumping behind her. She pushed past her mam, who was hovering in the hallway, crying. 'You choose him over me, Mam, and you lose me for good,' she said and dashed out of the front door. She ran down the street towards Granny Lomax's, wishing she could call to let Gianni know where she was going, but knowing that Jack might see her.

Chapter Fourteen

Cathy's lips stung like crazy as she sipped her tea. Her eyes filled with tears. She knew she looked a right mess and wondered what the hell she'd tell Debbie. It would have to be the truth, but she'd feel so embarrassed, and she'd also have to tell her *why* Jack had hit her. Then her secret would be out and her job at risk.

Granny Lomax stared at her over the rim of her mug. 'I still think you should give work a miss today, love.'

'I don't want to,' Cathy said, her voice wobbling. Gianni had promised to meet her under the Nobby Lewis statue after work. She could hardly go and stand outside the store and wait for him when everyone would be leaving, including her supervisor. She'd probably get the sack right away. 'I'll be fine, honestly.'

Granny Lomax got to her feet and put an arm round Cathy's shoulders. 'You shouldn't let Jack get away with it, Cath. Hitting a young girl like you. He needs stringing up!'

Cathy shrugged as her gran cleared the table and stacked the dishes on the draining board. 'Then Mam would be on her own and you know what that means.'

'Oh, they won't throw him in prison, more's the pity,' Granny Lomax said, running water into the sink. 'But he'd get a warning to stay away from you. Be best all round if they *did* lock him up and throw away the key. Alice would learn to cope. She'd have to. Anyway, if he shows his face round here he'll get what's coming to him. George next door said he'd have him.'

Cathy stood up and gave her gran a hug. 'He would, too.'
She smiled. 'Let's hope Jack stays away then. Don't want George
getting into bother on my behalf. I'll be a bit late home. I'm
meeting Gianni for coffee. Don't make me any tea in case we have
something to eat as well.' She kissed her gran on the cheek.

'Okay, love. Look after yourself, and if you see Jack hanging
around near work, make sure your boss phones the police.'

'So come on,' Debbie said, when she and Cathy were seated with
their lunches in the Kardomah Café. 'What happened? I hope
you're not gonna tell me Gianni did that.' All morning she'd been
dying to find out how Cathy had got her swollen and bruised lips.
But her friend had remained silent.

'No, of course he didn't,' Cathy said. 'I had a fight with my
stepdad.'

'And he hit you?' Debbie's jaw dropped. 'My dad *never* lifts a
finger to me. My mam would kill him.'

'Yes, well, my mam's scared of him, swine that he is. She sided
with him over me. I couldn't take it any more. I've moved in with
my gran.'

'What did you fight about?'

Cathy sighed. 'Promise you won't tell a soul? I mean it, Debs.
You really can't say anything to anyone.'

'I promise,' Debbie said and listened as Cathy explained.

'Oh, I'm gonna miss you.' She squeezed Cathy's arm. 'But I
can't say I blame you for trying to better yourself. I hope it works
out, Cathy, I really do.'

Cathy gave Debbie a hug. 'I'll miss you too. But we'll still see
a lot of each other. I'll be training locally. And…' she paused,
'Gianni and me – well – we're going steady. He asked me to be
his girl, yesterday.'

'Ooh,' Debbie squealed. 'How lovely. Can I tell Davy? And talk of the devil – he's just walked in with Mike.' She waved.

'Not a word about my new job,' Cathy whispered. 'I'll tell you more when we're back at work.'

Cathy smiled at Davy and Mike they sat down opposite. Davy flung his arms round Debbie and gave her a kiss, while Mike stared at Cathy, a frown on his face.

'What you done to your mouth?'

'Er, banged it on the sink. I slipped in the bathroom,' Cathy muttered, looking away from his piercing gaze. It was the same tale she'd told Dolores Redfern when the supervisor questioned her.

'Yeah?'

'Yes.' She nodded. 'Luckily I didn't knock any teeth out.' The look on his face said he didn't believe a word. He'd be giving her the third degree next. She changed the subject. 'I saw *Love Me Tender* the other night,' she said, remembering he'd seen the film. 'It was really good.' What she could remember of it, that was. How on earth she would manage to kiss Gianni tonight she didn't know. Her lips were too sore for anything other than a peck. She sensed Debbie's eyes on her and looked across the table.

'We're going tonight, aren't we, Davy?' Debbie came to her rescue. 'Seeing Elvis, I mean. We're looking forward to it.' She looked at her watch. 'We'd better get back, Cathy, or Dolly will be on the warpath.'

Cathy jumped to her feet and grabbed her handbag. 'See you again, boys.'

They hurried out of the café and Debbie linked Cathy's arm. 'Half an hour left,' she said. 'Let's go and look in Blacklers. I saw a nice dress last week that'd suit me. Might try it on if it's still there.'

'Thanks for that, Debs,' Cathy said. 'I'm sure you'd rather have stayed with Davy.'

'That's what friends are for.'

In Blacklers they searched the rails for the dress Debbie liked, but the assistant told them they'd sold the last one on Saturday. A full black skirt with white felted poodles embossed round the hemline caught Cathy's eye. It was perfect for dancing in and with a net petticoat underneath would flare right out when she next jived with Gianni. She held it against herself and looked in the mirror. There was a white shell top on the same rail that would look lovely with it.

'Try them on,' Debbie urged. 'They're really nice.'

The assistant showed Cathy to the changing room. She took off her uniform, slipped the top over her head and stepped into the skirt. It fell to her knees and was a perfect fit. She scooped her long hair up off her face. If she fastened it up with a rubber band and black ribbon into a ponytail she'd look really fashionable. She twisted this way and that, loving the way the skirt twirled out. The price tags weren't too bad – just under two pounds for both. A quick scrabble in her purse told her no. But maybe the shop would hold them until payday?

'Well?' Debbie said when Cathy came out of the changing room.

'They look lovely. But I don't have the money on me to buy them.'

'We can hold until Saturday with a ten-shilling deposit,' the assistant said.

'Okay.' Cathy beamed. 'Thank you.'

Debbie gave her a hug. 'You deserve a treat. We'll collect them Saturday dinnertime.'

'That's cheered me up,' Cathy said as the pair hurried back to Lewis's. 'Just need to go somewhere special to wear it now.'

'We can ask Gianni and Davy to take us dancing at the Grafton ballroom next weekend,' Debbie suggested.

'Good idea. I'll ask Gianni and you ask Davy later and see what they say.'

'Will you be finishing work at the end of August?' Debbie asked.

'Yes. Then I'll have a week off before I start my course. I'll be sixteen then.'

'My mam and dad are away that weekend. I'll throw you a leaving-work and birthday party on the Saturday. You can wear your outfit then as well.'

'A party. For me? Really?'

'Of course, really.'

Cathy stopped walking and her eyes filled. 'Oh, Debs, I don't know what to say. No one's thrown me a party for years.'

'Well *I* will and I'll enjoy spoiling you.'

Sniffling, Cathy threw her arms round her friend. 'Thank you.'

*

Gianni swept Cathy into his arms. He bent to kiss her lips but she turned her head to one side and his lips brushed her cheek. He tilted her chin and frowned. 'How's that happened?' He ran a finger gently over her bottom lip.

'I'll tell you in the café,' she said as he hugged her close. Staff members were hurrying by and shooting them curious looks. Cathy put her head down. They were joined outside the store by Debbie, Davy and Mike.

Gianni recognised the lad scowling as the one Cathy had been with at the Rumblin' Tum. He tightened his hold on her and scowled back as Mike muttered something under his breath. 'Sorry, did you say something?' Gianni asked.

'Mike,' Debbie said. 'Leave it. You've got the wrong end of the stick.'

'No, I won't leave it,' Mike said. He clenched his fists and took a step towards Gianni, who towered above him. 'Don't think you can get away with it and pretend nothing's happened.'

'What are you on about?' Gianni said.

'You, you greasy rocker bastard. Think you can get away with battering Cathy then acting like you care.'

Cathy gasped. 'Mike, you've got it wrong. Gianni didn't do this. And anyway, it's personal and got nothing to do with you.'

'Mike, come on, mate, time to go home.' Davy grabbed one of his arms and Debbie grabbed the other.

'See you tomorrow, Cathy,' she said as they led Mike away.

Gianni shook his head after them. 'Bloody nutter! How could he think I'd lay a finger on you?'

Cathy shrugged. 'Let's go to the Kardomah.'

'Your stepfather?' Gianni said quietly, after listening to Cathy's tale. 'I'll punch his lights out when I get my hands on him.'

'Gianni, no, you won't,' Cathy said. 'He's not worth it.' She paused and took a sip of coffee. She'd told him what had happened and of Jack's threatening behaviour, but that she'd taken control of the situation.

He stroked her hair. 'I'd still like to punch the bastard though.'

'No need. I did it myself.' She told him how she'd kneed Jack where it hurts most, and he laughed.

'That's my girl. I like a woman who can stand up for herself.'

*

Cathy waited in the hall with a holdall borrowed from Granny Lomax. Gianni was coming to pick her up and they were going to collect the rest of her things from Lucerne Street. He'd told her the bag would fasten onto the back of the bike and they could put her records and books in the panniers. She felt sick with nerves. It was a week since she'd last set foot in the house. But she couldn't leave it any longer; there was stuff she needed and she was running out of things to wear – assuming Jack hadn't slung everything away in a fit of temper. In spite of her mam siding with Jack, it would be nice to see her and the kids again; she'd missed them. She really hoped Jack would be out. 'I'm off now, Gran,' she called as Gianni sounded his horn outside.

'Right you are, love.' Granny Lomax came into the hall and gave her a hug. 'Please be careful on that bike. You know it scares the life out of me. Hold on tight to him. I'll see you later.'

Cathy ran outside. Gianni fastened her bag to the rear and helped her onto the seat. She pulled at the hem of her checked skirt, which had ridden up her thighs, and wished her jeans hadn't been on the washing line. Still, she had a spare pair at the house, thank goodness.

'Hang on tight,' Gianni called as they whizzed away down the road.

Cathy looked up at the windows and frowned as Gianni pulled up outside the house. The curtains were all closed and there was no sign of the little ones playing in the garden. 'Drive round to the back,' she said. 'Pull into the passageway behind. I'll go in the back door. Looks like they're out.'

'Well that's good, isn't it?' he said.

'It's unusual. They never go out as a family. Maybe Jack's turned over a new leaf now I'm not there. They might have taken the kids to the park.'

Gianni rode round to the back lane and pulled up at the gate. The curtains were closed at Cathy's old bedroom window too. A feeling of unease crept down her spine. What if Jack had done something bad to her mam and the kids?

She got off the bike and opened the creaky old gate. It had seen better days and needed a coat of paint.

'Hello, Cathy love.' A voice rang out from over the adjoining hedge. Millie's head popped up, hands full of wet washing and clothes pegs. 'Thought you'd left home? Your mam told me what happened, love and that you'd gone to stay at your gran's for a while.'

'I did, for now. It was getting a bit too overcrowded here.'

Millie switched her attention to Gianni and smiled. 'Sadie told me you two had started dating. It's not really before time.'

'Yes, we have,' Cathy said, feeling her cheeks heating. 'Have you seen my mam today? It looks a bit quiet.'

'She's not here, love. Brian is back from America for a short while and he came to get them all a couple of days ago. He's taken them to Blackpool to a little hotel for a few days' holiday. Alice needs it before she starts work again. She's put it off for another week while Roddy gets settled with my mam's neighbour. I'm surprised she didn't call you at your gran's to let you know all this.'

'No,' Cathy replied, 'she didn't, and neither did Brian tell me he was due home. But that explains the drawn curtains. What about Jack? Is he with them?'

Millie shrugged. 'He's gone, love. Alice was in the throes of chucking him out when Brian arrived. She gave him his marching orders and he left. No idea where he's gone. Good riddance I say. The steward at the Legion might have put him up, or one of his floozies.'

Jimmy's voice bellowed down the garden. 'Millie, have you done gossiping? This bacon is nearly burned to a crisp here.'

Millie rolled her eyes. 'Lift the frying pan off the gas then! I'm coming. See you two again.' She nodded at them both and disappeared indoors.

'Great, the house is empty,' Cathy said to Gianni. 'Can't believe Jack's gone. But why didn't Mam come and tell me?'

'Maybe Brian just wanted to get her away quickly while the dust settled,' Gianni said. 'I'm sure she'll tell you everything when she comes home.'

Cathy nodded. 'You wait here; I won't be a minute.' She took the bag off the bike and let herself in at the back door. She didn't want Gianni to see what sort of a state the place might be in, but to her surprise it was fairly tidy. She wrinkled her nose at the stale smell of a house that had been closed up for a while.

Upstairs in her bedroom she switched on the light. The naked bulb highlighted the stained walls and chipped paintwork. When she got her own place it would be a palace compared to this dump. She put her holdall on the bed under the window. As she folded clothes into it she hummed to herself and even allowed a little daydream to creep in, of what life would be like if she *did* marry Gianni. They'd have a nice house and a couple of children. Gianni would buy a car and they'd take trips to the seaside on Sunday afternoons. Then she remembered her nursing ambitions and sent the dream packing. She'd just bent to lift her records out of the small cupboard at the side of the bed when she became aware of heavy breathing behind her. The hairs on the back of her neck prickled and she turned to see Jack leaning against the doorframe, hand down the front of his grubby trousers. His bloodshot eyes and the boozy stench coming from him told her he was more than drunk, and he was leering at her.

'The wanderer returns,' he slurred, lips curled in a sneer as he limped across the room and grabbed her arm. 'Your mother and uncle chucked me out. But they're not here right now and the silly cow forgot to take the key off me.' He shook her roughly. 'This is all your bloody fault.'

Cathy tried to loosen his grip but his fingers dug into her arm and she squealed with pain. 'Let go of me!'

'Oh no, not this time, lady. You'll do as you're fucking well told.'

'I'll scream if you touch me,' Cathy said, feeling scared but trying not to show it. 'Gianni's outside. You'll be for it if you lay a finger on me.'

Jack laughed in her face and she gagged at the stink.

'Make you feel sick, do I?' He spun her round so she faced away from him. 'That better, Lady fucking Muck? You can't get me with your knee now.' He grabbed her other arm and threw her face-down on the bed. She screamed and wriggled but he gripped her like a vice and pushed her face into the pillow. He put his knee across her back while he let go of one arm to yank her skirt up. She tried to scream again but her scream was stifled by the pillow. She kicked out backwards and felt a sting across the backs of her thighs. His belt, he was hitting her with his belt. She was terrified now but knew she couldn't give in. She fought with all her might. She could hear him laughing, his hand squeezing her backside. The bed sank as he straddled the backs of her thighs.

Cathy tried to yell but could hardly breathe. She could feel him pressing against her. Her arms were pinned underneath her chest but as Jack's weight shifted slightly she managed to get one arm free and yanked as hard as she could on the closed curtains to her side. The lot came down, the curtains and the wire they were hanging from. As Jack was enveloped by the fabric, Cathy pushed backwards with all her might and screamed Gianni's name as loud as she could. Jack fell off the bed and crashed to the floor. Cathy jumped up as the door flew open and Gianni burst in.

'What the fuck?' He grabbed Jack up by the hair and aimed a punch in his face. Blood spattered from his nose and Gianni let him drop to the floor. He kicked Jack in the stomach and ribs and then, with one of his heavy biking boots, aimed between the legs. Jack howled and clutched himself.

Gianni pulled Cathy into his arms, where she sobbed against his chest.

'Oh God, Gianni, if you hadn't been outside…' She took a deep shuddering breath.

'Shh. Shh,' Gianni soothed, cradling her in his arms. 'Has he hurt you anywhere?'

'The backs of my legs are stinging.' She sniffed. 'He hit me with his belt.' She rubbed her arms where Jack's fingerprints were turning to bruises.

'I'm gonna call the police. Is there a phone here?'

Cathy shook her head. 'Don't call the police, please. You might get into trouble for half-killing him.'

'He tried to ruddy rape you. The pervert needs locking up. What if he tries it with someone who's not so lucky?'

Cathy looked at Jack, now curled in a ball, spewing his guts all over the carpet. His hands between his legs were covered in blood and he screamed with agony in between retches. 'I doubt he'll ever do it again.'

'Serves him bloody well right.' Gianni stood up and dug the toe of his boot into Jack's ribs. 'You should count yourself lucky Cathy doesn't want to report you. Lay another finger on her and I'll fucking kill you, make no mistake. You pathetic piece of shit.'

Jack put his hands up over his face and whimpered. Gianni spat on him and turned to Cathy. 'Let's get out of here.'

Chapter Fifteen

August 1957

Cathy removed the greaseproof wrappings from plates of sausage rolls, pork pies and sandwiches. Debbie had done her proud; there was enough food to feed an army. In the centre of the dining table stood a birthday cake, iced in white with pink roses round the edge and sixteen pink and white candles. Granny Lomax, in cahoots with Debbie, had secretly baked it and paid for most of the spread. Cathy hugged herself. She felt so lucky and as excited as a six-year-old. Her birthday had been a few days ago but she was loving all this fuss for her, and in Debs' parents' nice semi-detached too. Debbie hurried through from the kitchen with a dish of cheese and pineapple on sticks. She thrust the dish in Cathy's direction.

'Anywhere you can find a space will do,' she said, wiping her hands on her mam's flowery apron as the doorbell rang. 'Just got to get the cocktail sausages out of the oven now, slice the bread rolls and I'm done.'

Davy answered the door and let in some people from Lewis's and a couple of friends of his and Debbie's. The lounge soon filled and he loaded some records onto the radiogram turntable. The Everly Brothers' 'Bye Bye Love' blasted out as Cathy welcomed the guests, who handed over parcels, cards, hugs and kisses. She put the gifts on the coffee table to open later when Gianni arrived. In a cage, on a stand in the bay window, Debbie's mam's bright blue budgie Billy twittered and chattered away to his reflection in the mirror fastened to the cage. Cathy stuck her finger between the bars. Billy nibbled her nail and she tickled his cheek.

'Oh, you're a little love,' she cooed as Billy bobbed his head and did a silly dance up and down the perch.

'He loves music,' Davy said. 'Debs' mam's pride and joy, is Billy.'

'He's gorgeous,' Cathy said as the doorbell rang again and Davy left the room.

Cathy thought back over the last twenty-four hours. Her final day at Lewis's had been nice, with lots of good-luck cards and best wishes handed her way. Her mam had gone back to work now and she and Dolores Redfern had arranged a little lunch party for all the cosmetics-counter girls, with sandwiches and cakes courtesy of the management. Debbie had organised a collection, and the girls had presented Cathy with a bouquet of flowers and a silver fob watch with her name engraved on the back. She'd been overcome with emotion and told them it was a perfect gift for her new career.

Her mam and the kids had popped into Granny Lomax's on her actual birthday with cards and a bottle of her favourite *In Love* perfume, and a card from Brian with a ten-pound note enclosed. Cathy had never had so much money in her life in one go. Of Jack there had been no sign since Mam got back from Blackpool with Brian, who had now gone back to America. He'd put plans in place to help out financially, as he'd promised he would at the beginning of the year. When Cathy told them what had happened they wanted to involve the police, but she begged them not to. Her main concern was that Jack would report Gianni for beating him up and the police might not believe her. She was sure Jack would twist things his way and tell them she'd encouraged him. She felt it best to put it all behind them and get on with their lives. Millie's Jimmy had changed the locks on the house and put extra bolts on for security, and the chance of Jack showing his face there again was unlikely. And Millie said she'd be straight on the phone to the police if she ever saw him hanging around. Now all Mam had to do was get a divorce.

'Doorbell!' Debbie said, appearing beside Cathy and breaking her thoughts. 'Bet it's Gianni.' Davy went to answer. It was Mike and a couple of his mates, dressed to kill in smart shirts and suits.

Mike's face lit up as he spotted Cathy staring at him and he swaggered over.

Cathy accepted the glass of Coke Debbie handed her. She made to go past Mike but he put his hand on her arm.

'Happy birthday, Cathy,' he said, planting a kiss on her lips. 'You look great in that outfit.' He admired her new white shell top and black swirly poodle-trimmed skirt.

Cathy felt the heat rush to her cheeks. She didn't like the way Mike had just kissed her then, or that he was looking at her as though he could see through her clothes. Debbie had helped her get ready and curled her hair so it flicked out all around her shoulders, the crown lightly backcombed into a little bouffant. They'd painted each other's nails in a pearly pink shade that contrasted well with their black and white outfits. She knew she looked nice, Debbie and Davy had told her so, but Mike was making her feel uncomfortable.

'Yeah,' he grunted. 'You're wasted on that greasy biker.'

Before Cathy had a chance to react the doorbell rang again and Davy went to answer. This time it *was* Gianni, his arms laden with parcels.

She put down her Coke and went to greet him. He dropped the packages on the floor and swept her up in a bear hug, raining kisses on her face.

'You look and smell gorgeous,' he whispered.

'So do you.' He had on the black silk shirt he'd worn the night she'd first danced with him, and black jeans, and he smelled clean and spicy. 'How did you manage to carry that lot on the bike?'

'In the panniers. Come on, can't wait to see you open them.'

He carried the parcels into the lounge and they sat side by side on a sofa near Billy's cage. Cathy excitedly tore off the wrapping of the first parcel.

'Oh, it's lovely. Thank you.' She slipped the pretty silver charm bracelet onto her wrist and kissed him. Next was a book from his mam; a hardback version of Daphne Du Maurier's *Rebecca*. They'd talked about their favourite authors a couple of weeks ago. Fancy her remembering. The third parcel contained a sloppy Joe sweater in her favourite shade of red. The last parcel felt bulky but soft, and she opened it to reveal a black leather biking jacket.

'It's a girl's one,' Gianni said as she squealed with delight and slipped her arms into the sleeves. He zipped her into it, his eyes on hers. 'Keep you warm when we go out for rides.'

'Oh, Gianni, it's fabulous,' she cried, twirling round in front of him, ignoring Mike's scowls. 'Look, Debs,' she said as Debbie came back into the lounge to announce the buffet was ready.

'It's lovely,' Debbie said. 'It matches Gianni's, and it suits you, biker girl!'

'We'll try it out tomorrow,' Gianni said as Cathy grinned.

Cathy led him to the dining room, still wearing her jacket and ignoring Mike's mutterings about greasy bikers. 'Would you like a drink?'

'I'll have a beer, a small one. Don't drink a lot when I'm on the bike.'

'You can stay over,' Debbie said. 'Cathy's staying and Davy is too.'

'Oh, er, well, I er, wasn't after an invite,' Gianni stuttered. 'Depends what Cathy says.'

Cathy blushed and looked at him from beneath her fringe. He *could* stay; she'd like him to. They didn't have to do anything more than they'd already done, which wasn't an awful lot as they spent so little time alone. He knew how she felt about going all the way and he never pushed her, and since Jack's attack he'd been even more understanding. But even so, it would be nice to lie in his arms all night. The thought made her stomach loop, she'd imagined it often enough. And she was no longer underage.

*

Back in the lounge Debbie opened the window to clear the smoky air. She emptied the ashtrays onto the unlit fire. 'Mam doesn't like smoking in the lounge,' she said to Mike and his mates. 'Go in the garden please.' She frowned as they passed a roll-up between them, laughing at her disapproving stare.

'Come on, Debs, have a go,' Mike said, holding the joint out. 'It's just a little bit of weed from my Nigerian jazz mate at the docks. Enjoy. Relax a bit.'

'No thank you.' She walked out of the room and found Davy in the kitchen, pouring beer. 'Mike's smoking something he called weed in the lounge. It smells horrible.'

Davy's eyes lit up. 'He said he might be bringing some. Er, is it a problem?'

'Well, I don't know. Is it legal? He's in Mam's best room and it stinks. Ask them to go outside. They won't listen to me.'

Davy put down the bottle. In the lounge Mike was sprawled across the sofa and one of his mates was standing by Billy's cage, puffing smoke into the budgie's face. Billy was twittering and flapping his wings. 'Pack it in,' Davy said. 'You'll have the bird as high as a fucking kite. Take your stuff outside, or Debs'll cop it off her mam.'

Mike laughed and got to his feet. 'Bobby likes his birds as high as kites, don't you, mate? Gets more action that way.'

Davy shook his head as they left the room and Debbie came in. 'Thanks, love,' she said as Davy put his arms round her and gave her a kiss. 'Don't like Mike when he's with them lads,' she said. 'Put some more music on and we'll have a dance. I'll go and tell Cathy and Gianni to come in here.'

*

Cathy slumped against Gianni, hardly able to keep her eyes open. She'd had a glass of wine and it had gone straight to her head. He held her tight and she curled up in his arms. He kissed her, his hands moving over her body. She moaned softly and pressed herself closer. It was after one and they were alone in the lounge. Everyone had gone home and Debbie and Davy had disappeared upstairs. Gianni pushed her back against the sofa cushions, caressing her through the soft fabric of her clothes. He ran his hand up her legs and stroked her soft thighs above her stocking tops, desperate for more.

'Cathy, I know how you feel, but I really need you,' he whispered. 'Please.'

She looked into his eyes and struggled into a sitting position. 'You promised you'd wait.'

'I know.' He took a deep breath. 'I don't know if I can. I mean, well – spending the whole night with you – look, maybe it'd be better if I went home.'

'But you can't ride your bike. You've had too much to drink.'

'I'll walk.'

'It's too late. Anyway,' she stared at the ceiling for a few seconds, 'I don't want you to go.' She got to her feet, grabbed his hand and pulled him up.

In Debbie's bedroom Cathy watched Gianni drop his shirt, boots and jeans on the floor and sit down on the edge of the bed. He reached for her hand, pulled her towards him, slipped his arms round her waist and reached to undo her skirt. She shivered, legs turning to jelly as he undressed her. They tumbled onto the narrow bed, kissing and caressing each other. She groaned, wanting him as much as he wanted her, but also feeling terrified. He explored her until she cried out for more. This was going against all her principles but she couldn't fight it and didn't really want to. He looked into her eyes and she nodded as he pushed into her. She gasped at the sudden pain and bit her lip to stop herself crying out, conscious of how thin the walls were and of Debbie and Davy in the next room.

Gianni supported himself above her and looked down. 'You okay?'

'Yes,' she whispered, loving the feeling of him inside her now the discomfort was fading. His strong arms and the sprinkle of dark hair on his chest, the spicy scent of his aftershave mingling with her own perfume, sent shivers all over her; lost in the wonderful feelings as they moved naturally together. She wrapped her legs round him and kissed him hard, his tongue probing hers. She felt like she was floating, couldn't pull him any closer, and then something happened and her body went into spasm, like she was melting and falling off a cliff at the same time, then Gianni cried her name and pulled out of her, collapsing on top.

'Sorry,' he said, catching his breath. 'Didn't know we'd be doing this and I wasn't prepared.' He reached for his jeans, pulled out a hanky and wiped her stomach. 'Don't wanna put you in the family way.'

She didn't want that either and she smiled and snuggled into him. She felt wonderful and floaty and sleepy.

'Cathy.'

'Yeah?'

'I think I love you.'

She opened her eyes and stared at him. 'Do you?' She wasn't expecting that and couldn't believe he'd said it. Then a little bit of doubt crept in. She knew she wasn't his first, so did he say it to every girl after having sex because he felt obliged, or was she really special to him? Try as she might to block them, more doubts came creeping in. She shouldn't have done it. What was she thinking? But then, she reminded herself, she hadn't stopped. She had wanted it. Did that make her cheap? Would he think she was a tart now he'd got what he wanted?

'I do,' he said, breaking her thoughts. 'I mean, I *really* do. You mean everything to me.'

His face was serious and he looked like he meant it. But what if he was putting on an act? Then she thought about the lovely evening they'd had, dancing in his arms, and the thoughtful gifts he'd given her. How mature he was compared to Mike and his drunken mates.

She looked into his eyes and saw a light she hadn't seen before. He meant it. She traced a finger round his chin. 'Gianni, I think I love you too.' She could feel tears welling.

He kissed her hard and held her tight, burying his face in her hair.

*

Gianni awoke, disturbed by the sound of muffled voices and a door creaking. He got up, pulled on his pants and shirt and went for a pee, leaving Cathy curled up by the wall, still sleeping. As he came out of the bathroom he heard a wail and stopped to listen. The noise came from downstairs. The door to Debbie's parents' bedroom stood open and he could see the bed was empty. He looked at his watch. It was early, just after nine. Maybe Davy had to be home by a certain time and Debbie didn't want him to go. He stopped, hand on the bathroom doorknob, as he heard Debbie say 'What are we going to do?' and then muffled sobs as though she were crying against Davy's shoulder. He stood dithering for a while, wondering if he should go and see if he could help, then thought better of it. Maybe it was private.

Then a half-naked Davy ran up the stairs, his face white. 'Can you help me, mate?'

'Yeah, course, what is it?'

'The budgie. It's carked it. Debs is gutted. Her mam'll go doolally.'

'Well what can we do?'

'Get dressed for starters and then you can run me to West Derby to try and get another the same colour.'

Gianni shook his head. 'Where the fuck can we get a budgie at this time on a Sunday morning?'

'There's a fella breeds, buys and sells them over there. He advertises in the *Echo*. We just found the ad in the pet section. Hopefully he'll have one just like Billy,' Davy said, rushing into the bedroom and pulling on his clothes.

Gianni frowned but went to get dressed. Cathy was still out cold. He bent to kiss her forehead and tucked the sheet around her. She'd probably still be sleeping when he got back. 'Love you,' he whispered and closed the door quietly.

He followed Davy downstairs to the dining room, where Debbie had Billy laid on the table. She was sobbing and stroking his tummy. Her face crumpled as Davy took her in his arms and hugged her.

'Have you got a shoebox to put him in?' Davy asked.

Debbie got to her feet and rummaged in the sideboard cupboard. She took out a box and emptied policies and bills onto the table. She dug in her dressing gown pocket and pulled out a hanky, popped it in the box and laid Billy on top. 'This is Mike's fault. Those mates of his were blowing smoke at him last night. His little heart must have given out. I'll never forgive Mike for this.'

'Gianni's gonna run me to West Derby, love,' Davy said. 'We'll get another bird, don't you worry. Your mam will never know the difference.'

'She will,' Debbie wailed. 'Billy talked and sang. If you get a new bird it'll be younger and it won't know what to do. She'll guess it's not our Billy right away.'

'Not if we spend all day teaching it,' Davy said. 'We'll do our best, Debs. Make yourself a nice cup of tea. We'll be back as soon as we can.'

*

Cathy rolled over, stretched her limbs and reached for Gianni. She opened her eyes, stared at the empty space next to her and sat up, gazing blearily around the bedroom, but there was no sign of him or his clothes. She leapt out of bed, found her discarded clothing and got dressed as quickly as she could. Maybe he was in the bathroom. The house was silent as she opened the door and crept along the landing. The bathroom door stood open; the room was empty. She dashed in to use the loo, and washed her face, then looked into Debbie's parents' room, but that was empty too.

A sick and desolate feeling settled in her stomach. She hurried back to the room she'd shared with Gianni. Tears ran down her cheeks. He'd gone without even a goodbye. She flung herself down and sobbed into the pillow, where she could still smell his spicy aftershave. How could he? But what had she expected? He'd got what he'd waited ages for and was off to find the next conquest. Why had she trusted him? All that rubbish about loving her. What sort of an idiot was she? God, she was as much a fool as her mam had been when she'd taken Jack into her life. Well, that was it. No more men. She'd throw herself into her career and work as hard as she could to get to the top. She sat up and wiped her eyes, shuddering sobs racking her body. She got to her feet, packed her small overnight bag and went downstairs. Dithering in the hall about whether to take her new leather jacket or not, she heard crying coming from the lounge. Debs! Had Davy done the dirty and left *her* too? She dropped her bag on the floor and rushed into the room to find Debbie huddled on the sofa, her head buried in a cushion, sobbing heartbrokenly.

She sat beside her and touched her shoulder. 'Debs?'

'Oh, Cathy, how could he?' Debbie howled and flung herself into Cathy's arms.

Cathy stroked Debbie's hair back from her tear-stained face. 'Debs, don't cry. We don't need them. Can't believe they've done this to us. I'll never trust another boy as long as I live.'

Debbie pulled away and frowned. 'What, what do you mean?' she sobbed.

'Davy and Gianni,' Cathy said. 'They got what they wanted and both cleared off. We should have known better than to trust them.'

'Oh, Cathy, no, they haven't gone anywhere. Well they have, but it's not what you think.'

Cathy listened as Debbie explained what had happened to the budgie. 'Gianni's taken Davy on the bike to try and find a matching bird so Mam need never know what Mike and his mates did,' Debbie finished, wiping her eyes on a soggy tissue.

'Oh no!' Cathy's eyes filled again, for Billy, for her friend and also for herself because she'd shown so little faith in Gianni. 'I thought he'd left me,' she sobbed.

'No, why would he do that? He really cares for you, Cathy.'

'He told me he loved me last night. I need to learn to trust him. It's hard though, because of Jack.'

'Not all boys and men are like Jack,' Debbie said, patting Cathy on the arm. 'Gianni *certainly* isn't.' She stopped at the sound of a motorbike engine roaring up the road. 'They're back. Fingers crossed they've got another Billy.'

Gianni and Davy came into the room, Davy carrying a small brown box with holes in the top.

Davy opened it and helped a very similar budgie to Billy into the cage. The little fellow sat on a perch and looked around before tweeting and flying to the seed pot.

'He's the oldest they had. Similar age to Billy and as near as damn it to look at *and* he can talk. The man at the breeder's said he'd been brought to him by a guy whose mother died and he needed to rehome him. Dead lucky really because all the other blues were babies.'

'Oh, that *was* lucky,' Debbie said as Davy looked at Gianni and raised an eyebrow. 'What?'

'Well,' Gianni began, his mouth twitching at the corners. 'He swears a bit, but you can't really tell what he's saying when it's jumbled up with "Who's a pretty boy?" And his name's Joey. Maybe you can tell your mam one of your friends taught him "Joey" when he keeps saying it.'

Debbie smiled and shook her head. 'And maybe it might be best to come clean. We'll see how it goes. They're not back until Wednesday so it gives us time to work on him.'

Gianni put his arm round Cathy, who'd stayed quiet, and pulled her close. 'You okay, sleepyhead?' He ran a finger down her cheek. 'Tears?'

She nodded and led him out of the room and up to the bedroom. 'Sit down,' she said and sat beside him on the bed as he did as he was told.

'What is it?'

She told him the fear she'd felt when she woke to find him gone.

'Silly girl.' He kissed her and pushed her back onto the pillows. 'All I could think about while I was out was coming back here to find you waiting in bed for me and making love to you again. I told you last night, I love you. I'm going nowhere, Cathy.'

Chapter Sixteen

September 1957

Cathy glanced around the bedroom, checking to make sure she'd left nothing behind. Not that she had a lot anyway; her worldly goods fitted into two small cases and a cardboard box. Granny Lomax had bought her a second-hand record player and it was standing in the hall by the front door. Gianni was coming in a taxi at three to escort her to the nurses' home for the start of her new life. She couldn't believe the day was here at last. Tomorrow was induction day and her stomach did a little flippy dance at the thought. She had no idea quite what to expect, and felt nervous and excited all at the same time.

The week since the party at Debbie's had flown. Gianni had taken a two-day holiday from work and they'd gone to Blackpool on the Wednesday and on a trip into the Cheshire countryside on Thursday afternoon. She'd had the time of her life, riding pillion in her new jacket, hair whipping around her face. He'd told her every day, since her Sunday-morning wobble, that he loved her, and they'd made love again on the Tuesday and Thursday nights while his mam was out at her mother's. From being terrified of going all the way, she now found herself thinking about it and wondering when they'd get the next opportunity. She couldn't wait. She felt her cheeks heating. She jumped at a sharp rap on the door. Granny Lomax popped her head in.

'Now, have you got everything, love?'

'Think so. I'll be back to see you as soon as I can.'

Granny pressed two five-pound notes into her hand. 'Put that in your purse. It'll tide you over until you get your first pay.'

'Thank you.' Cathy threw her arms round her. With that added to Brian's ten pounds she was now so rich she felt like a pools winner. 'I'm really going to miss you. I've loved living here. You've spoiled me rotten.'

'I've enjoyed having you to spoil. I'll miss you too.' Her granny dashed a tear away as the doorbell rang. 'Here's your young man. All the best, my love. See you soon.'

Cathy gazed around the white-painted room that was to be her home for the next three years. It was smaller than the one she'd had at Granny Lomax's, but adequately furnished. The single bed took up one wall and a chest of drawers sat beneath a sash window. A narrow wardrobe, bookcase and a washbasin with a mirror above it took up the other wall. The bedside table was just big enough for her record player and the shelf beneath could house her records. The pale green cotton bedspread matched the curtains and contrasted with the dark green carpet on the floor. The sash window overlooked a small courtyard and through the windows of the opposite building she could see people in uniform, queuing with trays at a counter, and guessed it was the staff dining room.

On top of the chest of drawers was a white cloth bag with her name printed on. A note, pinned to the front, told her it was a laundry bag for dirty uniforms. Inside, Cathy found three blue cotton dresses, four white starched aprons and caps and an elasticated belt. On the back of the door hung a navy blue cape with red lining. A little thrill went through her and she turned to smile at Gianni, who was leaning silently against the washbasin watching her. 'I've got my uniform.'

'So I see,' he said, a twinkle in his eye.

'What?' She knew full well what was going through his mind.

'You know.' He smirked.

'Yes, I do, but not now. I'll sneak a set home with me.'

'And the black stockings and sussies?'

'Yes, stop it!' she said, trying not to laugh. 'Remember where you are.'

He sighed. 'I'd better go, hadn't I? Before Hatchet-Face chucks me out.'

'Gianni! Shh, she might be hanging around outside the door.' Cathy suppressed a giggle and moved into his arms. Home Sister, who'd shown them around, had made it quite clear that young men were not allowed in nurses' bedrooms, but Cathy had fibbed that Gianni was her brother and helping her to move in and Home Sister had given them ten minutes.

He kissed her, ran his hands down her back and squeezed her bottom. 'I love you.'

'Love you too,' she whispered, wishing they could try out the bed.

As she walked him to the front door, Gianni spotted a payphone in an alcove almost opposite Cathy's ground-floor room. He made a note of the number displayed on the dial.

'We can speak each night now,' he said. 'Let me know when you're allowed to come out to play and I'll pick you up.'

'I will.' She held him as they kissed one last time and said their goodbyes.

Cathy knelt on the floor and stacked her records under the table. The room looked more homely now she'd unpacked. A framed photo of her and Gianni, taken by Debbie at the party, stood on top of the record player, so she could look at him every night before falling asleep. She'd hung her clothes in the wardrobe and her toiletries and cosmetics were neatly arranged on top of the chest of drawers. The few books she'd brought were stashed on the bookcase shelves, alongside a couple of good-luck black cats bought in Blackpool.

Home Sister Judge had popped in with a reminder that tea for the new students would be served at six on the dot in the dining room and not to be late. She'd waved her arms in a vague fashion, and pointed towards the building across the courtyard. As she lurched away she'd reminded Cathy of a scarecrow, with her white hair poking out from beneath her lacy cap in all directions and her ungainly limbs. Cathy's tummy rumbled and she checked her watch. Still only five thirty; God, she was starving. She jumped at a knock on the door. Two teenage girls, clad in jeans and sloppy Joe sweaters, one blonde-haired, one dark, stood outside in the corridor.

'Hi,' the blonde said. 'I'm Ellie, this is Karen. Sister Judge sent us along. We're new too; arrived this afternoon.'

'Come in,' Cathy said and stepped back as they entered. 'Pleased to meet you. I'm Cathy.' She gestured to the bed. 'Have a seat.'

'Your accent tells me you're from around these parts,' Karen said, plonking herself down.

'Aigburth,' Cathy said.

'I'm from West Derby,' Karen announced. 'Ellie's from Cheshire, out in the sticks.'

'It's not,' Ellie said, laughing. 'I live on a farm in Crowton, but we do have shops and a pub in our village.' She laughed. 'Karen thinks we've all got straw in our hair and interbreed with the sheep!'

'Well, anywhere outside of Liverpool is foreign to me,' Karen said. 'So, who's the hunk in the picture with you?' She nodded at the framed photo.

'My boyfriend, Gianni,' Cathy said, feeling proud.

'Wow, lucky you. Been with him long?'

'A few months.'

'Is it serious?'

'Karen, you aren't half nosy,' Ellie said, nudging her in the ribs.

'Well, we've got to spend at least the next three years together, so we may as well get to know each other and the sooner the better,' Karen said good-naturedly.

'It's okay, I don't mind,' Cathy said, smiling at the easy way the two got along considering they'd only met today. 'Yes, it's serious. We love each other.'

'Not surprising,' Karen said. 'I wouldn't kick *him* out of bed.'

'Karen!' Ellie exclaimed as Cathy burst out laughing, taking an immediate liking to the pair.

'Do you two have boyfriends?' she asked.

Karen shrugged. 'I'm seeing a lad, but it's not serious. He's due to start uni in Manchester, so we'll probably just drift apart. Anyway, I'm looking forward to meeting new people. There's a few good dance halls and coffee bars in the city, so who knows. Must be some fit lads around.'

Ellie smiled. 'I split up with my boyfriend the other week so I'm free and single.'

'Do you know any lads going spare?' Karen asked.

Cathy thought about Mike and his mates. Karen looked like she'd be a good match for Mike, but after what happened to Billy... Mind you, a nice girlfriend might do him some good and she'd bet Karen would keep him on his toes. 'I know a few,' she said. 'Maybe one night we can go dancing at the Grafton and I'll introduce you to them.'

The phone in the corridor rang out.

'Do you think we should get that?' Cathy said.

Karen jumped up and hurried out of the door. She came back and said, 'It's a fella with an Irish accent, wants to speak to Mary Delaney.'

'Hmm, wonder which room she's in?' Ellie said. 'None of the doors have names on apart from Home Sister's. Ask him if he knows her room number.'

Karen hurried out again. 'He doesn't know,' she said, coming back into the room. 'I've told him to call later. Hope that phone doesn't disturb you, Cathy if it rings at all hours. You're the only one on this corridor. We're upstairs.'

Cathy frowned. 'Well, if it does I'll ask to be moved. Be handy though for Gianni calling me.'

'Is he Italian with a name like that?' Karen asked. 'He looks a bit foreign.'

'Half Italian. His mum's English. Romano, they're called.'

'Hmm, the summer fair that comes to Northwich not far from us is run by somebody called Romano,' Ellie said.

'It's Gianni's family fair,' Cathy told her. 'But his parents are no longer together. Gianni lives in the same street as I did, with his mam.'

'Has he got any brothers?' Karen asked wistfully, gazing at the photograph.

'Sorry,' Cathy said with a grin. 'He's an only child.'

'Pity!' Karen sighed. 'Ah well, shall we make our way to the dining room for tea? I'm famished.'

The dining room was packed but the girls found a free table by the window. They sat down with plates of poached eggs on toast and cups of tea. Cathy could see her room from here. A pair of dustbins stood beneath the window ledge.

Karen followed her gaze and smiled. 'Handy, you having a room on the ground floor. Front doors are locked at half ten, so if we're late back and you leave your window ajar, we can climb on the bins and get in that way.'

Cathy nodded. Half ten was a bit too early. 'We'd have to make sure no one was watching from over here.'

'There's blinds up there.' Karen pointed. 'They'll drop those when it gets dark. And,' she lowered her voice, 'we could sneak lads in and then let them out at the front door.'

Cathy felt her stomach do a little loop at the thought of smuggling Gianni into her room for a few hours.

'It's a bit of a risk,' Ellie said. 'I'm not doing it. Getting a place on the course means more to me than getting a lad. I've wanted to be a nurse for ever; I'm not wrecking my chances now.'

Cathy smiled. She understood Ellie's concerns, but still – a night with Gianni now and again was worth a thought.

After tea the threesome strolled down one of the long corridors to the communal lounge, where several girls were curled up on the sofas, listening to music. Two were waltzing to Tab Hunter's 'Young Love' and another pair were painting each other's nails, their hair done up in plastic curlers.

'Hey-up,' a girl with red hair said. 'New recruits. Come on in, girls. Grab a seat and tell us your names.'

They looked a friendly lot, Cathy thought, as they introduced themselves. There was much shuffling on the sofas to make room and she sat down next to Karen. Ellie flopped onto a chair opposite. The girl with the red hair introduced herself as Jean and Cathy smiled as she realised that this was the same woman who had broken her leg in the garden the day Roddy was born. She waited until Jean had finished rattling off the names of the others, pointing at each one in turn. The pair with the curlers were Linda and Fran and were getting ready to go on hot dates, Jean told them with a grin.

Then Jean looked closely at Cathy. 'Don't I know you from somewhere?'

'You do,' Cathy said. 'You broke your leg the day my brother was born.'

'Oh my God, it's Cathy,' Jean said. 'You did it, you took my advice. Well done, gel.' She announced to the others, who'd tuned in to the conversation, 'This young lady delivered her baby brother at the end of last year. It should have been my first district delivery, but as you all know, I was lying in the garden, having slipped on ice. Everybody dashed outside to see to me and Cathy was left to bring her brother into the world. She kept her cool at fifteen years old. She's cut out to be a nurse and she'll be a damn good one.'

Everyone cheered and Cathy felt overwhelmed. 'Thank you, Jean, all of you. I can't believe I'm actually here. And it's good to know you made a full recovery from your leg injury, Jean. Er, while I think on, does anyone know a Mary Delaney?'

'Yeah,' Jean said. 'She's one of the Irish nurses, but she's on a late. Finishes at nine. Why?'

'Somebody phoned for her,' Cathy replied. 'We told him to call back later.'

'Oh, it'll be her boyfriend. He never remembers what shift she's on. If the phone rings, leave it unless you're expecting a call yourself,' Jean advised. 'Otherwise you'll be up and down all night. It's nearly always for Mary or a girl called Astrid from Canada. *Her* callers don't seem to have a clue about the time difference. Report it to Sister Judge if it gets on your nerves. But treat yourself to some earplugs, just in case.'

'Thanks for the advice,' Cathy said. She looked around the comfortably furnished room, with huge windows that overlooked the gardens, and thought how much she liked it here already. She was looking forward to tomorrow and the induction.

'*Sunday Night at the London Palladium*'s on in a bit,' Jean said and got up to switch on the TV set, which stood in an alcove, one side of a huge old fireplace.

Cathy swallowed hard and felt a little pang as she thought of how she and Gianni had spent Sunday nights on the sofa at his place while his mum took a bath and had an early night, and how, once they were sure she'd fallen asleep, they'd enjoy petting sessions on the rug in front of the electric fire. She was missing him already;

they would have made love again tonight. Her stomach turned over at the thought. She felt an urge to hear his voice, and got to her feet before her eyes filled.

'Just going to make a phone call,' she told Karen. 'Won't be long.'

Karen smiled. 'Are you calling that good-looking fella of yours?'

Cathy nodded and slipped out the room to shouts of, 'She's in love' and 'Lucky her.'

Chapter Seventeen

The rules the Preliminary Training School group was to abide by were lengthy and strict, with a list of don'ts rather than do's, and if Gianni thought Sister Judge had a hatchet face, wait until he saw Matron's, Cathy thought. The woman had the thinnest lips, ice-blue eyes and a face that looked like a slapped backside. Today's nine o'clock induction with Matron and head tutor, Sister Carew, was an eye-opener. Resembling a large black bird, her long, prominent hooked nose like a beak, neat white lacy cap on top of her cropped silver hair, Sister Carew took great delight in quoting the rules, her cheeks pinking with excitement as she worked her way through them.

'This is worse than being in a convent,' Karen whispered to Cathy, just after, 'Any nurse found entertaining members of the opposite sex in their rooms will be faced with instant dismissal.'

Cathy nodded her agreement, making notes on her pad as the voice droned on.

'All cadets and student nurses must live on the premises for the duration of their training. No loud music to be played in the rooms after nine thirty. There must be no alcohol consumed on the premises. No makeup or nail varnish to be worn while on duty. All hair to be fastened up off the collar. Aprons and belts to be worn on the wards only. Dresses are not to be taken up any shorter than knee length'.

God knows why Gianni thinks nurses' uniforms are sexy, Cathy thought. They were starchy and itchy and anything *but* sexy.

No fraternising with doctors and male nurses on the premises. And finally, and said with the frostiest stare ever, 'Any student becoming pregnant during training will be asked to leave the hospital immediately.'

Karen raised her eyebrows, smirked and whispered. 'Bet they lose half the group each year!'

'Probably,' Cathy agreed.

Following dismissal, the class hurried to the canteen for a mid-morning break. Later they would be learning how to make a bed correctly, followed by taking notes on ward procedures. Tomorrow they would begin their six weeks in the Preliminary Training School, after which they'd take an exam and, depending on results; would be assigned their wards for the first of the eight-week courses.

Cathy removed her hat, kicked off her shoes and lay on her bed, glad to have finished for the day. Tomorrow would be busier but today had been mainly about taking notes. She rolled onto her side, willing herself to make a move, and stared at the stack of books on the floor waiting to be filed on her shelves in readiness for studying. At breakfast this morning, Karen had suggested that she, Ellie and Cathy should rent a flat close to the hospital when they'd got a bit of money together, but the rule that they live in the nurses' home for the foreseeable future put paid to *that* idea. They were allowed to stay at home during their two days off, but that was all.

Ah well, she'd get used to it; although this afternoon, while wrestling with starched sheets and hospital corners, she'd had a bit of a wobble and wished she'd stayed at Lewis's. She was missing Debbie's bright smile and non-stop chatter. Karen and Ellie were lovely and she was sure they'd all become good friends in time, but Debbie had been by her side since their schooldays, and right now Cathy felt like her right arm was missing. She wondered how the new budgie was doing and if Debbie's mam had realised yet that it wasn't Billy.

She got to her feet and took off her uniform, hung it in the wardrobe and pulled on jeans and a sweater. Time to head to the dining room. Gianni had promised to call her after tea and she couldn't wait to tell him about her day.

By the end of the first week, Cathy was a dab hand with the bed-making and hospital corners, which she practised on her own bed each morning. She'd taken temperature and blood pressure readings on one of the other students, and learned how to record them on a chart. They'd practiced bed baths on an unwieldy rubber dummy of no particular sex. Today the class had given injections to sandbags and oranges. Next week they were to spend a couple of hours a day on the wards, observing how the more advanced students and trained nurses used their skills. Cathy was looking forward to that. She'd enjoyed the anatomy and physiology lessons. It was interesting to learn how the various parts of the body interconnected to make a whole.

On Friday night Cathy packed a few clothes and toiletries and waited in the foyer for Gianni to pick her up. They were spending tonight and tomorrow night alone at his house. His mam had gone away for a few days with his gran. Cathy felt a bit guilty for lying to Granny Lomax and her mam that she couldn't come home for the whole weekend, but she'd told them she'd visit them both on Sunday afternoon. Granny had invited her and Gianni to tea. Meanwhile she would need to sneak in and out by Sadie's back door so as not to be seen on Lucerne Street.

Karen and Ellie joined her in the foyer while she waited for Gianni, and asked for directions to the Rumblin' Tum. Cathy had told them all about how she and Gianni got together there and they were keen to visit and have a dance and maybe meet a nice lad each.

'I'll write down the address,' Cathy said as Gianni's bike roared up the road and pulled up outside. 'Ah, here's Gianni now. I'll introduce you.'

She waved as he stepped into the foyer. He swept her into his arms and kissed her.

She clung to him and momentarily forgot about her friends waiting patiently behind her.

'Ahem!' Karen coughed; she had an amused expression on her face. 'Put him down for God's sake and let him take a breath.'

Cathy grinned and introduced them. 'I was just about to give them the address of the Rumblin' Tum,' she told him. 'They want to go tomorrow night.'

'Ah, well, we could meet you there,' Gianni said. 'It's dead easy to find. Take the bus from outside the hospital and get off near the Philharmonic pub. It's just round the corner on Hardman Street. We'll wait outside for you. Those two lads are on again playing guitars, so it should be a good night.'

'Oh great,' Ellie said. 'I love watching people actually playing instruments rather than just listening to records.'

'Me too,' Karen said. 'We'll look forward to it.

'You ready then?' Gianni smiled and picked up Cathy's bag. 'See you two tomorrow about seven thirty.'

'You will,' Karen said. 'Enjoy yourselves tonight. Don't do anything we wouldn't do.'

*

Gianni rifled through the box of papers and pulled out a photograph he kept hidden at the bottom. His dad, Luca, sitting astride an Indian Scout motorbike. The arm round his shoulders belonged to Uncle Marco, his dad's brother. The pair were posing outside the wall of death attraction. Gianni felt a thrill go through him. How he'd love to see his dad and uncle performing! But his loyalty to his mam overrode everything and he knew it wasn't possible – unless he could find out where the fair was at the moment and visit secretly. He looked up as Cathy stirred and mumbled his name. He pushed the box into the wardrobe and climbed back into bed, leaving the photo on the bedside cabinet. She snuggled close to him and he kissed her and stroked her hair from her face.

'What were you doing?' she asked.

He reached for the photo and showed her.

'Your dad?'

He nodded. 'And his brother.'

She sighed. 'Gianni, if you want to look for him, I'll help you. I know you don't want to upset your mam, but if my dad were alive and out there somewhere, I'd be desperate to find him.'

'The yearning to see him is overwhelming at times,' he admitted. 'I mean, I can go weeks and then wham, it takes over my thoughts completely.'

Cathy sat up and hugged her knees. 'Then do it. If you don't, and something happens to him, you'll never forgive yourself.'

'Not sure where to start,' he muttered, turning the photo over and over.

'Ellie told me the fair visits Northwich in the summer. It's only September; they might still be in the Cheshire region.'

He nodded. 'Maybe. They were here in June and they travel south late summer, or they used to.'

'You could look up town hall phone numbers. Fairs need permission to pitch up and I expect they get it from local councils. It's worth a try.'

'I suppose it is,' he said. 'I might make a start on Monday in my lunch hour. They've got directories from all over the place at work.'

'And I'll help you the best I can,' she promised.

'Cathy?' He leaned up on one elbow and looked into her eyes. 'You know I love you, don't you?'

'I do,' she said, smiling.

'Well, I've been thinking.' He swallowed hard and took her hand. 'Will you marry me?'

'Marry you?' She stared at him, wide-eyed 'God, I wasn't expecting that. We've only been together a few months. We're way too young. What about my training and stuff? I'm not supposed to get married while I'm a student nurse. And Mam and Sadie would never give their permission.'

'We don't have to do it yet. But now you're my girl, I'd like to make it official. We can get engaged. I'll save up to buy us a house while you're training. We can marry after you qualify. But we can get a ring now and then people will know you're spoken for.'

She frowned. 'Why do people need to know I'm spoken for? I'm not planning on going off with anyone. I love *you*.' She ran a hand down his stomach. 'I wouldn't be here with you now if I didn't.'

'I know.' He couldn't tell her he had a fear of losing her to someone better than he was. She'd think he was a right soft arse. But what if she met a doctor who fell for her and her for him? At least if she had a ring on her finger people would know she wasn't available and she might not get chatted up. But did that make him possessive?

'And another thing,' she said, 'I'm not allowed to wear any jewellery while I'm on duty. I'd be frightened of losing a ring.'

'Okay.' He sighed. 'We'll wait until you feel ready.' He pulled her close and rolled on top, looking into her eyes. 'I just want you to know that this relationship is for ever, for me.'

*

'You turned him down?' Debbie's jaw dropped. 'You must be mad. I'd bite Davy's hand off if he proposed to me.'

Cathy shrugged. 'It's not the right time, Debs. I've got over three years' hard slog in front of me. I love him, but I can't marry him for ages.' They were in the ladies' in the Kardomah. Gianni and Davy were waiting for them in the café. 'Anyway, I haven't really turned him down. We're still together.'

Debbie picked up her handbag and made for the exit. Hand on the door handle, she turned. 'You wouldn't even need to bother training to be a nurse if you married Gianni. You'd want for nothing, once he's finished his apprenticeship. You can settle down and have babies.'

'But that's just it,' Cathy said. 'I don't want to end up like my mam, struggling with loads of kids.'

'That'll never happen to you, Mrs Bloody Independent. And Gianni would never treat you like Jack treated your mam.'

Cathy chewed her lip. 'I'm not saying he would. But my dad died when I was young. Things happen in life that we've no control over. I want to make sure I can look after myself and any children we might have. You've never had to worry about stuff like that, Debs. I hope you never do.'

Debbie patted her arm. 'I understand what you're saying. I still think you're mad though.'

Cathy smiled and rolled her eyes. 'Let's go back to the lads. They'll wonder what the heck we're up to.'

'There they are.' Cathy waved to Karen and Ellie, who were standing outside the Rumblin' Tum and looking excited.

Cathy introduced everybody. 'This is my friend from my old job, Debbie, and her boyfriend, Davy. Meet Karen and Ellie.'

'Nice to meet you, girls,' Davy said and Debbie nodded her agreement.

'Right, pleasantries out of the way. Shall we go in?' Gianni said. 'By the way, the café's not licensed; soft drinks only.'

'That's okay.' Karen patted her handbag. 'We've got some voddy. Jean told us it wasn't licensed so we'll get some Coke and mix it. She's coming tonight with her sister. She said to bring our own booze and to look out for her so she can meet your lovely fella, Cathy.'

'Jean?' Gianni asked.

'The nurse who broke her leg in our garden and told me how I could train without doing O levels,' Cathy said. 'She's really nice. You'll like her.'

'Okay.' He nodded as they made their way into the smoky café. 'Go and grab us a table, girls, and me and Davy'll get some Cokes.'

Debbie hauled two tables together and Cathy helped her pull enough chairs round for everyone. There was a surge onto the small dance floor as the jukebox burst into life with Paul Anka's 'Diana'.

Karen grabbed Ellie by the arm. 'Come on. I love this.'

Cathy smiled as the pair made their way into the crowd.

'Nice girls,' Debbie said. 'Glad you've got someone to hang around with, Cathy.'

'Yeah, they're good fun, but I don't half miss you.'

'I miss you, too. I so wish you hadn't left Lewis's. Dolly's stuck that miserable Bridget Fowler on Max Factor with me.'

'Thought she was on Revlon?'

'She was, and now she thinks she's come down in the world. Snobby bitch. She's a right jealous cow over everything I say or do.'

'What she needs is a boyfriend,' Cathy said as Gianni and Davy appeared with a tray of drinks.

'*Who* needs a boyfriend?' Davy said, dropping a kiss on Debbie's lips.

'The miserable bugger who's on Max Factor with me now Cathy's left,' Debbie said.

'Huh, she'll be lucky.' Davy smirked. 'I mean, well you wouldn't, would you, mate?' He directed that at Gianni. 'That girl who was on the counter with Debs when you came in to meet us at lunchtime.'

'No thanks.' Gianni pulled a face. 'Bag-over-the-head job, that one.'

Cathy smacked his arm. 'Don't be so cruel,' she said, trying not to laugh. The music finished and Karen and Ellie came back to the tables.

Karen rooted in her handbag and gave Gianni the half bottle of vodka. 'Top us all up,' she said; she slurped some Coke out of her glass and the others did the same.

Cathy looked up as she heard her name being called. Jean was making her way across the café, a blonde girl in tow. Karen and Ellie got up to greet her and Davy pulled two more chairs over. Cathy looked up and smiled as Jean stood in front of her. She introduced her to Gianni, who had his arm round her shoulders, and Debbie and Davy. Jean pulled the blonde girl forward and introduced her as Brenda, her younger sister.

Cathy stared at Gianni as his face paled slightly and then his cheeks flushed. Brenda was the girl he'd been here with the first time she had come in with Mike, Davy and Debs.

Brenda chomped on her gum and grinned. She flung herself at Gianni and kissed him full on the lips, nearly knocking him off his chair. 'Not seen you around for ages. Have you been avoiding me, Gianni?'

'Er… no, of course not. This is my girlfriend, Cathy,' he said, extricating himself from Brenda's embrace.

Jean stared at her sister. 'You know Cathy's boyfriend, Bren?'

'Course I do,' Brenda said, with a smirk. 'We go back a year or two, don't we?'

Gianni took a large gulp of his drink. 'One or two,' he muttered.

Cathy stared at him. 'You used to go out with her?'

'No, I told you, we were just mates.'

Brenda folded her arms and looked at him. 'I'd say we were a bit more than mates, Gianni.'

Cathy picked up her bag and got to her feet. 'Excuse me.' She pushed past everyone and made for the ladies', tears pricking the backs of her eyes. The way the girl was looking at Gianni, Cathy knew they'd been more than mates. She felt sick. It was one thing knowing he'd had girls before her, but quite another to have one of them throw herself at him *and* kiss him to boot. She leaned against the sink, taking deep breaths. Debbie came in and stood beside her.

'You okay?'

'I will be.'

'Gianni's fuming out there. Just told that girl where to go. He's stormed off to the gents'.'

'Has she gone?' Cathy dabbed at her eyes with a tissue.

'Her sister took her over to the counter. Is she an ex?'

Cathy nodded. 'Her actions tell me she thinks she's still in with a chance. I mean, she could see he was sitting with his arm round me. Surely she must have realised I was his girl before he introduced us. I know I shouldn't feel jealous. It was before we got together. But I could have smacked her one right across her face.'

'Right,' Debbie said. 'That's the spirit. Now get back out there and show her that you and he are together. Otherwise, she'll be after him all night.' She grabbed Cathy's arm and pulled her towards the table.

Gianni had got back from his visit to the gents' and was looking anxiously around. His eyes lit up when he saw Cathy hurrying towards him.

He got to his feet and led her outside. 'I'm sorry about that. Me and Bren, well it was never anything more than a bit of fun, honestly. I wouldn't go there again if you paid me.'

'It's okay. I overreacted,' Cathy said. 'I know you've had girls before me. It was just the way she was so familiar with you.'

'She took *me* by surprise as much as you. I've had other girls, yes, but I've honestly never told anyone that I love them before. You're the one for me, Cathy and you know it.' He kissed her. 'Let's go back inside,' he whispered. 'Don't let her spoil our night.'

*

Cathy lay in Gianni's arms, spent from their lovemaking. She felt totally content and happy. She traced a finger down his cheek. The rest of the night had been fun, dancing to the two skiffle boys and their guitars. Ellie and Karen had had to dash away early to make the curfew, but she and Gianni had stayed on and then walked to the bus stop with Davy and Debbie. There'd been no sign of Jean and Brenda outside and Cathy was thankful for that and that they'd stayed away from their table the rest of the night. She couldn't help worrying that Gianni might be comparing her with Brenda. All the more reason to be perfect; and tonight he'd told her she was wonderful, which boosted her confidence. Gianni had dragged her straight up to bed when they got home and afterwards she'd almost told him that she'd changed her mind and would get engaged right away, but something stopped her. She sighed, closed her eyes and fell into a disturbed sleep.

*

Gianni awoke to find Cathy thrashing around beside him. She yelled and pushed him away, fighting to get out of his arms. Her eyes were closed but she lashed out and caught him on the chin. He shook her, gently at first and then firmly. Her eyes shot open and she stared at him, a look of panic on her face.

'Jack,' she cried. 'Where's he gone?'

Gianni held her as she began to sob. 'Jack's not here, sweetheart. You were dreaming.'

She shuddered in his arms. 'Oh God, he was trying to run me over with your motorbike.'

'Cathy.' He stroked her hair away from her wet cheeks. 'It was a dream, a bad dream.' He kissed her and calmed her down. 'Have you had dreams like that before?'

She shook her head. 'It was so vivid. I was really scared.'

'I know. But it was just a dream. You're here with me and I love you.'

She snuggled into him and closed her eyes again.

Gianni sighed. What a bloody night. He hoped the bad dream was due to her sampling vodka for the first time, and not the start of something that would become a problem.

Chapter Eighteen

Cathy sprang up off her bed and ran to answer the phone. She smiled into the receiver when she heard Gianni's voice. He sounded happy. 'It's good to hear from you. Did you have any luck tracking the fair down?' she asked.

'No. It was in Northampton recently and that's as far as I've got. I'll buy a map tomorrow and plot a route through the larger towns, and ring each council department.'

'Oh, well, at least you've made a start. What are you doing tonight?'

'I'm meeting Colin and Nigel for a pint. Why don't you come with us?' he suggested.

She sighed and twiddled her hair round her fingers. 'I can't. I've got studying to do after tea. Anyway, you'll enjoy yourself better without me there. I don't really know what to say when men start talking football and stuff.'

'Righto.' He laughed. 'Can you get out tomorrow then? Maybe just for a coffee?'

'Hmm, I'll have to see. Call me after work again. I'll try and get my studying done early. I told you it might be difficult for the first few weeks. If I can get out, I will.'

'Okay.' She heard him give a sigh. 'I love you. Hopefully see you tomorrow.'

'Love you too.' She hung up and went back to her room to change for tea.

*

Bloody hell! Who was knocking on her door at this time of night? Cathy tutted and glanced at the clock on her bedside table. Only nine; it felt much later. She got up and found Karen and Ellie outside.

'Jean's invited us to a dance at the hospital social club,' Karen said. 'It's only round the corner on site here. Do you fancy coming for an hour?'

Cathy looked back at the pile of notes on her bed. She was bored to tears of studying, and had just been wishing she'd taken Gianni up on his offer of going out. 'Okay, why not. Come in. Give me five minutes to put some makeup on.' She had on her jeans and the red sweater Gianni had given her for her birthday. Karen and Ellie were also dressed casually, so no need to get changed. 'Sit on the bed. Shift my notes out of the way.'

The pair flopped down. Karen picked up Cathy's notes and glanced at them. 'Blimey, you're making a right meal of this lot, Cath.'

'I want to make sure I pass those first exams,' Cathy said, squinting in the mirror to put on mascara.

Karen shrugged. 'Don't know why you're bothering, to be honest. You've got the chance of marrying the fittest lad around and you'd rather be here than settling down with him.'

Cathy frowned. 'There's plenty of time for that. I want to make something of myself first.'

Karen rolled her eyes. 'You must be mad,' she said, echoing Debbie's sentiments from the other day. 'I know what I'd be doing. You want to be careful he doesn't get tired of waiting and go off with someone else.'

'Gianni wouldn't do that to me.' Cathy blotted her lips with a tissue and turned to smile as Karen raised an eyebrow. 'He'll wait.'

'You sure about that?'

'Course I am.' She put on her jacket and grabbed her handbag. 'Jean's sister isn't going tonight, is she?'

'Doubt it,' Ellie said. 'Jean told us it's hospital staff only on a Monday night. We get to use the club facilities, including a bar. One of the junior doctors plays the records.'

Elvis Presley's 'Jailhouse Rock' was blasting out as the girls strolled into the smoky room. The dance floor was already crowded. Cathy bagged a table near the bar and they took off their coats and flung them over chairs.

'Vodka and Coke all round?' Karen shouted above the music.

'Just Coke for me,' Cathy said and Ellie nodded. 'Don't think you'll get served with alcohol at your age, Karen.' Cathy looked around to see if she recognised anyone. She spotted Jean and a couple of third-year students, talking to a group of lads. Jean waved and came over to the table.

She put her hand on Cathy's shoulder. 'Sorry about Saturday,' she began. 'I had no idea my sister and your fella had a past. Hope she didn't cause problems for you.'

Cathy shook her head. 'No, we're fine, really.'

'Good. Enjoy yourselves tonight. They're a nice crowd and you'll get to meet a few of our dishy young docs.'

'Oh good,' Karen said, returning to the table with the drinks. 'Could do with a bit of action.'

Jean went back to her friends and Karen sat down. 'What happened to the nice lads *you* were supposed to introduce us to on Saturday?' she said.

Cathy shrugged. 'Apparently they went to the Grafton ballroom. We'll have to take you there soon.'

Ellie took a sip of her drink and sighed. 'I feel like I've been living in a different world to you. All the places there are to go to in Liverpool. The most excitement I've had is dancing to fiddle players at the Young Farmers' dos.'

'That's what happens when you live out in the sticks,' Karen teased. 'We'll see about going dancing on Saturday, Ellie and hopefully Cathy and Gianni can come too.'

Cathy felt a little pang of guilt as she thought about Gianni and how he'd sounded a bit fed up when she told him she couldn't come out tonight. She took a sip of her drink. No doubt he'd got over it by now and was talking football and motorbikes with his mates.

The young doctor DJ said he wanted everyone up on the floor for the next song. Then Jerry Lee Lewis's 'Whole Lotta Shakin'' blasted their eardrums.

Karen pulled Cathy and Ellie to their feet and the girls were soon joined by others. A man with blond hair that flopped into his blue eyes grabbed Cathy round the waist and yelled down her ear that his name was George. She recoiled slightly from the smell of his boozy breath, which reminded her of Jack, but jived half-heartedly with him anyway. He accompanied them all back to the table and pulled up a chair next to her. She made an excuse and escaped to the ladies'. He was okay, but she didn't want to encourage him. When she got back Karen and Ellie were up on the floor again and he was still sitting there. Cathy sat down, twiddling the strap of her handbag. He was looking at her a bit too closely and it made her feel uncomfortable.

'Anybody told you how pretty you are?' he said, sliding an arm round her shoulders.

'Er, yes.' She wriggled as far away as she could without falling off her chair. Gianni had told her many times.

He grinned lopsidedly, stroking her hair. 'Are you enjoying your training? First year is it? Not seen you around before.'

She nodded. 'And you?'

'Second year,' he said.

'Oh right. Nursing or…?' There weren't many male nurses around, but she'd seen a couple in the staff dining room.

'Junior doctor. You from around these parts?'

She nodded. He had a funny accent, a bit fancy, not Liverpudlian like hers. 'Are you?'

'God, no.' He wrinkled his nose as though she'd suggested something revolting. 'I'm from Surrey.'

'Oh, right.' She wasn't too sure where Surrey was, but thought it might be down south, near London. 'Didn't you want to train nearer home?'

'I am doing. My parents moved to the Wirral a couple of years ago. Do you fancy going out one night?' He moved closer and offered her a cigarette.

He'd got his hand on her knee now and it was all she could do not to yell at him to move it. But she didn't want to show herself up. Thank God she'd got jeans on.

'Oh, erm, no thanks,' she said to the cigarette. 'And, er, I've got a boyfriend.'

'Suit yourself,' he said with a smirk and blew a cloud of smoke above his head. 'You look like the sort of girl who might enjoy a bit of fun.'

Cathy felt her cheeks heating. Did he mean she looked like a tart or something? Was she giving off the wrong signals? She chewed her lip, looked across the room and caught Jean's eye.

Jean gave a slight nod and mouthed, 'Need help?'

Cathy nodded back and breathed a sigh of relief as Jean got to her feet and sashayed over, wiggling her hips in her tight-fitting dress. George's eyes lit up as she put her hand on his arm.

'Now then, George,' she said. 'This one's spoken for. Keep your hands to yourself and stop bothering her. Come and have a dance with *me*.' She pulled him to his feet and Cathy let out a breath as he was led away. Jean glanced back over her shoulder and winked. Cathy smiled her thanks.

As George proceeded to whirl Jean around the dance floor, Cathy sipped her drink and wished she was back in her room, or out with Gianni. She didn't have the confidence the others had with lads. Maybe Gianni was right. If she'd had an engagement ring on, George probably wouldn't have wasted his time chatting her up.

*

Gianni went to the bar and ordered three more pints of mild. He didn't even feel like another but it was only half nine and Nige and Col did, and it was his turn to buy a round. He was missing Cathy like crazy after spending all weekend with her. He hoped she could get out tomorrow night. Unlikely though if she was studying hard. Trust him to fall for a career-minded girl. Ah well, that's what set Cathy apart; she was special, and maybe that's why he loved her so much.

'You okay, mate?' Nigel asked as Gianni brought the drinks to the table. 'You've been quiet all night.'

'I've got things on my mind,' Gianni said and sat down. He took a long swig from his glass, then dug in the pocket of his jeans and pulled out a handful of change. 'Just going outside to call Cathy,' he muttered.

'Thought she was busy, studying,' Colin said.

Gianni shrugged. 'Yeah, she is. But I still want to call her.'

He left the pub, ignoring Nigel's and Colin's raised eyebrows.

Some girl was in the phone box. He waited a few minutes, shuffling his feet, and then tapped on the glass, but she ignored him. She'd be in there gassing to her mate all bloody night at this rate. He could hear her out here, spouting the usual gibberish women talked when they'd had more than enough to drink. He'd seen her in the pub, knocking back pints of cider and all over the lad she was with, getting louder as the night wore on. Sod it. He opened the door. 'I need to use the phone. It's an emergency.'

She glared at him, said her goodbyes and hung up, giving him a filthy look as she came outside.

'Thanks.' He dashed in, reeling at the stink of cheap perfume and sweat, and counted out a few coins. He dialled the nurses' home and waited. Shit! Sister Judge had picked up. He asked to speak to Cathy and the line went silent. He heard the home sister banging on a door and calling for Nurse Lomax, and then she was back.

'Sorry, young man, no reply. She may be in the lounge. I'll pop a note under her door.'

Gianni thanked her and went back inside. Nigel and Colin were looking concerned and he guessed they'd been discussing his relationship.

'What is it, mate?' Nigel asked. 'Not like you to be so bloody miserable. You got her in trouble or something?'

Gianni shook his head. 'Nothing like that. Just missing her, that's all.'

'Bloody hell, you've got it bad for this one. Did you speak to her?'

'She wasn't in her room. I'll call her back later.'

'Ah, she's gone out without you,' Colin teased.

'She wouldn't do that. She's probably having a bath or in the lounge with her friends.' He ignored the look that passed between them and knocked back his drink.

At ten Gianni went outside again, but Cathy still wasn't in her room. Why couldn't bloody Sister Judge go and look for her? He slammed the phone down and went back inside the pub. As he took his seat and picked up yet another pint he didn't really want, Nigel went to the jukebox.

'Ha, very funny,' Gianni said, his lips twitching as his mates sang along to the chorus of the Everly Brothers' 'Bye Bye Love'. Cathy wouldn't leave him like the girl in the song. He supposed he was mad to get so bloody involved with a bird in the first place, but he couldn't help it.

*

'So, where were *you* last night?' Gianni asked as Cathy answered his teatime call. 'I thought you were supposed to be studying.'

'I was, I… er, I did,' she stuttered. 'I saw the note under my door that you'd called. Didn't ring you back because I knew you'd be out until late.'

'I called you twice.'

'Oh. Well, I didn't know that. But why?'

She seemed surprised and he realised his tone sounded accusing. 'I was missing you.' He sighed. 'Simple as that. Can you come out tonight?'

She was quiet for a moment, which bothered him.

'Okay. Pick me up about eight. I'll wait in the foyer.'

Gianni said goodbye and hung up, feeling slightly happier. His mam would be out, so they could come back here. He wolfed down the meal she'd left warming in the oven and shot upstairs to have a quick wash and shave. He killed the next half-hour by studying the map he'd bought earlier. He'd ringed the major towns down the centre of England in red, and had spent his lunchtime listing town hall numbers. Tomorrow he planned on making a few calls. He dug out the photo of his dad and uncle and felt a surge of excitement.

Gianni collapsed on top of Cathy and dropped a kiss on her lips. 'I love you so much,' he whispered. 'I really needed you tonight.'

She smiled. 'I needed you too. I hate not being able to see you as often as I did.'

'I guess it'll get worse when you go on proper shifts,' he said, flopping onto his back. 'At least you finish at four for the next few weeks, and get the weekends off.'

'We'll get used to it. I know three years is a long time, but we'll cope.' She sat up and leaned against the headboard. 'Why don't you show me your map and stuff?'

'In a minute,' he said. He had to ask her. 'So, are you going to tell me where you were last night when I called you?' He stared at her and her cheeks went pink. 'Did you go out with someone?' He shouldn't be asking her. Her loving actions in the last hour left him in no doubt of her feelings for him.

She let out a breath and nodded. 'I went to a dance with Karen and Ellie.'

He sat up next to her. 'I asked you out and you said no. Why did you lie and say you had to study if you knew you were going out with those two?'

'Gianni, I didn't lie. When you called, I'd no intention of going out. But then they invited me and I was fed up and wishing I'd gone out with you, but it was too late.'

'Where was the dance?'

'The hospital social club. It's for staff only on a Monday.'

'Oh, great!' He stood up and stared at her. 'Loads of randy young doctors and all you new nurses, eh?' He was gratified to see her blush even more. 'Why the red face? Did you get picked up by someone?'

She shook her head.

'I don't believe you. Who was he? I'll kill him.'

'Gianni, stop it. I jived with a lad; or rather *he* danced with me. I didn't encourage him or anything. I didn't even like him.'

She started crying and he felt bad and sat back down on the bed. This jealous feeling had never happened to him before and he didn't like it. He reached for her. He shouldn't be upsetting her. She loved him; her body language told him that. She was clinging to him, sobbing. He kissed her. 'Sorry. I can't bear the thought of anyone touching you or even dancing with you. You didn't go back to his room or anything?'

'Of course not. Jean rescued me by taking him off to dance and we only stayed a short time after that. I promise I won't go again.'

He shook his head. 'It's okay. I don't mind you having fun with your friends. I'm just feeling jealous, that's all.'

She smiled through her tears. 'Would it make you feel any better if I wore an engagement ring when I went out without you?'

He stared at her and a wave of relief washed over him. 'It would. But only if you really want to.' He couldn't believe she'd suggested it.

'I do.'

He kissed her and held her tight. 'I'll buy you a ring on Saturday.' He smiled; feeling like a weight had lifted. 'I guess I'd better get you back before the curfew. It's gone ten.'

*

Cathy pulled on her jeans and sweater while Gianni went to the bathroom. She felt a bit backed into a corner, but what did it matter? If wearing his ring made him feel more secure when she wasn't with him, it was a small price to pay. As he came back into the room, someone banged loudly on the front door.

'Oh no, your mam's forgotten her key,' she cried. 'Quick, get your clothes on and let her in.' She grabbed her jacket and handbag while he pulled on his jeans and T-shirt. They hurried downstairs and Gianni opened the door.

But it wasn't Sadie. Two grim-faced police officers were standing on the step. They asked if he was Gianni Romano and he nodded and stood back to let them enter.

'What is it?' Cathy grabbed his hand.

His face drained of colour and he shook his head as one of the officers cleared his throat and spoke.

'Mr Romano, we're sorry to have to tell you this. Your mother was involved in a road traffic accident tonight. She's in the Liverpool Royal Infirmary. We'll take you there right away, sir.'

Cathy gasped as Gianni stood still, his mouth open, but making no sound. 'Gianni, sit down. I'll get your boots and jacket.' She pushed him gently onto the sofa and dashed back upstairs.

'Is she badly hurt?' he asked as Cathy came back and helped him finish dressing. 'What happened?'

'She was hit by a car while crossing the road outside Sefton Library,' one of the officers said. 'I'm sorry; we don't know the extent of her injuries at the moment.'

'We'll both come with you.' Cathy grabbed Gianni's house keys from the coffee table. He needed her; the curfew and everything else could go out the window tonight.

Chapter Nineteen

Cathy clung to Gianni's hand as a solemn-faced doctor appeared at the door. A nurse had shown them into a small waiting room, brought them tea and told them someone would be with them shortly. Gianni hadn't spoken a word since they'd left his house and his face was as white as the nurse's apron. They sat silently side by side until the door opened and he'd grabbed her hand and sprung to his feet. The doctor told them his mam had died on the operating table. They'd done their best, he said, but she'd suffered a serious head injury and trauma to her chest area and stomach and had passed away without regaining consciousness.

Cathy thanked the doctor, who then left the room, closing the door quietly behind him. She sat Gianni back down and knelt by his feet, holding his hands. She didn't know what to say. His silence unnerved her and his eyes, wide and staring blankly at the wall opposite, made her wonder if he'd taken on board what the doctor had said.

The door flew open and Jean dashed into the room.

'Oh, Jean, thank goodness,' Cathy said, relieved to see a familiar face. 'I didn't realise you were on nights this week.'

'First night tonight and I'm standing in on casualty,' Jean said, coming into the room. 'God, I'm so sorry. I recognised your mother's surname and I've just spoken to the doctor and told him I know you both. He suggested I come and see you. Is there anything I can do to help?'

Gianni looked at Jean and nodded slowly, tears running down his face now. 'Can I see her?'

'Of course. Come with me.'

Cathy hung back, not wanting to intrude, but Gianni turned and held out his hand.

'I can't do this on my own.'

She swallowed hard and they followed Jean to a small room further down the corridor.

'Would you like some private time with her?' Cathy whispered as Jean opened the door and stepped back to let them enter.

He shook his head and she followed him inside, Jean bringing up the rear. A trolley, on which his mam lay covered with a sheet, stood by the back wall. Jean patted Gianni on the arm and turned back the sheet. She left them alone, discreetly closing the door.

Gianni stood with his head bowed and stroked a lifeless hand, tears dripping from his chin onto the sheet.

Cathy choked back her own tears. She'd never seen anyone dead before. She didn't know quite what she'd been expecting. Sadie looked like she was sleeping; her gentle face was pale and her hair, although bloodstained, was tidy. There was even a trace of her favourite blue eyeshadow on her lids. Cathy bit her lip and slipped her arms round Gianni's waist. She could feel him shaking.

'I'm going to leave you alone for a few minutes,' she whispered. 'You need to say goodbye to her by yourself. I'll wait near the door for you.'

Jean was outside in the corridor and caught hold of Cathy as her legs buckled. She led her to a chair and sat down beside her.

'It's never easy when it's someone you know,' Jean said, patting Cathy's hand.

'I can't believe it,' Cathy sobbed. 'I don't know what to say to him.'

'Let *him* do the talking,' Jean advised. 'Just be there for him. There'll be a lot of stuff to sort out. You'll be able to collect the death certificate tomorrow and then he can arrange the funeral. It will keep him busy and give him a focus for the next few days.'

Cathy nodded. 'Oh, God, we've just agreed to get engaged tonight, and now she'll never know.'

'Oh, that's such a shame,' Jean said sympathetically. 'Bet she's been waiting for him to meet a nice girl and settle down.'

Cathy smiled through her tears. 'Probably. Jean, what shall I do about my training? I'll have to go back home with Gianni. I can't leave him on his own. Who do I tell? I'm locked out now, and I'll need to get some stuff from my room. We were just getting ready to come back here when the police arrived.'

Jean sighed. 'I'm due a break in a few minutes and I've got my special pass key. You come with me to the nurses' home, collect what you'll need for the next few days and go back with Gianni. I'll see Home Sister first thing in the morning when I come off duty and I'll tell her what's happened. Then you can phone in tomorrow sometime and speak to Sister Carew. Don't worry about it. They'll allow you a few days' compassionate leave. She's your fiancé's mam. That's all they need to know.'

'Thank you.' Cathy looked up as Gianni came out of the room. 'You okay?'

He nodded. A bit of colour had returned to his cheeks. 'What do I do now?' he said, running a hand across his face. 'And you, Cathy. You're locked out. You'll be in bother.'

'I won't.' Cathy told him what Jean had suggested. 'Why don't you go back to the waiting room for a few minutes while I get sorted? Then we'll get a taxi to your house.'

'Okay.' Tears ran down his cheeks again. 'You won't leave me tonight, will you?'

Cathy jumped up and held him close. 'Of course I won't. I'll be as quick as I can.'

*

Cathy and Gianni sat up all night, crying and holding each other, waiting until they saw the lights going on across the street in Millie's and Cathy's mam's houses. Then they went to tell Sadie's friends the news.

Alice unlocked and unbolted the door at Cathy's urgent knocking, and Gianni brought Millie into the house.

'Sit down, Mam, Millie,' Cathy began and they sat side by side on the sofa, looking puzzled.

'What is it?' Millie began, her voice wavering. 'Has something happened?'

'I'm afraid we've got some really bad news,' Cathy said. Amazingly, her mam hadn't even questioned what she was doing here so early and why Gianni was with her. 'Sadie was knocked down,' she said, reaching for Gianni's hand. 'She died in hospital last night. There was nothing they could do to save her.'

The silence was deafening as Millie and Alice stared in disbelief at the pair. Gianni held Cathy tight, sobbing into her hair.

Millie spoke first. She got to her feet. 'Sit down too, you two. You both look like you've been hit by a sledgehammer.'

'It feels like it,' Gianni cried.

'Oh, Gianni, you poor boy.' Alice put her arms round him and held him tight while Millie comforted a weeping Cathy.

As the awful news sank in, Millie took charge. The kids were taken to school and Roddy to his minder. She hurried back to Alice's after stopping in next door at her house to phone Lewis's to explain why she and Alice would both need a couple of days' leave.

Alice had made hot, sweet tea and was trying to persuade Gianni and Cathy to at least have a slice of toast. 'It's going to be a long day. Just have a little bite and then I'll walk round to your gran's with you, Gianni. You will need all the strength you can muster for her, because she'll be heartbroken too.'

Gianni nodded. 'Will you come as well, Cathy?'

'We'll all go,' Millie said.

'And I need to go back to the hospital for the death certificate,' Gianni told them. 'They said it will be ready to collect today.'

By the next day, everyone who needed to be informed of Sadie's death had been contacted. A funeral director had been appointed and Gianni was told her body would be collected and placed in the chapel of rest tomorrow. Both Alice and Millie helped him to arrange the funeral and Millie said she would hold a wake for the mourners in her home.

Gianni and Cathy were glad to leave everything to them as they seemed to know what they were doing.

'You need to go and choose some nice flowers for the top of the casket, Gianni,' Alice had said. 'Pick something cheerful and bright, something that will suit your mam's personality. Millie and I will sort out a spray of flowers from her friends and neighbours.'

'She liked roses,' Cathy said, feeling the tears that were never far away begin to run down her cheeks again, as they stood in the flower shop on Lark Lane surrounded by buckets of flowers and greenery.

Gianni nodded. 'She did. Pink and white ones then, do you think?'

The lady took their order and told them the arrangement would be delivered to the house on the morning of the funeral.

'I can't face going back to the house just yet,' Gianni said. 'Let's walk to Seffy Park and get a bit of fresh air.'

They strolled hand in hand round the boating lake and then sat down on a bench. Gianni slipped his arm round Cathy's shoulders and pulled her close. 'I wouldn't have got through the last few days without you by my side,' he said. 'You've been my rock, so caring. Those patients you'll be looking after when you're trained won't believe how lucky they are. You're gonna make a fabulous nurse, Cathy.'

*

A week after Sadie's funeral, Gianni sat at the kitchen table, surrounded by the contents of his mam's box of private papers. He was going through it all to sort out insurance policies and house details. Cathy handed him a mug of coffee and kissed the top of his head. 'Thank you,' he said, slipping his arm round her waist. 'There's so much to do and think about. I couldn't have coped on my own.'

His mam had left a will. He was now a homeowner, and the mortgage would be paid in full with money from a policy. She'd also left him several hundred pounds in a building society account. He felt a bit guilty for feeling secure and comfortable about the future when she'd worked so hard and been careful with money for all her short life. The regular weekly deposits into the account were the same amount that he'd paid her for his keep. She'd been saving it for him instead of using it to help with the bills. He felt choked when he thought of how she'd done without so she could give him the best she could afford. He had a lot to thank her for and he hoped that, if he ever had a child of his own, he'd be as good a parent as his mam had been.

At the bottom of the box were her marriage certificate and a stack of cards and letters. He looked at one of the cards and saw that it was for him, signed by his father. He picked up another. There was a card for every birthday he'd celebrated, all from his father and all with loving messages, and he'd never seen sight of them until now. The letters were all addressed to 'Dearest Sadie' and brought tears to his eyes. His father had still loved her and Gianni, and never seemed to give up hope that maybe she still loved him too. Gianni shook his head. He wondered if she'd ever considered writing back. From the letters it would appear not. That saddened him even more. He'd missed out on having a dad. No child should have to endure that, even though he knew his mam had always believed she was doing the right thing. He sighed. By rights he really needed to let his father know Sadie had passed away. After all, they'd never divorced. His dad needed to be told he was now a widower. If only there was an address or a contact number for him, it would make life so much easier. All he could do was plod on with his plans to find the fair. He gave the letters to Cathy to read and went to make coffees for them both.

'These make for very sad reading,' Cathy said when he handed her a mug.

He nodded. 'They do.'

I have to go back to the hospital tomorrow, love,' Cathy said. 'I wish I didn't have to leave you, but I've some catching up to do for my coursework. I'll be home again on Saturday. Er, that's if you want me to come here.'

He nodded. 'Of course I do. Consider this your home now. It's a pity you have to live in at the hospital when you could be here with me.'

'I think you'll need some space,' she said. 'A bit of time to yourself. It's been hectic with people coming and going the last few days. And I expect you'll want to get back to work yourself soon.'

'Not really,' he said. 'But *I've* also got coursework to do and exams looming. I finish my apprenticeship late next year. After that I'll be a qualified draughtsman.'

Cathy smiled. 'You'll finish just as I start in earnest.'

'Ironical, isn't it?' He raised an eyebrow. 'Here we are, all set up for the future. A house of our own, money in the bank, and you can't even share it with me.'

'Oh, Gianni, I will, as and when I can. I'll stay here when it's my days off, I promise. Mam hasn't questioned me about me staying here at all, surprisingly.'

He nodded. 'Yeah, I know. I'm surprised too. But she knows I'll look after you. I'm just feeling a bit sorry for myself, that's all.' He was quiet for a moment. 'Can I buy you that ring at the weekend?'

'You can.' She smiled and gave him a hug.

*

Gianni replaced the receiver and sat back with a satisfied smile. He'd just spoken to a clerk at Poole Town Hall who'd told him the fair had been in town recently and had only moved on last week. Where to the young man wasn't sure, but Gianni felt like he was getting somewhere at last. His map was at home, so tonight he'd update his list and carry on trying towns down south. He'd done little in the last few weeks as he'd been catching up with work and studies. But his mind was made up; he was planning on packing in his job, taking a few months' break and trying to find his family. He was also hoping to persuade Cathy to go with him. There was no need for her to work; he had enough money in the bank to take care of things for ages. They could just go off, have a good time and maybe get married when they came back. Persuading her to give up her dream would be no easy task, though. There were times when he thought he'd cracked it but many others when he felt he was wasting his time. She was always loving towards him; and supportive when he had bad days and wanted his mam. But she was so stubborn about her career and her independence. Still, he had all weekend to work on her.

*

Granny Lomax placed a mug of tea in front of Cathy alongside a plate of home-made shortbread.

'Thanks, Gran.' Cathy took a sip of tea and sighed. It was Saturday morning, and she was getting her visiting out of the way before meeting Debbie for lunch, and then spending the rest of the weekend with Gianni.

'What's up, love? You've a face like a wet weekend in Blackpool.'

Cathy sighed and broke a piece of shortbread in two. She nibbled a corner. 'It's Mam. She's not right since Sadie died. She seems to have gone back downhill again. I popped in to see them all before I came here. She looked a right mess, not washed her hair, and the kids looked grubby and full of colds. I'm worried, Gran.

She's not coping at all. I don't know what to do. Millie said she hasn't been back in to work since the funeral either. Good job Brian is sending her some money each month. But that's not the answer.'

Granny Lomax shook her head. 'She's not really your problem, love. You need to be concentrating on passing those first exams next week and Alice needs to buck her ideas up and get back to work before she loses her job. I'll pop round next week and see if there's anything I can do to help. Now, how's that young man of yours? I must say, that ring he's bought you is beautiful. You just be careful you don't lose it when you take it off for work.'

Cathy looked at the engagement ring sparkling on her finger. She had to admit it was pretty. Gianni said the sapphire, surrounded by tiny diamonds, matched her eye colour. Her new friends at the hospital had oohed and aahed over it and Debbie had made sure Davy got an eyeful along with hints that *she'd* like one similar. 'Gianni's doing okay considering, thanks Gran,' Cathy replied. 'He has up and down days. He said it hits him most when he gets home from work and she's not there with his tea ready and waiting. He said the house feels empty. But he's got exams coming up, so he's studying, and he's also trying to find his dad and the fair. It's keeping him occupied.'

'Hmm.' Granny Lomax rubbed her chin and looked thoughtfully at Cathy. 'And what about you, now things have changed? Will you still do the three years of training? I bet he'll want to get married now he's got the house. He'll be earning good money soon, too. You'd want for nothing, love.'

Cathy frowned. 'Of course I still want to do my training. Why does everyone think that all women should be married and dependent on men? Look at the pickle Mam's in, and Gianni's mam struggled to bring *him* up alone. If anything goes wrong I want to be able to look after myself. I thought you, of all people, would understand that, Gran.'

'I know, love, I'm just saying. You'd have it easy compared to most young couples.'

Cathy rolled her eyes and finished her tea. 'I'd better go and meet Debs,' she said, taking her mug over to the sink. 'She's another one who'd take the easy way out. But I'm afraid that's not for me.'

Three plastic beakers and a bottle of Blue Nun waited on top of the chest of drawers under Cathy's window in the nurses' home. Friday evening; the end of the final day of their preliminary training. Karen and Ellie fidgeted on the bed and Cathy stood with her back to the wardrobe. 'Shall I go first?' she said, turning the white envelope over and over.

Karen chewed her lip and nodded but Ellie held up a hand.

'Why don't we do it at the same time? Get it over with in one go.'

'I feel sick,' Karen said, fanning her face with her envelope. 'I could be home for good this time tomorrow.'

'Well, looking on the bright side, your mam will be glad to see you,' Cathy said.

'Yeah, and I suppose I could go back to my old job. They said they'd have me back any time and at least I'd be able to stock up my wardrobe again.'

Cathy nodded. Karen had worked in C&A in the city and often told them about the next-to-nothing she paid for outfits with her staff discount. 'What about you, Ellie? What will you do, if…?'

Ellie shrugged. 'Go back to helping my dad on the farm, I suppose,' she said gloomily. 'And winter's on its way too.'

Karen looked at Cathy. 'And we all know what *you'll* do.'

'Do you?' Cathy frowned. 'Well, that's more than I do.'

Karen laughed. 'God, Cathy, you're hopeless. You'll marry Gianni, of course. There'd be nothing to stop you.'

Cathy smiled. 'Maybe. But come on, let's do it. One, two, three, go!'

The envelopes were opened and the letters inside carefully unfolded, to gasps of delight.

'Yes!' Cathy yelled. 'I'm in!'

'Me too,' Karen said, jumping up and down, and Ellie nodded, her eyes brimming with tears.

Cathy clapped her hand to her mouth. 'I've got the first of my placements. I've to report to B2 Men's Medical at eight am on Monday.'

'I'm on C3, Gynaecological,' Karen said, raising an eyebrow. 'That should be fun! What about you, Ellie?'

Ellie's grin split her face as she replied, 'A3, Children's ward. Oh, I was so hoping and praying I'd get that.'

'Well, that's it, girls. We're on our way.' Karen opened the bottle of wine and split it between the waiting beakers. She handed them round and they clinked them together. 'Congratulations to us all. We're almost proper nurses now,' she said. 'Here's to the future!'

Chapter Twenty

February 1958

Cathy patted the wrinkled skin with a soft towel and sprinkled talcum powder into the creases. Poor old man, she thought, gently fluffing out the powder so it wouldn't clog his pores. He smiled at her, toothless and helpless as a baby. She rolled him onto his side and rubbed a soothing cream into the base of his spine. The skin was inflamed and starting to break down. There'd be another bedsore if he wasn't turned and creamed more frequently. The one on his hip seemed bigger by the day.

Eighty-year-old Wilfred Wagstaffe was Cathy's favourite patient. When she first started her placements he'd been on Men's Medical, following a stroke, and now, paralysed down his left side, he'd been transferred here to Geriatrics. A widower, who'd lost his wife and only son in the Blitz, there was little chance he'd ever go home. He never complained, suffering the indignities with good humour, always grateful for everything she did for him. She pulled his gown down, placed a pillow behind him to prevent him rolling onto his back and covered him with a sheet.

'Are you warm enough, Wilfred? Would you like a blanket?'

He waved a hand in the air and shook his head slowly. Communication was difficult, but Cathy always managed to understand him.

'Okay, well I'll get on with my round. Nearly time for morning coffee. I'll come back and help you when it arrives.'

Wilfred smiled his lopsided smile.

Cathy pulled the curtains back from round his bed and pushed her trolley to the sluice to empty the bowl and bedpan. As she went into the adjoining bathroom to refill the bowl, she heard running water, gagging and groans of 'Oh dear'. She grinned to herself. Cadet Nurse Thomas was doing the denture round. It was the one job they all hated and it usually fell to the most junior nurse on the ward.

'You okay, Katie?' Cathy asked, trying her best to look sympathetic.

Katie Thomas was fresh from cadet training and doing her first time on denture-cleaning. She shook her head, fished in her pocket for a tissue and wiped her streaming nose. She took off her spectacles, rubbed them on her apron and wiped her eyes. She gagged again as she looked into the sink. 'I can't bear this. Just look at all that gunk.'

Cathy glanced into the sink and gasped. 'Oh my goodness, you've tipped them all in together.'

Katie looked confused and her cheeks went scarlet. 'I thought it would be quicker,' she muttered, looking down at the sets of false teeth, bobbing side by side in the water.

'I can see your reasoning,' Cathy said, trying not to laugh. 'But they're all mixed up now and God knows which set belongs to which pot.'

'They all look the same,' Katie said, her lips trembling. 'Oh, I'm a rubbish nurse.' Tears ran down her chubby cheeks and she dashed them away.

'No you're not. It's early days. Don't cry.' Cathy pushed the bathroom door closed and took a deep breath. 'Have you brushed them?'

'Sort of,' Katie said. 'I turned my head away and did this.' She made a scrubbing movement in the air with a toothbrush.

'Then I dropped them in there, in clean water.' She pointed to the adjacent sink.

Cathy scratched her head thoughtfully. 'Right, well, there's not a lot we can do about this other than shove them all back in the pots and dish them out to the patients. Come on, we need to be quick, Matron's due in for her round and Sister will be on our backs if the ward's not ready.'

Between them they refilled the denture pots and Katie placed them all back on the trolley.

'Cathy, thank you so much. I feel such an idiot.'

Cathy smiled. 'You're not the first to do it and you won't be the last. Go on, off you go and don't tell a soul. Fingers crossed most of them fit or we'll be in bother.'

At break time, Cathy joined Karen and Jean in the staff dining room for toast and coffee. Ellie was on a late and had popped into Pickford to do a bit of shopping. Cathy told them about Katie's denture mix-up and they laughed.

'I did it the first time I was given the denture round,' Jean confessed with a grin. 'Poor Katie. She'll get over it.'

'Has the postman been yet?' Cathy asked, spreading marmalade onto a slice of toast.

'Yeah, he was just filling the pigeonholes when we came through the hallway,' Karen said. 'Are you expecting something?'

Cathy shrugged. 'Gianni might have sent me a postcard.'

'Has he had any luck finding his father?' Jean asked.

'Not yet. The fair doesn't operate during the first couple of months of the year, but the clerk at the last town hall he tried told him they usually pitch up in Southampton just before Easter. It's at the beginning of April this year, so that's where he's heading at the end of this month. He's in Dorset at the moment. He needed a little holiday after everything he's been through.'

'Did he pack his job in permanently?' Jean asked.

'Yes. But he can always go back and finish his apprenticeship and qualify as a draughtsman.'

'Bet you're missing him,' Karen said. 'Shame you couldn't have gone with him for a dirty weekend or two.'

Cathy felt her cheeks warming and took a sip of coffee. She missed him like crazy and her body craved *more* than a dirty weekend with him. But she couldn't get a break other than her two days a week off, and was rostered to work all over Easter. At least Gianni had something to keep him occupied. When she'd spoken to him a couple of nights ago he'd told her he was enjoying sitting on beaches and sketching. He said he was missing her but loved exploring new places, and the freedom of just travelling around with no ties. He'd promised to send regular postcards from scenic villages and would call her when he could. He told her he was working on a special drawing at the moment, but wouldn't tell her what it was. She'd have to wait and see, he said.

'Are you coming to the social club for a dance tonight?' Karen interrupted her thoughts.

'Yeah, why not?' Cathy nodded. 'Right, I'm going back to work. See you here at lunchtime.'

'By the way, Cathy,' Jean began as Cathy got to her feet. 'Don't leave your window open when you're not in your room. Someone's reported a prowler. He was seen hanging around out there last night.'

'Oh, okay.' Cathy felt a little shiver go down her spine. She glanced across the courtyard towards her room. The window was closed. 'Thanks for the warning, Jean.'

Cathy hurried down the long, green-painted main corridor where the smell of disinfectant lingered and clung to clothes and hair, and past the kitchens that always stank of cabbage. She didn't like being the only one on the ground floor of the nurses' home apart from Home Sister, who wasn't always in her room at night anyway. She might ask to be moved if the prowler was seen again. She read the postcard she'd just picked up and hoped the postman hadn't looked too closely before dropping it in her pigeonhole.

Gianni had written that he was lying on his bed, looking at photos of her. Her stomach flipped, remembering how she'd recently posed in skimpy clothing for him. She'd refused at first, worried that someone in the chemist shop might see the developed film and recognise her. Gianni told her he'd try to develop them himself. Maybe he'd done that, or taken the film into a chemist while he was away where no one would know who they were. He said she was perfect model material because she posed so naturally, but there was no way she'd do it for anyone else. She'd die of embarrassment if any of those photos were ever seen by anyone other than her and Gianni.

Chaos met her as she entered the ward and put on her apron. She pushed thoughts of prowlers and naughty photos to the back of her mind. Sister rushed to pull the curtains round a bed while a team with a trolley barged past, nearly knocking Cathy flying. Her heart sank as she realised they were the curtains to Wilfred's bed.

'What is it?' she asked Cadet Nurse Thomas.

'Someone shouted "cardiac arrest",' the other girl whispered, her eyes wide.

'Oh no!' Cathy shot across the ward and slipped inside the closed curtains.

Sister pulled her back outside. 'Best leave him to the experts, Nurse Lomax. You can go in shortly.'

Cathy burst into tears as Sister led her to the office, muttering something about getting too involved with patients. She sat Cathy down and handed her a glass of water.

'He's got no one,' Cathy sobbed. 'It's so sad. He's a lovely old man.' She stopped as Sister looked at her over the top of her spectacles, opened her mouth to say something, then closed it as one of the team popped his head round the door.

'Ten thirty-two,' he said to Sister, who nodded her head.

She wrote down the time, thanked him and turned to Cathy. 'I'm sorry, Nurse Lomax. His heart couldn't take any more.'

Cathy sobbed into her hands. Sister patted her shoulder. 'I'd better make tracks. You stay there until you feel composed enough to resume working.'

Cathy looked up through her tears. 'Sister, may I help to prepare him? I mean, well, I've looked after him from the first day I started on the wards. It's my last chance to do something for him.'

Sister was silent for a moment. 'If you feel you can cope, that it won't upset you too much, Nurse, then yes. Come with me.'

Cathy took a deep, calming breath and followed her down the ward. This was the first laying-out she'd helped with, and the first death she'd experienced since seeing Sadie's body. She knew she had to get used to it. The thought of someone else preparing Wilfred for the morgue was unbearable.

'It was quick,' Sister said. 'He looks peaceful.' She went off to get the trolley and Cathy stood by the bed and stole a glance at Wilfred's face. He did indeed look peaceful. The thought of not seeing his lopsided smile again made her feel really sad.

Sister came back and between them they washed and prepared Wilfred and dressed him in a white shroud. Cathy brushed his thick silver hair and Sister put his teeth in. She struggled a bit with the bottom set. Cathy bit her lip. It was neither the time nor the place to say anything, and she didn't want to get Cadet Nurse Thomas into trouble.

'Well done, Nurse Lomax.' Sister patted her arm. 'I'll leave you to fill in the tags. Put one round his big toe, pin the other to the front of the shroud and then tidy the trolley away. I'll call the mortuary.' Sister bustled away.

Cathy stroked her hand across Wilfred's cheek, which was now cold. 'Goodbye, Wilfred,' she said, a catch in her voice. 'You've been a pleasure to look after and I'll miss you from the bottom

of my heart.' She took hold of the trolley and pushed it into the
sluice room, where the tears started again.

After the mortuary attendants had taken Wilfred away in a big silver
box on wheels, Cathy and Cadet Nurse Thomas stripped his bed.
They washed it down with disinfectant, dried it off and put fresh
bedding on. Cathy emptied his locker. There wasn't much in it: a
razor and comb, a wallet and a sepia photo Wilfred had treasured,
which was of a tall, handsome soldier, standing alongside a pretty
curly-haired blonde woman in a long white dress carrying a bunch
of mixed flowers. Cathy turned the photo over and smiled. Wilfred
and his new wife. The date, August 1914, meant the couple had
married during the early weeks of the First World War and probably before Wilfred went abroad. How hard it must have been to
have your new husband go away so soon after marrying him, never
knowing if he'd come home in one piece, or even if he'd come home
at all. But that was how it had been for her mam and dad too;
and Cathy had been on the way when Mam was left alone. So sad
that Wilfred's wife and adult son had both died in the next war.
But now they'd be reunited as a family. Cathy decided she would
attend Wilfred's funeral. After all, if she didn't, who else would?
She'd ask Granny Lomax to accompany her.

Gianni called as Cathy was making her way to the dining room at
lunchtime. The phone was ringing as she rounded the corner near
her room and sixth sense told her it would be him. Her heart leapt
as she picked up the receiver and heard his voice.

'Hi, darling,' he began, 'I'm really missing you, Cath. I'm going
to ride back up north later. I'll get a train to Southampton, Easter
week, and look for the fair. I can't go any longer without seeing
you. Can you get out tonight?'

'Yes, I finish at five, and guess what?' she teased. 'I'm off tomorrow and Wednesday, so I can spend the whole time with you. Gianni, I really need to see you too. I've had a bad day, so your timing couldn't be better.'

'Oh great. Be there as soon as I can. I'm setting off now and I'll stop and ring you when I'm a few miles away and you're off duty. We'll go straight to my place.'

They said their goodbyes and Cathy hung up, smiling. She couldn't wait. She hurried to the dining room to tell Karen she wouldn't be going to the dance tonight.

'Lucky you,' Karen said when Cathy explained. 'Bet he won't let you out of his bed for the whole time you're together.'

Cathy laughed. 'He'll cheer me up. It's been a rough day so far.' She told Karen about Wilfred.

'Aw, Cathy, I know you were really fond of him. If I'm off duty, I'll come to his funeral too. Just let me know the details when you get them.'

'Nurse Lomax,' Sister's voice called out as Cathy placed sheets on the shelves in the linen cupboard. She tutted. Now what?

'Coming.' She straightened her cap, smoothed down her apron, made her way to the office and took a seat at Sister's bidding.

'I'm updating your records, Nurse. You're due to leave this ward next week. You will report to D5, Men's Surgical, next Monday at eight am. I'm happy to say you've made good progress with us and I'll fill in my report accordingly. You have a kind and caring nature and I've no doubt you'll go on to make an excellent staff nurse or sister one day.' She stopped as someone knocked loudly on the door. 'One minute.' Sister got to her feet.

Cathy sighed. It was visiting time, when the patients' relatives were always knocking on the office door. Sister stepped out of the office and Cathy could hear a woman complaining about her father's dentures.

'Them bottom ones keep coming out! They're not his. He had small teeth. Them's big ones. They'd fit an 'orse.'

Cathy fidgeted uncomfortably on her chair. When she'd got back from lunch Cadet Nurse Thomas had told her that most of the patients seemed to have the right dentures as they'd all managed to scoff their meals without any problems. Mind you, geriatric patients were usually given mince and mash anyway, easy enough to slip down with or without teeth.

Sister came back into the room, looking agitated. 'Nurse Lomax, could you do a check and make sure each patient has their own dentures, please? There seems to have been a bit of a mix-up with Mr Darnley's.'

Cathy got to her feet and hurried out. Not many of the patients had visitors. A quick check told her they all had their teeth in and seemed quite comfortable. No one was complaining that they didn't fit, anyway. The teeth Sister had rammed into Wilfred's mouth had been a bit too small, she thought. Well, there was no way they'd get those back now. Wilfred's jaw would be well and truly closed for ever. She approached Mr Darnley's bed and smiled at his red-faced daughter. 'I've er, I've just checked with all our patients and they have the correct dentures,' she said, crossing her fingers behind her back. 'Er, your father's may be a bit loose because he's lost weight recently.' Did she sound convincing enough? The woman's face went redder still as she struggled for something to say. But Cathy got in first. 'Once he's home, I'd suggest a visit to the dentist. I'm sure that'll sort the problem out.' She nodded at the woman, knowing full well the poor man would be unlikely to go home, or need his dentures for much longer. Mr Darnley hardly wore them anyway. She turned and walked up the ward just as Auxiliary Nurse Grant came out of Sister's office. Cathy liked Nurse Grant. She was older than any of the student nurses and had been at the hospital since the Second World War. Many of her nursing tasks were menial as her training had been basic, but she put a smile on the patients' faces and had the patience to deal with most problems.

'Are you ready for off, Nurse Lomax?' Nurse Grant asked. 'I'm just heading for the sluice. Bedpan duty awaits me.'

Cathy had a sudden thought. She wondered if there might be a possibility of her mam training to be a nurse after all. She followed Nurse Grant down to the sluice room. Out of earshot of anyone else, she told her about the teeth mix-up and they both had a giggle.

'I'll keep my eye on Mr Darnley, don't you worry yourself. Such a shame about poor Wilfred. I know you were very fond of him.'

Cathy nodded. 'I was. Er, can I ask you a question?'

'Go ahead,' Nurse Grant replied, taking clean bedpans from the draining rack and beginning to load the trolley ready for her round.

Cathy explained how it had always been her mam's dream to be a nurse, but how that dream had never materialised due to circumstances beyond her control. 'Do you think it would be possible for her to get a job at her age now and maybe train to become an auxiliary like you?'

'I don't see why not. She could work part-time to accommodate her children's needs. And she'd get to wear a uniform and work on the wards. I love it, and although I don't do anything complicated, I'm working with the patients and that's what I always wanted to do. Tell her to give the main office a call and they can invite her in to discuss it.'

'Thank you. I'll do that. I'll see you tomorrow.' Cathy left the ward with a smile on her face. She couldn't wait to see her mam and tell her that there was a possibility she could still achieve her dream if she wanted to. It might buck her up no end; a bit of good news for a change.

Chapter Twenty-One

Cathy flung her arms round Gianni and he spun her round and round, dropping kisses all over her face. Ellie and Karen appeared in the foyer to wave them off.

'Look at you, all tanned,' Karen said, giving him a hug.

'I'm olive-skinned to start with,' Gianni said with a grin. 'It doesn't take a hot sun to get me really brown. The sea breeze does that. You can't beat sitting on a beach all day with nothing to do but sketch. But I've missed this one.' He squeezed Cathy until she squealed.

'Well, no guesses for how *you* two will be spending Cathy's days off then.' Karen smirked. 'I'll be catching up on my laundry and getting my hair trimmed, and Ellie's working. Boring. Have fun.'

'We will,' Gianni said, brown eyes twinkling. 'Ready, Cath?' He picked up her bag and she followed him out to the bike.

'It's cold in here,' Gianni said as they let themselves into the house. He wrinkled his nose. 'Can you smell fags, like freshly smoked?'

'Yeah,' Cathy said. 'But the house has been closed up for ages. How odd. It'll be all right when we open the windows. Let's switch the electric fire on to warm us up a bit first.' She went into the kitchen and shivered. There was a draught coming from somewhere, and the place was a tip. 'Gianni, come here, quick. I think you've had burglars or something.' Dirty dishes cluttered the sink, an ashtray filled with butt-ends sat on the table and the waste bin was overflowing with chip papers, tin cans and beer bottles.

'Shit, how the hell did they get in?' he said, joining her in the kitchen. The glass in the back door was smashed above the lock, with a hole just big enough to get a hand through. The key was missing and the door was locked. So the burglar had kindly locked up as he'd left, no doubt planning a return later.

'Call the police,' Cathy suggested, her heart skipping a beat.

'I'll go and check upstairs first. See if anything's been taken. Don't touch a thing in case there are fingerprints.'

Cathy sighed as Gianni ran up the stairs two at a time. She heard him banging around and then he was back beside her.

'Nothing seems to be missing, but the burglar's been sleeping in my old room and he's used the bathroom. There's a towel on the floor and the immersion's on.'

Cathy stared at him, open-mouthed. 'Well, the cheeky sod!'

Gianni shook his head. 'I'll call the police. I think we've got a squatter, a tramp or something. And I'll need to get that back door fixed and the lock changed. Bloody hell, bang goes our nice evening.' He felt angry more than upset at the prospect of a prowler. All the way home he'd thought of nothing but the wonderful night of loving he'd got planned.

Cathy gave him a hug. 'We'll soon have things sorted. You get on the phone and I'll nip to the corner shop and get some milk for a brew, and I want to pop over and check on Mam and the kids for ten minutes. I'll do that first.'

*

Cathy knocked on her mam's front door. Although she had a key, since Jimmy had changed the locks and put double bolts on, it was like Fort Knox to get in. Better safe than sorry though, just in case Jack tried to come back.

Her mam was pleased to see her and she looked a bit brighter than when Cathy had last been home. Hair freshly washed and her clothes were clean and tidy, as was the sitting room. Cathy explained about the auxiliary nursing positions at the Royal and her mam's face lit up with a big smile.

'So what you're saying is that my dream isn't completely over, I could still be a nurse?'

'You could, Mam. It's quite basic nursing, no injections or administering medicines or anything like that, but you'd be on the wards, mixing with all the other staff and looking after the patients' needs. Helping to feed those that can't do it for themselves, bed baths, making up beds, that sort of thing. What do you think? I know you've still got Lewis's to go back to, but maybe it's time for a change. The hours can be sorted to suit your needs so that you can still take care of the kids. I asked at the office after I'd spoken to the auxiliary nurse on my ward and they suggested you wrote in with your details and they'd send out an application form.'

'Thank you, Cathy love. I will definitely do that. I feel ready for a change. I really do.' She patted her hair into place. 'And talking of change, Johnny is coming down from Blackpool this weekend and he and Jimmy are going to sort the rooms out for me. The front room will be a sitting room again now Jack's gone and I'm moving back upstairs into the bedroom, and Roddy will go in Brian's room. If you ever want to stay there's a big sofa coming down in the van with Johnny, courtesy of his mam. She's having a new one. It'll fit nicely in the front room and it'll be comfy enough for you to sleep on for the odd night.'

Cathy smiled. Her mam's face had lit up at the mention of Johnny. It would be nice for her to see him again. New beginnings all round by the looks of it. Fingers crossed. 'I'd better get back to Gianni, Mam. He's had a burglary while the house has been empty.'

'Get away! I've kept my eye on the place and so has Millie.'

'Well, whoever it was broke in at the back door, so you wouldn't have seen anything. The police will probably be coming and I need to get us some milk. I'll see you tomorrow before I go back to the hospital.' She gave her mam a hug and dashed off up the street towards Lark Lane.

*

When Cathy got back and made them coffee, Gianni told her what the police had said on the phone. 'I felt a bit of a fool, explaining to the person who answered that I'd been burgled, but there was nothing missing, and all the thief had done was ransack the pantry and eat several tins of soup and beans,' he said. 'But I also told them my main concern was that the burglar would be back later and might prove violent if I had a go at him. Anyway, they're sending an officer within the hour.'

'Right, well we could do with a bite to eat.' Cathy handed him a mug.

'Yeah, I suppose we could.' He hadn't given food a thought. All he'd had on his mind was making love, although he thought now that maybe they'd eat out later.

Cathy sat down on the sofa and stretched out her legs. 'I'll finish my coffee and then go and get us a fish supper.'

'I'm sorry, Cathy.' He sat down next to her. 'What a pain! I'll swing for the bastard, spoiling our precious time like this.'

She put down her mug and took his from him, moved into his arms and kissed him. 'Once the police have visited and the door's been made secure, we'll have a good time, I promise.'

'Will we?' He looked at her, lips twitching with the beginnings of a smile. 'Why, what do you have in mind, Nurse Lomax?'

She laughed. 'Oh, seems like you've guessed, you bugger.'

'You haven't?' His eyes lit up.

'I have.'

'And the black stockings?'

'*And* the stockings!'

He grinned and squeezed her. 'Will you give me a bed bath, Nurse Lomax?'

She laughed. 'Cheeky. I knew that would put a smile on your face.'

*

Jack stood on the corner and stared as the police car left the street. Fuck it, the biker was back, and he'd bet his life he'd brought that bitch Cathy with him. He shoved his hands in his jacket pockets and shuffled up the opposite pavement towards the house, taking care to keep his head down in case any nosy neighbours were spying out of their windows. He'd been using the backs of the houses on his visits. He stopped and stared across at the biker's front room window. The lamps were on. Very cosy. He saw the biker stand up and pull the curtains across, but not before Jack caught a glimpse of Cathy as she got to her feet and flicked her hair back over her shoulders.

The room was plunged into darkness and seconds later the bedroom light came on and then the curtains were pulled across up there too. It appeared that Alice had no objections to her daughter spending the night with him. He shook his head and turned to walk back the way he'd come. He'd be unable to get into the house again, no doubt, as the biker would get the door fixed if he hadn't already. It had been good while it lasted: a warm, dry bed, food, somewhere decent to have a shit and a bit of a wash. Now he'd have to go back to the abandoned shed on the nearby allotments, sharing it with bloody courting kids. Well, he'd soon get rid of them; nothing like a bit of indecent exposure at the window to get the girls screaming. It had made him laugh as he'd hidden round the back while they hurriedly pulled on their knickers and legged it.

The shed was empty when he got there, the door swinging open. His old blanket was on the floor on top of some filthy sacks next to a used rubber johnny. Dirty little buggers, couldn't even clean up after themselves. He kicked it outside, manoeuvred the door into place and pushed the old broken armchair behind it. He flopped down, lit a fag and covered himself with the threadbare blanket. How had he ended up like this? It was that little bitch's fault. She'd never liked him from the day he'd married Alice. Snooty little madam, always looking down her nose at him. Spoiled by that bloody grandmother of hers. And Alice, what a waste of space she was, falling pregnant at the drop of a hat. Stupid bloody cow. He should divorce her and clear off. He would if he had the money. His thoughts turned back to Cathy and how the biker would probably be screwing her senseless right now. The heat rushed to his groin as he remembered her on her front beneath him, pert little arse in the air. He slouched further in his chair and shoved his hand down the front of his grubby trousers. He was lucky he could still get a hard-on after the kicking the biker had given him. All he needed now was a willing bint to practise on to make sure it stayed up, a permanent roof over his head and to get even with that little bitch once and for all. He knew which room she lived in at the nurses' home. He'd seen her, flaunting herself with her mates, prancing about in their uniforms in front of the window. They were all asking for it, and he liked the look of the little blonde tart she hung around with, too.

*

'I need to call Gran later,' Cathy said as Gianni brought a tray of tea and toast upstairs.

'Okay, we'll have breakfast first and then pop over and see her if you like. The joiner's putting a new pane of glass in the back door and he's changed the lock as well. I must remember to take the key out the next time we leave the house.'

They sat with their backs against the pink velvet headboard and ate their breakfasts. Gianni had moved into Sadie's old room and it was nice to have the space of a double bed. He'd told Cathy he might ask a mate to be his lodger and to share the bills, but hadn't bothered so far. Perhaps as well, Cathy thought, smiling as she surveyed the room with their clothes scattered in all directions. After the police had taken a statement, dusted the kitchen for fingerprints and gone away, that uniform had done the trick and cheered him up no end. Their lovemaking had been noisy, to say the least. He'd taken more photos of her in various states of undress and this morning he'd shown her some of the sketches he'd done from previous photos.

'Those sketches,' she said now. 'Don't let anyone see them, please.'

'I won't. They're for me, so I can dream about you and I don't have to use my imagination too much. I think they're fabulous, you are so beautiful, and you've no idea.'

'Yes, well…' They *were* fabulous, she had to admit. He'd copied the poses well, and now, at full sketchpad size, they looked classy, not like rude pictures at all. He made her look amazing. She still felt a bit uneasy in case they fell into the wrong hands, but she was proud of them *and* her body, and how good she looked. He still wouldn't show her the special drawing he was working on. He wanted her to wait until he'd finished it. She wondered what it could be that he wanted to keep it such a secret from her.

'Right,' Gianni said, picking up the tray. 'I'll wash up, you call your gran and tell her we're popping round and then we'll go out for a couple of hours. Shall we meet up with Debs and Davy at dinnertime?'

'Oh, yeah, let's.' Cathy slid out of bed and made her way to the bathroom.

*

There was no reply from her gran's number, so Cathy went to get ready while Gianni paid the joiner and tidied up the mess in the kitchen.

They rode into the city and had a wander around the shops. In Epstein's music store they listened to a couple of records in one of the booths and he bought her a copy of Buddy Holly's long-playing record *The "Chirping" Crickets*.

'I've been saving up for this,' she said, kissing him. 'Thank you.'

'I know. You've told me enough times,' he teased, hugging her close.

'I haven't,' she protested. 'I *was* going to buy it but I never seem to have any spare money.'

'Well, if I can't treat my fiancée to a gift now and again, it's a poor show,' he said as they left the shop. 'Right, shall we head over to the Kardomah?'

Cathy looked at her watch. 'Yep, Debs and Davy will be on their dinner break by now.'

*

Debbie and Davy were already eating when Gianni and Cathy got there.

'Mind if we join you?' Cathy said. She frowned. The pair looked a bit solemn and Debbie's eyes were red-rimmed.

'Feel free.' Davy moved up to let Gianni sit down. 'Nice to see you both.'

Cathy took the seat next to Debbie. 'You okay, Debs?' she asked, giving Debbie's arm a little squeeze.

Debbie nodded and then looked away as her eyes filled with tears. 'Not really,' she muttered.

'What's wrong?' Cathy raised an eyebrow at Davy, who was pushing his chips around his plate. He sighed and glanced over at Debbie.

'Shall I tell them or do you want to?'

Debbie wiped her eyes with a hanky. 'You tell them.' She sniffed.

Davy shrugged and pulled a slip of paper from his pocket. He gave it to Cathy. 'We've, er had a bit of news. And it's knocked us sideways.'

Cathy looked at the paper and gasped. It was the result of a positive pregnancy test from the local chemist. 'Oh, Debs!'

'I know,' Debbie wailed. 'My mam and dad'll go nuts.'

'I don't think mine will be too happy either,' Davy said, shaking his head.

'What you gonna do?' Cathy put her arm round Debbie's shoulders.

'We'll have to get married,' Davy said. 'Though God knows how we'll afford it or where we'll live.'

Gianni chewed his lip and looked at Cathy, who nodded. She knew what he was going to say. 'If it's any help,' he began, 'my place will be empty for a few months. I mean, it's not Buckingham Palace but it's a nice little house. You're more than welcome to stay there.'

Davy stared at him, open-mouthed. 'Do you really mean that? We'll pay you rent, of course. Oh, mate, you've no idea how grateful I am – we both are,' he added as Debbie nodded. 'It might make things a bit easier when we tell our folks, if I can say we've got the promise of a roof over our heads. Debs is terrified they'll make her give the baby away.'

'Your mam and dad would never do that,' Cathy said.

'They might,' Debbie sobbed. 'Andrea Carter down the road's gone to a mother and baby home in Hoylake and my mum was gossiping about her to our next-door neighbour and I heard them saying it's for the best.'

Davy reached for her hand across the table. 'I promised you last week I wouldn't let that happen,' he said. 'Now we know for sure, we'll tell them tonight and organise a wedding. Would you two stand for us? I mean, I know Debs will ask Cathy anyway, but would you do me the favour of being my best man, Gianni?'

'I'd be honoured, mate,' Gianni said, shaking Davy by the hand.

'I'll find out what days I'm off in the next few weeks,' Cathy said. 'It'll be a Saturday, won't it?'

Debbie nodded. 'The sooner, the better. I'm already three months gone. We kept hoping it would go away, but well, it doesn't, does it?' She sighed and blew her nose.

'No, indeed,' Cathy said, looking meaningfully at Gianni. They'd been lucky so far, *very* lucky. There was no way they'd be taking chances again; she'd make sure of it.

'You'd actually be doing me a favour if you moved into the house,' Gianni said. 'I've been broken into. Someone's been dossing down there. Got the locks sorted now, but it'd be good to know it was being taken care of while I'm away.'

'So it'll all work out well,' Cathy said. 'You'll be fine, Debs. You and Davy will make great parents.'

'Let's hope *our* parents are as positive as you two,' Debbie said, smiling through her tears.

Cathy smiled and got to her feet. 'I need the loo. Debs?'

Debbie nodded.

'I'll order something to eat,' Gianni said. 'What do you want?'

'Cheese on toast, please.'

Cathy led the way to the ladies'. 'So, how do you feel?' She leaned against the sink and stared at Debbie.

'Sick and fainty, most of the time.'

'No, I mean, how do you *really* feel? About well, getting married and stuff. You know, getting tied down at seventeen.'

Debbie shrugged. 'Terrified, but excited as well, in a way. I hope Davy doesn't think I've done it on purpose to trap him. He hasn't said he does, but what if he clears off and leaves me in the lurch?'

'Don't be daft. Davy loves you. Marriage might not have been in his plans just yet, but he won't let you down.'

Debbie sighed. 'It's so good of Gianni to let us have the house for a while.'

'Yeah,' Cathy said. 'Be good to have someone living there while he's away. It'll work out fine all round.'

'We'll put our names down for a council house,' Debbie said, squinting in the mirror and rubbing at the mascara smudges on her cheeks. 'Then when you and Gianni are ready to get married we can move out.'

Cathy laughed. 'No rush, Debs. It'll be years off.'

Debbie smiled wryly. 'That's exactly what *I* thought.'

Chapter Twenty-Two

March 1958

Gianni sat back and opened the packet of sandwiches Cathy had made. He was struggling to keep his eyes open as the train rattled on through strange towns and open countryside. They'd had a late night and then he'd been up early to drop Cathy at the hospital in time for her morning shift. In just over an hour he'd be in Southampton and looking for his dad. He felt nervous, apprehensive and excited all at the same time. The Easter Fair should be easy enough to find. The town hall guy had told him it pitched up on Southampton Common the weekend before Easter. He'd jump in a taxi and go straight there. He finished his snack and closed his eyes, thinking back over the last few weeks. Davy and Debbie had arranged their wedding for the second week of April to coincide with Cathy's weekend off.

He didn't envy Davy and Debbie's predicament, parenthood thrust on them when they'd only had a few months together as a couple. Once Cathy finished her training he hoped they'd do some travelling, maybe even emigrate to Canada or Australia before they settled down to start a family. The last few times they'd made love, Cathy had been a bit on edge and made it clear that he needed to be extra careful as she didn't want to end up like Debbie. He looked at his watch. Nearly there. He gathered his things together and reached his holdall down from the overhead luggage rack, his palms sweaty and his stomach lurching as the train clattered over the last few miles of track towards the station.

*

Cathy took off her uniform, wondering if Gianni had got there safely. He said he'd call her after seven if he could find a phone box nearby. It was only five thirty, time enough for a wash and a lie-down before tea. Karen was knocking on for her. Ellie was on nights this week but had said she'd try to join them for tea if she was awake in time.

Cathy pulled on clean jeans and a T-shirt and sat down on the bed to open the letter she'd found in her pigeonhole. It was typed on hospital headed paper and was a warning issued to all staff that they should not walk alone to the dining room late at night, and to always make certain they were in pairs when they came off late duty, as the prowler had been spotted several times recently, hanging around various areas of the hospital grounds, and mainly near the nurses' home. All staff were urged to be vigilant and make sure no ground-floor windows were left open in unattended rooms and also to check that fire doors at the top of the fire escapes were kept locked from the inside at all times. Cathy felt a shudder run down her spine in spite of the comforting tone of the last couple of lines, which stated that regular security checks of the grounds would be made on an hourly basis. She jumped as someone knocked on her door. It was Karen.

'Bit scary, isn't it?' Karen said when she saw the letter in Cathy's hand. 'Pity the nurses' home isn't directly attached to the hospital. It's that dark stretch of road in between that gives me the creeps. I know it's not far, but still…'

Cathy nodded. 'Yeah, we need to be careful. Glad I'm not rostered on nights for a few weeks. At least it's safe enough in the day with so many people around.'

'Did Gianni get off all right?'

'He did. He was really nervous this morning. It's such a big thing for him. I hope the family doesn't reject him. I don't know how he'd cope with that.'

'There's no reason why they should,' Karen said. 'His dad didn't leave Gianni. From what you say about the letters and cards Gianni found, his dad has spent years wondering about him. Anyway, how was your last night together? I was on pins in case Sister Judge realised you were out.'

'Sorry.' Cathy smiled. 'But it was good, thanks. Don't know what we'll do when Davy and Debs move in. They'll need Gianni's little room for the baby when it arrives.'

Karen raised an eyebrow. 'Don't envy them. Poor kids. Not even eighteen and tied for life. Not for me, thanks.'

'Nor me.' Cathy twisted a strand of hair between her fingers and crossed the fingers of her other hand behind her back.

'Right, come on.' Karen jumped up. 'I'm starving. Let's go and get something to eat.'

*

Gianni clambered out of the taxi and stood on the pavement, looking across the road to where the fair was being erected. A man was barking orders at a couple of youths who were setting up the dodgems. A further group of men were erecting a Ferris wheel on the far side of the common next to a smaller wheel that was already being tested, the cars swaying in the slight breeze as the wheel turned slowly round. Everybody looked so busy. Would he get in the way if he ambled across to look around? Maybe he should find a café and grab a coffee and a bite to eat and then present himself in an hour or two. The fair wouldn't be up and running fully until tomorrow, according to a poster he'd seen near the station. He decided on the coffee and then he'd make his way over to the common. There was a café nearby and he took a window seat and placed his order with the young waitress, who eyed him up and down as she licked her pencil suggestively and wrote on her pad.

He tucked into his double egg and chips, watching the goings-on across the road with interest. Would he be part of it one day? Did he want to be? He felt a bit of guilt as he thought about his mam and how she'd wanted so much more for him than fairground life. But the thoughts of travelling all over the country appealed. He hated being tied to one place.

Outside on the pavement again, and feeling slightly less nervous now he'd stilled his churning stomach with a meal, Gianni crossed over and made his way on to the common, passing between the huge silver caravans and brightly coloured, tarpaulin-covered trailers. Right across, near the smaller of the two Ferris wheels, he could see a huge yellow truck with 'Romano's Wall of Death Motorcycle Stunt Show' painted on the side in big red letters. A group of men were unloading and shouting at each other above the general racket and one man was giving instructions. The man turned and smacked a dark-haired, olive-skinned lad of about twenty round the head and swore at him. He spoke English with a foreign accent. Gianni grimaced and hoped that wasn't his dad.

The young lad turned and stared at him as he approached. 'Get lost, you. We don't open until tomorrow.'

He was immediately smacked across the head again. The older man nodded at Gianni. 'Can I help you?'

'Er, I'm looking for Luca Romano,' Gianni said, staring at the tall, slim man, who had dark hair streaked with grey and the same facial features as the young lad, including high cheekbones and a dimple in his chin. They were just like his own and they both had the same dark brown eyes too.

The man pointed to a caravan where another man of similar build and colouring was standing by the open door talking to a woman with long black hair. 'That's Luca, over there.' He turned back to shouting instructions and Gianni walked over to the man by the caravan.

The man turned and frowned and took a step backwards, almost falling over the woman, who gave him a shove on the arm. His mouth fell open and he stared at Gianni, who could feel his face getting warm at the close scrutiny.

'Luca Romano?' he managed as the man clapped a hand to his mouth, his face draining of colour. The man nodded; his eyes were wide.

'Gianni?'

Gianni nodded, swallowing hard. His dad; and he'd recognised him. But how could he not? They were two peas in the same pod, with only eighteen years between their ages.

Luca shook his head and turned to the woman, who was looking at him questioningly. 'This is my boy, Maria, my son, Gianni.' He flung his arms round Gianni and gave him a bear hug. 'I can't believe it. Come inside, come inside.' Luca pulled him up the caravan steps into a spotless interior. 'I've thought about this moment ever since your mother took you away. Oh, my heart's thumping so hard I can hear it.'

Maria followed them inside, took Gianni's bag and put it by the door. 'Sit down. I'll make some tea.'

Gianni felt a lump in his throat that threatened to choke him. He'd found his dad! He couldn't believe it. He was shaking. So was Luca. They sat side by side on an upholstered bench seat in front of a dining table, staring at each other while Maria bustled around in the kitchen area. Luca's face broke into a wide smile and he shook his head. A knock at the door was answered by Maria and the man from earlier popped his head inside.

'Luca, you coming to give a hand now?'

'In a while. I've got a visitor. Come in, meet my boy. Gianni, this is your Uncle Marco.'

Marco's face was a picture as Gianni shook the hand he offered. 'Gianni? After all these years? I should have recognised the likeness, he's the double of you and me. I never thought we'd see the day, Luca.'

'Nor I,' Luca said. Maria placed two mugs of tea on the table. 'I'll go and help outside. You two need some time on your own.' She looked pointedly at Marco, who followed her, promising to come back later.

Left alone, Gianni relaxed and took a sip of tea. Luca got to his feet, rummaged in a cupboard and pulled out a bottle of brandy. He tipped a liberal amount into the mugs and smiled.

'I think we both need it,' he said, patting Gianni on the hand. 'How have you been? What brings you down here? How is your dear mother?' Luca's questions tumbled over each other and all the time tears ran down his cheeks. 'I never forgot you, son. Every day I wondered if I'd ever see you again. I'd no real idea where to start looking. I sent letters to your gran's address. I don't even know if Sadie got them. She did a good job of going to ground. For years I studied the face of every young lad who came to the fair, hoping that one day…' He stopped and sobbed into his hands.

Gianni slung an arm round his dad's shoulders. To hear him saying those things meant so much. To know that his father still cared and had never forgotten. 'I, er, I need to tell you about Mam,' he began, and told his tale and how he'd longed to find the fair and his family, but while his mam was alive he couldn't do it. He told his dad all about his life, growing up in Liverpool and his education, and also told him he was engaged to the girl of his dreams.

'I respect all that you tell me, Gianni. You're a good boy. And you're a credit to Sadie. I'm so sorry for your loss. I always loved your mother. But all those years of writing to her with no reply, I gave up hoping in the end. I had to move on. Maria is my lady friend. She's widowed. We live together here. I was never able to marry her because I was still married to Sadie. Maria has a daughter from her marriage. Eloisa is a bit younger than you.'

Gianni and Luca talked for a while longer and then Luca asked him if he'd like to stay and see how the fair worked.

'I'm in no rush,' Gianni said. 'I'd love to look around. I need to find a hotel for a few days though.'

'No hotel,' Luca said. 'You stay here with us, your family. We'll make room.'

'Great. Thank you,' Gianni said. 'I spotted a phone box on the edge of the common. I need to call Cathy to let her know I've arrived and I can't wait to tell her I've found you.' As he left the caravan to make his call, Gianni's thoughts tumbled over one another. He couldn't wait to tell Cathy his news. He felt sad that he couldn't tell his mam that he'd found Luca and that he'd been made to feel very welcome by the family. It was such a shame that so many years had been wasted, for all of them.

*

Cathy turned over to face the wall and pulled the covers up around her ears. She was finding it hard to get to sleep tonight. Gianni's excitement, when he called her, had come over loud and clear. She was thrilled for him that he'd found his family, but she felt apprehensive too. He had itchy feet, was always telling her he wanted to travel, and she had a sick feeling in her tummy that he'd go off with the fair and she wouldn't see him for months at a time. Ah well, there was nothing she could do about it. It was his life and she was tied to Liverpool for another two years, at least. She closed her eyes and was just drifting off when someone hammered on her door. She sat up, slid out of bed and grabbed her dressing gown. The clock on the bedside table said one o'clock. Who the hell was knocking at this time of night?

'Hello,' she called, her teeth chattering with fright. What if it was the prowler?

'It's me, Karen. Let me in.'

Cathy opened the door and Karen practically fell into the room, a look of panic on her face.

'Get dressed, quick,' she babbled, picking Cathy's jeans and sweater up off the chair and throwing them to her. 'We need to go across to the hospital. Ellie's been attacked. She's in a bad way, but she managed to cry out for help. One of the night staff just came over to tell me they've taken her to Accident and Emergency. She's asking for us.'

Chapter Twenty-Three

Jack slumped onto his chair and slugged the last of the whisky he'd stolen from the off-licence. The stupid owner had ignored him when he came in and climbed a stepladder, pretending to arrange Easter eggs on the top shelf. Serves the ugly woman right that he'd pinched it. She shouldn't have flashed her fat legs and varicose veins at him. She'd left the whisky standing on the counter right under his nose. He chucked the empty bottle into the corner, belched loudly and drew his old blanket up to his neck. That blonde nurse had been an easy target. It had been worth getting pissed-wet-through in the rain. He'd been waiting for Cathy, but she didn't seem to be on night duty, so any bird would have done. But they'd all been in groups or pairs tonight for some reason. He'd been about to give up and go home when the little blonde appeared in front of him as he'd rounded the corner. She had her head bent against the rain, cloak wrapped tightly round her body, and ran right into him.

She'd been easy to grab and haul down the unlit ginnel between the morgue and the laundry. A smack round the head, and the threat that he'd kill her if she looked at him, had stopped her screaming and frozen her into submission. He'd pushed her to the floor and knelt between her legs. The uniform and stockings turned him on; her flimsy lace underwear tore easily as he yanked at them. She was easier to handle than Cathy, didn't struggle and fight him off. As he pushed into her and felt resistance, he realised he was her first. The feeling of guilt lasted mere seconds and he banged away until the powerful release came and he struggled to stifle his grunts and cries. The sudden noise seemed to bring her to her senses. He'd hardly finished coming before she started clawing at his face, yanking his hair, screaming and yelling for all she was worth. He smacked her hard across the mouth, splitting her lip, pulled up his trousers and got away as fast as he could with his limp.

He sighed now, closed his eyes and enjoyed the feelings of satisfaction washing over him for the first time in weeks.

*

Cathy and Karen sat with Ellie all night. She'd been transferred to a side room on the Women's Medical ward and didn't want to be left alone. They were also given leave from their duties the following day to keep her company. The police had questioned her and also the two nurses who'd found her. The description they'd given of the man had been vague, as he'd been halfway down the road when they arrived. Ellie had bruises on her back and buttocks where she'd been thrown to the floor, and fingerprint bruises on her thighs and arms. There'd been bloodstained fingerprints on her thighs. The policeman who questioned Ellie said they probably weren't clear enough to use in their investigations but copies were taken nevertheless. They'd also taken samples from beneath her nails and the hair that was clutched in her hands. A police guard was now on full-time duty at the hospital.

'He wants stringing up,' Cathy said as she and Karen went to get a coffee while a doctor had a talk with Ellie. 'The evil bugger. She didn't stand a chance. She hadn't picked up the letter about being careful. Someone should have waited for her at break time though. The rest of the ward staff knew, but nobody warned her.'

'It's Sister Norton's fault for making her stay until that patient stopped puking,' Karen said. 'She should have taken over and let Ellie go with the others. I hope she feels really bad now. That bloody policeman questioning Ellie was a right one though, wasn't he? Asking her if she was sure it wasn't someone she knew, a boyfriend or something, like it was all *her* fault.'

'Yeah, no wonder women don't report sexual attacks,' Cathy said, glad now that she hadn't reported Jack after seeing the way Ellie had been treated. Covered in bruises and bleeding, her underwear in shreds, and still the police had room for doubt. 'Men get away with murder. Ellie's parents are taking her home for a few days. I wonder if she'll come back.'

'I don't think I'd want to,' Karen said. 'But then again Ellie loves her job and there's nowhere else near enough to her home to finish training. God, I hope they catch him soon. No one's safe while he's on the prowl.'

*

Gianni wiped his dirty hands down his jeans. He stood back and admired his handiwork. The wall of death had been erected and he'd helped. He felt a sense of pride as his dad patted him on the back.

'Maria's got the kettle on,' Luca said. 'Let's take a break.'

The fair was due to open at six. Gianni looked around at what appeared to be, to his eyes anyway, total chaos. Men running around, yelling at each other and swapping tools. How on earth would it be ready in time?

'It might not look like it, but in a couple of hours we'll be up and running,' Luca said, as though reading his thoughts. 'Trial checks of each ride and we'll be ready to roll.'

Maria handed over mugs of tea as they sat down on the caravan steps. They were joined by Uncle Marco and the young lad from yesterday, who'd been introduced to Gianni as his cousin, Alessandro. Maria's daughter, Eloisa, joined them and Maria brought out a plate of sandwiches.

Eloisa looked at Gianni from under a thick dark fringe. Her eyes, chocolate brown, like Maria's, made him think of a spaniel his granny once had. Her wavy hair cascaded over her shoulders, and she flopped down on the grass next to him, tossing back her locks, revealing a lightly tanned neck and cleavage. Her long floaty skirt and colourful matching top were almost see-through and Gianni could see she wore no bra as she bent forward to help herself to a sandwich, flashing him an eyeful. He caught Alessandro staring at him, a look of jealousy in his eyes, and Eloisa grinned in his cousin's direction. Was she teasing Alessandro, or were the pair involved? She turned back to Gianni.

'Have you enjoyed helping this morning?' She smiled, revealing perfect white teeth.

She'd be great to sketch, Gianni thought, and then shook himself and answered, 'Yes, I've loved it. I'm looking forward to later when the fair opens.'

'Has Luca given you a job for tonight?'

'Er, no, not yet.' Gianni looked at his father, who was deep in conversation with Maria.

'You can work with *me* then.'

'Doing what?' Whatever she did, Gianni wasn't sure it was a good idea to work with her. He sensed rivalry with Alessandro and didn't want to get involved in any rifts after less than twenty-four hours with the family. Eloisa was a flirty piece, as he'd discovered last night when Maria had cooked a meal and she had come in from her fairground duties. She'd stared at him as Maria introduced them, batted her lashes and licked full glossy lips. She announced she was going out after dinner, ignoring Maria's pleas that she stay in and get an early night as tomorrow would be a busy day. Later Gianni had been shown where to sleep. Maria and his dad had a bedroom at the bottom end of the caravan. It was private, with a door, but the other beds were bunks in the living area, made up from parts of the seating arrangement. Gianni had been comfortable and drifting off to sleep when Eloisa had stumbled in as though drunk. She'd ignored him – or simply thought he was asleep, he hadn't worked out which – and had stripped off, swaying and humming quietly, wiggling her curvy hips and firm little backside in front of him, before pulling a blanket around herself and flopping down on the bunk near the dining table. He'd struggled to fight the rush of heat to his groin and taken several deep breaths.

Now his dad came to the rescue. 'Gianni, would you help out on the wall of death tonight? You can man the pay box.'

Gianni could feel the grin splitting his face. He'd been hoping his dad would say something like that. He'd love a go on the bikes, but no one had suggested it yet, although his dad had been pleased when he told him of his love of biking.

'Better than hook-a-duck hoopla, eh, boy?' Luca grinned as Eloisa pulled a face.

'I hate duck hoopla,' she said, getting to her feet. 'You know I want to ride the bikes. But you always say no, it's not for girls.'

'Behave yourself and be glad you have a job,' Maria scolded as Eloisa stormed off in a flurry of floaty skirts. Maria shook her head and gathered up the mugs and plates. 'Wilful little madam. She needs a slap on her backside.'

Gianni felt inclined to agree but kept his mouth shut. He jumped to his feet. He'd bet Eloisa was a handful to deal with. If his cousin was giving her one, he didn't envy him. Well he did, she was a sexy little bird, but she'd probably be a right tease, all take and no give. Not like his Cathy, who loved to please him. An image of her in uniform flashed before his eyes and he checked his watch. Mustn't forget to call her later before the fair was in full swing.

As Gianni prepared to leave the caravan, dressed in clean jeans and a white T-shirt ready for his evening duties, he caught Maria staring at him. She half-smiled and then looked away with a slight shake of her head. Gianni shrugged and ran down the steps and strode across the common. He felt a buzz of excitement, and adrenaline pulsed though his veins. Earlier he'd watched his dad and Uncle Marco do a practice run on the bikes and then Uncle Marco and Alessandro doing a routine together. He was dying to have a go. Hopefully tomorrow they'd let him. The Everly Brothers' 'Wake Up Little Susie' blasted from the overhead speakers and the lads on the waltzer waved as he hurried by. Everybody was so friendly and had welcomed him like a long-lost brother. He breathed in the heady mix of aromas, engine oil from the machinery, the sweet sickly smell of candy floss and the pungent scent of frying onions. Both Ferris wheels were standing ready and waiting to carry the first punters skywards. Everywhere he looked – the ghost train, the waltzer and the colourful galloping carousel horses – stirred something in his distant memory. This was it; this was where he belonged, not living in a two-up-two-down terrace, and stuck in an office all day. He passed the duck hoopla stand and Eloisa gave him a smile. He smiled back and she licked those luscious lips and tossed her hair back. He felt a twinge but fought it and carried on his way. That shouldn't be happening. Cathy was his girl and he'd never cheat on her. He'd tried to call her earlier but she wasn't in her room. Sister Judge had told him she'd push a note under her door. If he got time he'd try again, otherwise it would get too late, she'd be in bed, and he'd have to wait until tomorrow.

*

Cathy picked up the piece of paper that had been slipped under her door. Damn it, she'd missed Gianni's call by ten minutes, according to Sister Judge's message. She'd rushed back to the nurses' home especially. She hated not being able to call him back. But she wasn't sitting in her room all night on her own on the off-chance he'd call again. It was unlikely anyway as he'd probably be helping out with the fair's opening night. She hurried back across to the hospital, looking over her shoulder, even though it was still light, and re-joined Karen at Ellie's bedside. Her parents were coming in later to take her home.

Cathy sighed as she looked at her friend's pale face. Ellie had told them earlier that a doctor had advised her to take a month off and rest. She'd broken down and said she might not come back at all. She didn't think she could face it until she was certain the man who'd raped her was behind bars. She was terrified he might have made her pregnant.

Cathy couldn't even bear to think about what Ellie was going though and had been unable to sleep last night. Every time she closed her eyes she saw Jack's face leering at her. She'd been so close to becoming a victim, like Ellie. There were so many evil men in the world. She was lucky Jack had gone away and she had Gianni to take care of her.

Ellie's parents came and the three friends said a tearful goodbye, promising to call each other regularly. As they waved Ellie off from the car park Karen suggested a walk to the chippy.

Cathy linked her arm through Karen's as they strolled up to the main road.

'I don't feel like staying in,' Karen said.

'Nor I, but we're back on duty tomorrow and we need an early night,' Cathy said. 'Let's just get some chips and go and watch a bit of TV in the lounge.'

'Bet you're missing Gianni,' Karen said. 'I don't know how you can let him go off on his own, Cath. You could be enjoying yourself and meeting his family. It's not as if he doesn't want you with him. Is all this honestly worth it? After what's happened to Ellie I'm beginning to think it's not what I want, after all.'

Cathy shrugged. 'I'm not even sure myself at the moment. We've had a shock and it's made us think differently. Next week things might look better. And yes, I am missing Gianni, very much. But he's back soon for Davy and Debbie's wedding.'

*

'What do you mean danger?' Gianni stared at Maria, who'd just told him she sensed danger around him.

Luca laughed and patted her on the backside. 'She's trying to put you off having a go on the bikes tomorrow. Take no notice of her, son. They're only dangerous if you act foolishly.'

The three were relaxing in the caravan with a drink after the fair's successful opening night. His dad had just told him he could try the bikes tomorrow and see how he fared. Gianni felt excited, more so than he'd ever felt in his life. If his dad thought he was good enough to train up, it could be the start of a new career.

'It's not the bikes.' Maria interrupted his thoughts. 'I saw it surrounding you earlier. And then I saw it again in my crystal ball. There is danger to the one you love. You should be with her, protecting her.'

Gianni frowned. Maria's face was deadly serious. But he didn't go in for all that mumbo-jumbo malarkey and crystal balls stuff. It was a load of rubbish, wasn't it? He'd laughed at Cathy when she suggested having her fortune told by Gypsy Rose Lee when they had a day in Blackpool last year. He'd bought her a pair of lucky black cats instead, which now resided on the bookshelves in her room at the nurses' home.

'Maria, you're putting the wind up my boy. Stop it now,' Luca said.

Maria shook her head. 'There is great danger. You should take heed of what I tell you.' She put down her empty glass and went into the bedroom, closing the door behind her.

Gianni frowned and looked at his dad. 'Can she *really* see things?'

Luca nodded. 'She's a Gypsy with second sight, comes from a long line of fortune tellers. But don't worry, Gianni, now and again she gets things wrong. Probably just the sherry talking tonight.'

*

Jack stood on Lark Lane corner, his cap peak pulled low over his brow, watching people going in and out of the post office on the opposite side of the road. Pension day and there were hordes of them, mainly women, dressed in the pensioner uniform of headscarf, belted raincoat, thick stockings and beige shoes. He smirked. What the fuck did the old bats think they looked like? And there she was, coming out of the shop with her friend from next door. He'd seen them on washing day, hanging over the fence yapping to each other. They both had handbags looped over their arms, purses in outstretched hands, begging to be snatched.

Why didn't the stupid buggers put them in their bags before stepping outside? They didn't think, heads full of bloody gossip and the blue rinses they'd be having at the hairdresser's later. They crossed the road and headed in his direction. He slipped round the corner and waited. He could hear *her* suggesting they have coffee in the little bakery café. Jack rummaged in his pocket and took out the stocking he'd pinched off a washing line. A quick glance around told him no one was watching him. He took off his cap and pulled the stocking over his head. He heard their voices getting louder and he stepped in front of them as they rounded the corner. He snatched both purses and Ma Lomax's handbag. The pair appeared shocked into silence for some seconds, giving him time to shuffle down a nearby back alley. As he picked up a bit of speed he heard them screaming and shouting. He limped across to another alley between the rows of terraced houses off Lark Lane. He stopped for a few seconds to catch his breath, removed the stocking, pocketed money from both purses and rooted quickly in the handbag, grabbing a set of house keys, before tossing the lot over a nearby wall and then hurrying as fast as his wooden foot would allow. He'd be in agony tonight now, but it would be worth it.

When he was certain no one was following him he slowed down. At the top of the next road he got onto a bus into town. He made his way to the Philharmonic pub and ordered a pint of bitter, pie and chips and twenty Park Drive. He sat at a table towards the back of the vaults and picked up a discarded *Liverpool Echo*, dated yesterday. Halfway down the front page was a report of the rape of a student nurse in the grounds of the Royal Liverpool Hospital. Police were looking for a man in connection with the attack, but the given description was vague and sounded nothing like him. Jack lit a cigarette, blew a cloud of smoke above his head and half-smiled. Life wasn't too bad; he'd got money in his pocket now, a clean shirt on his back from the same washing line he'd nicked the stocking from, along with underpants, socks and a pair of jeans that fitted him to perfection. A swim at the university swimming pool had freshened him up and he'd picked up a decent leather jacket that some fella had put over the back of a chair in the café area. He didn't stink like the monkey house at the zoo any more and was hoping the housing officer would take pity on him and give him a decent council flat when he went to his appointment to assess his housing needs tomorrow.

The barmaid brought his food across and pointed to the paper. 'Shocking, isn't it? Poor kid, she's only seventeen. No woman's safe while *he's* on the loose.'

Jack nodded his agreement and squirted brown sauce onto his plate. 'They should string the bastard up by the balls when they catch him,' he said and checked her left hand – no ring. 'Why don't you let me buy you a drink, love?' He patted her backside and she didn't smack his hand away. He knew she wouldn't. He could tell an easy lay a mile off.

She smiled and fiddled with a blonde curl that had escaped her French pleat. 'Thanks. I'm due to finish in ten minutes. I'll join you for a spot of lunch, if you like. You can share your chips with me.' She tapped away on her stilettos, wiggling her backside in her tight black skirt. Jack grinned. If he liked? He certainly did, and hopefully the tart had her own place. He'd had no afternoon delight since Sheila had dumped him.

Chapter Twenty-Four

Alice didn't know who was more excited, she or Cathy, as they met on the long green corridor outside the ward Cathy was working on. Alice was on her way to an interview for an auxiliary nursing position and Cathy was off to the staff dining room for her morning break. The phone call to the hospital and the form-filling she'd had to do had so far paid off and Alice felt more excited than she'd felt about anything for a long time.

'I was hoping I'd bump into you before I go in,' she said, giving Cathy a hug. 'I've been haunting the corridor for the last fifteen minutes. I'm feeling so nervous, but excited as well. I can't believe this is happening, Cathy. I never thought I'd ever get a chance like this.'

Cathy smiled. 'It's just what you need, Mam; a complete change. You already look tons better than I've seen you look for ages. Did you get the house sorted, by the way?'

'Yes, I did. Johnny's mam's sofa looks smashing in the front room and Johnny painted the walls cream as well. It's all nice and clean now, no traces of Jack Dawson anywhere.'

'It's good to have a fresh start, Mam. If you get this job, it'll be the making of you. By the way, Gianni has found his family. He's with them now.'

'Oh, love, that's good to know. Sadie thought she was doing her best by keeping things from him, but by all accounts Luca wasn't a bad father. It was the lifestyle she found worrying.'

'Hmm, I know,' Cathy muttered as she linked her mam's arm and walked with her to the office, where Alice had been told to present herself. 'I have a feeling I may have the same problem, given time. Gianni is mad about bikes. He takes after his dad in more ways than looks. He said seeing his dad was like looking in a mirror. Right, Mam, here we are. Good luck. I might not see you afterwards as I'll be back on the ward. But will you ring me from Millie's tonight and let me know how you went on?'

'Of course I will. I have a good feeling about all this. Like I'm finally coming out of a fog I've been buried in for years.' She gave Cathy a hug. 'You be careful outside at night, love. That attack on your young friend was shocking. I hope they catch whoever was responsible, and that Ellie recovers eventually.'

*

Gianni stood in the bottom of the barrel, watching his dad roaring around the tops of the wooden walls. He took a deep breath as Alessandro tapped him on the shoulder.

'You ready?' He pointed to his Indian Scout bike, which was being loaned to Gianni for the first ride.

Gianni nodded and wiped his sweaty palms on his thighs. 'As I'll ever be,' he said as his dad came to a stop beside him.

'Ride as you would your own bike,' Luca instructed. 'Go round the base first and ease yourself up onto the first struts and when you feel confident, climb gradually. Off you go, son, and take it easy.'

Gianni started up the bike and, as instructed, rode round the black and yellow pie-shaped wedges of the floor. He whizzed past his dad, uncle and cousin, loving the pull and feel of the bike, and then he was on the lower wall of the barrel, whizzing round and round. The buzz was the most incredible feeling and flooded his body with adrenaline. He climbed higher and higher and wondered if there'd ever come a time when he'd feel brave enough to stand on the pegs and ride without hands as Alessandro did. He looked up and was shocked to see he was almost at the top of the wall. As he thundered round and round he could see the faces of fairground workers watching him behind the safety barriers, flashing by in a blur. He rode down the walls and came to a standstill beside his dad. A cheer from above made him smile. They were all clapping and shouting 'Bravo!'

He dismounted, his legs like jelly, but the feeling in his head was pure elation.

'Well done, Gianni.' His dad pulled him close and Uncle Marco slapped him on the back. Alessandro's congratulations were cooler than expected, but when he glanced up and saw Eloisa looking down at them he understood why. She waved and blew him a kiss, ignoring his cousin, who looked at her with an unfathomable expression in his eyes.

'When you re-join us after your visit home we'll start you in the show at the next venue,' his dad said. 'You're a natural biker; born to it. But then I thought you would be with *my* blood coursing through your veins.' He paused, and then added. 'That's if you want to be part of the act, of course.'

Gianni nodded, too choked to speak. But what would Cathy say? He'd be away for most of the year. Then again, she was tied to Liverpool with her training; otherwise she could travel with him.

'The rest of this week you must practise as often as you can.' His dad's voice broke into his thoughts. 'We'll get you your own bike in time. For now you can share ours. There's a spare one if you fancy tinkering with it and giving it an overhaul.'

'Be glad to,' Gianni said. 'I do servicing on my own bike at home.'

'Then the spare is all yours.'

*

'You look lovely,' Cathy said, fastening a corsage of maidenhair fern and cream rosebuds to Debbie's jacket.

'Do I?' Debbie looked down at her coffee-coloured linen suit. 'Not really what I imagined I'd be wearing on my wedding day.'

'Maybe not. But you still look nice.'

'Does my hair look all right?' Debbie fussed with her auburn hair, which was sitting on her shoulders in a neat flick. 'I had it trimmed a couple of inches the other day. Doesn't look too short, does it?'

'Looks fine. Is mine okay?' Cathy shook her head and her dark hair swished from side to side, long and glossy, setting off the deep rose-pink of the silk fitted dress and matching jacket that she'd borrowed from Karen. Fortunately they were the same height and size and they fitted like a glove.

'It's lovely and you look dead glamorous. Not like me, all fat and frumpy.' Debbie's eyes filled.

'Mascara!' Cathy handed her a tissue. 'Quick, blot those tears before you get smudges on your cheeks. And you don't look fat and frumpy at all.'

'Just pregnant.' Debbie sniffed. 'Maybe I should have worn that corset Mam suggested after all.'

'Oh, Debs, no, be proud of your bump. You shouldn't have to hide it.'

A horn sounded outside and Cathy looked out of the bedroom window. 'The car's here. Davy's dad's done it up really nice with ribbons and flowers. It looks quite weddingy.' She was trying her best to cheer Debbie up. There'd been a falling-out with her parents over the wedding plans. Debbie's mam had wanted a church affair for her only daughter, with a white dress and all the trimmings, followed by a reception at her dad's golf club, but Debbie refused when the wearing of a tight corset to conceal her growing baby was suggested. Her mam didn't want anyone to know about the baby. They could tell everyone it had come early once it arrived, she told Debbie. But Debbie had put her foot down and she and Davy had booked Mount Pleasant Registry Office, to be followed by a small buffet for friends and family at the Philharmonic pub.

Debbie's mam said she'd be ashamed to be seen in such places and refused to attend both events. Debbie's dad, saying little, had given money to help the young couple and taken her mam away for the weekend so she wouldn't have to face anyone.

Cathy couldn't believe Debbie's mam was being so uptight about the whole thing. She'd always thought her parents were fairly liberal. Debbie had told Cathy she couldn't wait to live in Gianni's house and she and Davy had already moved most of their belongings in. They were spending their wedding night at the Adelphi Hotel courtesy of Davy's parents. Cathy was glad as it meant she and Gianni could spend one night together before he headed off tomorrow to re-join the fair.

Cathy held Gianni's hand throughout the short ceremony, apart from when the registrar asked who had the ring and he stepped forward and handed it over. The registrar pronounced Davy and Debbie husband and wife, and Davy swept his new bride into his arms and kissed her.

Gianni squeezed Cathy's hand. 'Can't wait for our turn,' he whispered.

Cathy squeezed his in return. 'It'll be ages yet.'

'You never know.'

'Yes I do.'

'We'll see.'

Photographs were taken outside the civic building and then the party made its way to the Philharmonic pub.

Davy's dad took charge of the drinks and everyone raised a toast to the bride and groom.

Cathy put down her glass and made her way to the ladies' and Debbie followed her. 'You feeling better now, Mrs Ayres?'

Debbie laughed. 'Sounds weird. But yes, much better thanks. Your turn next.'

'No chance, you're as bad as Gianni,' Cathy said with a grin.

As they made their way back to the function room, Debbie tapped Cathy on the shoulder. 'Don't look now, but you're being watched.'

'What?' Cathy made to turn but Debbie stopped her.

'By the bar,' she said. 'Only ever seen him a couple of times outside Lewis's, but I'm pretty sure it's him. The funny foot gives it away.'

Cathy felt a shiver run down her spine as she looked at the man standing by the bar with a pint pot in his hand. He looked different, had grown his hair a bit longer and now sported a moustache, but it was him. *Jack.* She felt her stomach turn as he nodded and raised his glass in her direction.

*

Jack took a swig of his pint and smirked. She'd recognised him. She looked fitter than ever and that pink dress showed off every curve. He had to have her, if it was the last thing he did. He drained his pot and banged it down on the bar.

'Another pint, my love?' The barmaid picked up his glass, filled it and, looking over her shoulder to make sure the landlord wasn't watching, pressed his money back into his hand.

'Thank you, Lorraine,' Jack said. 'What time are you finishing?'

'About three,' she said. 'What would you like to do?'

'What do *you* think?' He raised an eyebrow.

'Again? You're insatiable. I've never known a man like you.'

'Bet you haven't,' he muttered. She was a good sort, was Lorraine. Five years his junior, she'd taken pity on him when the council place he'd been offered was not suitable. A small flat up five flights of stairs, no lift and a long waiting list for anything on the ground floor was no good to someone like him. Lorraine took pity when he'd told her his made-up tale of woe, how his wife had chucked him out in favour of a younger, fitter bloke with no disabilities. She'd offered him a bed for a couple of nights, and he was still there. She was okay, liked looking after him and was a good lover, but her tits were a bit droopy and her stomach wobbled after having two kids, who now lived with their father. Still, he couldn't grumble. She fancied him like mad, her backside was firm and she wasn't bad-looking. He was fed, watered and could come and go as he pleased without her nagging him to do anything.

*

'What's wrong?' Gianni pulled Cathy into his arms and held her close. 'You look terrified.'

'Jack's at the bar,' Debbie said, patting Cathy's arm.

'What? I thought he'd pissed off good and proper. What the fuck is he doing back in the area?'

'I don't know.' Cathy's lips trembled. 'But don't start anything, Gianni. I couldn't bear it.'

'I won't.' He sighed into her hair to quell his murderous thoughts. Maria's warning about danger came back to him, but he couldn't say anything to Cathy about that or she'd panic like mad. He pushed it to the back of his mind and smiled reassuringly. 'Well, he's not going to come through here. It's a private party, so let's try and enjoy the rest of the day for Debs' and Davy's sake.'

She nodded. 'Shall we get a bite to eat? I'm a bit peckish now.'

He led her to the buffet table and watched as she picked up a couple of sandwiches.

'That's not going to fill you up. Have a sausage roll too.' She looked really shaken and pale. He'd been shocked when she told him what had happened to her friend Ellie, and pleaded with her to take care around the hospital grounds. He guessed it brought back memories of what Jack had tried to do to her. Maybe the attack on Ellie was the danger Maria had seen. A sort of general warning from 'up there' to be careful. Cathy had a lot on her plate at the moment; exams looming, and worrying about her gran, who'd been robbed of her pension in broad daylight recently. What was Aigburth coming to?

*

Alice opened the envelope and pulled out a sheet of headed paper. She quickly scanned the contents and let out a yell.

Cathy, who'd popped round for a quick visit and to see the new-to-Alice sofa, was sitting at the table with a cuppa. She jumped to her feet. 'You got the job, Mam?'

'I did. Oh I can't believe it. I don't start for a month, but that's good as I can give my notice in at Lewis's in a couple of weeks and then have a week free to get organised here. My uniform will be ready to collect that week too. They took my measurements when I had the interview. I suppose that's to save time and me running to and fro.'

'Your hands are shaking,' said Cathy, smiling. 'Sit down and have your tea before it goes cold. I'm so pleased for you, Mam.'

Alice looked at the letter again. 'I'll have six weeks of basic training and then will be allocated a ward.'

'We may end up working on the same ward occasionally while you're training,' Cathy said.

'Now wouldn't that be lovely. And as the kids get older I can increase my hours as well. I should be able to get nicely on my feet in a few months.'

'It'll be the best thing you've ever done, Mam.' Cathy finished her drink and got to her feet. 'Right, I'm off to spend a bit of time with Granny Lomax.'

'How is she? You know, since she was robbed.'

'A bit nervous these days. I think it's dinted her confidence.'

'I'm not surprised. I hope they catch whoever it was.'

Cathy poured the tea and Granny Lomax put a plate of bacon rolls on the table.

They'd just started to eat when someone knocked on the front door. Granny went to answer and came back followed by a tall, skinny policeman.

'Sit down, young man. Cathy, pour him a cuppa, love. Would you like a bacon roll?'

'Oh, no thank you, just the tea will be fine.' He sat down at the table and took out his notebook. 'I'm sorry we've taken so long, Mrs Lomax,' he began, refusing sugar and nodding yes to the milk. 'But as you know, we recovered yours and your neighbour's purses, *and* your handbag—'

'And what about him?' Granny interrupted. 'The robber. Did you catch him yet? As soon as I got back home I had my locks changed. I knew he'd probably got my keys. The joiner had to break in for me. Did you ever hear anything like it?'

'We haven't caught him, but fingerprints show a match to prints taken at a break-in not far from here, so we're pretty sure he's local.'

'I bet he's from that estate up the road,' Granny said. 'There are all sorts of wrong'uns up there.' She nodded towards Cathy. 'Her young man was broken into a few weeks ago while he was away.' She rattled off Gianni's road name and door number and the policeman looked up in surprise.

'That's the same address I have here.'

Cathy stared at the policeman as a trickle of fear ran down her spine. It was too much of a coincidence, but… 'Gran, what was the man that took your purse like?'

Granny screwed up her face while she thought about it. 'Well, like I told them at the station, I didn't really see him because it all happened so fast and he had one of those stocking masks over his head. But he was even taller than you, young man, and he was wearing jeans and a black leather jacket, a bit like the one your Gianni wears on his bike, Cathy.'

'So you didn't recognise his face or his voice?'

'No, love, like I say, his features were all distorted with the mask and he didn't say a thing.'

Cathy nodded and sat back on her chair. Odd how the same prints had been found at Gianni's and on her granny's purse, and that Jack had turned up again out of the blue and had been wearing a black leather jacket the other day in the pub. But then again, he hadn't been around when Gianni's house was broken into, so it couldn't have been him; unless he'd been lying low somewhere.

'What is it, Cath?' Granny frowned. 'You look worried, love.'

'Well, it might be nothing really, but I er, saw Jack Dawson on Saturday. He was in the pub where Debbie had her wedding reception.'

'Turned up again like a bad penny, has he?' Granny pursed her lips.

'Jack Dawson?' The policeman nodded. 'That name's familiar. People have put it forward for a few pilfering jobs around the area. But he's difficult to pin down. No known address. Which pub did you see him in?'

'The Philharmonic, in town,' Cathy replied. 'He's my stepfather, but he and my mam split up and he, er, he left the area, well as far as we know.'

'Thanks for the information, young lady. I'll go back to the station and see what my sergeant thinks. We'll be in touch, Mrs Lomax.'

'If you need to talk to Cathy, she's a nurse at the Liverpool Royal Hospital,' Granny Lomax said.

'Okay, duly noted. Bad business up there recently with that young nurse. Do you know her?'

Cathy sighed. 'I do, she's a good friend. We started our training at the same time.'

'Well I hope, given time, she makes a full recovery.' The policeman said goodbye and Granny saw him out and then called out that she was popping to the bathroom.

Left alone, Cathy felt that trickle of fear run down her spine again. Gianni's break-in, Granny's purse theft and Jack's reappearance: surely it was all too much of a coincidence.

*

Jack was stuffing himself with fish and chips in a quiet corner of the Philharmonic, looking forward to some afternoon delight with Lorraine when she finished her shift at three. He swigged down a mouthful of bitter and dipped a chip in brown sauce. He looked up as two coppers strolled in and walked to the bar. They spoke to the landlord, who nodded in his direction, and then they were standing by his table.

'Jack Dawson?' The tallest of the pair spoke.

Jack looked up. 'Might be.' He shifted in his seat.

'We'd like you to accompany us to the station to help with our enquiries.'

'Me? Why? Haven't done anything wrong.'

'Well in that case, sir, it won't take up too much of your time.'

Jack shrugged and got to his feet. Lorraine was looking questioningly at him. 'Won't be long, queen. See you back at the flat.' He walked between the two coppers to the waiting police car. How the fuck had they managed to find him? The only person who'd seen him in here, apart from Lorraine and the rest of the bar staff, was Cathy. He knew the biker wasn't around at the moment and that the young couple who'd got married were living in his house, because he kept his eye on things. He'd been hoping Cathy might have moved in on her own so he could pay her a surprise visit. But it wasn't to be and hanging around at the hospital wasn't safe any more; it was crawling with cops at night. He'd no chance of getting his hands on her at the moment. The little bitch and Ma Lomax must have done the dirty on him, putting two and two together over the robbery and break-in.

*

Jack slumped low in a chair in front of two eagle-eyed cops, one of whom had told him why he was there and read him his rights. He was also told that matching fingerprints had been found on the purses and in the house belonging to Mr Gianni Romano. He'd known he should have worn gloves, but he didn't have any. They'd taken his prints as soon as they arrived at the station. It was only a matter of time until they matched them to the ones they'd got on file.

'Breaking and entering, stealing money and terrorising elderly ladies are serious crimes, Mr Dawson,' one of the cops said. 'If found guilty they carry a custodial sentence.'

Jack remained silent and stared at the ceiling. If that was all they were charging him with then he could handle it. A few months behind bars at the most and he'd be out. After all, he'd not used violence in either crime. No one had been hurt and what were half a dozen tins of soup and a few nights' bed rest? The old dears had only yielded a few quid between them. It hadn't lasted that long. He didn't even get the chance to rob Ma Lomax's place because the old bat had already had the locks changed when he'd tried. He looked up as another copper came in the room and whispered to one of the seated cops, who got to his feet.

'Excuse me one moment,' the cop said and followed the other one out of the room.

Jack continued to stare at the ceiling, wondering what the fuck was going on now.

The copper came back into the room with a grim-faced detective.

'Jack Dawson, can you tell us where you were on the third of April?'

Jack shrugged. 'How the fuck should I know. What's this all about anyway?'

'Are you sure you can't tell us where you were, Mr Dawson?'

Jack sat upright and chewed his lip. Was that the night he'd screwed the nurse? He couldn't for the life of him remember.

But they couldn't prove it; he'd left no evidence and she wouldn't identify him because she'd kept her eyes tight shut the whole time. He shook his head. 'I don't know.'

The detective nodded. 'In that case I'm arresting you on suspicion of raping Student Nurse Eleanor Jackson on the third of April in the grounds of the Royal Liverpool Hospital. You have the right to remain silent, but anything you do say will be taken down and may be used as evidence in court.'

Jack's mouth dropped open. 'You can't pin that one on me. You've no proof.'

The detective smiled. 'I think you'll find we have all the proof we need, Mr Dawson. New evidence has just come in from our labs, one perfect thumbprint that matches identically to a thumbprint found on the purses and at the home of Mr Gianni Romano. Now all we need do is check it with the fingerprints we took from you earlier, and if we have a match, then we have our man. You'll be held in custody until further notice.'

*

Cathy let in Karen, who had hammered loudly on her door. She'd just been enjoying a five-minute snooze before tea. 'What on earth is it?' Karen looked positively manic.

'They've got him. The rapist, they've caught him. It's just been on the news that a man they'd taken in for questioning about other crimes has been arrested for Ellie's rape.'

Cathy sat down on the bed, her legs turning to jelly. Since speaking to the policeman at Granny's the other day, she'd had this feeling of impending doom. She just knew who it was. 'Did they give his name?'

Karen shook her head. 'No, they just said a local man in his forties, but they didn't give Ellie's name either. They referred to the rape of a Liverpool student nurse. Cathy, what is it? You've gone white as a sheet.'

Cathy started to cry, deep shuddering sobs that racked her body. 'I think I know who the man is. I have to go to the police station. Will you come with me? Don't ask me any questions until we get there and don't say anything to anyone else.'

'Of course.' Karen looked bewildered. 'I'll just go and throw some clothes on and order a taxi.'

At the police station, and after a brief explanation of why they were there to the desk sergeant, Cathy and Karen were shown into an interview room. A policewoman brought them cups of tea and they were joined by two policemen.

In between sobs, Cathy told them she wanted Karen to stay and hear what she had to say. She told them her suspicions. That she thought her stepfather was the man who'd raped Ellie and that he'd tried to rape her, but she'd been too scared to report it. And now, how she felt so guilty, because if she had reported it he might have been locked up and wouldn't have had the opportunity to rape anyone else. She also said that she feared it was her he'd set out to attack, that she believed he'd been stalking her, although it had only just dawned on her that the prowler at the hospital had been Jack Dawson all along.

Karen listened quietly without saying a word and Cathy was sure she'd disown her once they left the police station. After she'd signed a statement one of the officers thanked her for being brave enough to come forward. They said they felt they'd enough evidence to convict Jack. The girls were taken back to the hospital by police car with a warning not to discuss the case with anyone at the moment.

Back at the nurses' home, Karen went to the dining room and got them some tea and toast and they ate it sitting silently side by side on Cathy's bed.

Cathy knew Karen didn't know what to say. Her friend looked numb and shell-shocked, just like Cathy felt. The hospital authorities would need to be informed, but maybe the police would do that. What an animal Jack Dawson was. He'd hurt so many people. If only her mam had never met him. Hopefully, now he was in custody, it was finally over.

Chapter Twenty-Five

June 1958

Heart in mouth, Cathy watched as Gianni mounted the bike and revved up the engine. He looked up and smiled, before setting off round the barrel floor. He roared onto the struts that looked so flimsy to her, like they couldn't hold one bike, never mind two. She'd been introduced to Gianni's family earlier, including his cousin Alessandro, who was now also revving up ready to join him. She had to admit they looked the part with their dark hair, red satin Russian-style shirts and black leather jeans, like twins, almost. She clutched the edge of the safety barrier as Gianni rode higher and higher with Alessandro travelling just below him. The heady smell of fuel and rubber filled her nostrils as the bikes thundered up the walls. The gasps and cheers of the crowd as the pair rode side by side. She clapped a hand to her mouth when Alessandro stood up on the bike pegs and put both arms out to the side to cheers and shouts – and then Gianni rose and mirrored his movements. Cathy thought she'd faint at any moment. This was so dangerous, but at the same time she felt herself swell with pride and her heart felt like it would burst. She caught a movement to her right and saw a girl with long dark hair watching the boys closely, then realised her focus was firmly on Gianni.

Cathy felt a twinge of jealousy when the girl blew him a kiss as he got off his bike and looked up. But his smile and wave were for Cathy and that made her feel better. He was beside her in a minute and they watched his dad and Uncle Marco doing their routine.

'What do you think?' he said, pulling her into his arms and dropping a kiss on her lips.

'It's exciting, but I was terrified for you,' she said. 'Oh, God, Gianni, it's so dangerous. Okay, you looked great, but I had my eyes closed for some of the time. I couldn't bear to watch.'

She saw the dark-haired girl staring at her over Gianni's shoulder, a look of scorn in her eyes.

'What's *she* staring at?' Cathy said, nodding in the girl's direction.

Gianni laughed. 'That's Eloisa, Maria's daughter. She wasn't around earlier when I introduced you to everyone. She's desperate to ride as well, but Dad won't allow it. Eloisa, meet Cathy, my girl.'

Eloisa nodded, but didn't speak.

'Shouldn't you be on your hoopla stall?' he said.

Eloisa rolled her eyes. 'I'm taking a break. My assistant's looking after things.'

'Which poor soul have you roped in today?' Gianni teased.

Eloisa shrugged. 'See you later.' She walked away, but not before giving Gianni wistful glances over her shoulder.

'What was that all about?' Cathy said. The girl clearly fancied him and Cathy didn't feel too happy about it. They had an easy banter between them. He'd told her he shared a room in the caravan with Eloisa, but for some reason Cathy had assumed she was a much younger girl of around eight or nine. Gianni hadn't mentioned age and she hadn't thought to ask. 'She's got a heck of a crush on you.'

'Don't be daft.' He looked away, cheeks flushing slightly. 'Come on, let's get out of here while I've got a few hours off. They don't need me again until tonight's show. Dad said I could spend some time with you.'

He led her down the steps and out onto the field, his arm round her shoulders. They were close to the area of Sefton Park they'd come to when he'd taken her out on his bike and she'd got wet in the rain and dried off at his mam's. It seemed a lifetime ago now.

'Shall we go and sit under the trees for a while?' he suggested. 'Be a bit quieter than up here. It's bloody heaving.'

Cathy nodded. The loud music blaring from speakers – coupled with so many people talking at once, kids squealing, girls screaming as the lads on the waltzer spun the cars round – was deafening.

There wasn't a soul around, not even a dog walker, as they lay beneath a shady oak tree and Gianni drew her into his arms. The music had followed them, but quieter, and the Everly Brothers' harmonies were soothing.

He smiled. 'Do you think there's a chance we might get a night together while I'm up this way?'

Cathy chewed her lip. It had been ages. 'Where though? Debs has got your old room ready as a nursery, so we can't stay there. And I don't want to stay in the caravan if you're sharing with that girl.'

'It's only temporary. I'll get my own caravan soon. Dad's looking out for a decent second-hand one for me. I'd be quite happy with a VW camper van, or something similar.'

Cathy frowned. 'But what's the point? I thought you were only planning on being with the fair for a short time.'

Gianni flopped onto his back and stared up at the sky through the leaves. 'Dad's offered me a share in ownership of the show. He and I will own fifty per cent and Uncle Marco and Alessandro would own the other half. Alessandro thinks we could take the show on the road without the fair. We could do that when everything else is packed away for the winter months. Take it to Europe maybe.'

Cathy remained silent while she digested this news. 'And what about us?' she said eventually.

He shrugged. 'I'll see you as often as I can. Whenever we're within riding distance I'll come up to Liverpool.'

'So once or twice a year, Gianni?' she whispered, feeling close to tears. 'Because you're not going to be that close for most of it.'

He rolled onto his stomach and stroked her hair from her face. 'There's another solution.'

'I can't do it,' she said. 'And it's not fair of you to ask. You know how important being a nurse is to me. Why can't you just go back to your job? Why can't we be normal, like Debs and Davy?'

He laughed and shook his head. 'Only the other week you didn't want that. Kids and stuff and being tied and stuck in Liverpool for the rest of our lives. You agreed you wanted to travel when I suggested it. You said you were as keen to see the world as I am.'

'Yes, and I still am. But I have to finish my training first.'

He nodded. 'And while you're doing *that*, I can work with the fair. I can't go back to sitting in an office all day after this. I love it, the freedom, and the thrill of riding.'

'I guess we'll just have to get used to being apart,' she mumbled. 'It's been a long six weeks though. I really needed you when the police caught Jack. I just wanted to feel safe in your arms.'

'I know and I'm sorry I wasn't there for you. Shall I book us a hotel room for tonight?'

'Gianni, it'll cost a fortune. There's nowhere that close so it would have to be the city centre and it will be really expensive.' She was silent for a few seconds. 'I can probably smuggle you into my room after dark. But we'd have to be really quiet, although Sister Judge is away this weekend, so that'll make it easier.'

His face lit up. 'You sure it'll be all right?'

She blew out her cheeks. 'Not really, but I've missed you so much.'

He crushed her to him. 'Oh, Cathy, I've missed you too.'

Cathy looked out of her bedroom window. The blinds were down in the dining room. She and Gianni had come back together following the evening wall of death show. She'd led him round to the back of the building and told him to stay out of sight until he saw the blinds drop. She pushed the window up and looked out. He was standing further down, his back against the wall. She beckoned and he crept silently towards her and climbed up onto the dustbin below. One push and he was in. She yanked the window down and drew the curtains across.

'Phew.' She sank onto the bed and he sat down with her. 'That was easy. Getting you out will be the hard bit. If we time it so that all the early staff are on duty and before the morning breaks start, I should be able to let you out of the front door. Karen will probably knock on for me for breakfast, so she can keep a lookout. And it's quieter on a Sunday.'

He laughed and traced a finger down her face, circled her lips with it and then trailed it down her front. He unzipped her jeans. 'I want you right now.'

'You too,' she said, grinning.

They stripped each other and rolled together on the narrow bed, kissing and exploring. Gianni knelt between her legs, looking down with a mixture of love and lust in his eyes. He suddenly clapped his hand to his mouth.

'Shit, haven't got anything with me and I so need you.'

'We can't stop now.' Cathy chewed her lip. 'I need you too. Just be extra careful.'

A tap on the door at eight o'clock was Karen calling for breakfast. Cathy was already up and dressed and she let her friend in. Gianni was still in bed, hands behind his head and covered with a sheet.

Karen grinned as he smiled at her. 'Had a feeling you might have a visitor,' she said to Cathy. 'How are we going to get him out?'

'When everyone's finished in the dining room, you can keep a lookout in the corridor and I'll smuggle him out through the front door.' Cathy took a quick peep out of the window and dropped the curtains back down. 'The blinds are already up, so he can't go out the way he came in.'

Karen nodded. 'We'll bring you some brekky. I'll try and get you a bacon butty and a coffee,' she said to Gianni.

'Thanks. I'll get washed and dressed while you two are out. Why don't you both come to the fair this afternoon? It's the last day. Give Debs and Davy a call and ask them along too. Not seen them since the wedding.'

'We will,' Cathy said. 'I'll call them later.'

'You okay, Debs?' Cathy asked as Debbie's face screwed up and she clutched her baby bump.

'Yeah, little bugger's kicking my bladder again.'

'We're hoping Everton will sign him up,' Davy said with a grin, his arm round Debbie's shoulders. 'Right little goer, he is.'

'*She*,' Debbie said. 'I'm sure it's a girl.'

Cathy laughed. 'Well whatever it is, you'll love it to bits.' They were all standing at the top of the barrel awaiting Gianni and Alessandro's performance.

Karen was staring at Alessandro. 'Those leather jeans look great on him. And you say he's Gianni's cousin?'

Cathy laughed. 'He is, but Gianni says he's a bit moody.'

'Moody I can cope with if the body's as fit as your fella's. I liked what I saw this morning in your room.'

'Cathy! Did you sneak Gianni into your room?' Debbie smirked. 'You'll be getting fired.'

'It was a one-off,' Cathy said, feeling her cheeks heating. 'We hadn't seen each other for six weeks and we had nowhere else to go.'

'More than a one-off if you ask me,' Karen teased. '*She* can't stop yawning and *he* looks ready to fall off his bike. Poor bloke was knackered when we smuggled him out. Probably didn't get a wink of sleep.'

Cathy grinned and changed the subject as Gianni raised a hand towards her and revved up the engine. He'd told her his dad had given the bike to him and he'd worked on it, and now it was as good as a new one. 'Ready, everyone, here they go.' She held her breath as Gianni circled the floor area and then, riding round and round, rose up the struts; as he mounted the walls Alessandro followed him. Cathy clutched Karen's arm, her teeth chattering. It was so hard to watch, but she couldn't take her eyes off Gianni, who was smiling, totally lost in the moment. He loved it, as much as she loved her nursing. There was no way he was going to give this up for her. If she wanted to hang on to him, she might as well get used to the idea.

'Let's go on some of the rides,' Karen suggested when Gianni and Alessandro took a break and joined them.

'I think we're going home,' Davy said. 'Debs is a bit wiped out today. She needs to put her feet up for a while.'

'Come to my dad's caravan and have a rest there,' Gianni said. 'Maria will be taking her break soon and she'll make Debs a cuppa while we have a few rides on things.'

'Thanks,' Debbie said. 'Be glad when this little devil's out and I can reclaim my body.'

'How long now, Debs?' Karen asked.

'Three months. It's flown, hasn't it?'

'Rather you than me.'

Debbie laughed. 'Yep, I know what you mean.'

Gianni led the way and introduced them all to Maria, who got a cushion from the caravan and put it on a garden chair for Debbie to sit on. Debbie wriggled and made herself comfortable, the cushion easing the small of her back. Maria went inside and brought out a tray of tea things and a jug of cold juice and glasses. It was a hot day, but the caravan was situated in partial shade under lofty trees and made a good spot for a rest.

Maria pulled a thin ribbon from her pocket. 'May I?' She smiled and pointed at Debbie's wedding ring. 'I hold it over your tummy and if it circles it's a girl, or swings side to side it's a boy. That's if you want to know, of course.'

'Really?' Debbie said 'Does it work?'

'Almost always accurate,' Maria said.

'Feel free.' Debbie gave the ring to Maria and placed her hands by her side. Maria threaded the ribbon through it and held the ring out. From hanging completely still, it began to swing from side to side.

Davy leapt up with excitement. 'Yes, it's a boy! Told you.'

'Congratulations.' Maria handed the ring to Debbie and went back into the caravan, leaving them to celebrate.

Debbie shook her head. 'It's a girl, I'm sure of it. That's just an old wives' tale. See, if I hold it out over Cathy's tummy it'll do exactly the same.' Maria had left the ribbon tied to the ring and Debbie held it out over Cathy. But instead of swinging from side to side the ring began to move in a circle. Debbie laughed. 'See, and Cathy's not even pregnant.' She held it over Karen but the ring stayed still, and when she got to her feet and tried it on Gianni and Davy the ring still didn't move. Everyone looked at Cathy, who insisted Debbie do it again. She lay back on the grass as Debbie held the ring over her tummy. As before, it moved in a circle.

Cathy jumped up and laughed. 'Just shows you, it's an old wives' tale. Right, take me to the waltzer,' she said to Gianni. 'Karen, you coming?'

'No, I'll stay here for a while. Give you two a bit of time together.'

'Okay.' Cathy looked over her shoulder to see Alessandro making his way towards them. She smiled. Karen would chat him up in no time. 'Come on, you,' she said, grabbing Gianni by the hand and pulling him with her.

'I saw your face back there,' Gianni said, as they walked away. 'Did it put the wind up you?'

'Of course not. Silly old wives' tale. There's no way, we haven't seen each other for ages.'

'Apart from last night.'

'Oh, for God's sake, Gianni, you were careful.'

He shrugged. 'Yeah. But would having my baby be such a bad thing?'

'No, I love you. But I don't want kids yet and neither do you. You said so.'

'You're right, I don't, but *you* looked horrified at the prospect.'

'Pack it in,' she said, stopping to pull him into her arms. 'Let's just enjoy the rest of our day together.'

Chapter Twenty-Six

It was almost like old times, Alice thought as she took the girls and Rodney to Granny Lomax's. It was Sunday morning and her shift was due to start in an hour. She absolutely loved her new job. She had recently finished her training and was currently working on the Children's ward. Granny Lomax had been to see her after Cathy told her Alice was going to be a nurse after all. Now Jack was out of their lives she'd agreed to help with the children should Alice require it. During the week Alice coped fine, as Marlene still did a school pick-up and Rodney went to his minder, but weekends, especially Sundays, were a bit difficult. But Granny loved being involved with them and she and Alice were slowly building a relationship again.

'Here we are.' Granny had the door open ready and welcomed them all inside.

Alice smiled at the aroma of baking wafting down the hall. 'You've been busy,' she said.

'Just a cake and apple pie,' Granny said. 'And I've got a nice leg of lamb for dinner. What time are you finishing today, Alice?'

'Three o'clock,' Alice said.

'Then there'll be a roast dinner ready and waiting for you too.'

Alice smiled. 'Thank you. I shall look forward to it.'

'If you see Cathy tell her there'll be plenty if she wants to join us.'

'She's been on nights and the fair's near Chester, so she'll be seeing Gianni later today, I would imagine.'

Granny nodded and sighed. 'No doubt. I know she worries herself sick with this job he's doing. And rightly so after what happened to my poor Terry. But what can you do? They have to live and learn, at the end of the day.'

'They do,' Alice agreed. 'Right, I'd better be off. You lot be very good, or else.'

'They always are.'

Alice raised a disbelieving eyebrow and hurried up to the bus stop just in time to see the one she'd needed pulling away. Damn it. Sunday morning and the buses were few and far between. She set off walking down Aigburth Road in the hopes she'd get one at the next junction, coming down the adjoining road. She ignored the beeping coming from behind her until a van pulled up and someone shouted her name. She spun round to see Johnny leaning out of the passenger-side window of Jimmy's van.

'I didn't know you were coming this weekend,' she said, her stomach looping as he opened the door for her to climb up beside him. She had no choice but to sit half on his knee and half on the seat, but Johnny didn't seem to mind.

'I'm helping Jimmy with a bit of a job he's got on. I arrived late last night, but your curtains were closed and no lights on. Didn't want to disturb you and risk waking up the kids by knocking on the door. Then Millie told me you were working today.'

'I am,' Alice said as the van pulled away. 'I just missed my bus, so you two are a godsend.'

Johnny laughed. 'Are you around tonight? I'm staying until Tuesday.'

'Yes, and I'm off tomorrow.

'Great, we'll catch up then. Perhaps get out while the kids are at school and have a bit of dinner if you like. Now get your foot down, Jimmy, lad. Let's get this girl to work.'

Alice couldn't stop smiling as the van sped off up the road; and she was still smiling as she walked down the green corridor to the

Children's ward. Johnny made her feel happy inside, like Terry had done. It was good to feel that way again.

*

Cathy straightened her apron and followed Nurse Toomey, the senior she was working alongside, into a curtained-off cubicle. It was her first night in the Accident and Emergency department and her heart went out to the little lad lying on the bed, crying his eyes out. He looked like he'd been hit full in the face with a heavy frying pan. Swollen lips, missing front teeth; his chin was gashed and his right cheek purple with the start of a massive bruise. The young woman accompanying him was also in tears as she explained to the duty doctor what had happened.

'He was out on the park with his three brothers,' she sobbed. 'Barry's me youngest, only just eight. They were all daring one another to jump off the swings when they got to a certain height. They pushed Barry's swing too high and shouted "jump" and he did, but he landed on his face, chin-first. Just look at the state of him. I'll swing for them little buggers when I get home. They've not an ounce of sense between them.'

Nurse Toomey patted Barry's mother's arm. 'Don't you worry, we'll get him patched up and in a week or two he'll be looking as good as new. Now those are his baby teeth so he'd have lost them soon enough anyway to make room for his adult teeth. First of all we'll get that chin stitched up.'

The doctor nodded his agreement. 'When you've seen to his chin I'd like Barry to have an X-ray on his neck and head. He's holding himself a bit stiff and I just want to make sure there's no damage. He's in pain so we'll give him something for that, and I'd like to keep him here overnight so we can observe him. With him landing face-down rather than on the back or top of his head I don't think there'll be any damage to his skull, but we'll get that checked out as soon as the X-ray results are through. Right, I'll leave you in the capable hands of my nurses and I'll be back to check on Barry later.'

Nurse Toomey bustled around laying out sterilised instruments on a trolley ready to stitch Barry's chin. Cathy cleaned his wound and picked out tiny bits of gravel with tweezers while his mother held his hand and tried to keep him still. In spite of a numbing lotion dabbed on his wound, Barry screamed the place down while his stitches were inserted. Cathy held on to his other hand and squeezed it gently. The cubicle curtains swished aside and the doctor beckoned for Cathy to follow him.

'You go, Nurse Lomax,' Nurse Toomey said. 'Nearly done here and then we'll get Barry up to X-ray. Ambulance is just arriving. I can hear the bells.'

Cathy nodded, said goodbye to Barry's mother and dashed over to wait with the doctor while two ambulance attendants brought in a young man on a stretcher, his head and face swathed in bandages, and rushed him into a small room where a team was waiting to attend to him. The young woman who had come in with him, accompanied by a policeman, looked ready to collapse and Cathy helped her to a seat. She spotted a wedding band on the woman's finger and presumed she was the patient's wife.

'Name, Eddie Crawford. Age twenty-two. Motorcycle accident,' one of the attendants said. 'Head-first under an oncoming lorry.'

The young woman grabbed Cathy's arm. 'That's my Eddie. He was on his way home from a late shift. Will he be okay, Nurse? Please tell me he will,' she sobbed as the doctor and the attendants exchanged worried glances that Cathy saw but thankfully Eddie's wife didn't. Cathy could see no sign of life from the young man on the bed, no rise and fall of his chest, no twitching limbs, nothing.

'Nurse Lomax, take Mrs Crawford into the family room and get her a hot drink, please.'

'I want to stay with my Eddie,' the woman cried. 'Please let me stay.'

'We're taking him straight to theatre, Mrs Crawford,' the doctor said. 'Nurse Lomax will look after you.'

As her husband was whizzed away down the corridor, Cathy led Mrs Crawford into the family room, which she realised was the one she and Gianni had sat in on the night Sadie passed away. The room was thankfully empty. A tray was laid with tea things and a kettle was already bubbling on a small electric hob that sat on top of a wooden cupboard. Cathy knew this was a common occurrence, making tea for relatives.

'Is there anyone I can call for you so that you're not alone, Mrs Crawford?' Cathy asked, spooning sugar into the hot tea. She settled her onto a comfortable chair and handed her the mug.

'Tina, please,' the woman said. 'There is no one else. Just me, Eddie and our little girls, and I've left my neighbour sitting in with them. They were already asleep in bed when the policeman came and knocked on the door. Ones just over two and the baby is five months old. Will my Eddie be all right, Nurse? He looked a right mess, blood everywhere and all those bandages. His poor face was all smashed up and he's such a handsome boy.' She sobbed uncontrollably and Cathy took the mug of tea from her in case she dropped it and scalded herself.

Cathy pulled a seat closer to Tina and held her hand until the sobs subsided. She looked at the clock on the wall. It was just after ten o'clock. She wondered how long it would take to operate on Eddie, if that were even possible. She felt shaken to the core, thinking that this must have been how her mam had been when Cathy's dad Terry was brought into hospital following his motorbike crash. She thought about Gianni and his terrifying new career and felt sick inside. This could be her at any given time. Most bikers chose not to wear helmets, and definitely not for the wall of death. If only someone would make them compulsory! But, she thought, even though it would save some lives, many bikers wouldn't take any notice. Like Gianni. He couldn't see any danger. When he called her and she listened to his tales of daring, she always cried for ages after the call ended. All it would take was one slip and that would be it; a fall from the top of that barrel would break his neck. She could understand now why Sadie had left Luca. She'd probably never stopped loving him, but couldn't live with the daily anxiety.

A knock at the door broke her reverie and the doctor, accompanied by the policeman who'd accompanied Tina to the hospital, came into the room. The doctor shook his head as Tina looked at him with hope in her eyes. 'I am so very sorry,' he began, but the rest of his words were drowned out by Tina's hysterical screams. The policeman caught her as she jumped to her feet and her legs gave way. He sat her down again and spoke to her quietly.

'We did everything we could,' the doctor told Cathy. 'His head injuries were too severe for survival. Mrs Crawford, you are welcome to stay here for the time being and then the policeman will take you home.'

Cathy took a deep breath as the doctor told her to go and join Nurse Toomey again and he would stay with Mrs Crawford for a while. She got to her feet and gently touched Tina's arm. 'I'm so sorry,' she whispered. It didn't seem enough, but words were never enough at a time like this. Nothing anyone could say or do was adequate. She left the room before tears started to fall. Nurse Toomey was waiting for her and between them they prepared Eddie Crawford for the morgue. Cathy let the tears fall then. There was no stopping them. Even Nurse Toomey's eyes looked suspiciously moist and she'd been in the job for over twenty-five years.

'This never gets easier,' Nurse Toomey said, a catch in her voice. 'Such a lovely young man. Hardly a mark on his body, but his head injuries were devastating. He'd no chance of survival. And now we need to make him look as presentable as we can for his poor wife to say her goodbyes. We'll leave all the bandages theatre have put on in place and just keep a little of his face free. The worst will be covered then.'

Cathy nodded. She didn't think she could bear this side of nursing. If she was going to survive it, she'd need to toughen up a bit to get through the next couple of years.

Cathy flung her arms round Debbie as she let them in and led them into the sitting room.

'Davy's out the back tinkering with a moped scooter he's bought off a mate,' Debbie said to Gianni. 'Why don't you go and see if he needs a bit of advice while Cath and me have a catch-up.'

As Gianni left the room Cathy joined Debbie on the sofa and looked around. As Debbie had said, Davy had painted over the old-gold walls with cream and it looked fresh and clean. Alongside some of Gianni's mum's furniture were some new pieces. The mix of period and modern worked well with the new red and cream Laura Ashley curtains and cushions made by Davy's mum.

'It's lovely in here, Debs,' Cathy said with a smile. 'You've made it look really homely and it's nice that you've still got some of Gianni's mum's things too.'

'Yes, we think so,' Debbie said. 'As long as it doesn't make Gianni feel sad when he comes to visit us. So, how are you? You look a bit washed out, to be honest.'

Cathy sighed. 'Okay, I suppose. I've just finished a week of nights and they've been heavy going.' She told Debbie about poor Eddie Crawford and how she couldn't stop thinking about his sad death.

'Oh, his poor wife,' Debbie said, her hand flying to her mouth. 'And their babies. I wish Davy hadn't got that bloody moped now. I know there's no speed in it, not like a motorbike, but even so, he'll be vulnerable in traffic.'

'Now you know how I feel every time I think of Gianni on the wall of death. I don't know if I can handle a lifetime of worrying.'

Debbie frowned. 'What do you mean? You don't want to stop seeing him, do you?'

'To be honest I don't know what I *do* want at the moment.' Cathy twiddled a strand of hair round a finger and stared at the ceiling. 'I love him so much it hurts, but I can't stand this lack of time together and the constant worry of him having an accident.'

'You need to be with him,' Debbie said, folding her arms across her huge belly. 'Give the nursing up, get married and go off with him.'

Cathy shook her head. 'No, I can't. I love my career, just like Gianni loves his. Neither of us is prepared to budge on that, I'm afraid.'

Debbie nodded and heaved herself to her feet. 'I'll go and put the kettle on.' She waddled out of the room.

Cathy followed her into the kitchen. She could see the boys through the window, kneeling on the floor in the yard, heads close together, fiddling with an exhaust pipe. Her heart leapt as she stared at Gianni's profile. His handsome face, the aquiline nose, like Luca's, and his thick dark hair that had grown long and wavy since he'd stopped having regular haircuts for the office. He looked up as though sensing her watching, and waved, his dark eyes crinkling at the corners and the dimples in his cheeks deepening as his smile grew wider. How she loved him! But was it enough to get them through the next few years?

'Sorry?' She turned to Debbie, who'd asked her a question.

'I said, when's Jack's trial?'

'Next week but one,' said Cathy. 'The police told me he'll be going down for a very long time. He's pleaded guilty, apparently. Don't think he's got much choice, to be honest, but pleading guilty is probably the only decent thing he's ever done in his life.'

'Let's hope they lock him up and chuck away the key then. How's Ellie doing?'

'She's okay. She decided to come back and is getting into the swing of things again. She still has flashbacks, but at least she's recovering and thank God she wasn't pregnant. That's a huge blessing.'

'Yeah, it is. She was lucky there.' Debbie banged on the window and beckoned. 'Those two need to come in and get cleaned up and I'll put the tea out. I've made a cheese and onion pie, a bowl of salad and my own recipe potato salad, too.'

'Oh yum, sounds good. Quite the little housewife, aren't you?' Cathy teased.

'You reckon?' Debbie said with a grin. 'Don't think Davy would agree with you. Two of his work shirts have got iron-shaped burns in the middle of the back. Good job he wears a jacket over them.'

*

'So you expect me to ride all the way back to Chester tonight?' Gianni shook his head. 'I'm tired; I assumed I was staying with you.'

Cathy looked away from his gaze and he frowned and grabbed hold of her arms. 'Cath, what's wrong? You've been distant all the time we've been out. Yesterday you said you couldn't wait to see me again.'

'It's awkward… you staying here tonight, I mean.'

'Why? I can sneak out early again like I did last time.' He stared at her but she didn't meet his eyes. 'I get the feeling there's more to it than awkwardness. Have you met someone else? Are you trying to break it off with me?'

She shook her head, feeling sick inside at what she knew she must tell him, knowing it would break both their hearts. 'There isn't anyone else. I love you, but I can't do this any more, Gianni. Every time you leave me I get the feeling I won't ever see you again. That it's bad news every time the phone rings. I can't cope with it. It's affecting everything I think, say and do. I've got more exams in six weeks and I can't concentrate on my studies.'

'I see.' He let go of her and took a step backwards. 'So, everything we've said to each other, everything we've done, the ring I gave you, none of it means anything? Well thanks, Cathy; at least I know where I stand now.'

Tears poured down her cheeks and she turned her head away as he looked closely at her.

He put a finger under her chin and tilted it. 'Why are you crying if you want rid of me? It doesn't make sense.'

She didn't answer and he continued, 'I can't give up the fair. Please don't ask me to. I'm happy for you to continue nursing and we'll get together when we can, but if that's not enough for you, I understand.'

'I'm sorry, Gianni,' she whispered, 'but it's not enough any more. Take care riding back.'

He took a deep shuddering breath, his face pale and his voice breaking as he spoke. 'Oh, I'm not going all that way tonight. I'll doss down at Col's or Nigel's and take off first thing, like I'd planned to do if I'd stayed here.'

'Okay, well, I'll see you around sometime.' She wiped her tears away with her fingers.

'You won't. If this is goodbye, then it's goodbye for good.' He grabbed her, kissed her on the lips and squeezed her like he'd never let her go.

He jumped on his bike and rode away without a backward glance, tears blinding him. That was the last thing he'd been expecting tonight.

*

Cathy watched Gianni roar away as the tears tumbled down her cheeks. She hurried into the nurses' home and ran upstairs to Karen's room. Karen and Ellie were ready for bed, sitting side by side with mugs of tea, as Cathy burst in.

'What wrong?' Karen gasped, putting down her cup and helping Cathy onto the chair beneath the window.

'It's over,' Cathy wailed. 'We've split up.'

'What? He's dumped you? The bastard!' Karen exclaimed.

'He hasn't,' Cathy sobbed. 'It's *me* that's dumped *him*.'

'You *are* joking?' Karen said. 'You want your bloody head feeling? Why have you done that?'

'Because he won't give up the fair and I can't handle not seeing him and worrying about him any more.'

Ellie shook her head. 'Then give up nursing and go with him, you daft thing. He adores you. Why would you choose to stay here, Cathy? You don't realise how lucky you are to have such a lovely and caring boyfriend.' She sat back against the headboard and folded her arms. 'I think you're bloody mad.'

'She is,' Karen chipped in. 'Bloody barking if you ask me, to choose this place over Gianni.'

Cathy shook her head. 'It's not just this place though, is it? It's the whole thing; I can do whatever I want when I've finished training. But if anything happened to Gianni and we had kids, what then? I can't run the risk of not being able to support myself. I saw what that did to my mam.'

'Yeah, well,' Karen said, shaking her head slightly as she looked at Ellie.

Cathy nodded to show she understood not to mention Jack's name. 'Right,' she said and got to her feet, feeling a sudden need to be alone with her thoughts and tears. 'I'm off to bed. I'm on an early tomorrow.'

'Night, Cathy.' Karen gave her a hug. 'A good night's sleep might make you feel differently and you'll change your mind.'

'I won't.' Cathy left the room and closed the door quietly behind her.

*

Gianni lay on his makeshift bed in the caravan, looking at the special sketch he'd been working on. It was taken from an old photograph of his mam, Alice and Millie just after the war and had captured the very essence of their youth. He'd planned to get two copies done and have them framed and give them to Alice and Millie on his mam's birthday. But that may mean bumping into Cathy if he went back to Lucerne Street and she was visiting. It had been a week since she'd broken off their engagement. He'd been so tempted to call her but had resisted. What was the point? She'd made her feelings quite clear. She couldn't handle his lifestyle. Leaving the fair for him would mean giving up his family after being so long without them, and they were all he'd got. It was his mam and dad all over again, although at least there was no child involved.

He'd spoken to Debbie last night and she said Cathy had been over on the Wednesday for tea and that she'd looked weary and pale. He hoped that was because she was missing him. Debbie told him to call for regular updates if he wanted to. He said he would, but maybe it was time to move on. No doubt Cathy would when those young doctors realised she was free. He felt sick thinking of another man pawing her, of her lying in someone else's arms all night. He punched the wall beside him and made a dent in the wooden panelling. No doubt Maria would give him earache when she saw it. The noise disturbed Eloisa, who turned over, muttering in her sleep. Gianni switched off the overhead light and lay on his side, willing sleep to come.

He awoke after a fitful night to find Eloisa sitting by his feet with her back to him. He could hear paper being turned and realised what she was doing. 'Give that back!' She had his sketch pad and was flicking through it.

'You're very talented,' she said, handing it over, an envious look in her brown eyes. 'Your girl is beautiful.'

'Yeah, she was.'

'Was? Has something happened to her?'

'We've split up,' he said, swinging himself out of bed. It was the first time he'd been able to admit it to anyone and it hurt, it hurt like hell. He grabbed his jeans from the floor as Eloisa shot him a lingering look. He turned his back to her and pulled them on. 'Where's your mum and my dad?'

'Outside eating breakfast.' She stood up and sashayed over to her own bed, wiggling her skimpily clad, pert little backside in front of him.

Gianni felt the beginnings of arousal and was glad he'd got his jeans on. Why was that happening when he was feeling so heartbroken over Cathy? It didn't make sense.

He joined his dad and Maria at the picnic table. His dad pushed a bacon roll towards him and Maria poured him a coffee.

'You okay, son? You look a bit down.'

He sighed and told them about his split with Cathy, his voice wobbling as he tried not to break down.

'I'm sorry to hear that, Gianni. We liked Cathy, didn't we, Maria?'

Maria nodded and looked at him. Gianni felt a shiver run down his spine as she stared, her eyes deep and unfathomable. 'You shouldn't let her go, Gianni,' she said. 'I still see danger. That girl needs you.'

Gianni shook his head. 'There's no danger. Jack's behind bars now. She's safe enough. Anyway, it's not up to me. Cathy's made her mind up.' He finished his breakfast and got to his feet. 'I'm off to practise with Alessandro for tonight's show.'

'Okay.' His dad patted his shoulder. 'We'll make it a good one. Tomorrow we travel to Sheffield. That'll put some distance between you and Cathy.'

Chapter Twenty Seven

Alice lifted the little girl back into bed and put the rail up on the side to stop her falling out. It was her opinion that this child should be in a cot still. At just over two she was too young for a bed and had already escaped and run off down the ward three times this morning. She was a cute little thing with her dark curls, mischievous blue eyes and a lisp. Alice pulled the bed table towards the child and put a bowl of puréed vegetables and meat in front of her. Molly had had her tonsils removed last week and was slowly being reintroduced to eating food with a bit more texture than soup.

'Now eat all that up, Molly, and you can have ice-cream and jelly for afters,' Alice cajoled as Molly screwed up her face in disgust. Alice scooped a spoonful up and offered it to her. Molly blew a raspberry on the spoon, splattering Alice's spotless white apron with the mushy mess. 'That was very naughty,' Alice said, trying not to laugh. 'Now, I'm going to leave you to do it on your own because I have to see to Peter now. You do a good job of emptying the bowl for me and I'll be very happy.'

She turned her attention to the little boy with the big sad eyes in the next bed. He'd had an operation to straighten his foot, which had been turned inwards since birth. She helped him to sit up and he smiled when she placed his meal in front of him. 'Can you manage, Peter if I cut your meat up into tiny pieces for you?'

He nodded and tucked in. Alice wiped away the gravy that had dribbled down his chin. She loved working in the Children's ward, looking after all the vulnerable little souls that passed through the doors. She really felt that she'd finally found her place in life. She had a lot to thank Cathy for. The suggestion that she try to become an auxiliary nurse had been the best idea ever. She was hoping to bump into Cathy in the dining room later. She hadn't looked too well last time she saw her, but Cathy had told her that she was just tired from working the night shift. She'd also told her that she and Gianni had split up. Alice felt sad that the young couple had let their careers get in the way of their relationship. But with the mistakes she'd made herself in life, she didn't feel that she was the right one to offer advice. Ah well, what will be will be, she thought as she pushed the trolley further down the ward to collect some empty plates and dish up the promised jelly and ice-cream.

*

Gianni could feel eyes on his back again. Eloisa! Since he'd told her his relationship with Cathy was over she'd haunted him. Everywhere he turned she'd be there with a big smile on her face, licking those glossy lips. He was fighting a losing battle and he knew it. He really didn't want to, but there was a feeling of inevitability about the whole thing. The fair had pitched up at Graves Park in Sheffield and everyone was busy erecting the rides. Eloisa hung around the wall of death, getting under everyone's feet and begging Luca for a go. He still refused, even though Alessandro said he thought she might be an asset to the show. He'd seen pictures in a magazine from the States where a young girl sat on the handlebars of a bike, waving to the punters, while the rider rode up and down the barrel walls. It was a show-stopper, according to the article. Maria also said no, she sensed danger for her daughter; but then again, Gianni thought, Maria sensed danger all over the bloody place.

The fair was due to open on Wednesday and at mealtime that night, Luca made an announcement. He and Maria had arranged to get married on Saturday at the local registry office and were taking a weekend off. It would be down to Marco and the boys to hold the fort while they had a one-night honeymoon to tide them over until the winter, when the fair closed down and he could take Maria to Italy to see her elderly parents.

Congratulations filled the air and Luca brought out a bottle of champagne.

'You kept that quiet,' Gianni said as he toasted the couple.

His dad smiled. 'It's about time I made an honest woman of her and we'll celebrate with a party next week after the fair finishes here.'

*

Saturday evening, Cathy made Debbie comfortable and went to brew some tea. Davy was out on a late works' do for someone's birthday and she'd promised to keep Debbie company and stay the night on their sofa.

'If the baby decides to come early, you can deliver it and that'll be two down and one to go for if you decide to take the midwifery course in time,' Debbie teased.

Cathy laughed. 'True, if they'll let me count them both. That's next on the agenda though. Midwifery training. It's something I really want to do when I'm ready.'

'So, how does your mam like her job at the hospital?' Debbie asked when Cathy sat down beside her and handed her a cuppa.

'She loves it,' Cathy said. 'She's also trying to sort out a divorce from Jack. She's seen a solicitor and because of the exceptional circumstances of her case, she might not have to wait years like she thought she would.'

'That's really good. She deserves an easier life.'

'She does,' Cathy agreed. 'Jimmy's brother Johnny is moving to Liverpool next month. He and Jimmy are setting up a property repair business. Mam's really thrilled as she and Johnny get on so well together. I'm just keeping my fingers crossed for them.'

'And I will too,' Debbie said. 'They make a lovely couple.' She jumped as the baby kicked her in the ribs. 'Ouch! I think Maria's right and this little one is definitely a boy with footballer's feet.'

'Maybe, if you believe all that stuff. Has Gianni called you recently?' Cathy asked, trying to keep her voice from sounding too interested.

'Err, yes, Davy spoke to him the other night. Actually, Maria and his dad are getting married today. The fair's in Sheffield at the moment. Gianni told Davy he's thinking of selling the house next year, and if he does he'll give us first refusal, if we can afford it. We'll try and scrape a deposit together.'

'Bet your parents would help, if you asked nicely,' Cathy said, feeling sick inside. If Gianni was thinking of selling the house there was little chance he'd change his mind and leave the fair.

'I wouldn't ask my mam for anything,' Debbie said, pulling a face. 'She still won't acknowledge the baby and she won't allow me to visit, even though it's not going to go away. Well, it's her loss. Davy's mam will be a fabulous granny. She's always buying baby things and she's knitting like crazy.'

'Are you and Davy still madly in love?' Cathy teased.

'Of course we are. Except he says it's like sharing a bed with a beached whale at the moment. Cheeky sod.' Debbie laughed. 'What about you, Cath. Are you missing Gianni?'

Cathy nodded and blinked rapidly. 'Yes, but I can't go backwards. If the fair means that much to him, then it's his choice.'

'I'm sure you could make it work if you tried,' Debbie said. 'He loves you like crazy and I know full well *you* still love *him*.'

Cathy shrugged. 'Perhaps he does, but it still won't work. We both want very different things from life.'

*

Eloisa was stretched out on her bed when Gianni came in. He nodded and went to his side of the caravan. He felt knackered.

It made a difference not having his dad around. They'd all had to work extra hard tonight.

'Would you like a drink, Gianni?' Eloisa slid off the bed.

'No thanks. Think I'll get straight off to sleep.' He caught his breath as she wiggled her way to the kitchen in a short and very tight white T-shirt and the skimpiest pink knickers he'd ever seen. He wished she'd wear something proper to sleep in. He swallowed hard as she poured a glass of wine, took a sip and then licked those bloody lips.

'Why don't you have a small glass to relax you?' she suggested.

'*I'll* get it,' he said. 'You go back to bed.'

When he turned from filling his glass, with more wine than he'd intended to, she was on his bed with his sketch pad in her hands.

'Why don't you draw *me*?' she said, pouting. 'I bet I could pose as well as your ex.'

'I'm sure you could,' he said, sitting down and reaching for the pad, but she held it in the air, her T-shirt riding up, revealing her flat stomach. 'Say please.'

'Stop messing about and give it to me.' He was angry now. He'd promised Cathy no one would ever see the sketches and he felt as though he'd betrayed that promise.

Eloisa handed him the pad and pointed to a sketch where Cathy lay naked on her front, hands under her chin, legs bent at the knees behind her and feet crossed at the ankles, smiling seductively from under her dark fringe, eyes wide and innocent. His stomach gave a lurch and he knocked back his wine in one go.

Eloisa's eyes were anything *but* innocent and he wondered how many of the fairground hands had screwed her.

She put down her glass, peeled off her T-shirt and stood in front of him. 'Shall I show you how I can pose like that?'

He stared at her generous but pert breasts and stayed frozen to his seat. His erection was instant and he wriggled to get more comfortable. She hooked a thumb either side of her knickers and slid them down, swaying from side to side. He moved over as she lay on the bed and adopted Cathy's pose, looking up at him with a smile.

'Come on, Gianni, get your pencil out for me,' she teased.

He threw off his clothes and pulled her up from the bed, his hands running over her body, mouth on her breasts. He lifted her onto the table and pushed into her. She wrapped her legs round his waist as he hammered away. There were no whispered words of love, nor gentle caresses or even kisses; it was just sex and her moans and squeals and clawing of his back told him she liked it. He almost hated her for enjoying it so much, but the sensations were immense and he couldn't fight it. She screamed and yanked his hair so hard when she came he was certain he'd have a bald patch there. He pushed her away and waited for his heartbeat to return to normal. That was wild, but he regretted it immediately; it left him feeling cold, with no deep satisfaction. Still, he'd needed the release and so had she, it seemed. He hoped it wouldn't cause complications. His heart would always belong to Cathy.

Chapter Twenty-Eight

September 1958

Gianni strolled back from the telephone box, his heart heavy. He'd just spoken to Davy and Debbie, whose baby was due next week. Talking to the excited pair made him long to see Cathy again. He planned to go back to Liverpool for a few days when the fair headed south next month. He wanted to give the pictures he'd had framed to Alice and Millie. He could try to time his visit to see the new baby for when Cathy might also be visiting. He was desperate to talk to her. He'd almost called her a few times but felt guilty for shagging Eloisa, although why he should feel like that when he was a free man, he didn't know. Cathy would be more or less finished with her exams. Maybe she'd agree to see him, spend a day out in New Brighton or something, just as friends if that was all she wanted.

Back at the caravan an argument was in full swing. Eloisa, yelling and crying at the top of her voice; Maria wringing her hands and shouting and wailing in Italian; and his dad, who was trying to make himself heard above the pair of them but seemed to be losing the battle.

Now what? Gianni turned to leave so they could get on with it, but Maria launched herself at him and slapped him round the face. He reeled backwards with shock into the table and looked at his dad.

'What the hell was that for? What's going on?'

'Maria, take Eloisa outside while I talk to my son,' Luca said, his face like thunder.

Maria led a sobbing Eloisa out of the caravan and Luca turned to Gianni. 'Sit down.'

Gianni did as he was told, a sinking feeling in his stomach.

'Eloisa tells us she is pregnant and that you are the baby's father,' Luca said, a muscle twitching in his cheek.

Gianni felt the blood drain from his face as he stared at his dad. 'No way! It can't be mine. She's been seeing Alessandro too.'

'I questioned her about Alessandro and she denies sleeping with him. They are just friends.'

'Yeah, so *she* says.' Gianni slumped on the bench, feeling sick. This couldn't be happening. It was a dream. He'd wake up soon.

'We look after the women in our community,' Luca continued. 'I expect you to do the right thing and marry Eloisa and take care of her and the child.'

*

Cathy stood in front of the sink and stared at her pale face in the mirror. The last day of exams, anatomy and physiology; how would she get through it? She'd never felt so ill in her life. She hoped the exam would be all theory and no practical with donated body parts to dissect. She felt sick and aching all over, as if she was coming down with flu or something. She pulled her cloak round her shoulders and set off to meet Karen and Ellie in the foyer.

'God, Cathy, you look rough,' Karen said.

'Oh thanks,' Cathy said with a wan smile. Her mam had said the same thing the other day. 'Cheer me up, why don't you.'

'Nearly over,' Elle said, linking her arm through Cathy's. 'Then you can have a week off to recover.'

'Jean suggested we go for a curry tonight to celebrate,' Karen said as they walked across the grounds to the PTS building. 'Year three finish their exams today as well.'

Cathy gagged at the mention of curry. The very thought turned her stomach. 'Think I'll give it a miss and have an early night with a hot-water bottle,' she said. 'Couldn't do a curry justice at the moment.'

'Oh well, maybe next week,' Karen said. 'Come on, in we go. Let's get it over with.'

Cathy lay on her bed, tossing and turning, trying to get to sleep. She was looking forward to the week's holiday. She'd promised her mam she'd go shopping in the city with her and she'd also promised Granny Lomax she'd help her paint her kitchen. Debbie's baby was due any day now and she was looking forward to celebrating with her friends. The week would fly by. If only she could stop her brain whirling round and get some sleep.

She woke at seven, still feeling rough, but ready for some tea and toast to settle her churning stomach. She slid out of bed, then felt dizzy and sat back down again. She shouldn't really go and see her mam and the kids if she was harbouring flu. The girls had only just gone back to school after the long summer holidays and the last thing her mam needed was them off poorly. Maybe she'd go and grab a tray of breakfast, bring it back to bed and stay there until she felt a bit better. She pulled her dressing gown on and shuffled to the dining room, hoping she didn't bump into any of the dishy young doctors as she knew she looked a mess, with her hair all over the place and no makeup on. The dining room was deserted, apart from the lady who ran the counter and the cook who was frying bacon. She was soon on her way back with a couple of slices of toast and a mug of steaming tea, glad to be away from the cooking smells as they turned her stomach.

No sooner had she downed the tea and toast than she was leaning over the sink with the tap running, puking it all back up. Oh God, what was wrong with her? She sat down on the bed again, head between her legs, until the dizziness subsided, and then lay back against the headboard, propped up by two pillows. She must have dozed for an hour as the next thing she was aware of, Karen and Ellie were knocking on the door. She let them in and sank back down on the bed.

'You still feeling poorly?' Karen asked, sitting beside her and smoothing her hair from her face. 'You look terrible. Shall I ask Sister Judge to get the doctor?'

Cathy shook her head. 'I'll be all right when I've had a rest.' She told them she'd puked up her breakfast.

The phone rang outside and Ellie hurried to answer it while Karen washed Cathy's face and hands and tucked her back into bed.

Ellie was soon back with a big smile on her face. 'That was your friend Davy. I told him you felt poorly so he said to tell you Debbie had a great big boy at three o'clock this morning over on Maternity. Nearly ten pounds, both doing well and they've called him Jonathon. He said you can go in and see them when you feel up to it.'

'Oh, wonderful.' Cathy's eyes filled with tears. 'Maria was right then.'

'Right about what?' Ellie said.

Cathy told her about the wedding ring thing and then she stopped, her eyes opening wide. 'Oh shit!'

'What is it?' Karen asked. 'You've gone paler still.'

'Nothing.' Cathy shook her head.

'Cathy, what's wrong?' Karen persisted, and then clapped her hand to her mouth. 'Oh hell, I think I know.' Karen told Ellie how the ring had swung over Cathy's tummy, but she'd dismissed the whole thing as an old wives' tale. Karen looked closely at Cathy. 'When was your last period?'

Cathy swallowed. 'Er, not sure.'

'Have you had one since Gianni stayed here that night?'

'No. About two weeks before.'

'But that was June,' Karen said. 'Bloody hell, no wonder you feel rough. You're pregnant!'

'I can't be,' Cathy said, struggling to sit up. 'I'm *always* late.'

'Yeah, but there's late and *late*! Didn't it dawn on you?'

'Not really,' Cathy said wearily. 'I pushed it to the back of my mind. I've been so busy what with work and exams; I've had no time to think.'

Karen grabbed the calendar from the wall and flicked back a few months. 'So that takes us from the first week of June and it's now the first week of September. You're about three months.'

Cathy began to cry and Karen pulled her into her arms and held her. Ellie sat on the bed, chewing her lip.

'You need to let Gianni know,' Karen said when Cathy had calmed down a bit.

'I can't do that. He doesn't want kids, not yet anyway.'

'Well, whether he wants them or not is irrelevant,' Karen said. 'He's having one and that's all there is to it.'

'Oh God, what a bloody mess.' Cathy lay back and sighed. 'I've no way of getting in touch with him and I can't do this on my own.'

Ellie patted her hand. 'Well whatever you decide to do, Karen and I will stand by you and I'm sure your other friends will too. Maybe you should talk it over with them when you go and see the new baby. At least you know you won't be passing on a bug now.'

'I thought Gianni kept in touch with Davy and Debbie?' Karen said. 'And you can write to him at that post office box number he gave you. Think about it. You have to make some decisions and you need help with that.'

'I might not be pregnant, maybe it's just worry and stuff…' Cathy said, trailing off. They both looked at her and shook their heads.

'It's not and you know it,' Karen said in her usual blunt manner. 'After that night of passion it's unlikely to be anything else. Right, we'll leave you to get some rest and come back later.'

'Don't tell anyone, please,' Cathy begged, grabbing Karen by the arm. 'I don't want to lose my job just yet. I need to sort out my head and decide what I'm going to do.'

Chapter Twenty-Nine

October 1958

Gianni tried hard to get Eloisa alone for a talk, but it was proving difficult. Maria appeared at every given opportunity and told him Eloisa must rest as she felt unwell. There'd been no wedding date decided on yet and Gianni had told his dad he'd rather wait until after the birth, when blood tests could be taken to prove he was the father. He knew there *was* a chance, but as far as he was concerned, it was a very slim one.

He listened as Maria and Eloisa spoke of wedding plans, but mainly in Italian. He wasn't fluent in the language, so he couldn't join in, but he got the gist of it. Maria wanted the wedding to take place as soon as possible to avoid any embarrassment to her daughter.

He supposed he could just get on his bike and piss off somewhere and leave them all to it, but then he'd be letting his dad down and he'd hate to do that. They'd grown really close until this happened and he'd never be able to show his face again if he did a runner. And then again, if the baby *was* his, he'd want some kind of involvement in its life. He'd grown up without a dad and he didn't want that for any kids of his own. Face it, he was well and truly trapped, and it wasn't a feeling that filled him with any hope for a rosy future.

*

Cathy sat on the sofa, cuddling baby Jonathon while Debbie mixed him a feed. She brought the bottle through and handed it to Cathy, who plugged it into the eager little mouth.

'He loves his grub,' Debbie said. 'Just like his daddy. 'You okay, Cath? You're looking a bit peaky.'

'I'm all right,' Cathy replied, looking down at the little face. Jonathon's look of bliss as he sucked the teat made her smile. She really should tell Debbie about her own predicament. A month had flown by since realisation had dawned and all she'd done was shut her mind to it and carry on as normal. The sickly feeling had passed and she felt better by the day, so it was easy enough to stay in denial for the time being. She wasn't showing much yet, just a slightly rounded tummy and bigger boobs; her clothes still fitted her fine and no one had made any comments about her gaining weight. She'd made her decision, but didn't know how the hell she was going to cope.

'You have to wind him halfway through,' Debbie said, breaking Cathy's thoughts. 'Then shove the teat back in right away before he gets a chance to kick off. They're complicated little things. Pity they don't come with an instruction book, but you soon get the hang of it.' She laughed as Jonathon belched loudly when Cathy patted his back. 'Can't believe he's only been here four weeks, it feels like for ever.'

Jonathon finished feeding and Cathy looked at Debbie, who had a rosy glow of contentment about her. Would *she* ever look like that? She doubted it. 'Debs?'

'Yeah?' Debbie looked up from the magazine she was flicking through.

'I need to tell you something, but Jonathon's gone to sleep, so don't yell out and wake him.'

'Okay. What's wrong? You look a bit mithered.'

'I'm er, I'm about four months pregnant.'

Debbie's mouth dropped open and her voice came out in a squeak. 'You're what?'

'I'm pregnant.' Cathy repeated. 'Four months.'

'Yeah, I heard you. I can't believe it. Why didn't you say something sooner? Does Gianni know?'

Cathy shook her head. 'No, and I don't *want* him to know either. *I* didn't know until four weeks ago, well, I guess I did, but you know how it is. I ignored it, like you do.'

Debbie nodded. 'Yeah, I know. Same as I did. But why don't you want Gianni to know? You are going to have it, aren't you, Cath?'

'Yes, but I'm going to lose my job and I don't know what I'll do for money. I need to tell my mam. I'm sure she'll let me stay with her. I'll just have to manage. Others do. It's not the future I'd planned, but there you go. With regards to Gianni, he didn't want to be tied down with kids and I'm not trapping him. If he comes back eventually, I'll tell him, but until then, well… and you know my feelings on the fair, I couldn't live that lifestyle and be worried sick about him every day, just like Sadie was with Gianni's father.'

'Oh, Cathy, that's not fair. You have to let him know. Give him the chance to tell you how he feels. I couldn't have done that to Davy. He dotes on Jonathon. It would have been cruel to leave him out of his life.'

Cathy stared at Debbie, whose eyes had filled. She looked down at Jonathon, sleeping in her arms, his little world safe and secure with two parents who adored him. Had she got the right to deny her own baby that love and security? She'd always said she didn't want to end up like her mam, in a poverty trap. But that's what was going to happen if she tried to cope on her own. Gianni *did* love her, she knew that, and she loved him. Their baby deserved the best she could offer it. But was the fairground life the right one? She guessed she'd never know until she gave it a try.

She nodded. 'Okay, I'll write to him at the box number. If I do it and post it tomorrow and someone picks up the letters in the next few days, he'll know by the weekend. If he gets in touch, then we'll take it from there. If he doesn't, well then I'll know the fair means more to him than I do.'

*

Alessandro sorted through the letters he'd been sent to collect. They were mainly for his dad and Uncle Luca. There was one for Gianni in a pink envelope, written in a girly hand. He frowned and turned the letter over. A return address was on the back. It was from Gianni's ex-girlfriend, Cathy. What the fuck did *she* want? The last thing he needed was for Gianni to clear off home, leaving Eloisa in the lurch. She'd be sure to pin the blame on *him* then. Alessandro knew full well the baby Eloisa was carrying was his – she was right about the dates – but he would keep his mouth shut on that score and let Gianni take the blame. He opened the letter and read it, his eyes widening. Cathy was pregnant and wanted them to try again. Fucking hell! He couldn't let Gianni see this. He needed him married to Eloisa and quick, before Cathy tracked him down. He shoved the letter into the envelope and took out his lighter, then pushed them both into his pocket as footsteps sounded on the caravan steps. It was his dad, coming to see if there was any business mail.

'Get out to the show tent and give that floor a clean,' Marco ordered. 'Too much oil on it. Go and wash it with hot water, and put extra cleaning fluid in the bucket.'

Alessandro did as he was told, and as the busy day went on and showtime arrived he forgot about the letter. The atmosphere between him and Gianni was frosty and they didn't quite gel as they'd done when Gianni first started to ride with him. Alessandro didn't care. He preferred it when his cousin kept his distance.

On the day the fair packed up to move on, one of the workers picked up a pink envelope, covered in oil and footprints. He pushed it into his overall pocket with the intention of trying to decipher the smudged name and address and who it belonged to when he had a minute – and then promptly forgot about it.

*

Ten days after she'd written to Gianni and having still not heard back from him, Cathy grabbed at a shelf in the ward linen cupboard and felt the floor coming up to meet her. She closed her eyes and slipped into oblivion.

'Nurse Lomax? Nurse Lomax?'

Someone was calling her name from far away, then her cheeks were being slapped and strong arms lifted her and whisked her to a soft bed. She opened her eyes cautiously and looked around. She was in a side room in the Women's Medical ward, her current placement. A burly porter stood just inside the doorway and Sister Delahunty was standing beside the bed, taking her pulse.

'Hey, Nurse, you gave us a scare there,' the porter said. 'Thought you were a goner.'

'Thank you, porter,' Sister said. 'I think we can manage now.' She dismissed him with a wave of her hand. 'Now then, Nurse Lomax, I think we need to get you checked over by a doctor. You banged your head when you fell. Have you eaten this morning? Your blood sugar levels might be low.'

Cathy nodded. This was it. Her secret was about to be discovered. Sister's lilting Irish accent was soothing, but she knew from rumours that the woman could be a right tyrant when crossed.

Sister left the room and Cathy felt tears rolling down her cheeks and sliding off her face into her ears. She wished now she'd let Debbie tell Gianni what had happened, but she'd made Debs swear to say nothing and Debs had kept her mouth shut when Gianni called her and Davy at the weekend. It was up to *her* to tell him though, and Debs said he hadn't mentioned the letter – so Cathy could only assume he didn't want to know or he'd not got it yet. Maybe the fair hadn't picked up their mail for a while. She'd been so sure he'd call her right away. The only other thing she could do was track the fair down, like Gianni had done all those months ago. The more she thought about it, the better she liked the idea. A young doctor popped his head round the door and her heart almost stopped when she realised it was posh George from Surrey who'd made her dance with him at the hospital social club many months ago.

'Don't I know you, Nurse?' he said closing the door. 'Ah yes, we had a dance. You're the one that's spoken for.'

Fancy him remembering. In spite of her problems, Cathy smiled.

'Sister tells me you had a fall and banged your head. Mind if I take a look?'

He examined her head, muttering that there were no cuts and bruises. He shone a torch in her eyes and nodded. 'No damage. So, *did* you fall or did you faint?'

'I think I fainted,' Cathy mumbled. 'I'm er, I'm actually pregnant.' There was no point in hiding it. He'd soon get to the bottom of her condition anyway.

'I see.' He sat down on a chair and smiled kindly. 'You do realise they'll chuck you off the course.'

Cathy's eyes filled. 'Yes.'

'And you want to go ahead with the pregnancy?'

'Yes, I do.'

'Okay. Well, I'll have to report this to Sister. I'm sorry. She'll come and have a word with you and tell you what to do next.'

Cathy swallowed the lump in her throat.

He went to the door and turned. 'Good luck, Nurse Lomax.'

Cathy smiled again, in spite of her tears. 'Thank you.'

'So where will you go?' Karen asked as she and Ellie helped Cathy to pack her things.

'I'm going to Mam's tomorrow and then I'm planning on trying to find Gianni.'

'Really?' Ellie said. 'Do you have any idea where the fair is at the moment?'

'No, but Davy and Debbie might. He calls them every couple of weeks or so to make sure the house is okay. They'll have an idea where he was the last time they spoke and I'll make that my starting point. I was hoping he'd have answered my letter by now, or called me. Maybe he doesn't want to know.'

'Or more likely he's not seen the letter,' Karen said. 'It's a bit hit-and-miss, this picking up mail when you're on the road. We've all seen how Gianni was with you. He never takes his eyes off you, loves you to bits. I'm sure the non-communication is because he doesn't know, not because he doesn't care.'

Cathy half-smiled. 'Let's hope you're right.'

'I think we've finished in here,' Ellie said. 'Let's go down to the lounge and then you can say your goodbyes. Jean's organised a little party. It's the last night we'll all be together for a while.'

Cathy felt the tears running down her cheeks. 'It's not been quite as bad as I thought it would be, this throwing me out thing, I mean. They were okay really. I've been told I can come back and finish my course after the birth if I want to.'

'And do you?' Karen asked.

'Maybe. I'll have to see what happens. I've no idea how Gianni will feel about the baby. My head is all over the place right now and I can't think straight. If he doesn't want to know, I'm not sure how I'd cope on my own.'

*

Gianni banged around, slamming tools down and picking arguments with people for no good reason. It was a grey and damp Monday morning towards the end of November and the fair was pitching up in Northampton for one of its last bookings before packing up for the winter months. On Saturday he was due to marry Eloisa in a civil ceremony that would be blessed in Italy in January when the family visited Maria's parents. Gianni hadn't had a single say in anything. He hadn't been near Eloisa since that one-night stand and neither did he want to. Some wonderful marriage this would be. He felt consumed with guilt and sadness at the way things had turned out and wished with all his heart that it were Cathy he was marrying. If the baby turned out to be his cousin's then he planned to make his escape, but until it was born he was stuck. There was no way he was consummating the marriage. He couldn't even look at Eloisa any more, never mind anything else. It was Christmas in less than a month and all he wanted to do was go home to Liverpool and catch up with his mates and hopefully Cathy – if she wasn't seeing anyone, that is.

He looked up as a woman came running into the tented area. He recognised her as Irene, the wife of Lenny, one of the many maintenance hands. The pair were fiery East Enders and their almost daily fallouts were a source of much amusement to the rest of the crew.

'Where's that bleedin' 'usband o' mine?' Irene screeched at the top of her voice.

Lenny's head popped over the top of the safety barrier he was erecting at the barrel platform. ''Ere I am, my sweet. What's up wiv ya?'

She waved an envelope in the air, a pink envelope. ''Ere's what's up wiv me. Who've you got up the duff then? You cheatin' bastard!'

'Yer what?' Lenny came down to the floor area, wiping his dirty hands on the legs of his overalls. He took the letter she thrust at him.

'It was in yer other overalls. I was gonna wash 'em and it fell out the pocket. It sez she's pregnant.'

''Oo is?' Lenny yelled, looking puzzled. 'Yer can't bloody read, yer silly mare, 'ow would yer know what it sez?'

'I can read *that* word. I'm not as thick as yer make out.'

A crowd had gathered as the pair went at it hammer and tongs. Irene calmed down when Lenny explained how he'd come by the letter. That he'd picked it up off the floor ages ago and forgot all about it. He told her he'd meant to try to find out who it belonged to.

Hand shaking, Gianni reached for the letter and amidst the oil stains and footprints he could just about make out the return address on the back. It was from Cathy. He'd known by the pink envelope, the same kind she'd used on other occasions she'd written to him. He felt the blood drain from his face as he read the opened letter. She was pregnant and wanted them to try again. He thought he was going to pass out. Someone brought him a chair and sat him down. The letter was dated September the twelfth. She'd think he didn't care. All those wasted weeks. The crowd subsided and went back to work. He looked up and saw Eloisa and Alessandro staring at him from the platform at the top of the barrel. Alessandro had picked up the mail ages ago and as far as Gianni knew it was the last lot to be brought to the fair. Realisation dawned and he leapt to his feet and shot up the stairs to confront his cousin. He grabbed him by the throat, lifted him off his feet and shook him hard before Alessandro even had time to blink.

'Did you steal that letter and hide it?' Gianni yelled.

Eloisa backed away and leaned against the barrier that Lenny had been in the process of erecting.

Alessandro made a choking noise, his lips turning blue. 'Did you?' Gianni shook him again and yelled in his face.

'Gianni, stop it,' Eloisa screamed, 'You'll kill him.'

'He deserves it. Are you in on this too?' He turned on her and let his cousin drop to the floor, clutching his throat and gasping for breath. 'That's *his* kid you're expecting, not mine.'

Eloisa screamed again as Alessandro got to his feet and launched himself at Gianni.

'It's not mine, it's yours, you bastard,' Alessandro yelled.

'No, Alessandro,' Eloisa cried. 'It's yours and you know it is. I'm sorry Gianni. It was his idea to blame you.'

'You little bitch!' Alessandro smacked her hard across the face and she lost her balance, grabbing for the barrier that hadn't been fixed to its moorings. She fell over the low platform wall and down to the bottom of the barrel, where she lay motionless, her body bent at an awkward angle.

'You've killed her!' Gianni yelled as someone ran from the tent, shouting for an ambulance.

'Yeah, right, it was *you* that hit her,' Alessandro started to say, but stopped as Lenny stepped out of the shadows.

'I think you'll find it was you,' Lenny said, jerking Alessandro's arm up his back and frogmarching him over to the stairs, where his father took over.

Chapter Thirty

December 1958

Gianni packed his things into the panniers of his bike, including his framed sketches for Alice and Millie, and said goodbye to his dad and Maria. Once they knew Eloisa had survived the fall and was out of danger, the family had talked long into the night and agreed he should go home and sort things out with Cathy. The wedding was called off and Uncle Marco apologised for his son's appalling behaviour. Although Alessandro was arrested and questioned, the police brought no charges against him, stating the fall was an accident due to the barrier not being installed properly at the point from where Eloisa fell. She'd broken her right leg, four ribs, suffered concussion – and had lost her and Alessandro's baby.

Gianni felt sorry for her; she'd been manipulated after all. But the relief was enormous and he was now free to move on.

'Keep in touch,' Luca said as he saw him off.

'I will. I'll let you know what happens. I might be back next spring, but I can't work with Alessandro again.'

'That won't be happening,' Luca said. 'Marco has arranged for him to go back to Italy. We've fired him from the act after what he's done. It will just be the two of us next year, unless you decide to come back.' He gave Gianni a hug and waved as he roared away.

*

Cathy stood on the corner by the park in Northampton and looked around. The fair had been here, someone told her, but about six weeks ago. She looked at the list Debbie had given her. The next venue was on the south coast in Brighton, miles away, and they would no doubt have moved on from there too by now. Maybe she should make her way south and stay in a bed and breakfast for a few nights until she could locate them. As far as she knew they stored things at a place in Kent over the winter. She would call Debbie and Davy when she got wherever she was going, and then when Gianni called them, they could tell him where she was. That's if he was bothered, of course. She looked in her purse and did a quick calculation of how long her money would last. Not that long, with train fares as well as accommodation costs; it was going down quickly. Both her mam and Granny Lomax had begged her not to go when she'd told them about the baby. They said they'd look after her. But she told them she had to find Gianni, no matter what. The weather was bitter cold and she pulled her warm coat around her. The buttons only just met; her baby bump had grown so much in the last few weeks. She'd only got three months to go now and wanted to be back in Liverpool for the birth. She picked up her bag and trudged to the railway station, where she bought a ticket to Dover, figuring they'd be near to the ferry port; she could recall Gianni saying his dad sometimes visited family in France and Italy. Then she treated herself to a cup of hot chocolate and drank it sitting in the warm waiting room until the train arrived.

*

Gianni pulled up outside the nurses' home and rang the bell on the front door. Sister Judge appeared, eyebrows raised questioningly.

'Is Nurse Lomax on duty today?' he asked, feeling slightly intimidated as the woman swept him with a scornful look.

'Nurse Lomax left the hospital a few weeks ago,' she told him. 'I suggest you contact her at home.'

'Thank you.' Gianni sighed as the woman closed the door. Home? Where was home? Cathy didn't really have one, apart from the odd night she'd spent at her mam's or Granny Lomax's. Would she have gone to either of them? He wondered if Karen and Ellie were around; they'd still be in touch with Cathy, surely. He hung around for a while, but there was no sign of the girls and he was getting some funny looks as people walked by. He guessed they were all a bit wary of strangers since Jack's attack on Ellie. He decided to call on Debbie and see if she knew anything. Davy would be at work, but Debs might be in. He should have rung them before he set off from the fair, but he'd been in such a hurry to get on his way, he'd forgotten.

Debbie let him in with a welcoming hug. 'Oh, Gianni, am I glad to see you. Come and sit down and I'll make you a coffee. You look frozen.'

He sat on the sofa and warmed his hands in front of the fire, glad to get a welcome and not a cold shoulder.

Debbie came back into the room and handed him a mug and a mince pie.

'Do you have any idea where Cathy is?' he began. 'She's not at the hospital any more.'

'She got asked to leave,' Debbie said. 'Did you get the letter she wrote a while ago? She's been looking for you.'

'I did, but only just.' He told Debbie what had happened, about his mistake with Eloisa and the disastrous consequences.

Debbie's hand flew to her mouth. 'Oh, Gianni, what an awful mess for you. But it's all over now?'

'Yes, it is,' he said. 'I feel sorry for the girl, but there was nothing in it. I cannot tell you how I felt when I finally got Cathy's letter in my hands, just before I was supposed to get married. I was distraught.'

'I'm sure you were. Now, I haven't spoken to Cathy for a few days but she's going to ring on Friday and let me know she's okay. She was heading to Northampton and then Brighton and finishing up in Kent. That was her plan anyway. None of us wanted her to go, mad fool that she is. She's six months gone now and she should be resting, not trudging round the country in this cold weather.'

'I feel so bloody guilty about the whole thing. If only I'd called her to keep in touch. I just thought she wouldn't want to know.'

'Well, you know how stubborn Cathy can be,' Debbie said. 'She might not have even wanted to speak to you. Are you going to go and look for her?'

Gianni nodded. 'I'll set off in the morning, make my way to Kent by train; she won't be able to ride on the back of my bike with her bump. It'd be too dangerous. She'll never bloody find the storage place. *I* don't even know where it is, I've never been. If she calls, tell her to make her way to the ferry port at Dover and wait there for me. She'll be able to find that easily enough and she can keep warm there. I'm going to pop over and see her mam in a minute. Is it okay if I stay the night here and leave my bike in the backyard?'

'Of course,' Debbie said. 'Davy'll be relieved to see you.' She stopped as a loud cry sounded, and she raised her eyes to the ceiling. 'That's his lordship's afternoon nap over. Back in two ticks.'

Gianni knocked on Alice's door just as Millie popped her head out of her own front door.

'I thought it was you,' she said, closing her door behind her and stepping over the small garden wall in between the two houses as Alice opened the door.

Gianni was swept inside to hugs and kisses from his mam's two best mates.

'Are you going to go and look for Cathy?' Alice asked, her eyes filling as she told Gianni to sit down on the sofa. 'She wouldn't listen to me not to go. She's so stubborn.'

Gianni nodded. 'Yes, I'm setting off in the morning. Er, I wanted to give you these while I'm here.' He handed over two flat wrapped parcels as they both looked at him in surprise. 'It's nearly my mam's birthday; so they are for you to remember her by.'

'We'll never forget Sadie,' Millie said and Alice nodded her agreement.

They unwrapped their parcels and gasped with surprised delight as they stared at the white wooden-framed copies of the beautiful sketch Gianni had done of their late friend and themselves.

'Oh my word,' Millie said. 'I remember us having the photograph taken not long after the war ended. How lovely. Oh you are so clever, Gianni. It's beautiful. Thank you.'

'Wonderful,' Alice said, her voice husky with tears. 'I'll treasure this for ever.' She put the framed sketch on the mantelpiece and smiled. 'Now I can talk to her every day. Thank you so much, Gianni.'

'You're both very welcome. I found the photo in my mam's box of papers and stuff. I love it.'

'Now all you have to do is find my girl, and bring her back home so that she can give birth to mine and Sadie's grandchild safely,' Alice said. 'And no matter how stubborn she is or how much she protests, just put your foot down and get her home.' Alice and Millie wrapped their arms round Gianni in a group hug.

'I will,' he promised. 'I'm never letting her go again.'

*

Cathy knocked on the door of a guest house, its brightly lit vacancy sign casting a welcoming light onto the dark street. The door flew open and a blonde-haired woman in a black dress covered with a frilly paisley-patterned apron peered out into the night and smiled.

'Yes, love, how can I help you?'

'Can I have a room for the night, please?'

The woman looked her up and down, her gaze resting on the baby bump. Cathy felt her cheeks warming as the woman also stared at her ring finger. She still wore the ring Gianni had given her for their engagement and had turned it round so the gold band looked like a wedding ring.

'Just the one night, is that, Mrs, er…'

'Romano,' Cathy said without even thinking.

'I'm Mrs Brown. Are you one of the fair people then?'

'Yes, I'm the daughter-in-law of one of the owners. I'm er, meeting up when they arrive to store the fair.' Where did that lie come from? She'd never told lies in her life. It just tripped off her tongue.

'Ah, well, in that case you'd better come in, love. They should be here in the next day or two.'

'Thank you.' Cathy knew she only had enough money for one night, if she wanted to eat tomorrow, so hopefully the fair would arrive the next day. But how could she ask the woman where the storage farm was when she was supposed to know? She'd better think about that one and quick.

The woman rattled off the cost and told her it was one shilling extra if she wanted a hot bath. A cooked breakfast was an extra one and sixpence. Cathy hesitated for a moment and then agreed to the whole package. She needed a bath to relieve her aching back, and leaving here with a hot breakfast inside her seemed a good plan. It would keep her going most of the day until she found the farm.

The next morning, Cathy woke from the best sleep she'd had in ages. She felt warm, refreshed – and ravenous. She got up and dressed herself slowly. Breakfast was served between eight and nine and it was almost eight thirty. She was dreading having to leave this cosy room and go out into the cold again. She drew back the curtains and gasped. A fine layer of snow had fallen overnight. It all looked very pretty but the thought of going out and wandering the streets filled her with despair.

Downstairs in the dining room several men in suits were finishing their breakfasts as Mrs Brown hovered in a pink nylon overall, her blonde hair fastened up into a neat pleat.

'Come and sit here, Mrs Romano,' she called as Cathy hesitated by the door.

She made her way to a table in the front bay window that looked out onto the street.

'Sit yourself down, love. Would you like the works? Two eggs as well, for that little one there?' She nodded at Cathy's bump.

'Please.' Cathy could eat a horse, she was that hungry, and the more she ate now, the longer she would last before she needed to buy another meal.

A man at the table across from her smiled. 'Are you related to the fair folk, my dear?'

Cathy nodded and poured a cup of tea from the pot Mrs Brown placed in front of her.

'She's joining them up at Bridges Farm later,' Mrs Brown told him. 'Isn't that right, love?'

'Yes, that's right.' Cathy smiled. Brilliant. Bridges Farm? She could find out where that was easily enough.

As night fell again and more snow along with it, Cathy felt her legs wouldn't carry her any further. The farm was miles from where she'd stayed and she'd spent the last of her money on snacks and drinks that were stored in her bag for later. This was the daftest idea she'd ever had in her life. Why hadn't she listened to her mam and gran and Debbie? Gianni would have come to her eventually, even if only to tell her he didn't want to be with her. Tears ran down her cheeks at that thought. He'd probably met someone else by now and would be horrified when she presented herself and her lump to him.

She started to sing a song to cheer herself up as she slipped and slithered along a path that was turning icy as the temperature plummeted. Whoever said it was warmer down south should try walking miles in this. She was wearing all the clothes she'd brought with her – three pairs of warm socks and knickers, maternity trousers with an adjustable waistband that Debbie had given her and two baggy sweaters with a T-shirt underneath – and she still shivered. She changed the song she was singing from Perry Como's 'Catch a Falling Star' to Buddy Holly's 'Heartbeat.' Except all that made her do was think of Gianni and how he always made her heart beat faster when he kissed her.

She rounded a bend and saw a sign warning, 'No Trespassing'. There was a stile by the side of the gate and she squeezed through it and clambered down onto a path. Up in the distance a large house sat on top of a hill. Lights twinkled in the downstairs windows but other than that there was no sign of life. Not even a cow or a horse. There was certainly no sign of the fair. No big trucks or caravans, no tyre tracks in the snow, nothing. She stood for a moment wondering what to do. She needed a wee desperately, and was weary and cold. To her left stood a small brick barn. It looked deserted. Dare she? A kick in her ribs reminded her that she should; it wasn't just about her any more. Little Lucy had done nothing but kick and wriggle all day. Must have been the extra egg at breakfast. She knew her baby was a girl. Well, Maria had said so, hadn't she? And apparently she was never wrong. And Gianni's Italian granny had been called Luciana and Cathy loved the name.

Cathy opened the barn door and crept in. The place smelled sweet, not damp, and she saw the bales of hay piled up along the back wall. So there must be animals somewhere on the farm. It was dry and not as cold as outside. She breathed a sigh of relief. It would do just fine. She scattered some hay from one of the bales into a corner. It would be nice to lie on rather than the hard earth floor. A tartan rug, slung across a low beam, caught her eye. It looked like an old horse blanket and would probably be a bit scratchy, but it would keep her warm. She lifted it down and spread it across the hay. A twinge in her tummy reminded her that she needed a wee and she went outside and squatted down behind the barn. How bloody undignified. How the hell had she ever got into this state of affairs? She shook her head and got to her feet. All the airs and graces she'd adopted, not wanting to end up like the other girls, and here she was, six months pregnant, unmarried, weeing in the open air and sleeping in a barn. She went back inside, lay down on her makeshift bed and rummaged in her bag for a snack. Surely the fair would be here tomorrow. If it wasn't, she had no idea what she'd do next.

*

Gianni got off the train at Dover and found a place to stay for the night. Tomorrow he'd head for the farm on the off-chance that Cathy had made her way there. He must be getting closer to her by now. She'd be calling Debbie today with an update, so it wasn't long to wait. The fair should be arriving within the next twenty-four hours anyway and if Cathy was in the area she'd see it and follow them. That thought gave him some comfort and he fell asleep as soon as he settled down.

*

Cathy woke very early the next morning. To her dismay she'd wet the bed. Well, the blanket. As she got to her feet, though, more fluid trickled down her legs and she realised her waters had broken. She felt a wave of panic; the baby wasn't due for weeks yet and she was alone with no money. She sat back down again and started to cry. There was nothing she could do but keep still until someone came by. Walking wouldn't help; she needed to keep off her feet to give her baby the best chance of survival. Pains started low in her back and around her lower stomach. Labour pains. She curled into a ball, drawing her legs up, anything to try to stop it happening; but nothing worked. The pains were getting stronger. The sound of an engine stopping outside the barn caught her attention. She yelled out for help and the door flew open. A burly man in a long brown coat, a bright yellow bobble hat on his head, stepped inside.

'Please,' Cathy called. 'My baby's coming and it's too early.'

'Lord above,' the man said, a look of panic on his red face. 'Stay there, love and I'll get the wife and an ambulance.'

*

Debbie dropped the phone onto its cradle and turned to Davy. 'That was Cathy; she's in a hospital in Kent. She went into labour but they've managed to stop it for now. She's lost some of her waters, but she's okay. I've told her Gianni's looking for her and that he'll call us today. She said to tell him where she is and for him to get to her as soon as he can.' Debbie burst into tears and Davy put his arms round her. 'Oh God, after all this, I just hope that baby's going to be okay.'

'I'm sure it will be, love,' said Davy. 'It's got its mother's survival-instinct blood in its veins. It'll be just fine.' He let her go as the phone rang again and she snatched it up. 'It's Gianni,' she whispered. She told him what had happened and hung up with a satisfied smile. 'He knows where the hospital is, there's a sign right by the phone box. He's on his way.'

*

Cathy opened her eyes as the door creaked open and Gianni slipped inside, dressed in a paper gown. He smiled as he closed the door.

'Oh, Gianni.' Cathy reached out her hand, relief washing over her. 'I'm so sorry I told you we were finished. Please forgive me. I love you.'

Tears tumbled down his cheeks as he reached for her and held her. 'I love you too and there's nothing for you to be sorry about.' Her tears mingled with his as they sobbed against each other's shoulders. He felt so relieved, but it was mixed with guilt at what she'd gone through on her own.

'I believe I'm about to meet my baby,' he said as the door opened again and Cathy was told she was being taken to the delivery suite.

'You are,' Cathy said, clinging to his hand. 'I'm just hoping it makes it. They tried to stop it coming but it's not worked.'

'It will make it. It's a fighter like its mother.'

*

Gianni looked on in awe as his tiny dark-haired daughter was whisked to the other side of the room. Cathy had insisted he should stay with her in the delivery suite and the midwife had agreed that it was okay, given their exceptional circumstances. Tears rolled down his cheeks and he didn't bother dashing them away. He dropped a kiss on Cathy's lips. Her eyes were anxious as they both listened for a sound. And then it came, a thin reedy cry, like a kitten, and they both cried with it.

'She's fine,' the midwife shouted across the room. 'Just needs a few nights in Special Care and building up a bit and she'll be good to take home. She's only just a fraction under four pounds. Now then, have we got a name for this little lady?'

'Lucy,' Cathy said, smiling at Gianni. 'Luciana Sadie Romano. Those are her great-grandmother and grandmother's names. But we'll call her Lucy, eh, Gianni?'

He nodded, tears still running down his cheeks. 'Dad will be thrilled with that, and so am I.'

Back in her room Cathy clung to Gianni as they talked and caught up with each other.

'I'll never let you go again,' he told her. 'It's been a nightmare without you.'

'I know, for me too. I'm so sorry.'

'I told you, you've nothing to be sorry about, Cathy. Six of one and half a dozen of the other, as my mam would have said.'

'Funny how Maria was right,' she said, smiling. 'About her being a girl, I mean.'

'Yeah, and she said she could see danger where you were concerned too. I dismissed it because I thought she meant Jack, and *he* was banged up. Bloody hell, I should have listened to her.'

'Where will you stay while I'm in here?' she asked.

'Tonight I'll stay where I stayed last night and then hopefully in my dad's caravan, when it arrives.'

'Okay. Don't forget to call Debs and my mam and Granny Lomax, and if you can let Karen and Ellie know too, that will be nice.'

'I will.' He took her hand and twisted her ring round on her finger. 'So, we're still engaged, are we?'

'Do you want to be?'

'No.' He shook his head. 'Not any more.'

'No?'

He laughed as her face fell and he dropped kisses on her lips. 'No,' he repeated. 'Definitely not. What I want more than anything in this world right now is for you to say you will be my wife. And this time I'm not taking no for an answer.'

'I won't say no,' she said, smiling.

'What about your career?' He raised an eyebrow. 'It was all you ever wanted.'

She shrugged. 'They said I can go back when I'm ready.'

'Did they? Then I'll do my best to help you fulfil all your dreams, Nurse Lomax.' Gianni dropped another tender kiss on her lips. 'But you'll be Nurse Romano by then.'

A Letter from Pam

I want to say a huge thank you for choosing to read *The Nurses of Lark Lane*. If you did enjoy it, and want to keep up to date with all my latest releases, just sign up at the following link. Your email address will never be shared and you can unsubscribe at any time.

www.bookouture.com/pam-howes

To my loyal band of regular readers who bought and reviewed *The Shop Girls of Lark Lane*, thank you for waiting patiently for the third in the series. I hope you'll enjoy catching up with Alice, Sadie, Millie and Cathy. Your support is most welcome and very much appreciated. As always a big thank you to Beverley Ann Hopper and the admins and members of her FB group Book Lovers, and Deryl Easton and the members of her FB group The NotRights. Love you all for the support you show me.

A huge thank you to team Bookouture, especially my lovely editorial team, Abi, Natasha and Ellen for your support and guidance and always being there, you're the best, and thanks also to the rest of the fabulous staff.

And last, but most definitely not least, thank you to our wonderful media girls, Kim Nash and Noelle Holten, for everything you do for us. And thanks also to the gang in the Bookouture Author's Lounge for always being there. As always, I'm so proud to be one of you.

I hope you loved *The Nurses of Lark Lane* and if you did I would be very grateful if you could write a review. I'd love to hear what you think, and it makes such a difference helping new readers to discover one of my books for the first time. I love hearing from my readers – you can get in touch on my Facebook page, through Twitter, Goodreads or my website.

Thanks,
Pam Howes

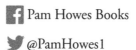

Pam Howes Books

@PamHowes1

Acknowledgements

As always, my man, daughters, son-in-law, grandchildren and their partners. Thank you all for just being there and understanding when I'm up to my stressed-out eyeballs. I love you all very much. Xxx

Thanks once again to my lovely 60s Chicks friends for their friendship and support. And a big thanks to my friends and Beta readers, Brenda Thomasson and Julie Simpson, whose feedback I welcome always.

And last but by no means least, thank you once more to the band of awesome bloggers and reviewers who have given me such wonderful support for my Mersey Trilogy and again with the first three books in the Lark Lane series. It's truly appreciated and without you all an author's life would be a difficult one.

Lightning Source UK Ltd.
Milton Keynes UK
UKHW041926211119
353992UK00001B/92/P